JULIA DEFIANT

THE WITCH'S CHILD, BOOK 2

CATHERINE EGAN

ALFRED A. KNOPF

NEW YORK

Visit us on the Web! randomhouseteens.com

Educators and librarians, for a variety of teaching tools, visit us at
RHTeachersLibrarians.com

Library of Congress Cataloging-in-Publication Data is available upon request.

ISBN 978-0-553-53335-4 (trade) — ISBN 978-0-553-53336-1 (lib. bdg.) —
ISBN 978-0-553-53337-8 (ebook)

The text of this book is set in 13-point Adobe Jenson.

Printed in the United States of America
June 2017
10 9 8 7 6 5 4 3 2 1

First Edition

For David—

it can't have been easy being the littlest,

or captive to my relentless story making,

but every story of mine is still for you

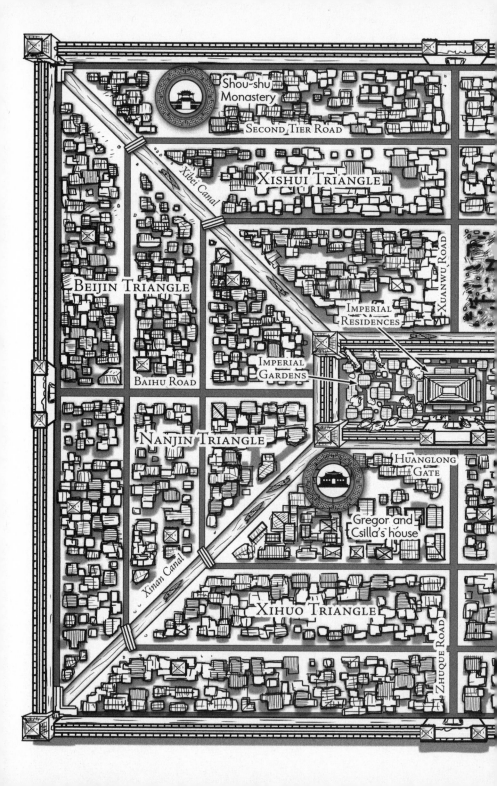

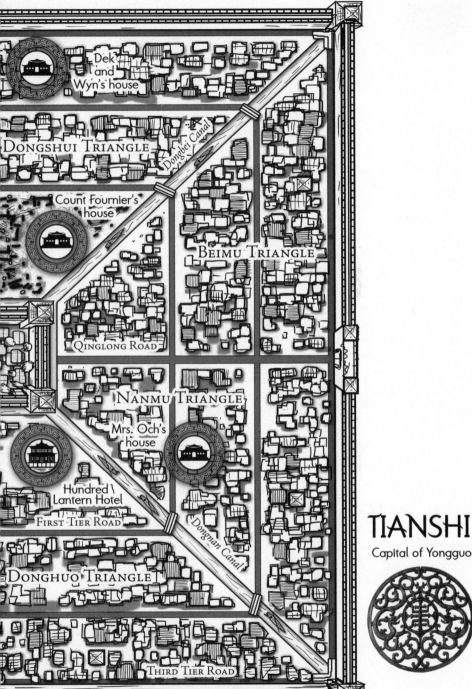

Dek and Wyn's house

DONGSHUI TRIANGLE

Dongbei Canal

Count Fournier's house

BEIMU TRIANGLE

QINGLONG ROAD

NANMU TRIANGLE

Mrs. Och's house

Hundred Lantern Hotel

FIRST TIER ROAD

Dongnan Canal

DONGHUO TRIANGLE

THIRD TIER ROAD

TIANSHI

Capital of Yongguo

PEOPLE, PLACES, AND THINGS

Ammi: A witch; Julia and Benedek's mother

Professor Baranyi: A scholar, once jailed for heretical writings, now employed by (and devoted to) Mrs. Och

Benedek: Julia's brother

Bianka: A witch; Theo's mother

Casimir (Lan Camshe): One of the Xianren, seeking to reassemble all three parts of *The Book of Disruption*

Csilla: An actress turned con artist; Gregor's lover; a member of Esme's gang

Esme: A Spira City crime boss, now employed by Mrs. Och

Count Fournier: A Fraynish aristocrat living in Tianshi; Lady Laroche's nephew

Frederick: A brilliant young student; Professor Baranyi's assistant

Gangzi: The elected leader of the Shou-shu Council

Gennady (Zor Gen): The youngest of the Xianren, imprisoned by Casimir; Theo's father

Gregor: An ex-aristocrat con man working for Esme; Csilla's lover; a drunk

Agoston Horthy: The prime minister of Frayne

Jun: An able spy; Count Fournier's associate

Ko Dan: One of the Shou-shu monks; a famous witch

Lady Laroche: A witch; the head of the Sidhar Coven in Frayne

Lidari: A general of the Gethin; Marike's associate

Ling: A smart young woman from Tianshi; Benedek's girlfriend; Mei's sister

Marike: A witch; the first Phar and founder of the Eshriki Empire

Mei: Ling's sister; Wyn's lover

Mrs. Och (Och Farya): The eldest of the Xianren, trying to keep Theo (and the third fragment of *The Book of Disruption*) out of the hands of her brother Casimir

Pia: Casimir's terrifying assassin, sent to Yongguo to find Theo . . . and Julia

Si Tan: The grand librarian of Yongguo, a position second only to the emperor's

Lord Skaal: A dignitary from Frayne; an associate of Agoston Horthy

Theo: The toddler son of Bianka and Gennady, with a fragment of *The Book of Disruption* bound to his essence

Wyn: An orphan and a crook; Esme's adopted son; Julia's ex-lover

Zara: A Fraynish girl hiding in the Shou-shu Monastery

The Ankh-nu: A double-spouted clay pot made to transfer the essence of a living being from one body to another

The Book of Disruption: The first written magic and origin of magic in the world, said to have been written by Feo, spirit of fire, and broken into three pieces by the other elemental spirits

The Eshriki Empire: A powerful witch empire three thousand years ago whose rulers called themselves the Phars

The Gethin: An army of creatures brought into the world from Kahge and given physical form by Marike, the first Eshriki Phar

Kahge: A magic-infused reflection, shadow, or image imprint of the natural world created when *The Book of Disruption* was split into three

The Lorian Uprising: An unsuccessful revolution in Frayne eighteen years ago aimed at replacing King Zey with his more moderate brother, Roparzh

The Ru: The elite warriors who guard the Imperial Gardens

The Shou-shu Monastery: A monastery in Tianshi, capital city of Yongguo, currently led by a monk named Gangzi

The Sidhar Coven: A Fraynish coven of witches—of which Julia's mother, Ammi, was part—involved in the Lorian Uprising

The Xianren: The immortal siblings, sometimes allies and sometimes enemies, each charged with protecting a portion of *The Book of Disruption*: Casimir (Lan Camshe), Gennady (Zor Gen), and Mrs. Och (Och Farya)

JULIA
DEFIANT

Above the wasted plains of the earth, after the battle was done, Haizea, goddess of vengeance, and Tisis, goddess of mercy, stood side by side and argued over which of them was needed.

"I will give the vanquished strength," said Haizea. "Look, down there, a young mother—her dress torn open, her husband dead. She kneels before the body of her murdered child. I will give her my whirlwind so that she might strike back at those who stole her joy."

"And then?" said Tisis. "Enslaved to the whirlwind, will she tear other children from their mothers, will she pillage and murder also? The enmity between these people cannot be brought to an end with vengeance. I will bring her my cup and let her drink. In mercy and forgiveness may she find peace, and give peace to future generations."

"Some things cannot be forgiven," said Haizea.

"Some things cannot be avenged," said Tisis.

"Then what good are we?" asked Haizea. "Why do they call for us and call for us, in times of war and in times of peace?"

The two goddesses went down to the plain, where the bodies of

1

the dead and the dying lay strewn. Tisis offered her cup to those who would drink, and to those who would strike back a hundredfold, Haizea gave her whirlwind. Then they came to the young mother they had argued over. She knelt in the dirt and looked up at them, her dark eyes reflecting their blazing glory. They told her: "Choose."

ONE

When did I first go over a wall that was meant to keep me out? I don't even remember. I've spent my life scaling walls. I've made a career out of what used to be just mischief—going where I am not supposed to go, seeing what I am not supposed to see, being someone I'm not. It has taken me farther from home than I'd ever imagined. This is a fine wall, tall and strong and tiled on top, and this is my third time going over it.

The sun set an hour ago, and the streets are already empty. I take a rope with a five-pronged hook at the end of it from my bag and step back a few paces, eyeing the wall and measuring the rope out. Then I give the hook a whirl and toss it up. It flies neatly, scraping against the stone on the other side and catching on the tiles at the top. I tug to make sure it's firm and then walk up the wall, hand over hand along the rope. Straddling the top of the wall, I coil the rope around the hooked head and tuck it back into my bag.

From here I can see the whole city, the broad, paved streets and peaked rooftops surrounding the Imperial Gardens at the center. This is Tianshi, capital of Yongguo, seat of the greatest empire the world has ever known. Within these walls, in the northwest of the city, lies the Shou-shu Monastery, famous for its bronze bells and long-lived monks. It is a maze of dark temples and alleys around the Main Hall— almost like a miniature version of the city itself.

If I look east, I can see all the way to the Dongshui Triangle, the slum where my brother is hiding out with my ex-lover. I ate supper with them last night, and Wyn was in a poor mood. He'd had too much to drink and called me unforgiving, which seemed funny at the time.

I shoulder the bag with the hook in it and slide both my legs over to the monastery side of the wall. I've thought a great deal about forgiveness and what is forgivable. Still, I've yet to tell him *I forgive you*, because even though I have, he wouldn't understand. When Wyn talks about forgiveness, he means having me back in his bed. It means something different to me. It means everything to me. It's why I'm here, ten thousand miles from home, dropping from this wall onto the gravel path below.

⁓

Getting here was no small matter. We crossed half the world in two months, by ship and by train, by horse and by camel, by riverboat and by donkey cart and on foot. We saw wonders I never knew existed: the white palace floating on the lake in Beru, built for the king's favorite concubine; the spiraling rock formations in the Loshi Desert; the Kastahor Mountains, cloaked in ice.

One evening, a few weeks into our journey, I found my brother, Benedek, sitting on the cooling desert sand, watching the sun setting behind the Eshriki Pyramids. Our tents and camels were just out of sight, over a dune. He smiled up at me and said something in Yongwen. This was Professor Baranyi's rule, that we speak only Yongwen on the journey, and if he ever tired of giving us lessons on steamships or in bedsits, he didn't show it. But I was having none of it here, alone with Benedek. To my chagrin, he'd proved a much more adept student than me.

"Can we just speak bleeding Fraynish for once?"

"You need the practice."

"Well, I don't want to practice with you."

It was always a relief to be alone with him—really, with any of my own crew, but with Dek in particular. It was the only time I could be at ease. The rest of them—well, we were careful with each other, and I was conscious every moment of trying to win their trust, if not their friendship, and conscious too that they could never really trust me. Not after what I'd done.

"I was saying that they're remarkable," said Dek, gesturing at the pyramids with his good arm. "You know, the part we see is just the very tip of the pyramid, poking above the sand. The rest, underneath the ground, is absolutely vast."

"Really?" I said, startled.

"No." He snorted. "Pea brain."

I punched him on the shoulder.

"Do you know what Mrs. Och said yesterday when she saw them?"

"What?"

"She said, 'I remember when they built those.'"

He laughed. The sun sank behind the pyramids, the golden light that suffused the clouds and the sand and the pyramids themselves deepening to crimson. He asked me, almost casually: "Do you suppose they'll forgive you if you find him?"

He didn't need to explain who he meant by *they* or by *him*. But the question took me aback all the same. He'd clearly been waiting for a moment alone with me to ask.

"I don't know," I said.

"Will you forgive yourself?"

"No."

"I wish you could."

"If wishes were horses," I said, shrugging it off, and he let it go. We watched the light fade in silence.

The truth is that the question of forgiveness fuels my days and plagues my nights. Goodness was not something I gave much thought to until I relinquished any possible claim to it. Am I evil, as Frederick once suggested? There is no way to remake the past. The very best I can strive for, the work of every day now, is to be a good person who once did an evil thing.

If atonement also happens to be fun, well, that is just good luck. I land on the path and set off at a light jog behind the monastery library. The monks retire to their sleeping quarters at sundown, so I don't need to worry about running into anybody. In my pocket, I have a wrinkled copy of the monastery map that Mrs. Och obtained for me. I've looked around enough to know it is inaccurate. Tonight's task is to fill in the gaps. If some parts of the monastery are secret, unmapped, it's a fair guess that that's where I ought to be looking.

I make my way through the southern end of the monastery, avoiding the Treasury, the only place where guards are posted both day and night—not monks either, but proper imperial guards. There are three hundred–plus monks here, and they all look much the same to me, with their crimson robes and shaved heads, their gaunt, hungry faces. I am looking for one man: Ko Dan. This is complicated, since I don't know what he looks like or anything else about him besides his name and the fact that a year and a half ago he worked a terrible magic that needs undoing. Perhaps most important, I don't know that he'll want to be found.

The monastery buildings are made of ancient wood from Yongguo's northern forests, where the trees are black as pitch and a hundred feet tall. The rooftops are bright blue tile, though in the dark, they look as black as the wood. I turn right at the west wall, passing the sleeping quarters, several minor temples, the broad road leading to the Main Hall, and the elaborate Garden of the Elements, behind which lies a well-tended vegetable plot and a small house with a light flickering inside.

Three nights in a row, when the rest of the monastery is dark, there has been this one light. Through the window I see the same old man sitting at his desk, writing. His face is wrinkled as a prune. He writes very quickly, as if agitated, page after page. He is wearing the crimson robe that all the monks wear, but he has a long braid down the back of his shaved head and a golden medallion on his chest.

When I told Mrs. Och and Frederick about the old man, they agreed it was probably Gangzi, elected leader of the Shou-shu Council. Anyone seeking to enter the monastery must obtain special permission from Gangzi, and my understanding is that this permission is so special it is never actually granted. Not even the emperor can come here unless Gangzi says so; the monastery is under Yongguo's protection but not its jurisdiction. Women are expressly forbidden to enter under any circumstances, and I admit that just sweetens the job, as far as I'm concerned. For all that, it is easy enough to get in. Just a wall, and no guards besides those at the Treasury. Only the wrath of the empire and magic-using monks to worry about if I get caught, and I never get caught. Well—hardly ever.

The prune-faced man folds the paper, addresses it, seals it with wax, and adds it to a bamboo basket nearly overflowing with letters. He dips his brush and sets about writing the next one. I'd like to get my hands on one of those letters and see what he's frantically writing about night after night, but I daren't enter the little house while he's there. I leave him to his work.

The Hall of Abnegation (Frederick's translation) stretches the entire length of the northernmost wall. I pause between the hall and the swallow coop, tilting the map in my hand so I can catch a little of the moonlight to see by, when the ground shifts right in front of me. I step back against the wall of the swallow coop, stifling my cry of surprise.

A flagstone rises up from the path and is eased aside soundlessly. A shadow emerges from the ground, fluid and swift. The shadow replaces the flagstone without a scrape or a clink and slips away from me, down the alley. Talk about luck. I follow, heart galloping now with the thrill of the chase, even though I don't know who or what I'm chasing yet.

We come to a wall about twice my height. Walls within walls within walls in this city. The shadow goes up and over it like a spider. I make a quick circuit of the wall. It forms a rectangle, fewer than two hundred paces right around, and there is a painted door facing south—locked. The wall is roughly made, the stones uneven enough that I can clamber up them easily, if not as smoothly as the shadow I'm stalking. I fling my leg over the top, lying flat to look down on the courtyard below.

At the center of the courtyard sits a modest house. Bamboo runs around the inside of the wall, thick and green. I see no sign of the shadow I followed here, but two figures are seated at a table in the candlelit garden. They are playing Zhengfu, a strategy game with tiles, similar to the Fraynish game of Conquest. The larger of the two figures is singing softly as she plays. So much for no women in the monastery. The tune is familiar—and then I catch a snatch of it and am shocked to realize she is singing in Fraynish. I know the song from my own childhood. It's a depressing ditty about the weeping moon following the sun round and round, pulling her dark cape of stars behind her and longing for day. *Why so sad, Mistress Moon, why d'you cry?*

The other figure is so small I'd have guessed it was a child, except that she is smoking a pipe. She smacks down a tile, then scoops the singer's tiles off the board with a little bark of triumph. The singer laughs and they rise to their feet. By her voice and posture, I reckon the pipe smoker to be an old woman.

The singer blows out the candles, and they head toward the house, the old woman carrying something long and bulky I can't make out in the dark. I climb down the wall as fast as I dare, using the bamboo to steady myself, but the feathery tops of the stalks shake and rustle as I descend, and the singer looks back, calling out in Yongwen: "Is someone there?"

The old woman makes a beeline for me, and I realize she's holding an old-fashioned blunderbuss. She pries between the bamboo stalks with it, the tip of the muzzle just skimming my shoulder. Her face is only a foot from mine, peering this way and that. It is a stern face, if slightly blurred from my perspective, with great scraggly eyebrows. She looks right at me, but she doesn't see me, of course.

After checking the wall and the garden, she returns to the girl at the threshold of the house, and together they go inside, the girl casting a last look my way over her shoulder. I ease myself through the bamboo stalks and dash across the courtyard. They leave the door open to the chirping night insects, and so I slip in after them.

They pass through the main room to a smaller room sparsely furnished with a bed, a wardrobe, a dresser. There is a large wooden barrel to one side. The old woman takes the lid off, and steam pours upward from the hot water within. The girl is still humming her Fraynish tune, and by the lamplight, I can see her New Porian features, her fair skin and light-colored eyes. She cannot be much older than I am—eighteen or nineteen at most, I'd guess. She is thick-shouldered and plump, rather matronly in figure, but with a face ill suited for plumpness—too severe, with a small, pinched mouth and a long nose made comical by her round cheeks. She is dressed in a wide-sleeved robe of embroidered silk, like the upper-class ladies of Tianshi wear, her mousy brown hair held back with jade clasps.

The old woman says something I don't understand, and the girl laughs again, breaking off her song. In spite of my weeks of immersive study with Professor Baranyi, now that I am here, I find everybody speaking far too quickly and not following the linguistic rules of Yongwen as I've learned them at all. It is difficult to catch more than a snippet here and there.

The girl begins to undress. I've seen enough of the place, and it offends even my admittedly dinged sense of propriety to watch her take a bath, so I slip out to look for the shadow I followed here.

I find him outside, crouched on the roof, still as the night. I watch him for a few minutes but he doesn't move, and so I go over the wall, more slowly and quietly this time, and run back to the swallow coop. I reenter the visible world, so that everything pulls sharply into focus around me, and search for the flagstone the shadow came out from under. At first I'm just breaking my fingernails on stones that won't budge, but then I find the right cracks in the ground and pull it up.

Looking down the hole, I see nothing but darkness. I reach in and feel steel rungs—a ladder. I'm not going down there without knowing more, but I am curious to see what my spy will do if he thinks he's been discovered. So I leave the tunnel open, the flagstone lying there on the path, and I step back against the wall of the swallow coop, where the birds chirrup softly in their nests.

I vanish and wait.

TWO

I don't hear the shadow coming—that's how good he is—but I see him standing there, looking down at the open tunnel, his face hidden by a hood. Then he bends quickly to replace the flagstone and makes for the east wall of the monastery.

My shadow-spy goes up the wall and over it, and the first whisper of fear ghosts through me, cold in my veins. I've only known one person who can go up a wall like that, and I don't fancy meeting her like again. Me, I need my hook and rope for this wall, and so I wait a minute or two, hoping he'll be out of earshot but not yet out of sight. When I get to the top of the wall, I scan the streets for a panicky second or two before I spot the shadow heading toward the Xuanwu Road. I drop down to the street and hurry after him, into the Dongshui Triangle, still vanished in case the shadow looks over his shoulder, which he doesn't.

This part of the city has a reputation for robbery, assault, opium, and illegal magic. The streets are mostly empty, but in an abandoned lot ahead, next to a collapsed wall, several figures are crouched around a bonfire. My spy keeps going, looking neither to the right nor to the left. A couple of the figures rise to watch him. One of them speaks, but my spy says nothing in return, does not even glance their way. I speed up, closing the gap between us somewhat. The rest of the men around the fire rise now, and there are more of them than I'd realized—eight or nine. They are climbing over the broken wall, streaming after my spy, shouting jeers. One of them smashes a bottle on the road. One of them draws a knife.

I can't decide if I should call out a warning about the knife, try to help. But it becomes clear very quickly that my spy, whoever he is, needs no warning, nor any other kind of help from me.

He tosses something casually over his shoulder and then bolts. It looks like a small pottery jar. It shatters on the road, and a buzzing swarm explodes up out of it. I fling myself up on the wall at the side of the road, and the men scatter, shouting and fleeing, a cloud of angry wasps in pursuit. I dash along the wall to the corner and see the shadow running south. Stars, but he's fast. I jump off the wall and go after him.

He slows down when he reaches the first tier of the Dongshui Triangle, the section closest to the Imperial Gardens. Iron tracks for electric trolleys run along the three tier roads, dividing the city's elegant neighborhoods from the shabbier ones, which are farther from the Imperial Gardens. I hang back but keep him in sight. This part of the city was burned sixty years ago when a group of old, wealthy families revolted against the meritocracy, and it has a haunted feel. The once great courtyard houses are collapsed, their walls broken, the charred buildings open to the night sky. A few homes survived the fire intact, but those are somehow the saddest of all, standing lonely and empty among their ruined neighbors.

My spy heads toward one of the undamaged houses. His hand on the door, he looks over his shoulder for the first time. The moon is out and I can see the shadow's face clear enough. He is just a boy, no older than me, with sharp cheekbones and a rather fierce expression. His eyes cut across the street, passing over me. Then he opens the door and disappears inside.

I stand in the road a minute, looking at the closed door. I'd hoped that the monastery's secret spaces would turn up Ko Dan, but I know from experience that sometimes the thing you hope to find does not look the way you expect it to at first. In any case, I have two things to report to Mrs. Och tonight. First, a Fraynish girl who stays up late playing Zhengfu. And second, that I am not the only spy with an interest in the Shou-shu Monastery.

THREE

Since I'm in the neighborhood, I decide to drop in on Dek before going back to Mrs. Och's house. When we arrived in Tianshi, Mrs. Och split our group into three and sent us to different parts of the city. Her insistence that I live with her, Bianka, and Frederick came as a surprise—I'm not sure if I should take her wanting me close as a sign of how much she needs me or how little she trusts me. Perhaps a bit of both. Either way, I'm stuck living with the people who have the most reason to hate me.

Esme, my boss since I was a little pickpocket in Spira City, and her colleagues, Gregor and Csilla, are renting an elegant house in the first tier of the Xihuo Triangle, overlooking the canal. Gregor is posing as Lord Heriday, a visiting scholar, which is laughable. Professor Baranyi, our Yongguo expert, is acting as his official translator and, behind the scenes, his coach. I don't envy him the job of trying to teach a drunken ex-aristocrat con man how to fake an intellect, but the professor has been remarkably patient. Esme is acting as their manservant. We tried her out as a lady's maid, but in all her six-foot-tall fierce-browed splendor, she was predictably unconvincing. Gregor-as-Lord-Heriday is requesting permission to visit the Imperial Library. If Ko Dan does not turn up in the monastery, Mrs. Och reckons there will be records in the library to give us an idea of where he's gone.

Dek and Wyn, in the meantime, are meant to be digging up rumors—and, just in case, weapons—from the rogues and hustlers in the seedy Dongshui Triangle, but as far as I can tell, they are just going to lots of shady bars to get drunk and calling it reconnaissance. If I'm lucky, they'll have found some real coffee. I know Wyn has set finding coffee beans in this city of tea at a high priority.

The front door is ajar, and I go in without knocking. A lantern hangs from a hook on the wall, and the two of them are sitting at the table in their shirtsleeves—but not just the two of them. I freeze in the doorway, wondering if I should turn around and slip out before they see me.

There are two girls with them. One of the girls is playing cards with Wyn. She has cynical, low-lidded eyes, and her face paint has seen too many weary hours. Dek is practicing calligraphy, bent over a sheet of rice paper with a girl in an ancient-looking silk tunic a few sizes too big for her. Her gleaming blue-black hair is in an untidy knot on top of her head, and I can't see her face at first.

"Hullo, it's Julia," says Wyn, looking up at me. So much

for slipping away unseen. I step inside. I can smell bitter green tea, so I guess I am out of luck on the coffee.

Dek turns and breaks into a smile. His dark, curly hair is tied back. Usually he only does that when he's working, the rest of the time letting his hair fall over his face to hide the Scourge scars and blots around his missing eye. I'm a little surprised to see it tied back in the company of two girls.

"Working late?" he asks, nodding at my bag with the hook and rope inside. I shrug it off and put it down by the door. The girl next to him turns to face me now, looks me up and down. I can see right away that the two girls must be sisters, but this one is younger and prettier than the girl playing cards with Wyn.

"I didn't know you'd have visitors," I say.

"We're making friends in the neighborhood," says Wyn. He jerks a thumb at the older girl, who is resting her chin in her hand now, looking vaguely relieved to be abandoning the card game. "This one is Mia. Or Minnie. Or something."

"Mei," says Dek. "And her sister, Ling."

"It's hard to keep the names straight," says Wyn. "D'you want some tea, Julia? It's good to see you. Why can't you come live with us? We're lonely out here."

I refrain from saying that they don't look lonely.

"Mrs. Och wants me close," I say. "You haven't found coffee, then?"

"No such luck," Wyn sighs. "People just laugh at me when I ask for it."

One of Mrs. Och's tree pipits comes hopping across the

table and gives his knuckles a peck. We use them to send messages, birds being easier to enchant than most animals, according to Mrs. Och. Wyn was skeptical, muttering about how messenger birds are not uncommon and that instructing a bird by magic seemed simply lazy. The magic makes him uneasy, but he quite likes the birds themselves, which are only really tame with him, having fallen victim to his charms, as so many of us do.

The younger girl, Ling, brings me tea in a chipped cup, still staring at me with naked curiosity. The sleeves of her overlarge tunic nearly cover her hands, but when I take the cup from her, I notice her left hand is bandaged up to the knuckles. Her fingers are chapped and ink-stained, the nails bitten to the quick.

"We met them at a bar and brought them back here for their scintillating conversation and funny stories," says Wyn. He nods at glowering Mei. "This one has had us in stitches for hours."

"So you've been out this evening," I say, sitting down and looking at Dek's calligraphy. "What is the dark underbelly of Tianshi like?"

"Dark and underbellyish," says Dek, tousling my hair so some of the pins come loose. I swat his hand away.

Wyn adds: "Turns out these two lovelies have got an uncle who has some dealings with the monastery. Nice fellow."

I make myself meet his eyes, mainly so it's not obvious that I am always trying not to look at him. His eyes are a grayish green, the color of the sea after a storm. We've always guessed that his people were from North Arrekem or some-where thereabouts, because of his dark skin, but who knows where he got those eyes. He doesn't know either, since his earliest memories are of the awful orphanage he ran away from. Csilla says his beauty is wasted on a man, and indeed there is something almost too pretty about his perfect lips and cheekbones, the arc of those dark eyebrows. It's not his beauty that slays me, though. It's the humor of his face I've always loved, the way he seems to be laughing at himself and the world, like he's in on a big joke, *the* big joke of human existence. Wyn radiates joy at being alive, and the feeling is contagious. Being with him was a joyful thing. Until I found him in bed with another girl, that is.

"He smuggles in tobacco and liquor for naughty monks," explains Wyn when I don't reply. Too busy getting lost in those eyes. Honestly, pull yourself together, Julia.

"Oh, so this is actually work, then, is it?" I ask.

Dek laughs.

"No harm in mixing business with pleasure," says Wyn. "What have you been up to?"

"The usual mischief," I say lightly. "Listen, can you find out who delivers mail to the monastery and who takes letters out? There ought to be a *lot* of letters going out every day."

"We'll look into it," says Dek.

Mei is rubbing her face like a sleepy cat, leaving black smudges around her eyes. Ling takes the brush from Dek, dips it in the inkpot, and writes something on his rice paper.

I don't know anything about calligraphy, but even I can see she's good at it. There is an easy flair to her characters that Dek's painstaking calligraphy lacks.

"What is that?" he asks in Yongwen. "A saying, a name?"

Ling tilts her head to one side, smiling as she answers him. No Fraynish girl has ever looked at Dek like that. In Spira City, Dek was an outcast, marked by Scourge. His scars, his missing eye, his withered arm and leg, were all sure signs of the illness that had terrorized Frayne. But Scourge never had such a strong foothold in Yongguo. There are cripples here, as there are cripples everywhere, and Dek is only one of them. His foreignness is more remarkable than the crutch he walks with or the puckered map of blots and scars on the right side of his face.

"It's a saying," says Dek, translating for Wyn and me: "Destiny must be hunted."

Mei, smudge-eyed and stifling a yawn, says, "Ling is very clever," and adds something about the Imperial Gardens that I can't understand.

"What did she say?" I ask Dek, annoyed that the conversation seems to be switching over to Yongwen.

"Ling has a tutor," says Dek. "She works as a dishwasher, but in her free time she studies literature and philosophy. Her family thinks she might pass the examinations and get them a place in the Imperial Gardens."

Ling stares at her own calligraphy, the expression on her face almost angry now, and I study her again. The system in Tianshi is peculiar in that the ruling class is not hereditary.

Power and prestige are not passed from one generation to the next but rather earned through a system of examinations. Anyone, even a peasant, may apply to take the Imperial Examinations. If they pass—showing a breadth of knowledge and also demonstrating excellence in at least one area of specialty—then both they and their entire family may live within the Imperial Gardens, that walled enclave of privilege at the center of the city. A family with a gifted child might pour all their resources into educating and preparing that child for the examinations. It is a huge gamble for a poor family, and naturally the wealthy have the significant advantage of money and time for tutors and study. But if Ling is truly exceptional, then even though she's a dishwasher from Dongshui and her uncle is a smuggler, her family might rise to the very top of Yongguo's society.

The most extraordinary contrast to Frayne here in Yongguo is that witchcraft is viewed simply as another kind of talent and can also earn you a place in the Imperial Gardens. While witchcraft is governed by strict laws, witches are highly respected, and a licensed witch may use her power in service of the empire. If my mother had been born here instead of in Frayne, she might have been a member of the Imperial Court. She would not have been drowned in the river like a rat.

Ling and Dek are leaning over the sheet of rice paper, heads almost touching, speaking Yongwen rapidly together. I understand the story of her hands now—the chapped skin and the ink and the close-bitten nails, hidden in her sleeves again. Mei has moved closer to Wyn and is resting her head on his shoulder. All at once, I feel very awkward.

"I should get back," I say, rising.

"You just got here," says Wyn.

"Mrs. Och will be wanting a report. Thanks for the tea."

"We'll find coffee in this blasted city, Brown Eyes. I swear it on my life!" he says dramatically. He doesn't call me Brown Eyes so often anymore.

"Good night," says Dek. "Be careful."

I give him a wave, shouldering my bag, and try to be happy for him that he's got a pretty girl to pass the evening with.

Halfway home, I am sure I'm being followed. I can't see anybody; it's just a feeling. It may be no more than jitters, but I go the rest of the way vanished anyway.

FOUR

Even the animals are quiet when I return to the modest courtyard house in the Nanmu Triangle that serves, for now, as home to Mrs. Och, Bianka, Baby Theo, Frederick, and me. Spira City would be brilliant with gas lamps at this hour, but Tianshi is nearly pitch black. There is the odd flicker of a lantern here and there, the dim glow of a candle in a window; the rest is darkness. I think of home: the winding streets of the Twist, raucous laughter spilling out of the brothels, half-starved cats stalking rats, the smell of spice and snow and smoke. The sounds and smells are all different here: wet stone from the afternoon rain, which came down in a torrent while the bells of Shou-shu chimed their magic for it; lamp oil and chicken shit; the click of dice and low voices behind courtyard walls. Where Spira City comes alive at night, Tianshi nestles down close to the earth, the people withdraw, the lights go out.

A slight rustling and whispering greets my arrival, a hint

of smoke from the small folds of paper tucked into the cracks in the wall. Spells. If it were someone other than me coming through the door, the whole household would be woken by now. Ours is a simple three-sided courtyard house, though the front wall facing onto the street is thick enough to disguise it as a proper courtyard house with living quarters on all four sides. I pass through the gate and straight into the yard, where the cantankerous goat we bought for milk looks up at me curiously. The chickens are sleeping in their enclosures, the messenger tree pipit chirruping in its cage. The servants' quarters, kitchen, and washrooms along the sides of the courtyard are dark, but a lamp glimmers inside the main house.

"Can't sleep?"

He looks up, startled. Frederick always has a look about him like you've just jumped around a corner and shouted something obscene, but right now he is genuinely surprised. He was too deep in his book to hear me come in.

"I don't sleep much, to be honest," he says. "It always feels like such a colossal waste of time. Anything interesting?"

"Very," I say, leaving my bag in a corner and throwing myself into the chair next to him. "What do you make of a Fraynish girl, about my age, living in the monastery?"

He frowns. "Are you sure?"

"Of course I'm bleeding sure. It's not an easy mistake. I saw her, and I heard her singing a Fraynish song. There was somebody else spying on her too. He came up through a tunnel under the monastery. Lives in Dongshui."

Frederick raises his eyebrows and puts his book down on the table, a sign I've really got his attention. It's very irritating when he keeps hanging on to his book while you talk and you know he's just waiting for a chance to get back to it without seeming rude. Poor Frederick has been very book-deprived since we left Frayne. He bought a book he couldn't even read at a shop in Ishti, just because he wanted one to hold, I suspect, though he claims it was because he wanted to study classical Ishtan.

"Odd sort of coincidence. I wonder what Mrs. Och will make of it," he says. He hesitates a fraction of a second before adding: "You're sure the spy was a man?"

"A boy, I reckon. My height."

"But male."

"He was wearing trousers."

"So are you," he points out.

In Yongguo the peasant women often wear trousers, and I must say I've rather taken to it. I'd never given much thought to the impracticality of women's clothing until I started dressing like a boy. I am wearing black for nighttime creeping: a pair of cotton trousers that button at the waist and ankles, a loose tunic of the sort women in the countryside wear, and peasant boots, a shoe with a length of tough fabric that wraps to midway up the calf. I've got my knife tucked into the bindings, and I leave the bottoms of my trousers unbuttoned so I can reach it easily. My hair is pinned up on my head, but the pins pinch, so I loosen them now, letting my hair fall over my shoulders.

"Got a pen?" I say. "I should sketch the layout while it's fresh in my mind."

Frederick fetches me a cartridge pen from his box of writing supplies, and I lay out the wrinkled map next to a blank piece of paper. I draw a more complete map, marking the Fraynish girl's secret courtyard and the spy's tunnel by the swallow coop. I hand it to Frederick when I'm done.

"Impressive," he says.

"Gangzi, if it's him, is still writing loads of letters," I say, looking at my map over his shoulder. "I've asked Wyn and Dek to find out who takes out the mail. We might be able to nab a few and see what he's writing about. I'd like to get into the Treasury too. It's got a steel door and two guards on duty right through the night."

"We're here for a man, not Gangzi's correspondence or treasure," says Frederick.

"You never know where a clue might turn up. What sort of thing do magic-using monks stash in a treasury, anyway?"

"I've no idea."

I stretch my legs and get up. "Well, enjoy your book. I'm going to get some sleep. Unlike you, I find sleeping to be one of the absolute best uses of my time."

I am leaving the room when he says: "Julia."

Frederick met me as Ella—a compliant, illiterate housemaid. I was a spy in Mrs. Och's house, digging up secrets, and he was rather taken with that fictitious person. I know he will never be as fond of Julia as he was of Ella, but the way he says my name tells me he no longer sees her when he looks at me. If we are not exactly friends, crossing half the world together has afforded us a kind of ease with one another. He looks different now than he did back in Spira City. He was a gangly youth when I met him, all arms and legs, but the months of hard travel have added a layer of muscle that suits him well. His fair beard has grown long, and his face is sunburnt, which has the effect of making his eyes look even bluer behind his spectacles. I lean against the doorframe, waiting for him to say what I know he is going to say.

"You're sure . . . you aren't worried, then, about this spy?"

He doesn't say her name, but I know he's thinking of Pia. I know because I think about her all the time as well. The last time I saw her, she was broken on the ground, bleeding from the knife I'd stuck in her gut, but I know better than to believe that was the end of her. We all know that Casimir, her employer, isn't going to let us go with his prize. He'll be searching for us here.

"It wasn't her," I tell him.

He nods, looking relieved. "Good night, Julia," he says. "Well done."

I leave him to his book and tiptoe into the dark of the room I share with Bianka and Theo. I feel blindly for my nightgown hanging from a nail in the wall and change as quietly as I can. Little Theo stirs, and my eyes adjust to the darkness enough to see him lying on a mat, curled against Bianka. A sash around his waist is tied to her wrist. She has stitched a spell into the sash, writing with thread that it shall not be undone except by her hand, and she checks the needle she sewed it with every night to make sure it is unbroken and that the spell will hold. It is the only way she can let herself sleep; she will not risk having him stolen from her a second time. And yet she agreed to have me, who stole him first, share their room. If she hadn't, I would have had to bunk down with Mrs. Och, so I am doubly indebted.

I lie down gently on my own sleeping mat, barely two feet from Bianka, who once counted me her direst enemy, and Theo, who has never understood enough to blame me. He looks an ordinary boy, not even two years old yet, with corkscrewing dark curls and a smile to melt lead. But woven into his being is such magic as could undo or remake the world, if put to proper use. Marvel at *that* when he's spilling his milk or pulling your hair.

"Lala," he murmurs when I lie down, his eyelids fluttering.

"Shh," I whisper, reaching across the gap between our sleeping mats and giving him my finger to hold. He wraps his little fist around it and is back asleep in seconds.

Sleep takes longer for me. I stare at the softness, the absolute peace of his face at rest—no fear at all, tucked against his mother, no idea of how he is hunted across the world, no awareness of the magical fragment Ko Dan hid inside him, bound to his essence, and which we only hope Ko Dan can take back out. I watch him breathing in the dark, and I swear by all the holies, as I do every night, that I will keep him safe. I'll make it right.

FIVE

"Good morning, Julia. You had an eventful night, I hear."

Mrs. Och is next to the hearth, a stone-lined pit in the center of the room, wearing a black Tianshi-style robe embroidered with golden birds. She is examining the map I drew last night. Her back is straight, her eyes bright and alert. There is an unusual vigor about her. I know what that means, even before I look at Frederick slumped over the table, his face a sickly gray. He raises one hand in greeting and lets it drop again.

"And you've had a busy morning already," I reply, unable to keep the bite out of my voice.

I know he agrees to this, but still it makes me angry—perhaps at myself, as much as at her, for refusing to give her any of my own life force. She is dying, though very slowly, her power waning—and Frederick, Professor Baranyi, and Bianka all volunteer their own strength when she needs it. Bianka weathers it best, of course, being a witch, but

Frederick has no unnatural powers. It is horrible to see her vivid and sprightly while he slouches there so diminished, without even the strength to read. He speaks of it very rationally, how we need Mrs. Och and she needs strength. But I remember what it felt like when she took mine by force—albeit to save our lives—and I cannot bring myself to give it to her willingly.

Either she doesn't notice my tone or she ignores it deliberately. She looks up at me, and I feel a sick little jolt at her still-unfamiliar face. For two weeks now she has appeared to be an elderly lady from Yongguo, her white hair knotted on top of her head, her accent matching whatever region we were passing through. Still, I can't get used to this changeability of hers.

"Describe to me the girl you saw in the monastery."

"My age. Brown hair. Fancy clothes." I fold my arms across my chest. "Do you know why she's there?"

I am good enough at reading faces, but I have never been able to read Mrs. Och's, no matter what she looks like.

"No," she says. "But you had better keep an eye on her."

"D'you think she has anything to do with Ko Dan?" I ask.

"I doubt it."

"Then why should we care about her?"

"I care about a great many things," she says mildly.

I bite back a sarcastic retort as Bianka comes in with an apron full of eggs and Theo at her heels. He is tugging at her skirt and begging, "Egg? Egg?"

"No, you may not hold one," she snaps, maintaining her

31

stride and half dragging him along with her. "Last time you broke them, d'you remember? And then you had to go without your breakfast."

He gives me a sly look and murmurs, "Lala umma egg."

I glare back warningly and am glad he can't really talk yet. In fact, I slipped him most of my breakfast that time. For such a little thing, he certainly has an appetite.

"Egg," he sighs again, in a very world-weary manner. Bianka kneels by the hearth and begins to crack them carelessly into a pan, not bothering about the bits of shell. I've had months to get used to Bianka's cooking.

Giving up all hope of holding and probably smashing an egg, Theo comes to me. I scoop him up and plant a kiss on his soft, golden cheek. Bianka shoots us a wary glance. I can't blame her, but I can't resist him either.

"We need more bread" is all she says.

"Julia will go to the market today," says Mrs. Och. She's quite fond of that construction, *Julia will*, and employs it freely. I give Theo another squeeze and pretend to take a bite of his fat neck while he chortles.

"At nightfall you will go back to the monastery. Enough mapping. I want Ko Dan."

"So do I!" I half shout, startling Theo, who wriggles free of my embrace, affronted. "What d'you think I'm doing there every night? There are three hundred of them, and I don't even know what he looks like! *You* told me not to be seen. What am I meant to do, go up to them one after another and say, *Hullo, which of you is Ko Dan?*"

"Do not be insolent."

She turns her cool gaze on me, and I quake. Most of the time she just looks like an old woman, even if her features vary. But I've seen her look like something else altogether, well beyond human, and there are moments when she looks at me and I feel the full force of her centuries upon centuries, her potential for transformation, the ancient, fading power hovering just behind the kindly face and still eyes.

"I just don't know what I'm supposed to do," I mutter.

"You are a resourceful girl, Julia. Find him. *How* is entirely up to you. I ask only that you remain unseen, particularly if there is another spy about."

Bianka stirs the eggs, not looking at me. Frederick's eyes are closed.

"I'll go get bread," I say curtly, and then, because I am angry and because I can do it, I vanish right in front of her. It wouldn't have worked, once—but I've learned a thing or two about what I can do since then.

Nothing changes in her expression—or nothing that I can see—but I hear Theo cry out, a muffled sound, and I feel a stab of regret. Bianka reaches for him, and I walk out, banging the door shut so they know I've gone.

We entered Tianshi on false papers, and we are all trying to stay out of sight as much as possible—easier for me than for the others. I follow the narrow road outside our gate to the Dongnan Canal and walk along it, toward the market.

To reach Tianshi from anywhere, you must cross either the desert or the sea, and its forbidding walls, famous the world round, are visible for miles, forming a rectangle around the great city. They call it the Heavenly City, and it is indeed a marvelous place. The bells of Shou-shu are chiming, a merry sound for fine weather. The sky is a distant, impossible blue, the sun pouring down on the brightly colored tile rooftops and the green leaves of the persimmon trees. The incantations on the bells were inscribed by long-ago witches; struck in a particular way, in a particular order, they can change the weather. That is why drought and other natural disasters so seldom strike Tianshi. The city and the forests and farmland surrounding it sit lush and green at the edge of the vast desert. The bells call and the rain comes. The bells warn, and the dust storm withdraws. So they say, in any case.

The smaller branches of the trees are wrapped in twists of paper, and some of these little slips are blowing along the street, having come loose from whatever branches they were fastened to, bearing somebody's dearest wish written out in elegant Yongwen characters. It's still odd to me, seeing customs long banned in Frayne flourishing out in the open in Yongguo—like the little shrines to the elements along the roads, or men walking about with tattoos visible on their hands, necks, even faces. I continue along the canal, which is full of narrow, painted boats, their gunwales hung with charms, everything slightly blurred by the haze of my vanishing, while the slender trees loose swirls of petals as well as wishes onto the breeze.

Not so long ago, my vanishing seemed a simple thing, a trick, a gift, and I never sought a reason for it. I thought of it like a pocket in the world, available only to me. A single step back into that space and I was hidden in plain view—from ordinary eyes, at least. There were exceptions: My friend Liddy, in Spira City, could still see me. Then Mrs. Och, and Theo too. But I've learned that the space I used to vanish into is merely the edge of somewhere else. And I've been practicing.

Another step back—my surroundings growing hazier, sound coming a bit muffled and distant—and not even the likes of Mrs. Och can see me. I tried it out on her on the steamer from Nim. "Tell me when you can't see me anymore," I said, and pulled away—carefully—one step, two steps. She didn't say anything, but I saw fear in her eyes when I returned to the world, and while I'm not exactly proud of it, I confess I felt a ripple of triumph. This power is all I've got, and with her I was always powerless. Not anymore.

Three steps back: My perspective begins to scramble, lose focus, and I feel a tingling, a loss of sensation that starts in my extremities. Four steps: I disappear into a dizzying vantage point from which my senses take in everything, from every direction, but I can't find or feel my own body—I don't *have* a body there. I've been practicing this too, because it's one way to get over a wall. From that unsettling nowhere, if I can focus in on a particular spot, I can return to my body there instead of where I started out. For example, on the other side of a wall. Still, I prefer the more traditional means of breaking and entering. Disappearing so completely leaves me feeling shaky and a bit sick. Always, I'm terrified I might not find my way back to my body.

And there is another place even beyond that. I have not dared return to it since I was in Casimir's fortress, where he broke my wrist and all the fingers on my left hand, told me how he watched my mother drown, threatened to cut me open and murder my friends before my eyes. Then, fueled by terror and pain and despair, I wanted only to escape my surroundings and my *self* entirely. And I did.

I still dream of those burning streets. I see my own hands, which were not human hands, and I remember how it felt, and I know that there is something in me I do not understand. The gift I've always taken pride in, *reveled* in, turns out to be the tip of something dark and vast and terrifying. I know it is there, at my back—that I must be something other than what I have believed, if I can enter there.

My desire to know what I can do—what I *am*—and my fear of knowing the same have been pressed up against each other for months. Now I have an idea—something that might lead me to Ko Dan. I've pretended to be many things I'm not. I try to tell myself this will be the same—a pretense—but my heart tightens in my chest just thinking about it. There's fear, yes, but something else too, something I can't quite name—a sort of quivering thrill, like that feeling when you stand at the edge of a high ledge and you almost think you might step off it just to see what it's like to fall.

SIX

To pass the time on the ship that was carrying us along Ishti's great Mohasi River, Professor Baranyi told us the story of Haizea, Ishtan goddess of vengeance, and Tisis, goddess of mercy, arguing over a bereft mother after a battle. We asked him, "So what *did* she choose?" and he said, "Isn't that the whole of the human story? That choice?" This earned him a blank stare from Wyn, an eye roll from Bianka, and a chuckle from Frederick. I was struck less by the story than by the illustration he showed us in a book of the goddesses on their holy hill, watching the battle. Tisis was lovely, her hair like a river, stars on her skin, holding out a cup that overflowed with light. Haizea's hair coiled around her head like snakes, and her eyes were black caverns dripping blood. In one hand she held a whirlwind like a sword. Her hands and feet were clawed.

It was the hands that made me shiver, reminding me of the glimpse I'd had in that other place, high above the burning city, of a hand that was not my own at the end of my arm, holding the gun I would use on Casimir's witch, Shey. While Professor Baranyi pontificated on the parable of the goddesses, why they so often appear together in stories and in art, I stared at the picture of Haizea, looked into her bleeding eyes, and saw something I recognized. Today she will be my inspiration and my disguise.

There is a gap between the Hall of Abnegation and the monastery's north wall, where I've smelled tobacco early in the evening. I go there now and tuck myself against the wall, vanishing. Monks are not meant to smoke, of course. The Shou-shu monks practice something called selflessness, which is not exactly what it sounds like, but maybe that's just the poor translation. They strive to transcend the physical world, all of their bodily needs and worldly attachments. It is said that those who achieve selflessness live for hundreds of years, and that they do not eat or feel pain or desire—although *somebody* is eating those swallow's eggs and the vegetables in Gangzi's garden. In any case, the goal is immortality without the need for sustenance—the triumph of the spirit over the body. The greatest leader of Shou-shu was a man called Li Feizi, who is said to have lived a thousand years before one day walking out of the monastery to the holy mountain Tama-shan, where he perhaps remains to this day. Gangzi claims to be four hundred years old. I have my doubts, and anyway I can't imagine what the point of living forever would be if you're just going to stay shut up in a monastery not eating or feeling anything. I am not in the least surprised that out of three hundred monks, there are a few novices who are doing their time here for prestige, with no intention of taking the lifelong vows, and for whom a secret smoke break is a welcome reprieve from trying to transcend all desire and whatnot.

I hold the image of Haizea in my mind, half hoping that my smoking monk will not come tonight. But eventually he does, squeezing into the gap against the wall and trying to surreptitiously light his little pipe. He is young, and I suppose that can only make it easier. Then again, if he is too new, he may not know anything. I ease myself back into the world next to him, and his features come into focus. He gives a little squawk and drops his pipe.

"Oath breaker," I say in what I hope is passable Yongwen. I practiced it with Frederick this afternoon, once he'd recovered a bit from Mrs. Och's draining him. Even if I can deliver my lines, though, I can't be sure that I'll understand whatever this young monk might have to tell me.

He turns to flee, and I grab him by the shoulder. Here it is. I take a deep breath and yank him with me. One step— two—three—four—oh Nameless, help me—five: it feels like falling—back through the membrane of that edge-of-the-world space, back to the void in between, back to the place I swore I'd never revisit.

Kahge. That's what Mrs. Och's youngest brother, Gennady, called it—the hell of Rainist cosmology. But the idea of it is older than that. Whether he was right or not, it is *farther* than I remember. In Casimir's fortress, it felt as if that place and the world were almost overlapping—I could see them both at once, could slip from one to the other and back again in an instant.

But this is different. I feel as if we are spinning in nothingness for a long time, the monastery and the city and the sky all around us at odd angles, and the monk screaming and then silenced, voiceless. For a horrible minute or two I think we are lost in the void, *lost*.

Then we are through. The boiling river is swollen, and Spira City, half formed and in flames, lies on either bank. Still Spira, no matter where *I* am—and I wonder why. We are standing on a boat that moves fast through the water, its ragged sails full even though there is no wind, only the still air steaming. The young monk falls to his knees, gibbering. My hand on his shoulder is a hooked, dark thing with black claws.

I am shaking with horror at the world transformed, *myself* transformed, but at the same time I feel a rush of something like triumph. Maybe just because I can do it. Not only by accident or in the madness of mortal terror but on purpose, with intent: I can pull another person right out of the world with me. Oh, what *am* I? And also, what power!

I spit the Yongwen words out, my voice hoarse and unfamiliar: "*Where is Ko Dan?*"

He stares at me, uncomprehending, and I think I've overdone it, terrified him beyond usefulness. I give him a shake, not too hard, but his bones in my grip feel absurdly fragile.

I am afraid I might snap him in two by accident. Easy, Julia. Focus. I repeat the question: *"Where is Ko Dan?"*

He stammers an answer that I can barely hear over the roar of flames sucking up the air, over the roar of my heart.

"Again!"

He is telling me he doesn't know. Hounds, what a waste this will be if he knows nothing at all. Now he is talking, but so fast that I don't understand.

"Where? Where? Where?"

He repeats his answer over and over, wringing his hands, and this much I do understand: Ko Dan is gone. Disappeared. My heart sinks. The monk is weeping, pouring sweat. I think he has pissed himself, and frankly I'm not far from doing the same. I manage the bit I memorized this afternoon, though:

"I am Haizea, goddess of vengeance, and I will drown the world in blood and fire if you betray me. If you speak of this, the first blood will be yours. Do you hear me, human? Secret, secret, secret!"

He promises, sobbing loudly. Even if he does tell, he'll be thought mad. When I look up, the boat is moving in slow circles. On the shore, a tall, cloaked figure with the face of a fox and enormous antlers reaches an arm toward me. Shadows gather behind him, monstrous shapes taking form through the smoke, tusks and snouts and curved teeth.

"Lidari," crows the fox-faced figure, pointing right at me with his human hand. What the bleeding stars *are* these things? The other voices join in with awful screeches and roars: *"Lidari! Lidari!"*

I yank the whimpering monk back, away, spinning through emptiness and at last falling hard against the monastery's north wall, behind the Hall of Abnegation. The monk's knees give way instantly, and he sits, huddled and damp, staring up at me. I watch my hand pick up his pipe, stick it in his mouth, fetch his scattered matches, light it for him.

"Good man," I hear myself say in my own voice, putting a finger to my lips. "Not a word."

At first I think that I am all right. I can go to Kahge—or wherever it is—then come back to the world and be on my way. I'm just a little wobbly. But as I round the corner of the Hall of Abnegation, I start shaking so hard I can't walk anymore. I lean against the smooth wood of the hall, clenching and unclenching my fists, struggling to breathe. All I can hear is the rush and buzz of my blood.

My dirty fingernails bring me back to myself. I stare at my shaking hands—but they are just my hands, a girl's callused hands, broken fingernails. The image of those great hooked claws clutching the monk rises up in my mind, and my gorge rises too.

A basic rule of spying is to leave nothing behind—no sign that you have been there. But I leave the contents of my stomach on the path by the Hall of Abnegation before I can gather myself up and make my way home.

SEVEN

"Stoy," says Theo, imperious in the way that surely only royalty and small children can be, pushing my breakfast off my lap and plunking himself down there instead.

"You're going to get me filthy!" I object, but I pull him close anyway, drawing comfort from the feel of his skin and my own—ordinary, human. And yet we have this in common, Theo and I: something inside us that is neither ordinary nor human at all.

In Theo's case, it is part of a book—*The Book of Disruption*. Mrs. Och says that long ago, when everything had a will and an essence of its own, the spirit of fire, called Feo in Fraynish lore, wrote magic into the world, disrupting the natural order by giving herself dominion. The original power grab, in other words. The other spirits joined together and subdued Feo. They couldn't completely destroy the book she'd made, but they managed to break it in three. Then they birthed the immortal Xianren—Mrs. Och, Casimir, and

Gennady, as I know them—and charged *them* with guarding the fragments of the Book, keeping them separate, and keeping order in a world now overflowing with magic. That's the story anyway. Millennia passed; the spirits dwindled and became part of the earth. The fragments of the Book changed shape too—Casimir's became a lake, Mrs. Och's a great tree, and Gennady's a shadow that clung to him. As their power faded, the Xianren had to reckon at last with the inevitability of death. Let's just say Casimir hasn't faced it gracefully. He decided to reassemble the Book, the source of magic in the world, turn it back into text, and harness its power. He already has two fragments: his own, and Mrs. Och's, which he stole.

He almost got the third, as well. Gennady, with the help of the monk Ko Dan, tried to hide his part of the Book from Casimir by binding it to his son's essence and then leaving Bianka and Theo behind so nobody would ever know. It was a ridiculous bit of overconfidence—secrets that big are hard to keep. When Casimir figured out what had happened, he hired me to kidnap Theo. I didn't know that was the job at first, but when it came down to it and Pia threatened my life and the lives of those I loved if I didn't obey Casimir, I proved myself a gutless pawn and did as I was told.

Every day, I wake up with that fact: I took Theo from his mother, and from safety, and I handed him over for silver. I nearly got him killed. Granted, I got him back too—but he's not yet safe. Not until we find Ko Dan and get the Book fragment out of Theo. Then it will be up to Mrs. Och to keep her brother from assembling the fragments. I intend to see Theo safely out of the whole business.

Now I hold him against me and rock back and forth a little. His legs are muddy, and he is wearing nothing but a dirty shirt that hangs to his knees. He looks quite the little urchin, except for how well fed he is, round-cheeked and dimpled at the knees and elbows. He goes about shoeless and perpetually underdressed, never seeming to feel the cold, but today the air is balmy and springlike and so I am having my breakfast on the steps outside. Or I'm trying to, anyway.

"Lala umma wap Teo," he says comfortably. "Stoy."

"Please," says Bianka, washing dishes by the pump.

"Pees," repeats Theo mechanically.

"All right," I say, laughing.

My mother used to tell us stories, Dek and I curled against her body in the bed for warmth. I hadn't thought about them in years, but now whenever Theo asks for a story, they return to me whole, emerging from the depths of my memory like glittering beasts rising up from the bottom of the sea, freighted with all the fears and wonders of my girlhood.

When I tell my mother's stories, I can't see her face, but I remember her intonation, her dark hair falling over her shoulders and brushing against my cheek. I remember her hands illustrating the story: clever brown fingers that became birds flying, soldiers marching, a spider pouncing, the breeze wafting, or the moonlight filtering down.

"Once upon a time," I say, and Theo sticks his thumb in

his mouth, "there was a fisherman called Tomas. He married a beautiful girl and they had a beautiful son."

"Sun!" cries Theo around his thumb, pointing at the sky with his other hand.

"Not that kind of sun," I say. "A boy, like you."

"Teo," he agrees, and goes back to sucking his thumb.

"Yes. So one day Tomas is out fishing when he feels a tug on the line, and he reels in a great big silver-blue fish, twisting about on the end of the hook." I mime reeling in a fishing rod, and Theo mimes along with one hand. "The fish lands on the rocks—*whap*—and says to the man, 'What do you want?' Well, the man is ever so surprised. Fish can't talk!"

Theo cackles. He's too young to understand the stories, but he seems to like them anyway.

"So he takes the fish home, fills a big pot with water from the well, and puts the fish in the pot. The fish swims in circles and asks him the same question again: 'What do you want?' It starts him thinking. At first Tomas thinks that maybe he already has everything he wants. He has his lovely wife, his lovely son, his lovely house on a lovely island. But the more he thinks about it, the more he thinks that none of that is what he wants most deeply. He doesn't want to waste his wish, and surely a fish that can talk is a fish that can grant wishes. So he tells his wife: 'Wife, this life is not the life for me. It does not fulfill my deepest wish. I must go and seek my heart's desire. Please take care of this fish until I come back.'"

Bianka has stopped washing the dishes and is watching

us with a complicated expression I can't interpret. Her hair, normally an unruly black cloud around her face, is tied back in a kerchief, and it makes her face look smaller, somehow diminished. She does not discourage Theo's affection for me, or mine for him, but I can only imagine how she feels seeing me with him. Still, she knows—I am sure she knows; I have told her and it was the truth and she believed it— that I would die before letting anyone harm him again. It's a strange thing to love a child so helplessly. It's different from every other love that I've known. When he laughs his beautiful, crescendoing laugh, I think my heart will crack right open. I could live on that laugh and nothing else.

"Go on," says Bianka. "What happens then?"

"Well, Tomas goes off and he travels the world. He has a great many fine adventures, but he keeps traveling to find his deepest desire. Years pass and he grows old. He is too tired to travel anymore. He goes home and finds his wife packing all her things. He asks her where the fish is. She tells him that she killed and ate it the night he left. Without Tomas to provide for them, they were very poor, but when their son was grown, he went to the city to seek his fortune. He was very clever and became a rich man. Now, she tells Tomas, she is going to live with him in his big house in the city so she can spend her old age in comfort. Tomas remains alone in the falling-down house on the island, and every day he thinks of that beautiful fish twisting in the air long ago and of the moment the fish spoke to him, when everything still seemed possible."

I stop, and Theo pulls his thumb out of his mouth.

"The end," I say lamely.

"Dee enn," he repeats, and slides off my lap, running to chase the chickens around the yard.

"Another of your mother's stories?" asks Bianka, staring at me.

"I don't know any others," I say, half apologetically.

They are odd stories to tell a child—they are odd stories in general—but Dek and I loved them when we were little. When my mother finished telling us that story, we were outraged, berating Tomas for his foolishness, for not seeing that he had everything he wanted already. But Ma said, "I think we are all like that." I can't say that I agree. I can think of times in my own life when I was so happy I only wished that nothing would ever change. Before Ma died, before Dek had Scourge. And then later, with Wyn, for a while. But I think my mother could relate to Tomas—his restless heart, his aimless longing.

Tiring quickly of the chickens, Theo goes and bangs on the gate with a stick.

"Mama!" he shouts. "Owwwwwd."

She shakes her head at him and sighs. "We're going to go mad if we have to stay cooped up in this courtyard much longer."

She looks so unhappy, squatting barefoot in the mud by the pump with the dirty dishes stacked next to her. She has been very low since I told her last night that Ko Dan was missing.

"I'll help wash up," I say. Theo gives up on the gate and comes over to splash under the water and get in the way. We laugh at him and wash up together and it almost feels natural, like we are friends—except, of course, it can never really feel that way.

Nearly clean now from the pump, shirt soaking, Theo runs squealing across the yard while we dry the dishes and carry them into the kitchen. Bianka heads back out ahead of me. From our makeshift scullery I hear her cry, *"Theo!"*

I run for the door, heart in my throat. She is bolting across the yard after him. Somehow he has gotten the latch of the gate open with his stick. He sees her coming and runs out into the road, shouting with glee. Before I can get across the yard, she has him, pulling him back in, slamming the gate. Her face is all twisted up and she is shouting at him: "Never run off! Never!" She whacks him on the backside. He squirms free of her and runs to me, grabbing my leg and howling with rage. Bianka stalks past us and then drops down on the steps, clutching her head in her hands and letting loose a ragged scream that dissolves into sobs.

Theo stops hollering and stares at her in shock. He can't understand any of it, of course—why he has to stay shut up in here or why his mother reacts with such ferocity when he tries to stray out of her sight. He can't feel that piece of *The Book of Disruption* fused to his flesh and blood and his innermost self. If anyone can take the text out of Theo without killing him, it will be the man who put it there. But if

Ko Dan has disappeared from Shou-shu, we are without leads or any idea of where to look for him.

"Theo, my darling," Bianka sobs, reaching for him. He lets go of me and dives into her arms. She pulls him close, covering his curly head with kisses; he buries his face in her neck. I leave them there, a horrible pit forming in my stomach, and go back into the main house.

"Ah, Julia," says Mrs. Och, smiling at me. A tree pipit is perched on her shoulder, and she is holding a rolled-up slip of paper. "We need to find you a dress."

"We do?"

"Yes. Gregor has been granted an appointment with the grand librarian."

EIGHT

Later that afternoon I am at the elegant courtyard house in the Xihuo Triangle with Csilla's knee in my back while she pulls my corset on so tight I can hardly breathe. It's an item I rarely bothered with in Spira City and have not worn at all these past two months, traveling and dressing like a boy. I straighten my shoulders and grimace.

"Nice to see a waist on you again," says Csilla, pleased with her work.

"I don't know. I always wanted a brother," says Dek, who has come by with a sleek, nickel-plated pistol for Esme from a weapons dealer in Dongshui.

Esme laughs at my expression. Easy for her, dressed as a manservant. I'd begged to simply go along vanished, but Mrs. Och preferred to have a role for me just in case, reasoning that I could always vanish if need be but could not spring into existence if I started out vanished.

"I was getting used to breathing freely," I grumble. "I think

I might stick to men's clothes from now on. Take a leaf out of Esme's book."

"Oh, please no," says Csilla. She yanks my hair back so hard I yell and fastens it deftly on top of my head.

"A brother I could call Jules. We'd be a fearsome pair," continues Dek, carefully oiling the barrel of the pistol.

Csilla pinches my chin between her thumb and forefinger and frowns at my face, as if it isn't up to snuff. "Honestly, Julia, you're not bad-looking if you'd just put in a little effort."

"Well, we aren't aiming for beauty today," says Esme. "Plain as plain will do just fine. Julia ought not to attract too much attention."

No fear of that with Csilla nearby. She has been a great boon to the single New Porian dress shop in Tianshi. Today she is wearing a low-cut gown made of watered silk, with a ruffle of lace along the bust, her hair a fountain of white-gold curls. She is utterly contemptuous of the fashion in Tianshi. The women look like they are wearing drapes, she says. I thought so too when we first arrived, watching the ladies in their wide, stiff robes trotting around on dainty silk shoes. But the funny thing is that if you spend some time in a place, you start to see all its strangeness as natural, and I can imagine now how absurd and immodest Csilla's dress might appear to the dignified drape-women of Tianshi.

Csilla dresses me in a plainer gown than her own, a dark blue piece that buttons to my chin, the idea being to make me look as young, and therefore as harmless, as possible. It is still the most elegant dress I've ever worn, and I do not like it. I am meant to be Ella Heriday, Lord and Lady Heriday's daughter, an educated girl and my father's secretary. I look like a miserable governess. I try to take a deep breath, and think that the appearance of a trim waist is hardly worth this feeling of having my lungs locked up.

"I suppose if you've been off buying weapons, you haven't found out who collects the mail from the monastery yet," I say to Dek.

"I have, actually," says Dek. "Or Wyn has, I should say. A government employee brings the mail and takes it out twice a week, and there's a basket of letters bearing Gangzi's seal every time. Anything in particular you want?"

"I'd just like to know what he's writing about. Can you get me one?"

"I reckon we can buy one off the mail carrier," he says. "Mrs. Och gave us loads of money for bribes."

Gregor wanders in with a bottle, more than half empty, of the amber-colored persimmon wine *shijiu* in his hand, and Csilla spins me to face him.

"What do you think of your new daughter?" she asks. He looks me up and down, unimpressed.

"Don't know why you're taking so much trouble with her clothes. Nobody's going to look twice at her anyway."

I suppose I can't fault him for saying what I was just thinking myself.

"Put that bottle down," says Esme. "You can't turn up drunk."

She is the only one who can say it. Esme and Gregor have a long history, dating back to the so-called Lorian Uprising, in Frayne, the year before I was born. Esme's husband, Gustaf Moreau, was Gregor's best friend and a leader of the uprising. Gustaf was captured and hung, along with countless others, the uprising was crushed, and somehow the grief and failure has kept them bonded all these years after. Gregor's expression darkens, but he doesn't argue with her. He puts the *shijiu* on the lacquered side table, throws himself down on the settee, and then looks at the bottle.

"No point going in sober," he says. "I'm supposed to be a Fraynish aristocrat, remember? I grew up with the Fraynish aristocracy. They're drunk all the time."

"Maybe in *your* family," says Esme. "But you're supposed to be a scholarly nobleman, not the drunk, idle variety."

I try to catch Dek's eye, but he has gone back to polishing Esme's gun, studiously avoiding looking at me.

"Rotten stuff anyway, *shijiu*," says Gregor, still gazing at the bottle with a terrible longing. "Flaming Kahge, but I miss whiskey. What I'd do for a nice bottle of whiskey. Or rum. Give me rum. Anything but this fruity *shijiu* stuff. Barely taste it."

"Then stop bleeding drinking it," says Esme.

Csilla powders my face, her dark eyes bottomless and blank.

"Gregor's right, nobody's going to look at me," I say, but she keeps at me like I'm a painting she's working on.

Professor Baranyi comes in, and immediately the mood changes, becoming not exactly hostile, but guarded. When he sees me, the professor looks faintly surprised, as if he'd forgotten I'd be joining them. I wonder if he finds it as uncomfortable lodging with my gang as I do lodging with his. Probably slightly less so, since none of mine have any reason to want to murder him in his sleep; still, I reckon we'd both love to switch.

"Ah! Hello, Julia. Nice to see you," he says.

I doubt it is particularly nice to see me, but I say hello back politely.

"Is Mrs. Och well?"

"Much as usual," I reply.

"Well!" He looks around nervously, his eyes darting between Gregor and the near-empty bottle of *shijiu* a few times. "Are we ready?"

"Ready as we'll ever be!" declares Gregor, rising with a flourish but spoiling it by staggering a little and then giggling.

Even drunk, Gregor cuts a dashing figure. He is tall and broad and graying at the temples, and while his drink-ravaged face could not be called handsome anymore, he has a kind of charisma about him that can at times affect even those of us who know him and his weaknesses all too well. He makes a fine Fraynish aristocrat. Whether he can pose convincingly as a scholar is another question altogether, and I have my doubts, even though the professor has been coaching him for weeks.

Csilla slips her arm through his to steady him.

"You look *marvelous*," he tells her, and she softens against him.

When I was little, I thought Csilla impossibly glamorous, and she and Gregor struck me as very romantic in their moony-eyed devotion to one another—particularly compared to the endless quarreling I remember between my own parents. As I got older and lost some of my illusions, I came to see that drink has always been Gregor's one true love, and that Csilla's glamour is like lacquer painted over a brokenness I can barely fathom. Still, even knowing that they are bound above all by their shared disappointment—with life and with Gregor himself—when I see them gazing at each other this way, I envy them a little. I miss being in love and thinking it such a fine and unassailable thing.

NINE

The Imperial Gardens are guarded by elite warriors called the Ru. Their lightweight, flexible armor covers all but their eyes. They stand with feet planted apart, eyes fixed straight ahead, gleaming weapons strapped to their chests and backs, double-pointed spears in their gloved fists. Wyn and I tried to make fun of them when we first arrived in Tianshi, but the truth is, there is something terrifying about them.

At the great Huanglong Gate, Gregor presents our invitation from the grand librarian to the Ru, and we pass under the twisting, gold-plated dragon that stretches over the top of the gate, its wide crimson mouth pointing down as if to gobble us up. The Imperial Gardens are reputed to be one of the wonders of the world, and indeed, stepping inside those grounds is like entering an enchanted fairyland. There are tiered waterfalls, ponds flashing with red-gold carp, walkways made of pale jade and lined with flowering trees, and brightly feathered birds that watch us from the branches above with an unsettling intelligence.

The Imperial Residences sit on a huge pedestal at the center of the gardens. Arranged around this pedestal, among the lakes and wooded paths and flower gardens, are the homes, studios, laboratories, and so on, of those citizens clever and talented enough to have earned a place here. The buildings are all white, which has a rather blinding effect, while the Imperial Residences are painted bright red, with gold-plated tiles on the sweeping rooftops.

A small troop of the Ru leads us up the steps to the Imperial Residences and an open-air pavilion overlooking the gardens. A tall, powerfully built man in an elegant silk robe, his long beard shot through with gray, is peering through a magnifying glass at a scroll spread across the table in front of him. He is holding what appears to be a needle. He looks up as we approach, then puts aside his instruments and, to all of our surprise, greets us in fluent Fraynish.

"Welcome to the Heavenly City, Lord Heriday," he says in a gravelly but pleasant voice. "I am Si Tan, the grand librarian of Yongguo."

Frederick explained to me that the grand librarian, officially head of the Imperial Library, functions almost as the prime minister does in Frayne—he is second only to the emperor. In fact, though, Yongguo's emperor is quite a young man, and it is said that the grand librarian and the empress dowager are the true powers behind the throne. Si Tan certainly looks like a man who is confident of his authority. He shakes Gregor's hand and raises Csilla's to his lips. She drops a deep curtsy.

"I thank you, I thank you!" booms Gregor. He claps Professor Baranyi on the shoulder, and the professor stumbles a bit. "I brought my translator, but it seems we have no need of him!"

I feel a flutter of anxiety at that. We'd all assumed that the professor would be the main communicator and Gregor merely a mouthpiece, a face. If the grand librarian speaks Fraynish, Gregor will have to bluff rather more effectively than we'd expected.

Si Tan looks at each of us in turn as Gregor introduces us. I do my best to appear unmemorable—the dull, bookish daughter—but still his eyes rest on me, drink me in. I feel as if I'm being memorized and explored. He is an intimidating size, and in spite of his scholarly beard, fine robe, and impeccable manners, there is something of a brute about him, I think. The way he moves like a giant cat, the way he flexes his large, powerful hands, the hardness around his eyes.

"Lovely place you've got here," says Gregor. He glances at the scroll on the table. "Doing a bit of writing, are you?"

"Come, I will show you," says Si Tan, waving him over. "I think miniaturism is not a popular art form in Frayne."

"Minia-whatsit?" says Gregor, bending over the long scroll. "Flaming Kahge, what's all this?"

I crane around him to look. The scroll is covered with beautiful rows of calligraphy, but there is a bright band of color all along its edges. Si Tan hands Gregor the magnifying glass. He peers through it and exclaims, "Hounds, how by the stars d'you do *that*?"

"A visiting artist from Piram introduced the form to Yongguo. We invited many artists from Piram to the city after that, to teach miniaturism." He offers the magnifying glass to each of us in turn. The colorful border is, in fact, a long and complicated illustration. There are boats on rivers, peasants crossing bridges, soldiers on horseback—all of it so tiny that to the naked eye it can hardly be made out at all, and yet I see with the magnifying glass that the soldiers are frowning, that the woman with the bucket of water on her head has a dreamy expression on her face.

"I am only an amateur, of course. It takes years to master the technique," says Si Tan.

"I should think so," blusters Gregor. "What's the bleeding point?"

If this is his impression of a scholar, I think he needs more practice.

"The point of art?" asks Si Tan, smiling faintly.

"It is tremendously clever," says Csilla quickly. "You're quite right that it hasn't reached Frayne. I have never seen anything like it."

"This is the story of a hero we call Muhan, who vanquished giants invading Yongguo from the north," says Si Tan.

"Giants?" says Csilla. She is holding Gregor's arm very tightly, like she's trying to restrain him. "Is it a true story?"

"A legend," he says. "But there is a kind of truth in such old stories, though your Fraynish king may not agree."

I can feel Professor Baranyi's agitation coming off him in

waves. He is like a cabriolet driver watching his vehicle roll down a hill without him to steer it.

"Very interesting," says Gregor, more subdued now. Perhaps Csilla has been pinching him.

"May I offer refreshment?" asks Si Tan, putting aside the scroll.

Gregor brightens immediately. "Splendid! Thank you, yes! It's thirsty weather, isn't it?"

The afternoon passes slowly, in awkward politeness and sipping tea, which has Gregor very glum and disappointed. I am glad now that I did not come vanished, as there is a tray of delicate wafers that melt to a sweet powder on the tongue. I help myself to as many as I can while the others make idle chat. Esme has to nudge me to get me to stop reaching for more, which seems unfair, since the tray is still half full and nobody else is eating any. I notice Si Tan looking over at Esme a number of times, trying to catch her eye, with the air of a boxer sussing out his opponent. He doesn't believe she's a servant, I think anxiously. This is a man who recognizes authority when he sees it, no matter how it's dressed.

Finally, wanting a drink very badly by now, Gregor runs out of patience and interrupts the conversation about architecture that Csilla is managing quite well to say, "Well now, my dear man, we are here to see if we might visit your famous library."

"Ah yes," says Si Tan, his eyes alert, the polite expression on his face shifting subtly. "You are interested in Shou-shu. Tell me."

"Well, yes, that's just it. The hierarchy is what I'm writing on. How monks rise in the ranks, how they keep their authority separate from the empire, that sort of thing."

Si Tan folds his big hands together in a gesture that to me seems full of menace, although I can't say why. "Most scholars want to know about the bells," he says. "Or the longevity of the monks."

"The organization of the place is my real interest," says Gregor. "Not the magic. I want to know how it functions on a, er, *human* level."

"Then why Shou-shu in particular?" asks Si Tan.

"Why? Because it is the most important sect, residing within the most powerful city in the world," says Gregor. He is not doing so badly, I think, even if it all sounds memorized. I am watching the professor out of the corner of my eye, but he is managing to keep his expression neutral. "They govern themselves, keep their numbers small, and have managed it for thousands of years without revolts, dissent, or trouble with the empire. Fascinating."

"You are interested in leadership?" Si Tan asks. "In Gangzi, head of the Shou-shu Council? Succession, perhaps?"

"Yes, yes," says Gregor enthusiastically. "How the leaders are chosen. How they wield their authority. What the rules are. That sort of thing."

"Your past work is largely on New Porian monks, I understand," says Si Tan. "They are subject to the state's authority, are they not?"

"Yes," says Gregor. "Very different system. We don't call

them monks in Frayne, but holies. They run the temples, but they answer to the Crown, yes."

"And it is the same in other New Porian countries?"

"Similar. They all answer to the heads of state, yes, all the holies."

"New Poria proclaims the ultimate authority of the Nameless One, and yet does not place its holies on equal footing with its kings and queens," remarks Si Tan.

"No, indeed, very true, bit of a contradiction, isn't it?" says Gregor, beginning to get nervous a good few minutes after the rest of us have started to sweat.

"You wrote a book on these . . . holies, you call them? The hierarchies within the Fraynish temples. Tell me about your findings."

Gregor blusters through some of what the professor has coached him on. Si Tan asks him one sharply pointed question after another, and with each answer Gregor seems to be floundering more. He does not sound like a man discussing his life's work. He sounds like a man terribly anxious to not say the wrong thing and being as vague as possible. I think I can feel us collectively beginning to panic. Since Esme isn't looking at me, I snatch three more wafers and stuff them into my mouth. I don't know what the penalty is for coming to the grand librarian under false pretenses. Si Tan grows more and more stern and specific. He asks for names. He asks for dates. Twice he corrects Gregor, showing us that he knows more than we'd reckoned about what the professor had hoped would be an obscure topic.

"The Holy Findis, two hundred years ago, wrote a dictum on the relationship between the king and the temple that was condemned, but he was not executed for treason after the trial. What was his defense?"

I have never heard of this case, and apparently neither has Gregor. Si Tan has stopped pretending this is a conversation. It is a test, and he wants us to know it.

"His defense?" says Gregor faintly.

Csilla is getting a wild look on her face.

The professor can't bear it anymore. "I remember taking notes on his trial defense for you, sir," he interjects. "You took a rather surprising position on it, as I remember. That he was not trying to save his life, but to offer a new way of looking at Crown and temple. He believed he *would* be executed for saying that the temple was the root of the tree and the Crown was the trunk, the people of Frayne the branches. But, in fact, the Crown rather liked the metaphor. Perhaps a poor understanding of botany allowed them to take it as a compliment . . ."

Si Tan turns his gaze slowly to the professor, who trails off a bit at the end. He has done Gregor no service here. We are all silent. Then Si Tan rises.

"It has been a pleasure meeting *all* of you," he says with chilling politeness.

He goes to his table, writes something on a scroll, and stamps it with his seal. We all just sit there, frozen. He rolls up the paper and, pointedly ignoring Gregor, hands it to Professor Baranyi.

"Here is my seal and permission," he says. "A man named Fan Ming will call on you tomorrow. He will be your guide and take you to the library. There are no restrictions—you may enter any part of the library and examine all the records you wish to see."

He bows to the professor and then to Esme while a stunned Gregor scrambles to his feet and bows back. I feel a little ill. He's figured us out completely, including who is really in charge here.

"Now, please, stay awhile, enjoy the view. I will ask someone to bring you dinner."

With that, he walks away from us, his elaborate robe trailing on the ground behind him. Esme shoots me a look from the corner of her eye. I pop one last wafer into my mouth and disappear in his wake, following him down the path and into the red building across the way. He walks down a corridor that opens into a room all hung with silk, so it looks like a bright cocoon. Reclined on something that is half seat, half bed, resting against a pile of cushions, is a tremendously large old woman, her white hair coiled snakelike upon her head. Her piles of thick, brilliantly colored clothing give an impression of utter shapelessness, as if there is no human form at all beneath them. Her face is powdered to a ghostly white. A hand with clawlike gold fingernails emerges from the mass of silk. She uses this hand to hold the long tube of a hookah to her lips, inhaling languorously and blowing out plumes of blue smoke that fill the room with their sweet smell.

Si Tan waves his hand in front of him to clear the smoke. He enters with no ceremony and sits himself down next to the woman. I follow him into the smoke of the room, willing myself not to cough. He leans close to her, murmuring in her ear. She smiles a little, like he is telling her something funny, and answers in a rasping voice, speaking out of one half of her mouth. The other half of her face is immobile.

I curse my terrible Yongwen. What good am I as a spy when I can't bleeding understand anything anybody says? Then, to my surprise, this powerful, elegant man lays his big head in her lap and closes his eyes. She strokes his hair distractedly and carries on smoking.

TEN

I lie in bed listening to Bianka's breathing, Theo's breathing, the screech of cicadas in the trees outside. I try to relax, sleep, but my mind is galloping on and on so fast I can't bear to be still. I sit up before I've really thought it through, slip my nightdress off, and creep over to where my tunic and trousers are folded in the corner. I am halfway dressed when Bianka's voice comes out of the dark: "What are you doing?"

"Can't sleep," I whisper. "I'm going to go poke around the monastery."

I've had an idea. A bad idea, but I can't shake it.

Bianka sits up, watching me in the dark as I pull my boots on, wrap the straps around my calves, and fasten my knife to my right leg.

"Shouldn't you check in with Mrs. Och before you go running off?" she asks.

"She's asleep," I say, which may or may not be true and

is not really an answer to her question anyway. "I won't be long."

She doesn't argue with me. I shoulder my bag with the hook and rope and slip out into the main room. The house is dark except for a light under Mrs. Och's door. Surprised, I creep closer and press my ear to it. I hear the low murmur of a male voice. It sounds like Professor Baranyi, but I can't make out what he is saying. I stand there for a moment, bag over my shoulder, undecided. Then I go outside, sliding the door shut as quietly as I can behind me, and vanish—two steps back—by Mrs. Och's window. She keeps the paper blinds lowered, but they are uneven enough that I can peer through a crack at the bottom. Mrs. Och is at her table, hands folded in front of her. Frederick and Professor Baranyi are seated opposite her, leaning forward.

I take a shaky breath. I've been practicing vanishing, it's true, but still, there are things I am not confident of being able to do with any finesse. If I can see a place, I can move myself there by vanishing—kind of like jumping out of my body and jumping back into it somewhere else—but whether I can do it without alerting Mrs. Och is another question. It's risky, but that's never put me off before. I'd like to know what they're talking about so secretly in the middle of the night and why Bianka and I were not invited. I put down my bag and pull back, out of my body.

The courtyard scatters below me. I can hear the chickens breathing, can feel the warmth of the goat, his heart thudding comfortably behind sturdy ribs. I find the crack of light beneath the blinds, and the three people in the room. As soon as I focus on the opposite end of the room, the dark corner where the sliding door leads through to Mrs. Och's sleeping chamber, everything turns around and I am somewhere over the room—no, I am in the corner. I can never leave my body behind without terror, and the panic is so physical that it's difficult to stay vanished. I draw myself back against the wall, comforted as soon as I can feel my body again, the wild galloping of my heart—I'm still here, I'm still me, though vanished two steps from the world. They are blurred and their voices are muffled, but in the quiet of the room, I can just make out what they are saying.

"I'm honored." This from Frederick. "I've spent half my life dreaming of going to the Imperial Library!"

I stifle a laugh. I'll bet he has. Typical Frederick: when other boys were fantasizing about sailing the seas or joining the army, he was dreaming up library visits.

"We will need to tread very carefully," says Professor Baranyi. "Si Tan may have granted us permission only to see what we are really going to look for in the library. It might be best if Frederick and I go alone, acting as representatives of Lord Heriday."

"No," says Mrs. Och. "The permission is in Lord Heriday's name. Gregor needs to be there. You should take Esme and Julia as well, in case it is a trap."

"May I suggest that we tell Julia what I am doing there?" says Frederick. "She might be able to help. I should like to ask her questions."

"Not yet," says Mrs. Och. "Let us see what we find first."

"If I'm to research her power, surely she will want to know more about it as well, and she could provide useful details. . . ."

So that's it. I bite down on my lip hard, a stream of nasty names I'd like to shout at Mrs. Och running through my head.

She cuts him off: "Not yet. Do not make me repeat myself."

His mouth hangs open a moment, and then he closes it.

"The only recorded case of any creature crossing from Kahge to the world is that of the Gethin army," says Professor Baranyi, jumping in awkwardly. "We know that the first Eshriki Phar, Marike, brought the Gethin into the world three thousand years ago, but we do not know *how*. So you should begin your research with the Gethin and with Marike, but cast a wide net. Any texts dealing with Kahge—there will surely not be many—should be useful."

My knowledge of history is shaky at best, but even I know about the Eshriki Empire and Marike, the witch who founded it. It is a cautionary tale in Frayne of the evil days when witches ruled the civilized world. As for the Gethin, I know more about them than I'd like. In Spira City, I was hunted by the last of that tribe, and I shot him through the heart.

Frederick removes his spectacles and rubs his hand across his face. He looks exhausted.

"Are we sure that she disappears to *Kahge*?" he says.

"Whether the Gethin truly came from there is a matter of dispute, after all. Whether Kahge *exists* is a matter of dispute."

"If only we could ask Gennady precisely what he saw when she took him there," says Professor Baranyi.

"We could ask *Julia* what she sees," says Frederick, a note of impatience creeping into his voice. Oh, Frederick, I'm going to have to buy you a present or something.

"We will most certainly have a conversation with Julia when we know a little more," says Mrs. Och, not bothering to hide her irritation. "I have no doubt of Kahge's existence, nor do I doubt that Gennady would know it if he saw it. We—the Xianren—have always felt something beyond the world, something connected to our fragments of *The Book of Disruption*. I can feel the edge of things, and something beyond, but I cannot *go* there, as Julia claims she can."

I want to shout that I never claimed anything, but I keep quiet. I need to hear this.

"The only serious study of Kahge on record was conducted by Yongguo's philosopher-witches," says Mrs. Och, addressing herself mainly to Frederick now. "You will find these in the library. When *The Book of Disruption* was split into three, it was like an explosion of magic, too much for the world to contain and withstand. We think of the consequences in terms of the disruptions it left in the world—witches, magical creatures and objects—but the creation of Kahge was arguably the greatest consequence. The force of the Book's breaking created a kind of shadow—like an image imprint of the world—that we call Kahge. It lies apart from the world, and yet it is connected, and magic drains out of the world *through* Kahge, or so the philosopher-witches believed. I can say from my own experience that the world now is *less* magical than it was in the immediate aftermath of the Book's breaking, and I accept the theory that magic is draining slowly away—fading, just as the Xianren are fading. As for Kahge, the philosopher-witches claimed that life arose there but that they were half lives, like a reflection of life here, insubstantial. Still, somehow Marike is said to have brought the Gethin from Kahge, making an otherworldly and nearly immortal army to serve her empire, and the Gethin, whatever their powers, were certainly corporeal."

She pauses, and I wonder if, like me, they are all remembering that night in her house in Spira City, the Gethin's sad eyes, the way he felled us, one after another, and my lucky shot that brought him down.

She continues in a softer voice: "Witches and others have tried to reach Kahge since Marike's time, to access that overflow of magic, but none have succeeded. If Julia can truly move between the world and Kahge, I do not know what the implications are, for her or for the world. My inquiries about her mother before we left Frayne led nowhere. Everybody had a story about Ammi, but nothing to suggest that she was anything more than a clever and charismatic witch whose primary loyalty was to the Sidhar Coven. No, this is something unique to Julia herself, and I wish to know why."

I'm nearly choking on my fury now. That she is research-ing my abilities without telling me is bad enough, but inves-tigating my *mother* and keeping it a secret too?

"I will be looking for clues of Ko Dan's whereabouts in the library," the professor says to Frederick. "It will be up to you alone to see what you can find out about Kahge, any stories of creatures crossing over."

"I'll do my best."

"I trust you will be discreet," says Mrs. Och, her tone icy, and I know she means, *Don't tell Julia.* I stick my invisible tongue out at her.

He nods. I suppose I can't blame him—it's not as if he didn't try—but I'm annoyed anyway.

"Go home, my friend," she says to Professor Baranyi. "You will need to be well rested tomorrow."

Frederick and the professor bow to Mrs. Och and go out. I stay and watch her for a minute or two, but she just sits at her desk, not moving, hands folded in front of her. Lurking invisibly in her room is starting to give me the creeps, so I go over to the window and peer out at the shadowy figures of Frederick and Professor Baranyi in the courtyard. I fling myself out of my body again—oh hounds, but I hate this feeling—and the courtyard is expanding below me, if there *is* any me left, and yet I can hear Frederick's voice as if he were whispering in my ear:

"I do not like it. She should know about it, since it con-cerns her."

I return to myself by the corner where Theo likes to pee,

jarred back into my body, vanished only one step from the world.

"Mrs. Och is right," the professor says. "I understand your feelings, but there is no point working the poor girl up until we know more. There is always the possibility that what we discover will be dangerous."

"Dangerous how?" asks Frederick.

"I don't know," says Professor Baranyi wearily. "Let us see what we find, and then we will discuss it. Get some sleep, Frederick."

They bid each other good night, and Professor Baranyi goes clomping off down the road while Frederick goes back to the main house and lights a lamp. He'll be up all night reading, I reckon. As for me, I am in a righteous fury, and more than ready to stir up some trouble.

ELEVEN

I start out at a jog, but soon I'm running full tilt down the empty streets, running so hard my legs and lungs ache. I am sick to death of reporting all my movements to Mrs. Och anyway, and if she's undertaking investigations without me, I am more than able to do the same. My chest fills with something like the exhilaration I used to get when out burgling or just roaming Spira City with Wyn. I felt so free back then.

The trolleys stop running at sunset, and so I have to cross the city on foot. I go over the monastery wall with my rope and hook and vanish next to the flagstone through which I saw the spy emerge two nights ago. I'm not in a waiting mood—far from it—and it's only a hunch that the boy is a regular visitor to the Fraynish girl's secret courtyard. But my hunch is right. It's less than an hour before he appears, quiet as a shadow, in the alley. As soon as he bends to lift the flagstone, I step into view, placing my foot over it. He leaps away and pulls from his belt a stick sharpened to a ferocious point. I hold up my hands to show I'm not armed. I won't deny I enjoy appearing this way, as if out of nowhere.

"I'd like a word with you," I say in Fraynish. I figure if he's spying on a Fraynish girl, he's likely enough to speak the language. But he doesn't answer. He bolts. *Blast.* I take off after him. If I can't catch him, this will have been fun but essentially pointless.

I catch up to him as he reaches the east wall of the monastery. I grab him by the shoulder, and he hits me in the face with his elbow, sending me reeling backward. He is nearly flying up the wall. I pull back, out of my body and over the wall, landing a little too hard, breathless and queasy, on the other side. I'm waiting for him there when he comes over. I hold my hands up like I'm surrendering.

"Hullo again," I say.

For a moment he just stares at me, his eyes round and terrified. Then he moves so fast that I don't have time to react; he spins me around and slams me into the wall. He's got me pinned, with the sharp stick pressed against my ribs. This is not exactly how I'd planned it. I'm realizing I hadn't planned it very well at all. All this disappearing and reappearing has got me feeling very queasy, but this isn't a position I care to linger in, so I pull away from the world again, vanishing out of his grip. He stumbles into the wall with a startled cry, and I return to myself a safe distance behind him.

"Over here," I say.

He spins around and draws in a sharp breath, putting

the stick in front of himself defensively. At least he hasn't thrown a jar of wasps at me yet. I rub my side where he jabbed me with the stick. He broke the skin, but it isn't serious.

The Yongwen words are clumsy in my mouth, and I hate to sound a fool at a moment like this, but I ask him: "Do you speak Fraynish?"

"Who you are?" The answer comes in strongly accented Fraynish, thank the Nameless.

"I'm sorry I frightened you," I say. "I just want to talk. Without you trying to kill me with a stick."

"Why?"

"I want to know who you are and what you're up to. And I'll bet that now you'd like to know the same about me. I thought we might be able to help each other out."

When he doesn't reply, I suggest: "We could get something to eat. I don't suppose you know where a girl can find coffee in this city?"

He lowers the stick slowly, and I try not to let my relief show.

"You walk in front," he says. "I tell you where to go."

There is no coffee. We sit on either side of a low table and drink tea from tiny, steaming cups. It is a hole-in-the-wall tea shop if ever there was one—just three tables, and a wizened old woman behind the counter. The place is empty, which is not surprising, as it's closing in on midnight now. The old woman brings us bowls of white rice and little dishes with bony fish and steamed eggplant in a sweet sauce.

The boy puts his pointed stick down on the table and lowers his hood. A long black braid hangs down his back, as is the fashion among young men in the city. His face is all sharp angles, his brows dark slashes over coal-black eyes, his full lips an incongruous softness in an otherwise rather severe countenance. He eats quickly with the two eating sticks they use in Yongguo, his eyes never leaving my face. I follow suit, somewhat clumsily. I'm hungry after all that jumping in and out of the world.

"What's your name?" I ask him.

He hesitates a fraction of a second before saying: "Huang."

I doubt that is his real name. He looks at me expectantly.

"I'm Ella," I say.

He finishes his meal, puts down the eating sticks, and stares at me, waiting.

"Who's the Fraynish girl you're watching?" I ask.

He blinks and says skeptically, "You do not know who is she?"

"If I knew, I wouldn't be asking you."

He shakes his head. "No. First you talk. Who you are? What you are doing here? How you can disappear?"

"The vanishing thing is just . . . something I can do. A trick. A bit of magic." Something that would get me killed in Frayne if I was found out but that I can admit to more freely here. "I'm looking for somebody in the monastery. Since you seem to spend a good bit of time there, I hoped you could help me."

"Who you are looking for?"

Well, here it is. Mrs. Och would be furious, but creeping about and speaking to nobody has gotten me exactly nowhere so far, and I don't know if it's just that he's armed with nothing more than a pointy stick, but I'm betting he doesn't work for Casimir.

"Ko Dan. D'you know him?"

He frowns at me. "He is not there."

"But you know who he is? You've seen him before?"

"He is important man there. Then he go away."

"When did he go away?"

"Year and half," he says.

Not long after putting Gennady's piece of *The Book of Disruption* into Theo, then. Gennady told us that Ko Dan put the fragment into Theo soon after he was born. The magic bound it to Theo's very essence so completely that it would live and die with him. According to Gennady, Ko Dan wanted to murder the baby immediately, thus destroying the text and putting an end to the whole business. But instead Gennady put Bianka and Theo on a train and disappeared from their lives, figuring nobody would ever find them. Only an unwed mother and her child, nobody important. As for Bianka, she didn't know at first what Gennady had done, that her child would forever be hunted by the world's immortals. Seems like the sort of thing you ought to tell a girl once you've knocked her up, if you ask me, but

79

nobody has ever accused the Xianren of being overly considerate. If anyone has made worse choices than me in love, it's Bianka.

"Where is Ko Dan now?" I ask.

"I don't know. Why you want him?"

"I'm working for a Fraynish lady who needs his help," I say, which is more or less true. "You don't have any guesses where he might have run off to?"

He shakes his head. Blast. Well, I still want to know about the girl in the monastery.

"Now your turn," I say. "What are you up to?"

"I cannot tell you."

"I just told *you* what *I'm* doing."

He shrugs.

"Fine. Who do you work for?"

"I cannot tell you," he says again.

I give him an exasperated look, and he cracks the slightest smile, a dimple appearing in one cheek, which makes him look suddenly younger and less ferocious.

"Maybe your boss would like to meet me. Tell him you ran into a charming, witty, semi-attractive Fraynish girl with the ability to appear and disappear right before your eyes. That might interest him, don't you think?"

Incorrigible, I scold myself. He shows you a dimple and you start flirting.

He nods, pressing his lips together like he's trying not to laugh. "I think, maybe," he says.

"Does your boss speak Fraynish?"

He nods.

"All right. Tell him I want to meet him, and see what he says. How will I find you again?"

He gives me a wry look. "I think you know."

"I mean, perhaps you could leave me a message somewhere."

"Here." He nods toward the old woman behind the counter. "Old Thien can keep secret."

"All right. I'll check in with Old Thien soon."

He is drumming on the table very fast with his fingers, a restless tic. "You do not know who is the girl in Shou-shu?" he asks again, like he doesn't believe me.

"No," I say. "Why don't you tell me?"

He shakes his head. I laugh, and he cracks a small, cautious smile again, the dimple reemerging.

"How about the Treasury?" I ask. "Do you know what they keep in there?"

He shrugs, his eyes narrowing. "I am not thief."

"Neither am I," I assure him hurriedly. At least, not anymore. Still, whatever part of me drew me to thieving in the first place can't quite let go of that locked, guarded door.

"You are witch," he suggests.

"I'm not," I say.

He casts his eyes down for a second and then looks up at me, touching his fingers to his own jaw, to the same spot where he hit me with his elbow. Very seriously, he says, "I am sorry I hurt you."

Stars, this boy. Handsome, mysterious, quick on his feet, and now *sweet*. I struggle not to give him a melty look.

"No, it was . . . I shouldn't have approached you like that. I'm all right."

He knocks back the last of his tea and rises. I get up as well and pay Old Thien.

"Glad to meet you, Huang," I say once we're outside.

"Good night, Ella," he says.

Impulsively, maybe because I am hoping for another glimpse of that dimple, I say, "Oh hounds, look—it's Julia, actually."

This time he smiles for real—a luminous smile that changes his face completely. It's the kind of smile you can't help smiling back at. Two dimples, though the left one is deeper.

"I am Jun," he says.

TWELVE

Our guide, Fan Ming, is a handsome man with a clear brow and intelligent eyes. He speaks Fraynish well, but formally and with great care, which makes him seem earnest and a little dull. When he switches to Yongwen to speak to the professor or Frederick, he is quite different, gesticulating and cracking jokes, making them laugh.

The Imperial Library is not in the city at all, to my surprise, but housed inside the holy mountain, Tama-shan, a day's journey north of the city on horseback through the forest. I'm relieved to find that our guide is such a pleasant, scholarly sort of fellow. It's obvious that Si Tan saw through Gregor's attempt to present himself as a scholar, but if we were being led off into the woods to have our throats cut, I don't think Fan Ming is the type of person they'd send to do the job. Then again, appearances can be deceiving, as I well know.

We leave the city through the Xuanwu Gate, under the

massive carved black turtle entwined with a snake. Outside the vast walls, makeshift markets and shantytowns have been built up close to the city. Sellers shout to us to come and try their goods, men sit in rows having their beards trimmed, old women pass us stooped double under heavy loads of firewood, and the stink of meat and fish hangs in the air, the lesser cuts and day-old catches being sold to those who can't afford the city's finer fare. We go to the stables just beyond the raucous market to rent our horses, then mount up and set out riding north. There are a few villages farther out, but we soon pass through all of these and travel the broad path through the forest until suppertime. I have never ridden a horse before. Thankfully, women in Yong-guo do not ride sidesaddle—an idiotic idea if ever there was one—but ride as men do, wearing trousers under a stiff, split robe that separates for the purpose of riding but falls to the ankles when one stands upright.

Even so, by the time we set up camp for the night, an hour's ride from the holy mountain itself, my tailbone feels as if it has been hammered up into my spine, and I can hardly walk. Tama-shan, rising out of the woods ahead of us, is crimson in the evening light, pointing like a finger at the sky. The spring nights are still cool, and so we build a fire, even though we've brought rice balls and dried fish with us and have no need to cook anything. The sky darkens, the stars come out, and we watch the mountain light up as the witches of Tama-shan lay their elaborate fires, writing out spells of safekeeping in flame.

As those distant fires appear on the mountainside, the temperature drops sharply. The trees around us tremble and shake their leaves. Our fire leaps upward, spitting sparks, and the river foams and rushes, as if trying to flee whatever is happening on the mountain. A foul wind sweeps over us, through us, and is gone as quickly as it came, but it leaves us all shivering and queasy, the trees and the grass bristling strangely, the rocks and the water bright even in the darkness.

"You feel that?" says Frederick, awed.

"The Tama-shan witches are strong," says Fan Ming, poking at the fire with a stick.

It's something I cannot get used to—that there are legitimate, important jobs for witches in this country. That one could discover in oneself such a power and find a way to use it profitably, openly, rather than hiding it.

When our fire begins to go down, Frederick heads in among the trees with a lantern to collect more wood, and I follow him.

"So Mrs. Och really thinks we'll be able to find out what's happened to Ko Dan at the library?" I ask him once we're out of Fan Ming's earshot.

"It's a fair bet," he says cheerfully. "Almost everything is a matter of public record in Yongguo—births, deaths, marriages, changes of domicile, all that. You can trace the movement of any registered citizen through library records, and copies of all the Shou-shu records are kept there as well. We should be able to find some hint, at the very least, and hopefully the professor will be able to disguise the real purpose of our research. Tremendously helpful that you found out how long ago he left."

I did not mention Jun last night but said I'd overheard that Ko Dan had gone missing a year and a half ago.

"And what will you be doing at the library?" I ask bluntly.

He gives me a startled look and says, "Why . . . helping." Then he bends over hurriedly to gather some branches. Frederick has always been an appalling liar.

"And you're feeling entirely better, then . . . after the other day when Mrs. Och took your strength?" I ask, letting him off the hook—for now.

"Oh, I'm fine."

We gather sticks in silence for a moment. I can tell he is trying to put some distance between us, but I follow him again.

"I wish you didn't let her do that to you," I say.

"I know," he sighs, finally looking right at me. "I choose to do it, Julia. To help her. And honestly, I'm quite recovered."

"It's horrible. She didn't used to do it in Spira City."

"She had more opportunities to rest and gather her strength then. This journey has been very hard on her."

"Or maybe she's developing a taste for it."

He shakes his head. "It's one way that I can be useful. I can't do what you can do, but I can give her the strength she needs when she needs it. She is a force for good, Julia. She has saved so many lives."

"She didn't save my mother."

It sounds absurd and childish as I say it. I don't know how to explain the revulsion I feel at this ancient immortal drinking up the energies of the young, or the uncomfortable mixture of fear, resentment, gratitude, and awe I feel for Mrs. Och. I bite my lip and wait for him to chide me, but he doesn't. When I look up to meet his eyes, they are all compassion and concern, none of which I deserve—not from him.

"Sorry," I say. "I'm being stupid."

"I wish you could trust her," he says. "She trusts *you*, you know. And with less reason, if I may say so."

I accept the rebuke. I can't answer it, after all, even if it stings. He's right—I don't trust her, and he knows perfectly well that she does not really trust me either. She may be a force for good, as he says, but she is mercilessly pragmatic, and I cannot forgive her for trying to keep from me knowledge of my own mother, of my *self*.

I follow him back to the camp. All evening, as we eat and talk, our fire leans in the direction of Tama-shan, ignoring the direction of the breeze and rising alarmingly high at times, the smoke streaming toward the fires on the mountain like it is being called that way. In the morning, the writing on the mountainside is black and smoldering, the spells still visible.

THIRTEEN

Having risen at dawn, we reach the mountain before the morning dew has dried and tie our horses up at the edge of the forest. A middle-aged woman dressed in a peasant tunic sits on a stump by the cave that leads into the mountain. She is busy whittling something with a fierce-looking blade, but she looks up as Fan Ming approaches. He bows and shows her the letter of permission with Si Tan's seal. She glances at it, not stopping her whittling, and then looks over at us. The corners of her mouth turn down, but she nods curtly toward the cave, and in we go. Fan Ming leads the way, and Esme and I take up the rear.

Odd sort of library, if you ask me, though I'll grant you, I've never been to the regular kind either. The passageway slopes sharply downward, and then the tunnel turns into steps. They spiral around and around, deep underground, and the air gets colder.

"Suppose the punishment for trying to get into the library

under false pretenses is to be buried underneath it?" I whisper to Esme, but she shushes me. Then she stops and I run into her back, which is fairly like running into a solid wall. Fan Ming is exchanging greetings with someone else. Lanterns are lit, which is blinding for a few moments and then a relief. The tunnel walls look paler than I would have expected and are entirely smooth. The roof over us is high and vaulted. I think I see bats hanging up there.

We have reached the bottom of the stairs at last, and whoever is up ahead leads us along a straight passageway that opens into a painted cavern. The paint is so bright it looks wet in the lamplight. Demon gods glower down at us from the high ceiling; a sea dragon snaking along one wall attacks a ship manned by naked sailors; a giant octopus-like creature squats over a castle and appears to be shitting ink all over a bunch of squalling courtiers. I am gaping around at the walls when Esme nudges me. I hadn't gotten a good look at the figure who met us at the bottom of the stairs, but now I see her, hooded and kneeling on the floor, writing in a leather-bound book. There comes the smell of salt water— startling, so far from the sea—and a grinding sound from the stone walls. A door opens where there was no door before, the painted stone shifting aside.

Professor Baranyi holds up his lantern, peering into the darkness, and asks Fan Ming a question. Fan Ming says something about Shou-shu. Together they enter this second, smaller cavern, and they come out soon after, arms full of books bound in leather and flexible bamboo. These they set on a stone shelf at one end of the painted cavern. The professor has the sort of avid look on his face that I associate with gamblers off to the racetrack. He and Fan Ming are rather forgetting to pretend that Gregor—the supposed scholar—has anything to do with this at all.

Frederick says something to Fan Ming in Yongwen, and I recognize the word for Kahge. Fan Ming nods in agreement.

"If you are comfortable here," he says to the professor and Gregor, "I will take Frederick to the old part of the library. If you need anything, Bao Wei will help you."

Esme scowls at the witch, still kneeling on the floor with her legs tucked under her. Traveling with Bianka, and indeed traveling through Yongguo, has led my old crew to a new perspective on witches, so feared and reviled in Frayne, but still, I can see Esme does not want Fan Ming to leave them with *this* witch.

"Of course," says the professor. "Thank you very much."

"I'll come with you," I pipe up, joining Frederick over by Fan Ming. "I could help take notes."

Frederick and the professor exchange a stunned look, and then Frederick stammers, "Ah, no, thank you, Miss Heriday, that won't be necessary."

"I should like to," I say firmly. "It will be very good practice for me." Before he can protest again, I turn to Gregor. "What say you, Father?"

Gregor stares at me in confusion for a moment and then, because he doesn't know what to do, looks at Esme. She gives him a slight nod.

"Miss Heriday should stay with us," begins the professor, recovering from his surprise, but Gregor cuts him off.

"Not at all, it will be an interesting experience for her to explore the library a bit. Go on, my girl."

I smile, triumphant. "Thank you, Father."

Frederick and Professor Baranyi gape at each other but there is nothing they can do. Gregor is supposed to be the authority here, and they can hardly countermand his decision regarding his own daughter.

"Follow me, then," says Fan Ming. I shoot Esme a grateful look and she cocks an eyebrow at me. I'm going to have to explain this to her later.

The passageway we came along branches off into more tunnels and more painted caverns. After several turns I begin to worry I might not be able to find my way back to the others on my own. I do not at all like being this far underground. Frederick clears his throat a few times, glancing nervously at me, but I keep a brisk pace behind Fan Ming and do not look at him.

We reach a much smaller, plainer cavern, where a large woman, presumably one of the librarian-witches Frederick told me about, dozes in the corner. Simple shelves are carved into the walls, and these shelves are filled with bundles of slender bamboo strips nearly the length of my forearm. The woman's eyes snap open when we come in. Fan Ming bows low to her, speaking in very formal Yongwen. She nods and waves a hand toward the shelves, as if giving him permission.

"Many of the writings on Kahge are very old and must be handled carefully," says Fan Ming, taking out one of the bundles and untying the silk around it. The writing on the strips looks almost pictographic compared with the elegant modern Yongwen script I've grown used to seeing.

"May I?" asks Frederick, taking one of the strips in his hands like he's receiving a great treasure. I look at the paintings on the walls and my heart gives a jolt. At eye level there is a black-skinned woman clothed in gold holding a small bowl with two spouts; something white swirls out of the spouts. Next to her, a great many shadowy, white-eyed warriors, shining blades held aloft, are descending a hill topped by fire. The Gethin. I quiver a little inside. Encountering one of them was bad enough. I can barely imagine an army of them. No wonder the Eshriki Empire ruled half the world for so long.

"What is that?" I ask, pointing at the picture.

Fan Ming translates my question for the librarian-witch, then tells us her answer: "That is Marike bringing the Gethin into the world."

"The fire on the hilltop is meant to be Kahge?" asks Frederick, and Fan Ming nods.

I think about the Kahge I have seen—Spira City burning, and those revolting creatures alongside the steaming river, pointing at me.

"What does *lidari* mean?" I blurt out.

Frederick looks startled. "It is a name, is it not?" he says. "One of Marike's generals, or her advisor?"

Fan Ming asks the witch. She answers briefly, and he says, "Yes, Marike's prized general, one of the Gethin."

"So the Gethin *came* from Kahge," I say. "But could they go back and forth . . . between the world and Kahge?"

Again Fan Ming asks the librarian-witch. She shakes her head and answers at length, and then he says: "No, they were bound here by their bodies. A physical body cannot go over to Kahge, though it has been speculated that the *essence* of a Gethin might return to Kahge once its body was destroyed. There is no consensus on that, however."

But I *do* have a body in Kahge. I think of what Mrs. Och said: *If Julia can truly move between the world and Kahge, I do not know what the implications are, for her or for the world.* Thinking too closely about it makes me nauseous with fear.

"And that is the great question, is it not?" says Frederick. "Not only how Marike brought them across, but how she gave them their monstrous physical form?"

"Yes," Fan Ming translates. "It is a mystery none have been able to solve."

"This is older than any writing I've seen," says Frederick, returning to the bamboo strips. "Translating it will take more time than we have today. May I transcribe some of them?"

"Of course," says Fan Ming. "I will help you select those that seem most relevant." He pauses, as if struck by a thought. "The earliest recorded reference to Kahge is carved on a stele. Perhaps I could take Miss Heriday to make a rubbing while you start here."

"Very kind of you!" exclaims Frederick.

I try to catch his eye—I am not keen at all on being separated farther in this warren of tunnels and caverns beneath the mountain. But Frederick barely looks up from the bamboo strips, and I have no choice but to follow Fan Ming out of the cave. If he tries anything, he'll get more than he's bargained for, that's certain.

We climb a different stairway, winding upward until I am quite breathless, and come out into a vast cavern open to the light. The whole cavern is full of standing stones, tall and narrow like gravestones. I find myself blinking and squinting at the great oval view of the world through the opening at the far end of the cavern. We are facing south, and I can see over the forest we came through, the great walls of Tianshi off in the distance.

"The forest of stele," says Fan Ming, gesturing grandly at the standing stones.

He takes me in among them, most of the stones as tall as I am or taller, and I can see that they are all carved with text, some fresh and new, some ancient and worn. Before a very old stele, he sets down his basket and takes out a brush. He cleans the surface of the stone, then lays a sheet of rice paper over it.

"Please hold it still," he says, and I do. From his basket he takes what looks like a ball of dark wax and begins to carefully rub the surface of the rice paper with it, so that the inscription on the stone emerges pale amid the dark smudging on the sheet. When he is done and the text is clear on the paper, he rolls it up and hands it to me.

"There you are."

A cloaked figure calls to him from the entrance to the cavern.

"Excuse me a moment," he says to me. "There is something I must take care of, and then I will take you back to the others. Please—have a look around. There are many beautiful stones, and the air is fresher here than below."

"Thank you," I say, and watch him go. At first I am a little on edge, not sure of the meaning of his bringing me here and then leaving, but it's true it is more pleasant than in the claustrophobic tunnels underneath the mountain. I go to the edge of the cavern to look out over the forest, fingering the scroll he gave me. Perhaps this sheet of rice paper holds all the secrets to this power of mine, if it is a power and not a curse. I just need to make sure Frederick explains it to *me* before he tells Mrs. Och anything.

I feel as if I'm being watched. I turn around and nearly tumble off the ledge in my fright. Standing there is a woman—I think it is a woman—but she has no eyes, just a mass of dark stitching where eyes ought to be. Her head is smooth and hairless, every inch of her tattooed with writing. She wears a sleeveless tunic that hangs to her knees, and her arms and legs too are covered in black ink, the writing winding about her limbs. The air crackles as she moves through it.

"Fan Ming said I could rest here," I babble in Fraynish, forgetting every last word of Yongwen that I know.

"Show me your hand," she says in Yongwen. I don't dare

refuse, and so I hold out my hand to her. I see the little blade in her hand too late. She nicks my finger and pulls the blade away with a smear of blood on it. I cry out, trying to step around her so I'm not on the edge of the cliff. She snaps the fingers of her other hand, conjuring a little flame, perhaps with the characters tattooed on her fingertips, and holds the knife in the flame. My blood sizzles, and she says to me: "Your mother was a witch. Drowned."

That stills me. I clutch my bleeding finger and say, "Yes."

"Your father?" she asks.

"Just a man," I say in Fraynish. "Not much of one either."

She shakes her head, not understanding me, and barks: "Speak Yongwen."

I struggle for the words. All that study, and every last bit of it has flown.

"My father ... man," I manage in stuttering Yongwen. I cannot think of the word for *ordinary*, which would have been too much of a compliment anyway.

She sniffs the knife. The fingers of her free hand move in the air. It takes a minute to register what she's doing, and by the time I realize she's writing, it's too late. I've only ever seen one other witch who could work magic by simply writing in the air with her fingers. I try to move away from her but I cannot move at all. My thoughts have gone thick and slow as molasses, struggling to crawl along through a heavy, dark space. She raises my arm to her wrinkled lips, and then out comes a black tongue and she licks my wrist. Everything in me recoils, and I almost remember something—a way out, another place—but my mind is slowed and dim, and the thought slips away almost as soon as it comes.

The witch pads closer and puts her arms around me. Muttering to herself, she feels the knobs in my spine, lifts my hair to her face and sniffs it. I stare at the tiny, spidery writing running along her cheekbones, down the bridge of her nose, across her forehead, covering every bit of her. Even the stitching over her eyes, I realize, is not random but a mass of tiny threaded script. *Who are you?* I want to say, but I can't find a way to speak. She presses her thumb to my forehead and everything goes black.

FOURTEEN

I am kneeling on the pitching boat before Bianka while Theo traps a marble under a cup. My voice is thick with unshed tears: "I'd die before letting anything happen to him again. I swear to you, I'd die first." And she reaches for my hand.

Pia takes Theo from my arms, shuts the door in my face, and I am standing in the hall with a bag of silver.

I take the book off the shelf in Professor Baranyi's study—Legends of the Xianren I—and open the heavy tome in my lap.

I fire the gun and the Gethin falls. Mrs. Och is bleeding against the wall. I crawl over her wings to finish him off.

The fire is warm, the coffee is good, and Gregor says to me: "When the client wants to see you, I'll let you know."

* * *

A blur of images and memories rushes through me, spills out of me, like my life flashing before my eyes, slowing down for certain scenes and then speeding up, racing by. A flood of color, a bright burst of laughter, a scream, my heart racing— I think I will burst with feeling it all at once—my bare feet on the cobblestones, the moon rising over Mount Heriot, music pouring out of the temple, honey on my tongue, a hand on my cheek, waking with the morning light, all the lost moments returned to me and snatched away again in the space of half a breath.

And then it stops.

I am sitting on the steps up to our flat above the laundry, eating an apple I've stolen. My mother was taken the night before, and I do not know what to do. I am horribly aware of my heart in my chest, its relentless thud-thud-thud. *Dek and I had been to stare at the outer walls of the great prison, Hostorak, but we were just children—what could we do? My father stumbles down the stairs past me, a scarecrow in his raggedy clothes, his hair unkempt, his face ruined by opium. He looks back at me, but barely, half a glance over his shoulder, not meeting my eyes. "Forgive me," he mumbles, and then he is gone, and that is the last time I see him.*

Again the blur of sensation and emotion, my life speeding backward, and halting years earlier:

I am shouting for my brother, and he comes, he always does. Two older boys have caught a cat and shut it in a box. They are looking for tinder to burn it, and the cat is howling in the box like it knows what they have in mind. When I tried to free the cat, one of them hit me right in the nose with his fist, and now my nose is bleeding all over my mouth and chin and pinafore. When Dek sees me, he is ablaze with fury. I tell him in a great sobbing jumble what is happening. Oh, the splendor of him striding down that street, the way he knocks those boys' heads together—never mind that they are both a year older than him—the way he sends them scurrying. He lets the cat out and tries to pat it, but it scratches him across the face. We come home bleeding but triumphant, and our mother looks at us and sighs. More laundry.

And back, and back:

They are quarreling, my ma and pa. He is searching the room, tearing it apart, and she is shouting at him, and Dek is shouting at both of them, but Pa is simply fixed on pulling open cupboards, looking in the kettle, pulling the mattress off the little bed, leaving our small home a ruin. He is looking for money. My mother grabs his arm and he shakes her off, and Dek lunges at him, roaring, and he gets knocked aside too. I am about two years old. I am crying, but nobody hears me, and then it is too awful for crying and I draw myself away from them. I hadn't known I could do it, but suddenly they are all a bit blurred, muted. I feel safe. My father goes storming off, and my mother and Dek are righting things about the flat when Dek says, "Where's Julia gone?" She looks around, her eyes moving right past me, and the same with him. They look and look but they do not see me sitting right there against the wall, still as a mouse, holding my breath. It seems obvious to me that they should not be able to see me. It seems like I have always known this hiding place in plain view was there for me and me alone. I watch them search for me, and my ma sends Dek running to look about the neighborhood, and then she looks so lost that I pity her, and I go and throw myself into her arms. I expect her to embrace me, to be relieved and happy, but she pulls me off her, holding me at arm's length and searching my face, her eyes wide and amazed, looking at me hard, like the answer might be there, and I am crying again—I just want her to hug me, to tell me it's all right, it's going to be all right.

It is all wanting and terror and joy, the world huge and bright, and then a darkness unlike anything I've ever known, a rushing and roaring in my ears. I emerge again, but this is different:

I am kneeling on the red earth with my mother, Ammi. But it is not me—I am not her child. A rocky crag looms over us, a little black house at the top of it. Far behind us and below us, the world is like a moving painting of itself, half real. She holds in her hands a small clay pot, almost like a teapot but with two spouts, one on either side of it.

"I have it," *she says to me.*

"We are almost ready," *she says to me.*

"Can I trust you?" *she says to me.*

Her dark eyes, her pretty mouth. I see her so clearly, and she seems to pulse with life. I envy it, I am hungry for it, and I will do anything, anything at all.

Her hand on my face. The warmth of her.

"You won't fail me."

It is a statement, not a question. She is fearless and lovely. Leaving me with my longing, she wades into a river of mud and disappears into the world. A gurgling voice above me says, "You need to go back. They are waiting for you."

And I wonder what I will tell them. I wonder if I will really betray them. But I know the answer to that. Her eyes, her skin, her beating heart, those little buildings far below, the whole story of human existence unfolding all at once, all the time—fear is nothing, loyalty nothing, next to my desire to be whole.

I open my eyes and am vaguely surprised that I have eyes to open. I am sprawled numbly at the center of everything that has ever happened to me, all of it spread out to be examined by this witch's nimble fingers—except that last one, which is not my memory at all but someone else's, of somewhere I've never been or dreamed of. The witch is squatting on my chest and I can hardly breathe. Her tattooed hands work through the threads around me and all over me—or are those ribbons, or what are they?

Then I remember the thought that eluded me before: I can disappear. But the effort it would require feels quite beyond me. I watch the witch, so preoccupied with her task, and I notice the little knife strapped to her wrist.

I can't move my arm *in* the world, but I can pull it out of the world—just that part of me, just past the edge of things, far enough to be free of the spell paralyzing me. I vanish my arm, then swing it up and snatch her little knife. I stick the blade into her arm. She squawks. It's a stupid thing to do.

The knife is tiny, can make no more than a small puncture, and she has me immobile on the edge of a cliff.

She takes hold of a fistful of my hair and knocks my head against the rock. Suddenly I can hear a lot of talking, and it seems to me that maybe this noise has been going on for a long time. She gives my head another bang. Fan Ming is standing a few feet away, shouting. He is pressed against some invisible barrier in the air, trying to reach us, and there is Frederick behind him, also shouting. The witch ignores them and bends over my face. She bites my cheek, hard. The pain clears my head, and I pull my whole body back, blurring the world, freeing myself of whatever binds me. I shove her off me with all the strength I have. She sprawls on her back, grinning, my blood on her lips.

I make a desperate scramble toward Fan Ming and Frederick, feeling that surely this is all a dream, a nightmare. I find myself in Frederick's arms, and his voice, which is both too loud and oddly far away, is asking me if I am all right. Fan Ming is gesticulating wildly now, shouting at the witch. She raises her arms up above her head, fingers working. I whisper, "*Run*," but none of us move, and then small winged shapes are diving down from the ceiling of the cavern, filling the air. *Bats.* Frederick shoves my head into his jacket and we are on the ground, me gasping for breath inside his coat, my face close to the rock. I feel a few vicious pinprick bites on my back, my legs. I thrash and yell in the darkness of Frederick's coat and then they are gone.

Frederick helps me to my feet. He is trembling and white-faced and the arm he shielded me with is bleeding. The witch is walking off among the standing stones. I try to make words, but my mouth feels thick and furry, my mind too heavy. I lean against Frederick and think about my mother, how clear she was in the memories the witch pulled out of me—a clearer picture than I've had in years—but that last one wasn't *my* memory, so whose was it? I'd half forgotten her face, its lively expression, the warmth of her gaze, the humor of her mouth. Ma, the luminous center of my world until she was gone—and it seems to me now that everything has been askew and all wrong ever since then, including me.

I wonder later if I fainted, but I'm too embarrassed to ask. Frederick carries me back to the painted cave below, where Professor Baranyi is standing at the shelf making notes and Gregor is pretending, not very convincingly, to be absorbed in a book.

Esme sees us first. Her face doesn't change, but the pistol Dek got her seems to leap from the holster at her side into her hand—she is pointing it straight at Fan Ming's forehead.

He blanches, raises his hands, and says in a rush: "A witch attacked Miss Heriday. Not one of the Tama-shan librarian-witches—I do not know who she is. I am sorry, but we must leave immediately. It is not safe, and I have no authority here."

"He's right," says Frederick. Esme lowers the gun slowly but does not holster it. I notice then, with some relief, that Fan Ming is holding the rolled-up stele rubbing he made for me. I thought I might have dropped it off the cliff when the witch appeared.

"A little more time—" begins Professor Baranyi, but Esme shuts him down.

"We're leaving now."

꩜

Professor Baranyi begged to prolong our stay, then asked for a private word with me, but Fan Ming and our witch escort, Bao Wei, were firm in ejecting us quickly from the library, and they flanked me the whole way out. With Esme on their side, the professor gave up, and now he looks very glum and unhappy on his horse.

As soon as we are back on the road in the forest, me slumped on a horse in front of Frederick, I feel better. When I sit up straighter, he says, "All right?"

"Yes," I say, relieved to find I can speak easily again. "I don't know what that blasted witch did to me."

His voice is low, close to my ear. "Fan Ming brought me up to the forest of stele, and you were . . . I don't know how to explain it . . . you were tied up on the ground, but the knots and bindings were not of any earthly matter. It was as if you were tied up by darkness, and all around you pieces of light and shadow were moving across the ground, and that witch was stirring through it all with her fingers."

I don't dare tell him what I saw, what I remembered. Not until I understand it a little better myself.

"Nameless only knows what she was doing. I hope you found *something* worth almost dying for in that place."

He gives a shaky laugh and says, "I think when all this

is over, I'm going to get a nice, quiet job at some obscure, second-rate university somewhere."

"You won't," I say. "You'll keep on doing horrifically dangerous and difficult things for Mrs. Och."

He laughs properly this time. "You're probably right," he says. And then, more gently: "What about you? What will you do when this is over?"

"I don't know," I say. "I reckon that depends."

"On what?"

"On how things turn out."

There is a heavy pause, full of all the terrible ways this *might* turn out. But even if we succeed, the truth is that the future terrifies me. Say we find Ko Dan. Say he fixes all this, and Theo is safe. Can I go back to Spira City? And if I can, then what? Back to a life of crime in the Twist? Or turn my back on that old life and become a barmaid, fending off desperate old coots night after night? I can't imagine a future for myself, a grown-up life I'd be glad to inhabit.

And beyond all that, it depends . . . it depends on what it means that I can disappear, that the world's edges are porous, but only to me.

"Why did you insist on coming with me in the library?" he asks.

I tell him the truth: "I overheard Mrs. Och asking you to research me. I want to know the answers too."

He is quiet for a bit. At last he says, "It is unusual for her to encounter something she cannot explain. I think it worries her."

"It worries me too," I say. "I thought it was all a great lark, a piece of brilliant luck, my vanishing trick, until I stumbled into Kahge. If that's what it is."

"Well, perhaps you can tell me . . . how it feels, what you see?" He's been dying to ask, I can tell—held back only by Mrs. Och wanting to keep me away from my own secrets.

I *do* trust Frederick, but it is hard to find words for how it feels. I tell him what I can—the steps of vanishing, the way it feels to lose contact with my body, how I am different in Kahge, Spira City aflame. And haltingly, I tell him about the creatures at the side of the river, screeching the name Lidari. Lidari, one of the Gethin, Marike's prize general thousands of years ago.

"I know that witch in the library said that the creatures in Kahge don't have bodies, but they *did*," I say. "They didn't look like the Gethin, though. What happened to Lidari, anyway?"

"He served Marike for centuries," replies Frederick. "Mrs. Och would be better able to tell you about her. Marike was the first real threat to the authority of the Xianren. Before that, every human empire had at least made a pretense of obedience to them. The Eshriki Empire was the beginning of the end of Xianren rule. Indeed, at one point, at the height of her power, she even imprisoned them and tried to reassemble *The Book of Disruption* herself."

"I remember reading about that in Professor Baranyi's study," I say. I hadn't understood what I was reading at the time. "She couldn't read the Book, though, could she?"

"No. Only the Xianren could read it and reassemble it. They outlived her empire, of course. The story is that Casimir hunted down Lidari, executed him, and sent his head to Marike. However, these legends are rarely the whole truth of the matter."

"So why would those . . . *creatures* in Kahge be shouting Lidari's name?"

"I've no idea," says Frederick, sounding ridiculously cheerful. He loves having baffling questions to dig into. "I hope that the transcriptions I made will be revealing once I translate them all."

I think again of the little pot my mother was holding in the vision I saw—like the little pot Marike held in the painting on the library wall. I don't dare ask about that—not yet.

"And you'll tell me what you find," I say. "No matter what Mrs. Och says."

A long pause, and then he says, "I'll tell you."

The cool forest passes by us, Tama-shan receding as the city walls approach. I try to take comfort in being myself, in my own body, safe among friends—more or less safe, more or less friends. But my skin is still crawling with residual fear as I think of what I saw in the cave, that other self, not me, whispering with my mother, plotting and longing . . . for what?

FIFTEEN

We make it back to Tianshi just before the city gates close for the night. Fan Ming exchanges polite farewells with the professor and Frederick. Gregor has all but given up pretending to be Lord Heriday, since Fan Ming pays him no attention anyway. Then Fan Ming turns to me and says, "I am relieved you were not badly harmed, Miss Heriday. I am so sorry I could not prevent what must have been a very frightening experience."

Could not, would not, did not. I meet his eyes and thank him in my best polite Yongwen, but I'm thinking that if I'm ever alone in a dark tunnel with him again, things will go very differently. He promises us that he will report the "incident" to Si Tan, though I suspect that Si Tan orchestrated the whole thing.

We part ways with Gregor and Esme when we reach the second tier road, as we are going in different directions.

"Come see me in the morning," says Esme to me as we say our goodbyes, and I nod, wondering what on earth I will tell her to explain why I'm so interested in Frederick's research. Having people like Mrs. Och or Frederick know the awful depths of what I can do is one thing, but I'm afraid of how differently the people I love might look at me.

The moon is high and bright when the professor, Frederick, and I arrive at the house in Nanmu. Mrs. Och and Bianka are waiting up, and as soon as they see us, Bianka cries, "What happened to your *face?*"

I lift a hand to the scabby imprint of the witch's teeth on my cheek. "Somebody bit me," I say flatly, and then add: "A witch."

Mrs. Och raises her eyebrows.

"Julia was assaulted by a most powerful and unusual witch," says the professor. "Fan Ming seemed very shaken by it, but it is possible he was involved."

"Fan Ming took me to that cave and left me there," I say. "He knew."

"Come, sit by the fire," says Mrs. Och. "Describe to me what happened."

I feel very uncomfortable with all of them staring at me, but I tell them what the witch looked like, the way she sniffed and licked and bit me, the way she tumbled my memories about like she could pull them from me and examine them. I don't mention that last memory of my mother, the one that wasn't mine.

"Perhaps that is why we were granted access," says Mrs. Och when I am done. "Si Tan wanted to know who was prying around his library and for what. Now he will know not only what we are here for, but who you are and what you can do."

Who *am* I? What *can* I do?

"Julia wanted to assist me in my own, separate investigation," says Frederick cautiously, and Mrs. Och turns her most terrible gaze on him. He does not quite meet her eyes, but he carries on, stumbling only a little. Oh, Frederick—stalwart and true, you are. "We spoke of what she sees and experiences when she crosses over to Kahge. She saw some beings . . . creatures with physical form. They were calling out the name Lidari."

"Ah," says Mrs. Och. And that is all.

"Will you describe the creatures you saw, Julia?" says Professor Baranyi.

I do my best, though it makes me shudder to think of the misshapen beasts emerging from the mist, that antlered thing pointing at me with its human hand. I watch Mrs. Och as I talk, and I do not like the look on her face. The look of locking me out. Whatever she thinks about all this, she is not telling me.

"I'm sorry you've had a fright, Julia, but what about Ko Dan?" Bianka breaks in impatiently. "I thought this trip to the library was to find out where he's gone."

A look I can't interpret passes between the professor and Mrs. Och. Then he clears his throat and replies, "The Shou-shu records do indeed show Ko Dan taking a trip to Sirillia a year and a half ago, for the purpose of meeting with Zor Gen of the Xianren."

"We already know *that* from Gennady," snaps Bianka. Her nerves are clearly frayed. "They stuffed this magical book inside my son while I was sleeping."

"Indeed," says the professor. "Upon his return, Ko Dan was reprimanded—officially, for the misuse of a magical object. He was exiled to Tama-shan for meditative penance, the plan being that he would return to the monastery when he and Gangzi agreed he was ready. Now, I did find a new note in another record book suggesting that Ko Dan sent Gangzi an appeal requesting permission to return. There is no record of Gangzi's answer, but the appeal was registered only a few weeks ago. Of course, we have no way of knowing how accurate these records are. They might have cut his head off and put something rather prettier on the books. Given Si Tan's suspicion of us, we must also consider the possibility that the records were altered for our benefit and are intended to mislead us."

"But if it *is* true, then Ko Dan was *there* in Tama-shan?" cries Bianka.

My heart plunges into my stomach. To think we might have been so close to him and let the chance slip by! No wonder the professor didn't want to leave. I don't see how we'll get back inside the library. Si Tan isn't going to issue permission again, and while I am generally confident of my breaking-and-entering skills, a mountain aflame with protective spells is not something I want to take on.

"I tried to get us more time," says the professor helplessly.

"We need to confirm this version of events," says Mrs.

Och. "Dek and Wyn should press their contacts, find out what the rumors in the city are."

I hold back a snort, since their *contacts* seem to consist of a few barkeeps and two pretty girls.

"If we can be sure that Ko Dan is in the library, I will go there myself," says Mrs. Och to Bianka. "But we must be *sure*. Once I reveal myself, we will have only a short time to act. Now it's late. We will decide on a course of action in the morning."

And so we are dismissed. Frederick and Professor Baranyi go to make up a bed for the professor in the servants' quarters, as it's too late for him to go back to the house in Xihuo, and Mrs. Och retreats to her room, closing the door. Bianka looks at me and sighs.

"She didn't tell me the truth about Gennady or Theo until she had to," she says. "She likes to keep things to herself."

"I know," I say.

I stay awake for hours. Only when I'm sure there will be no secret whispered council about the True Nature of Julia—or anything else, for that matter—do I let myself sleep.

SIXTEEN

I feel as if I've barely put my head down on the pillow when I'm woken by Theo's crying. He has pulled off his diaper and wet the bed, and Bianka is cursing a blue streak.

"Dipe umma *noooo!*" screams Theo when Bianka tries to pin a new diaper on him. He wriggles free of her. She sticks herself with one of the pins and begins cursing again. I leave them to it, wearily stripping the sheets off their mat and tossing them in a corner. I lay a spare blanket down to act as a sheet.

"We can wash those in the morning," I say. "No point trying to do it in the dark."

"*We?*" says Bianka. "Me, more likely. You'll be off doing whatever you do all day, intrigue and whatnot, and I'll be stuck here like always."

She is trying to hold Theo down, but he slams his head into her mouth and wriggles skillfully out of her grasp, fleeing across the room. She gasps with pain, raising a hand to her lip.

"Little rotter," she says, fighting back a sob. "Come here and put your diaper on."

"Dipe umma NO!" roars Theo. No doubt he's woken the whole household by now—not that Mrs. Och or Frederick is going to come to our aid.

"Look, how about I tell you a story while your mama fixes you up," I say.

Theo is standing in the corner of the room now, starkers, but he regards me warily, considering this.

"Yes," says Bianka with desperate enthusiasm. "Won't that be nice? You love Lala's stories, don't you, darling?"

"Stoy," he says, like it's his idea.

"I've got a good one you've never heard before," I say.

He comes plodding over, suspicious, still ready for a fight. I half want to laugh at how the powers of a witch and a vanishing spy combined are barely enough to get a tot into a diaper. But then, like always when I offer him a story, one comes up from the depths, all its details intact, every word that my own ma whispered to me all those years ago when we lay abed together in the dark nights.

I tell them about a princess so beautiful and so rich that noblemen the world over sought her hand in marriage. Her parents urged her toward various useful alliances, but she declared that she would only marry the man who brought her the Cup of Life, a magical cup said to grant its keeper immortality. Her parents were very angry, thinking this

115

was a ploy of hers to never have to marry anyone. When they accused her of this, she admitted it freely, saying she preferred to stay unmarried and rule her own kingdom after they were gone. But one day something came to the palace—a creature half man, half dog, with a cloak made of darkness and ice—and he claimed to have in his possession the Cup of Life.

I pause. Like all my mother's stories, it is relentlessly grim. But Theo is quiet and diapered now, nestled against Bianka while she strokes his curls, so I carry on: "The princess quaked when she saw the thing that had come to see her. His dark boots seemed hardly to touch the ground, his cloak brought a terrible cold into the warm hall, and his face was that of a beast. He held in his clawed hands a simple cup of red clay, and she knew that to accept it and to accept him would indeed mean that she would live forever."

Theo's eyes are drooping closed, his breathing slowing down. I keep my voice to a soft monotone.

"Her parents pressed her to refuse and tried to cast the thing out, but their guards were frozen in time, unable to move. 'If you accept this,' said the beast, 'you will belong to me and you will never die. If you refuse, you will belong only to yourself, but soon your flesh will rot and your bones will turn to dust in the earth.' The princess shuddered to think of this fate. Better to live forever, whatever the cost. 'I accept,' she said, and she reached for the cup. The instant her fingertips touched the cup, it swallowed her up and she disappeared inside it. The beast tucked it back into his cloak and left the palace. Neither the princess nor the beast with the Cup of Life was ever seen again."

Oh, Ma, what *were* you thinking, telling us such tales? I lie there waiting for sleep to come, but then Bianka's voice comes instead, not sleepy in the slightest: "Such horrible stories you tell."

"They're the only ones I know."

I think again of the look on my mother's face in the vision or memory I had of her holding that double-spouted pot: *I have it.* Was it something so powerful she feared it might swallow her up? But she didn't seem afraid. She was never afraid. Even standing on the barge before the roaring crowd that day, her eyes roving over the people but never falling on me, held tight by Dek as I screamed and screamed, my world splintering around me. She must have been afraid, but she did not *look* afraid.

"My gran, who raised me, was not much one for stories," says Bianka. "Perhaps because all the good ones stink a little of folklore. She was a royalist, very taken with King Zey and his philosophy. She was too practical a woman to be telling me tales."

"What about your parents?" I ask.

"It's not a pretty story."

"That's all right. I mean, I don't mind. You needn't tell if it's . . . if you don't want to."

"No, it's not that," she says. "I never knew them, and so, while I think it sad, it is just another sad story about other people. My gran and granddad came to Frayne from

North Arrekem. They bought a dairy farm and my ma was a proper little milkmaid, but then a hired hand forced himself on her. He ran off afterward and left town. Nameless knows what became of him. My poor ma tried to get rid of me in the womb, but I held on, very stubborn. After I was born, she fell into a great sadness. She was unmarriageable now, and far too young to be caring for a babe, and some women, well, after having a baby, they can get awfully blue. That's how it was with her. She hung herself when I was a few weeks old. My gran and granddad raised me, and I loved them, but I never felt right in that little town that was all a-whisper about my ugly beginnings. My gran died of a fever when I was fourteen, and it was just impossible, me and my granddad alone and him such a quiet man. I still feel awful about it, but I left for Nim a year later, made my way as a dancer and cabaret singer. I never had the courage to go back and tell him I was sorry. I don't even know if he's still alive."

"When did you know that you were a witch?" I ask her.

A little laugh in the dark.

"Oh, first time I held a pen, I knew," she says. "Perhaps even before then. When I saw my granddad making notes in his ledger, keeping his accounts, I thought I *must* know how to do it. I told him I could keep the ledgers if he taught me to read and write a little, and so he did. And *then* I knew. I could feel it whenever the pen touched the page—how the paper became everything and the ink was my will and the world might bend to what I wrote. I didn't dare write anything to

118

make it so, not until a calf I was fond of fell ill. Then I wrote on a scrap of paper *Missy don't die.* The whole house smelled of the magic, and I was terrified. I ate the paper I'd written on, and my gran and granddad never suspected, though they fussed and worried about the smell for a day."

"And Missy?" I ask.

"She got well again, but I was so feverish I couldn't get out of bed for a week. So I learned I could do it, and I learned what it cost me. It was too big a spell to start with—the saving of a life. I learned to hide it—how I couldn't burn, how strong I was—and I swore off writing anything. Too dangerous, too painful. I wanted to be a dancer, not a witch."

"If we find Ko Dan and he can help, might you stay here in Yongguo?" I ask. "Or somewhere else where witchcraft isn't punished?"

"No," she says. "Frayne is home, for all that it's no place for a witch. I'm a witch only by accident, not by choice. I've no true desire to write magic, never mind the way my fingers itch when they get hold of a pen. I want to go back to Nim."

"But what will you do?"

"I don't know. I'd rather keep myself than go back to being a rich man's mistress, though there's always money in that. If I could just get home, I'd find my feet. I have friends that would help us while I sort things out. If I save up enough, I could even open my own music hall by the sea. Oh, I don't know, I only want to have a life again, be done with this nightmare."

I think of all the women I've known. Scraping by in the

Twist, most of them, hawking their wares at market, scrubbing the privies of the rich, and so on. I used to swear, when I was little, that I would never be like them, nor even like Ma, her hands rough from washing, all those hours of rinsing and hanging and folding. Now I am surrounded by women who have forgone the well-trod path, the ordinary ways of being a woman in the world: Esme, with her criminal empire; Bianka, dancing and going about with rich men; Csilla, in the theater and Nameless knows what else before she left it all for Gregor. But I can't see among them any path that I might take.

"What about you?" she asks me, as if she's heard my thoughts.

"I want to go home too."

"And you'll have plenty of gold," she says, without cruelty. "You'll be all right."

It sounds foolish, trite, but I must say it anyway: "I'm not here for the gold."

"Oh, I know that," she says, and she reaches across the narrow gap between our sleeping mats, takes my hand, and draws it over Theo's chest, rising and falling, so that we are holding hands over him. "I wonder now if I can truly call the people I knew back in Nim my friends. They don't know what I am, and if they did know, I expect they'd turn me in."

"They might surprise you," I say, just to be kind. We both know how unlikely that is.

"I'm grateful to Mrs. Och," she continues. "I owe her my life, and Theo's. But I also know that, like Casimir and like

120

Gennady, she cares about something *in* Theo, not Theo himself—that bit of book they're all obsessed with. To me, he's not a bit of book, he's my darling boy." She squeezes my hand so hard my fingers hurt, the fingers Casimir broke, and her voice lowers a notch. "You took him from me, and I thought I wouldn't rest until I killed you myself. Even after you got him back, I thought about just ending you for what you did to him." Her grip tightens, and I bite my lip so as not to cry out. "There are moments, still, when I see you together and I think to myself, If she could do that, who knows what she could do? And yet—Mrs. Och has only ever helped me, but she doesn't love him. Everybody is here for something else—for money or adventure or their own purposes. You are the only one, besides me, who really loves him. You are the only one who came here for Theo."

She loosens her grip on my hand, and I let out a shuddering breath. "I do love him," I say.

I mean to go on, to say that I know she will never be able to trust me, to tell her how I despise myself for what I did, but I stop. It's all been said; there's no point saying it again. She is silent so long, eyes closed, that I think she has gone to sleep after all, her fingers slowly sliding from mine. When she speaks, her voice is thick and drowsing.

"I will *never* forgive you," she murmurs, slitting one eye open. "But you might be my only real friend. Isn't that funny?"

The eye drops closed again. I lie still until her breathing deepens, and then I slowly withdraw my hand. She does not stir, her hand resting alone now over Theo's heart. I lift myself on one elbow to look at them. The magicked sash is still around her waist, but she's forgotten to tie it to him. Careful not to wake him, I wind the other end of the sash around his fat little wrist and make it fast, binding him to her.

SEVENTEEN

Wyn turns up in the morning with bad news in the form of a drawing. Not his. It is a sketch of Mrs. Och, Bianka, and me.

"This is plastered all over the city," he says, startling me at the henhouse, where I'm fetching eggs for breakfast. He looks altogether too good in Yongguo-style dress. His hair is getting a little wild, though. He hasn't had a haircut since the one I gave him months ago, bundled in our coats and perched on the roof outside his attic room—the spiky rooftops of the Twist around us, the autumn sky bright—back when we were happy, and I was just a girl who could vanish, and everything still seemed simple.

"Word is, you can ask for Shun Yi at the Hundred Lantern Hotel if you've seen any of these nefarious characters. Nice reward offered too."

I snatch the paper from him. There we are, the three of us in a row on the page.

"Not a good likeness of you," he adds. "Whoever did it botched your chin completely. And your expression—you've got quite a sappy look there."

It's not a flattering picture in the least, and, indeed, I'm looking uncharacteristically soulful, but it is me, without a doubt.

"Only the three of us. It's got to be Casimir. Where did you get it?"

"Snatched it off a wall. They're everywhere. But I reckon we don't need to worry too much. Mrs. Och doesn't even look Fraynish anymore, Bianka never leaves this courtyard, and you can be invisible. Who's going to identify any of you?"

"Si Tan, the grand librarian, saw me just the other day!" I snap at him. "Blast. I'd better show these to Mrs. Och. Are you staying for breakfast?"

"Of course! You've got eggs! Dek and I ought to get a chicken or two."

"You'd never remember to feed it," I say, taking up the basket.

The picture sets everyone on edge.

"It is Casimir," Mrs. Och agrees. "He would guess that we might come looking for Ko Dan. I would not be surprised to find his agents here."

"You don't think he might be behind Ko Dan's disappearance, do you?" I ask.

"Possible," says Mrs. Och. "But I think unlikely. Casimir holds no real sway here."

"It could be Agoston Horthy," I say, a bit desperately. The Fraynish prime minister frightens me less than Casimir does.

"I think not," she says. "Horthy does not know *you*. Besides, he would not pursue Theo so far beyond his borders. He does not know what he is."

"What he *is*?" says Bianka sharply. "He *is* a little boy. It's just that he's got something else stuffed inside him too."

Theo is sitting on the floor gnawing on something that looks like a rock but which I hope is a potato. He looks up, curious, aware that he is being discussed. I can't help feeling we ought to be more careful what we say around him now that he is picking up so many words.

"Only Casimir would go to the ends of the earth to find him," says Mrs. Och, ignoring Bianka. "We need to know who he has sent and how extensively he has infiltrated the city. Julia, you will investigate."

"I'll need money," I say.

Mrs. Och fetches me a chain of coins on a red string. In Yongguo the coins all have holes at their center and they are carried in clusters like this.

"Will this be enough?"

I nod, and slip the coins into my pocket.

"Come on," I say to Wyn. "I need your help this time."

Wyn finds a boy, aged ten or so, selling bunches of flowers from a little broken-down cart at the edge of the canal. Mrs. Och's coins are enough to buy the whole lot of flowers and more: an errand. Wyn's Yongwen is appalling, but he manages to convey the basic idea to the boy, showing him the picture and pointing out Mrs. Och as she used to appear back in Spira City. The boy is to say he saw a woman like her in the West Market. He should push for his reward, but not too hard. We don't want the fellow getting hurt; I just want a look at Shun Yi.

The boy does a happy jig and babbles very quickly, and Wyn says, "All right, all right then," clapping him on the shoulder. The boy wants to know where to find Wyn afterward, to report back, but Wyn tells him never mind that.

I am invisible, or all but, in that edge-of-the-world space. The boy darts off, and I am after him. He is a clever dodger, glancing over his shoulder often to check if he's being followed, taking back ways and crowded lanes. I slam into a woman carrying a basket of radishes, and that's it, I'm back in the world, everything pulling into focus, but I'm going to lose the kid if I don't run, so I run, leaving the woman shouting insults after me and collecting her radishes out of the gutter. I slip back to invisibility as we clear the alleyways, struggling to match the boy's pace while I'm vanished.

The Hundred Lantern Hotel is a many-storied building of gleaming yellow wood not far from the Imperial Gardens, its rear balconies overlooking the Dongnan Canal. It is easy to spot on the busy road because it really does have a hundred red lanterns hanging outside. I follow the boy into the main dining hall. The beefy barkeep makes to swat our boy away, but the kid dodges his hand, talking fast. The barkeep is halfway to cuffing him on the ear when he freezes at something the boy says. He lowers his hand uncertainly and beckons the boy to follow. He does, and so do I, vanished behind them.

The private eating rooms are along the side of the dining hall. The boy is bouncing on his toes, wriggling with the thrill of the coins in his pocket, the mystery of his assignment. The barkeep pulls back a curtain. The boy goes bouncing inside, with me close behind him, and then all his bounce and verve are gone.

I nearly run for it, but I'd have to move the curtain and then I'd be caught. I stay still against the wall, breath frozen in my throat.

There is Pia, those awful mechanical goggles emerging from her face where eyes should be. I smashed them with the hilt of my knife in Casimir's fortress, but somebody has repaired them since then. She is unchanged: ghastly pale, a helmet of black hair hanging to her jaw, long leather-clad limbs. I know, though, that underneath she must be different from the first time I laid eyes on her. There must be a scar on her belly where I stuck my knife. Or maybe not. What do I know about her, really? Maybe I left no mark. Maybe I could never really harm her.

The boy is speechless. We could have warned him, if only we'd known—and we should have known, but I didn't want to think it.

She speaks Yongwen, not well but competently, very formally—textbook Yongwen that even I can understand.

Fraynish is not her first language either. I don't know where she's from. It's impossible to imagine Pia as a little girl in a foreign country, speaking some language like it belongs to her.

"Sit down. I won't hurt you."

He is shaking all over. He has never seen anything like Pia, and now I'm sorry we collared him off the street.

"I *will* hurt you if you don't tell me what you're doing here," she says in her high, clipped voice, her too-correct Yongwen. "No games. The truth."

Wyn gave him money, with no threat of consequences for betrayal, and looked altogether nonthreatening compared to this. What fools we were.

The boy is speaking dialect and I do not understand him at all, but I know he's selling us out.

"Did you see this woman or not?" asks Pia, jabbing the picture of Mrs. Och with her finger.

"No," he tells her, head hanging.

"Describe the man who gave you money."

He babbles, presumably about Wyn. I daren't move, I daren't breathe.

"Fraynish?"

The boy doesn't know.

"Only a man?" asks Pia, frowning. "You did not see the girl in this picture? They did not ask you to come back to them afterward?"

"No," says the boy. He carries on, and I don't know what he's saying, but I know what Pia is thinking. I watch her thinking it, I watch the understanding click into place in her expression, the tension firing through her limbs. She looks around the small, curtained room, goggles whirring. The boy stops talking and stares at her. She stands up, hand on the long, curved knife at her hip. She draws it and the boy screams.

"Julia!" she calls, and I startle, jostling the curtain. She can't see me, but she turns sharply, fixing on the place where I am standing. "There you are," she hisses.

I run.

EIGHTEEN

"Well. Blast."

It's not yet noon, but Wyn pours himself a glass of *shijiu* and offers me one. I shake my head, trying to steady myself. I fled straight back to their place in Dongshui from the Hundred Lantern Hotel and am still catching my breath.

"At least now we know," says Dek. "We're not really in a worse position than before."

"She knows we're here," I say. "She knows *I'm* here."

I'm thinking about how I knifed her and shut the trapdoor on her in Casimir's fortress. I'm thinking she's going to find me and cut me into pieces.

"She already knew that," says Dek. "Or she wouldn't be here. Tianshi is a big city. We can stay out of sight until we wrap things up."

"Now she knows what I look like," says Wyn. He's never even met her, but he's as shaken as I am.

Dek snorts. "What did the boy tell her? Foreign? Dark? Nobody is going to find you."

"That narrows it down a good deal," says Wyn. "I'm sure he mentioned devilishly handsome. That narrows it down even more."

"There are hundreds of foreigners in Tianshi," says Dek. "We'll keep a low profile."

"We *haven't* been keeping a low profile. I'm very memorable! A little asking around and she'll know where we're holed up. Hounds. We should talk to the girls. Let them know to keep their mouths shut."

"I doubt they need to be told," says Dek. "But we'll talk to them."

So Mei and Ling were not just one-time visitors.

"Maybe we should move," mutters Wyn.

Dek sips at his *shijiu*, makes a face, puts it down. "Julia—she can't really get to you, can she? I mean, you can just disappear if she gets close."

"Only if I see her coming," I admit.

I've explained to Dek a little about how I've learned to vanish farther, more completely, though I did not go so far as to tell him about Kahge, or whatever that place is. I told him mainly so he'd stop shadowing me so closely while we were traveling.

"You should take this."

He reaches under his sleeve, and I realize he's unfastening the wristlet filled with capsicum gas that I used to wear. One squirt temporarily blinds an attacker—and hurts like a demon too. I put a hand on his wrist to stop him.

"No, you keep it. I've got my knife, and I can vanish, like

you said. Besides, it's not much use against Pia. Those goggles protect her eyes. If she has eyes."

"We could get you a pistol," says Wyn. "Doesn't get much more effective than that."

I grimace. "I don't like them. And I don't want to put a hole in anybody anyway. I just want to make sure Pia doesn't find us before we find Ko Dan."

"Agreed," says Dek. "But look, I've been working on something else that might come in handy."

Dek is a wizard at designing weapons and other useful gadgets. He fetches a box full of finger-length darts with hollow ends and shows them to me.

"I got these from the circus. They use them for sedating animals. A bit of sleeping serum inside the hollow end, fasten the plunger back on, and then jab someone with the point while pressing the plunger. It'll knock them right out. A little tricky to gauge the right amount, but it should be a good, nonlethal way of dealing with a threat. Also, less noisy than the capsicum gas, which tends to lead to lots of screaming. I haven't tried it out yet—I wanted to use Wyn for a test run, but he objected, the coward. I'll give you a few just in case."

"Thanks." I watch him fill them carefully from a vial, one-handed, the open dart in the crook of his thumb, his other fingers managing the acrobatic feat of pouring without the thumb. I know better than to offer to help. Dek is very clever with the one hand he can use.

"By the way, we talked to the mail carrier yesterday and

made him a very generous offer," he says as he transfers the serum to the darts. "He was absolutely terrified. Wouldn't give me one of Gangzi's letters for love or money."

"I don't remember you offering *love*," says Wyn.

"Well, your Yongwen is terrible. How badly d'you want one, Julia? Now we've got this serum, we could knock him out and steal the whole basket."

"I don't even know if it's important," I say. "But if you can get one without hurting him, and without too much risk, I'd like to see what Gangzi's so busy writing."

"The mail goes out again the day after tomorrow," says Wyn. "I'll nick one for you, easy." Then, to Dek: "I *told* you we should have just stolen it, instead of trying to bribe him."

"I liked the novelty of bribery," sighs Dek. "But I suppose theft is where your talents lie."

He caps the last of the darts and makes a *ta-da* gesture with his good hand. Wyn picks one up and looks at it.

"All right, so if Pia turns up, we *might* be able to knock her out if we're tremendously lucky and she doesn't kill us first," he says. "But what are we going to tell Mrs. Och? Will she think we botched it, letting Pia know we're here?"

"I need to think," I say.

But there is nothing to think about. The only thing to do is to find Ko Dan and get out of Tianshi before Pia finds us, and while I know Mrs. Och might not like the way I'm going about it, I've got a contact now and I'm going to use it.

Old Thien has a note for me with an address on it. The note is written in Fraynish—not by Jun, I reckon, as the Fraynish is flawless and the handwriting that of an educated person—and explicitly instructs me to come alone. I can't say I like the sound of that. Dek and Wyn like it even less.

"The bleeding stars we're letting you go alone," says Wyn. "It could be a trap."

"We'll come armed and stay out of sight," says Dek. "Whistle if you need us."

I am unsure—it will annoy Jun if he discovers it—but in the end, I agree. He may have swoon-worthy cheekbones and dimples to die for, but that's no reason to trust him.

The address we arrive at isn't the house I saw Jun go into the other night. It is in the same part of Dongshui, though. The place is a wreck, a burnt-out shell. Nobody lives there, that much is obvious. The fellows settle behind a wall just up the road. I go vanished into the ruined house, through its courtyards and gutted rooms. Nobody. But when I go back outside, I see him, a blurry silhouette waiting in the bright, empty road. I suppose I'm showing off, but I get close to him before stepping back into the visible world, startling him. He pulls out the stick he jabbed me with before. I might have found his wielding a stick funny if my side didn't still hurt whenever I moved.

"That's unfriendly," I say. "I thought now we'd had tea, there wouldn't be any more of that."

"The note says come alone," he says. "You are not alone."

"You almost speared me with that stick the other night," I say. "That sort of thing makes a girl nervous."

His eyebrows go down in a scowl. No sympathy there. I shrug and whistle. Dek and Wyn emerge from behind the wall, pistols visible at their belts, and saunter over to us.

"I only want to meet your boss," I say. "But I think I'm allowed a bit of protection."

His mouth gives a mocking quirk. "That is not protection."

I don't have time to reply or ask him what he means by that. Very casually, he takes something from the pouch at his waist and tosses it into the road at Wyn's feet. I flinch, but it isn't a wasp nest like the one he threw the first night I followed him. We all stare at it—it looks like a grayish rock—and then a bolt of white flame shoots out of it, crackling. I leap back with a cry, momentarily blinded. There is a pistol shot, and Dek shouting, "Don't *shoot* him, you bleeding fool!" and then, "*Oi!*"

He is quick as anything, I'll give him that. He yanks Dek's crutch away from him and swings it at Wyn's head, landing such a blow that Wyn staggers and falls to one knee. Jun hits him again with the crutch and wrestles the gun away from him, then swings back toward Dek and shouts, "Drop gun!"

Dek is collapsed in the street anyway, has only just gotten his gun out. He lets it go.

"Stop it!" I shout.

Jun is breathing hard, his brow shining with sweat. Dek's

135

crutch is in one hand and Wyn's pistol is in the other, pointed at me.

"Don't move," he says, and the flare of white fire shrinks and vanishes. The thing in the street looks like a blob of black sludge now. Wyn groans, head in his hands. Dek is all right, though, and pulls himself to standing against the wall.

"That went well," he says to me.

"Shut up," I reply.

"Your friend shoot at me," Jun says accusingly.

"You set fire to the street," I say—realizing belatedly that the flame gave off no heat. "What *was* that?"

"I take *you* to meet boss," he says, ignoring my question. "Not them."

Wyn gets slowly to his feet. He looks rather sick. Jun tenses, but when Wyn makes no move, he tosses Dek's crutch back to him. Dek catches it awkwardly, says, "Thanks."

That's when I decide that I trust him—because he didn't hit Dek, and gave him back his crutch. Still pointing Wyn's gun at me, he snatches Dek's gun off the ground and tucks it into his belt.

"Now you go," he says to them.

I say, "It's all right. I'll be fine."

"I don't like this," says Dek, hitching his crutch back under his armpit.

But since Jun has both of their guns, there is really no argument to be had. They shuffle off, glancing over their shoulders anxiously. I give a jaunty wave to reassure them, and then they are out of sight. Jun lowers the pistol, and I relax a little.

"You know the house?" he asks.

"So do they," I tell him. I showed it to them on the way here, and if they try to stage a rescue, I'd rather he not be startled.

"Go," he says, and we do, to the house I remember from the night I followed him back.

NINETEEN

We pass through the outer sections of the house and through an unkempt courtyard to the inner house, which is dark and decaying. The walls have holes in them. The floor is unswept. A mouse skitters out of sight as we enter. Jun dead-bolts each door behind him. I don't say that if Wyn and Dek turn up, locked doors won't keep them out. He knocks on a door at the end of a cobwebbed hall and calls out in Fraynish: "Boss, I bring the girl."

A singsonging male voice answers: "Bring her in, then, dove!"

This room is as poorly tended as the rest of the house, the once opulent furniture frayed and stained. At a desk by the window sits a Fraynish man in his fifties, or perhaps a little younger, but aged by debauchery. He wears a double-breasted waistcoat that, like the furniture, has seen better days, and he peers at me over a pair of crooked, gold-rimmed spectacles. The whole house, including its main occupant, gives the impression of past wealth and current decay.

"Julia, is it?" he says.

"Yes," I say.

"Real name?"

"Yes."

"I am Count Fournier."

He rises and comes around his desk toward me with springing steps, holding his hand out. I am startled to notice that he is in his stocking feet and his stockings have holes in them—a big knobby toe poking out the end of one. He is tall and bowlegged, with a gut that strains the buttons of his waistcoat. His features droop downward, as if the flesh of his face simply hasn't the energy to stay stuck up on his head any longer, and this gives him a rather sad expression. I take his sweaty hand, and he plants a kiss on my knuckles. I wonder if I am supposed to curtsy, but it seems silly in trousers.

"Charmed," he says. "Always a pleasure to meet someone from the homeland. May I offer you a drink?"

"No thank you."

"No? Very well. Do sit down."

I sit on one of the sofas, sinking deep into the ancient cushions, dust pluming up around me and making me cough. It smells like mold and cat piss, though I don't see any cats. Count Fournier sits across from me in a gigantic chaise, slinging one leg over the other. Jun stays standing by the door, pointing Dek's pistol at me as if I might suddenly attack the count. I wish he'd put it down.

"I'm going to tell you what I *know* about you first," Count Fournier says pleasantly. "And then I'll tell you what I *think*.

You may tell me how much I've got right. Won't that be fun?"

"Sounds like a barrel of laughs," I say.

"Let us begin. You are Fraynish. It is your native tongue. You are a witch of some kind. You have not been in Yongguo long, and you speak the language only slightly. You have entered the Shou-shu Monastery secretly on multiple occasions. You are working for somebody with power and political interests rooted in Frayne. These things I know. Here is what I *think*. I think you are a low-class girl, probably from Spira City, judging by your accent, and, in that case, probably from the Twist. I think you have been instructed to find out what you can about the Fraynish girl in the monastery and about anybody involved with her. I think you know exactly who she is. I think you probably know a fair bit about me. I'd wager even odds that I will have to kill you shortly."

I decide, as he reaches the end of this little speech, that I do not like him much at all.

"What do you think of my guesses?" he asks.

"You're partly right," I reply. "But you've got it all wrong regarding the girl in the monastery and yourself. Also, I'm not a witch. Like I told Jun, I'm looking for the monk Ko Dan. I don't know anything about you or the Fraynish girl."

"That is a convenient story," he says. "But not very believable."

I see Wyn's face at the window for a second, waggling his

eyebrows at me, and I stiffen. I hope they don't come bursting in while Jun has the gun on me. I'd rather he not be startled with his finger on the trigger.

"Here's what I know about *you*," I say. "You're Fraynish nobility, but you're broke, and you've been stuck out here a long time. You're frightened because, whatever you're up to in the monastery with this Fraynish girl, you think I've found you out. But we've got different things going on, and we might even be able to help each other, if you could trust me."

He waves a hand at Jun, who lowers the pistol, looking relieved. "Go on, then," he says.

"I work for a Fraynish lady. . . . I can't tell you who she is, but she *is* very powerful, and finding Ko Dan is important to her. I reckon you've got connections in the city. I thought we could make a deal. If you'll do a bit of digging about Ko Dan and share with me whatever you find, I'll help you however you'd like. I'm sure you could think of something useful a girl who can vanish might do for you."

He takes this in.

"You really don't know who the girl in the monastery is?"

"Should I?"

He grins. His teeth are yellow. "I expect your employer knows—this powerful and important lady you work for."

"Maybe she does, but she didn't see fit to share it with me."

"What religion are you?" he asks, quite out of nowhere.

"I was raised Baltist, in the loosest sense," I reply.

"What does that mean, 'in the loosest sense'?"

"I was raised only in the loosest sense."

I feel Jun watching me closely. If I had to guess, I'd say he knows just what I mean.

"You are too young to remember the Lorian Uprising," says Count Fournier.

I'll bet an exiled count was on the wrong side of that rebellion, and I think I see the way to win him over.

"I was born the year after," I say. "But I heard stories of it. My parents and my employers were on the side of the revolutionaries back then."

He leans back, clasping his hands around one knee, and looks at me a long time, as if wondering whether to believe me.

"Have you heard of Gregor Chastain, or Esme and Gustaf Moreau?" I ask.

He looks properly surprised for the first time. "I knew Gustaf. Everybody knew Gustaf."

"If you lived in Spira City, then you know that after he was hung, his wife, Esme, took over the Twist. I worked for her, growing up. Now I work for someone else, and so do Esme and Gregor. It has nothing to do with your girl in the monastery."

"Gregor Chastain and Esme Moreau would know who she is," he says slyly.

"Well, I could bring them by, if you'd like," I say, a little too carelessly.

"*Could* you, now?" he asks, real interest in his eyes. "They are in Tianshi? How remarkable!"

"I just want to know about Ko Dan," I say, anxious that I've said too much. "I'll bring friends over, do a bit of spying for you, scare somebody you'd like scared, make you dinner, whatever you like, if you'll tell me what you know about Ko Dan."

"My dear girl, I do not know anything about Ko Dan."

I could kick myself for naming Esme and Gregor.

"So I'm wasting my bleeding time, am I?"

A click from the door. I leap to my feet as Jun spins around, raising the gun.

"Don't shoot!" I beg him, and the door swings wide, but there is nobody there. "Stop!" I call to Dek and Wyn, who are presumably in the hall. "Don't do anything!"

But then Wyn comes charging in with a sheet of scrap metal in front of him. Jun hesitates, which makes me think he's probably never fired a gun before. Dek appears in the doorway, pointing a little single-handed crossbow that used to belong to Professor Baranyi, and shoots him in the shoulder. Jun gives him a woozy look, tries to point the gun, then fumbles and drops it. He stares at the gun on the ground. "Faaa . . . ," he mutters, reaching for it, eyelids drooping, and then he falls, unconscious.

I skid to my knees next to him, feeling for a pulse. I can't breathe until I find it, steady in his wrist.

Wyn snatches up the pistol and points it at Count Fournier, tossing aside his scrap metal. The count sighs like somebody has just broken a teacup.

"Is Jun going to be all right?" he asks.

143

"I hope so." I shoot an evil look at Wyn and Dek. "I wasn't looking for a rescue."

"We couldn't be sure," says Wyn. "It didn't look entirely friendly in here."

He's got a darkly purpling bruise on his temple, but otherwise he seems to have recovered pretty well from being clocked on the head earlier. He helps me lift Jun onto the smelly sofa. Jun's head flops back, his mouth hanging open. He looks much younger this way, and I resist the urge to smooth back the strands of black hair that have fallen in his face.

"He'll be fine in an hour or so," says Dek, although he sounds less sure than I'd like. He told us himself that it's difficult to gauge the right dose with sleeping serum.

"He's not going to be happy with us when he wakes up," I say.

Wyn gives me an odd look. "Does it matter?"

I shrug. I'd been hoping for another of Jun's brilliant smiles, and instead it's been all scowls and pointing pistols. Of course, it shouldn't matter. We're not here to make friends.

"I suppose now you'd better answer some questions," I say to the count.

"I hope it's safe to assume that you two are not with the Fraynish delegation that arrived the other day," he says, looking Wyn and Dek over. "You don't look it."

He knows well enough that a Scourge survivor is an outcast in Frayne.

"They work with me. We don't know anything about any delegation," I say.

"We'd like to know, though," says Wyn, giving his pistol a little twirl.

"Somebody very high up, my contacts tell me," says Count Fournier. His voice is smooth, but I notice his fingers are trembling. "There have been delegations sent before, of course. They've been petitioning Gangzi and the emperor for permission to search the monastery for close to a year now."

"Why don't they just send somebody over the wall if they want to look around?" I ask. "It's hardly fortified."

"Because the Fraynish Crown fears Gangzi, and rightly so, but you never can be sure—they might fear the girl even more. That's why Jun has been spending so much time there. Keeping an eye."

"So she's someone important, this Fraynish girl?"

"Yes," chuckles the count. "She's important. King Zey has fallen ill. Have you heard?"

I hadn't. We haven't had news from Frayne since we left two months ago.

"He is an old man, and the doctors can do nothing more for him. A distant cousin has been named heir. But there are many who would agree that the girl in the monastery has a greater claim to the throne."

I stare at him blankly.

"She is King Zey's niece," he says. "Prince Roparzh's daughter. Her name is Zara."

It takes a minute for this to sink in. I remember the old story of a baby princeling smuggled out of Frayne when Prince Roparzh, King Zey's brother, was hung along with his wife and older children after the Lorian Uprising. I'd always assumed it was a wishful rumor. The revolutionaries had hoped to oust Zey and place his brother on the throne. Prince Roparzh was a Lorian by marriage, and certainly a more moderate man, without Zey's passion for stamping out every last glimmer of folklorish ways.

"Hounds," breathes Wyn. "That's a twist, isn't it? What in flaming Kahge is she doing *here?*"

"She has been raised, guarded, and educated in hiding, by witches and those allied with them," says Count Fournier. "There was a great network of us across the world working to keep her safe. Have you heard of the Sidhar Coven?"

"Yes," I say. Dek and I exchange a look. Our mother was a part of it.

"My aunt, Lady Laroche, is the head of that coven," he says eagerly, clearly proud of the association. "She brokered the deal with Gangzi a couple of years ago. We thought no place more secret, more secure than Shou-shu, which is protected by the empire but not answerable to any outside authority. But I have heard nothing from my aunt in over a year, have received no money, and I do not know if she is still alive." He speeds up, the floodgates open now: "This new Fraynish delegation will try to offer Gangzi something in exchange for the princess, make a deal, and if he believes his agreement with my aunt has expired, then perhaps they will succeed. If I had any connections left, I would get her out, but all my contacts have gone silent this past year. Many of the witches who organized the princess's escape in the first place have been hunted down by now. I am running out of money. Jun is the only employee I have left. I have no means with which to return home. . . ." He trails off. His hands are shaking badly now.

I gesture at Wyn to lower his pistol and he does.

"You see, you do need help," I say. "I'll talk to our employer. She has money and connections, no doubt about that. She might even know something about this Lady Laroche, your aunt. But I want you to ask around about Ko Dan. See if there are any rumors about where he went. If you can find something out for us, I'll bet my employer can help you and your princess. She's quite good at dodging the Fraynish Crown."

"You're really here for Ko Dan?" he asks wonderingly.

I nod.

"I confess I had some idea of who you worked for, though I couldn't be sure of her purpose." He slips from his pocket the picture of me, Bianka, and Mrs. Och that's plastered around the city. Of course. *Blast.*

"Jun recognized you from this picture," he says. "I don't know who this woman is." He points to Bianka, then slides his finger over to Mrs. Och. "But this—*this* is Och Farya of the Xianren." He looks up at us, eyes glinting.

I don't know whether to confirm or deny it, so I say nothing. Wyn and Dek follow my lead, their expressions blank.

"Her relationship with the Sidhar Coven has been . . . uneven," he says. "But overall she has been a friend to witches. Nobody told me . . . I assumed when I saw this that she had come for the princess. I couldn't be sure of her intentions—if she is working with or against the coven this time."

"Neither," I say. "She's here for Ko Dan."

"Well." He licks his lips. "That is a surprise. I remember Ko Dan, you know. When we were in talks with Gangzi about the princess, Ko Dan was always there too. He was Gangzi's right-hand man—his shadow, some of them used to call him. I will see what I can find out."

I look at Jun laid out on the sofa, his mouth soft.

"We're all right, then?" I ask. "There's been a bit of knocking each other about, but I think we ought to have a go at being friends."

"I couldn't agree more," he says. A different tune, now that the gun has changed hands, but never mind. I don't have to like him to believe what he's told me so far.

"I'm sorry about your boy here," says Dek, nodding at Jun. "We were worried about Julia."

"You don't have to worry about me," I say. "I can always disappear if things get bad, like you said before."

"I know," he says. "It's more than a bit ridiculous, me limping in to rescue you. But I do worry anyway. I can't help it. It's my vocation, I think—worrying about you."

The count watches us with interest, his spectacles sliding down his sweaty nose. "Jun told me how you disappear and reappear at will," he says.

148

"It comes in handy," I say shortly. "We'll be in touch soon."

"Won't you have a drink before you go?" he asks.

"No time," I say, ignoring the disappointed looks I get from Wyn and Dek. They've noticed the whiskey on the side table, of course. "Come on, fellows."

We all shake hands, very chummy now, and leave Count Fournier filling up a glass alone.

TWENTY

Csilla greets us at the door of the elegant house in Xihuo and takes us through to a grand, open-air room overlooking the inner courtyard, with its flowering bushes and its small pond choked with water lilies. Professor Baranyi is next to a wan-looking Mrs. Och on the settee. Esme and Gregor are standing. We arranged the meeting by tree pipit, and everyone is here but Bianka and Theo—who are not to leave the house in Nanmu—and Frederick.

"Where's Frederick?" I ask, looking around for him.

"He did not want to leave Bianka and Theo unattended," says Professor Baranyi.

I refrain from rolling my eyes at the idea that Frederick might be any kind of protection for Bianka, and I say: "Well, we've got news. Good and bad."

"Start with the bad," says Gregor, sitting back with a glass of *shijiu*. "As is traditional."

"Pia is in Tianshi," I say. "And she knows we're here too."

"You saw her?" asks Mrs. Och sharply.

"Yes. She doesn't know where we're living, but she's here and she's looking for us. That's the bad news."

"You're all right, though?" asks Esme. She's looking at Wyn, his bruised, swollen face.

"That happened later," I say. "We're all right."

"*You're* all right," says Wyn, but he says it good-naturedly.

"The good news?" asks the professor faintly.

"We've found out who that girl in the monastery is. At least, I think we have." I pause for effect, but nobody says anything. "Well, according to my source, her name is Zara, and she's King Zey's niece. The rumors about a royal baby smuggled out of Frayne after the Lorian Uprising were true, seems like. She's here, and the Fraynish government already knows about it. There's a delegation trying to get permission to get into Shou-shu or have the princess turned out."

A short, stunned silence, and then they are all bursting with questions. I try to explain about Count Fournier and Jun. I can feel Mrs. Och's eyes on me, and I know she's probably furious that I've been doing all this behind her back, but I don't care. I feel quite important, bringing such monumental news. Esme and Gregor keep exchanging this wondering, peculiar look, like they've just remembered something about each other that's been buried a long time.

"I'd heard rumors about the princess in Yongguo," says Mrs. Och at last, her chilly voice breaking in and silencing the others. "I did not know for certain they were true.

Certainly, a baby girl was born to Zey's brother just before the uprising. We all knew what was coming, and I helped arrange for her to be taken out of Frayne. But I lost track of her years ago. I heard she died of a fever somewhere in Ishti more than a decade back, but then talk about her surfaced again in the Far East. If it is true, it is good news indeed."

"And King Zey is dying," repeats Esme. She looks at Gregor again—a helpless, resigned look this time. He is clutching the bottle of *shijiu* to his chest like a child clings to a favorite toy. "Who is left?" she says.

"There are many in Frayne who did not join the Lorian Uprising but who have no love of Agoston Horthy," he says fiercely. "Even among the aristocracy, there are those who would support a viable alternative to Zey and his ilk. And Princess Zara—if it is her—has a greater claim than some far-off cousin they've dug up."

"Does it really make such a difference?" asks Wyn. "This king or that queen, I mean."

Gregor pounds the table with his fist. "She is a Lorian princess!" he cries. "First of all, she has a *right* to the throne. Besides that, it would mean a sea change in Frayne, the change we fought for. Freedom of religion and thought! Imagine that! A Frayne that doesn't spend all its resources hunting down and drowning witches? That doesn't trample over its old traditions? Somebody who would flick off that murderous dog Agoston Horthy!"

"All right, all right," Csilla murmurs, patting his arm soothingly, but he is not soothed in the slightest.

"How can you say it makes no difference?" he cries, pointing at Wyn, who puts his hands up in mock surrender.

"This count thinks she's in danger, though," I break in. "He'd heard of Gustaf, by the way."

"Everybody who knew of the uprising knew Gustaf," says Esme calmly. She never speaks of her dead husband, or the child she lost to Scourge around the same time.

We are all quiet for a moment. Then Gregor stands up. He is flushed and trembling, but not from drink or lack of drink. There is something in his expression I don't recognize, have never seen. Like he might weep—and not in a drunken, maudlin way, but tears of real, sober, great emotion. He goes to the edge of the veranda and pours the whole bottle of *shijiu* out onto the ground. Then he comes back in and fetches three more bottles from the pantry and takes them and pours them out as well. Csilla begins to cry; she goes to him, and he folds her in his arms. They stand there weeping and clinging to each other, him rocking her in his embrace.

It's an affecting scene, I'll say that. I look at Esme, and her expression is odd, uncertain. Gregor has given up the drink before, many times. He always means it, and he always goes back to it in a matter of days. Csilla is the only one, besides Gregor, who ever believes it will last.

"And Ko Dan?" asks Mrs. Och, ignoring the dramatic scene. "Any word?"

I shake my head.

"This count Julia found has got connections," says Dek.

He can tell I'm on dangerous ground with Mrs. Och. "I bet he'll turn something up for us."

She nods. "Very well. You will pursue the matter with your new friends."

"What about the princess?" asks Esme.

Mrs. Och folds her hands in her lap. "The princess," she repeats, and then, unexpectedly, she smiles. "Why, we will take her back to Frayne and give her the throne."

TWENTY-ONE

When at last our group breaks up, I try to slip out quickly with Dek and Wyn, but Esme calls me back: "Julia. I need to speak with you."

"Come for dinner after," says Dek to me, giving my shoulder a reassuring squeeze.

I nod and follow Esme reluctantly to the bamboo bench in the outer courtyard. We sit, and she says nothing, waiting. She used to do that when I'd done something bad as a kid, like breaking a window or stealing something I wasn't supposed to steal. She'd sit me down and look at me with that flinty gaze of hers, waiting for me to confess. I cracked every time, and I crack now. I tell her the truth. Just not all of it.

"Mrs. Och has got Frederick researching my ... the vanishing thing. She wants to know why I can do it, but she's going about it behind my back. And I want to know too."

"Did he find anything?"

"Maybe. He's got to translate it all."

"I don't like it. This witch targeting you in the library too. Why you?"

"If Si Tan saw those pictures . . . I was the only one from the pictures that was there at the library."

"Julia." She puts her big hand on mine, and I stare at her scarred knuckles. Her gentleness is always vaguely surprising. I've seen those fists in action. "You are entitled to your secrets. But if you are in trouble, you must tell me. I have money. We can go home anytime. We don't owe Mrs. Och a thing."

"And the princess?" I say.

"I want to see it through. But I reckon we could manage it without Mrs. Och."

"You don't want to get on the wrong side of her."

"No, I don't. But if you're in danger, I'll do what needs doing. I can get you clear of all this."

"All right."

"Promise me you'll tell me if you need help."

"I'd better go," I say. She lets go of my hand.

I grew up with Esme's power and certainty at my back. The sorts of things that happened all too often to girls in the Twist never happened to me; no man would have dared to lay a finger on me. First I was Ammi's daughter, and then Esme's ward, and I felt safe and strong as a result. But we're beyond all that now. For all that her fists are like anvils and she's the fastest draw in the Twist and clever in ways you'd never suspect, in spite of all the folks who owe her favors and the money she's got stashed away—not even Esme can protect me from Casimir, or Mrs. Och, or the truth.

When I get to the little house in Dongshui, Mei and Ling are already there. I force a smile, biting back my annoyance. There is so much I want to talk over with Dek and Wyn, but we can hardly get into it in front of the girls, even if they don't speak Fraynish. Mei is ladling a sweet-smelling soup into bowls, and Ling is bent over a book, messy hair hanging in front of her face, while Dek strokes the back of her neck absentmindedly.

"Julia! Look, the girls have spent the day catching turtles and they've made a soup!" Wyn says this with false enthusiasm, fetching another bowl for me, and then pulls a horrified face behind Mei's back. Without turning around, she elbows him in the gut and he yelps. She says something in her dour voice, and Dek laughs.

"I'm not going to ask for the translation," says Wyn, sitting down.

Dek supplies it cheerfully anyway—"Barbarian"—as Mei puts the pot back on the stove.

"Quite a day," says Dek, raising his eyebrows at me meaningfully. I suppose that's as close as we're going to get to talking it over. But I'm starving, so I pull a chair up to the table and dig in with the others. I don't know what turtles are supposed to taste like, but the soup is hot and hearty, which is all I really need from a soup. I knock it back.

"Don't forget to breathe," Wyn says in mock horror. Mei says something approving, and Dek laughs again. Maybe I'm the opposite of a barbarian.

I look at my brother—relaxed, laughing, *happy*, one arm slung over Ling's shoulders—and an uncomfortable memory of our journey over the Kastahor Mountains comes back to me.

We took that route because Mrs. Och and Professor Baranyi feared those mountains less than trying to cross Xanuha, a mountainous country between Ishti and Yongguo. Xanuha is ruled by fierce warriors who overthrew a witch-led regime a hundred years ago, and they have defended themselves for centuries against the vast empire hulking on their northern border. They are apparently not welcoming to strangers, and even less so to magical strangers. But there was no beast that could carry us across the Kastahor Mountains, and Dek could not walk it. Bianka, being by far the strongest among us, had to carry him, like a child, on her back while the rest of us took turns carrying Theo. She never complained of the burden—she kept us all alive on that journey, conjuring the fire that kept us from freezing each night—but for Dek it was humiliating. I remember his face in the icy wind, tight and pale, thin-lipped. It was the hardest leg of the journey for all of us, and I was so preoccupied with my own suffering that I had little left over to think of him.

We set our camp one day at the base of a glacier that shone blue in the sunlight, and while we ate our meager supper, we watched half a mountain collapse, a day's journey or more away from us. The roar of it was deafening, the shape of the landscape changed, and we were still and somber because we were witnessing the ease with which this place could bury us. My awe at the beauty of the mountains had worn off quickly. Every inch of me hurt, and I was hungry all the time, worn down to a nub of the girl I'd started out as—that girl bent on atonement, with courage to spare for making right her wrongs.

"I hate this place," I said to Dek.

He rubbed his leg grimly and said nothing.

"Does it hurt?" I asked him.

"It always hurts," he grunted, the first words he'd spoken in days. "I'm used to hurting."

"Well, I'm not."

"Lucky you."

I don't know why I said it. I wish I could take it back. I said: "I don't feel lucky. I wish someone would carry *me*."

The white-lipped glare he gave me! I sobbed like an idiot, tears freezing on my face as soon as they fell, and he said nothing, returning to his silence.

But he changed when we reached Yongguo at last, as we crossed the grasslands and then the desert, stopping in settlements and cities where he was no more unusual than the rest of us. His money was accepted in the markets, nobody recoiled at his touch. I watched something open up in him, and somebody like my brother as he used to be reemerge. Somebody who laughs easily, somebody strong and self-assured.

I caught a moment alone with him when we were camping a few miles from the city walls and blurted without preamble: "I'm sorry about what I said." I didn't say *two weeks ago, in the mountains.* I didn't need to. He tucked my hair behind my ear and said, "You never need to say sorry to me."

Watching him now, I think I understand properly how terrible Spira City has been for him these past ten years. It didn't occur to either of us that there might be some other place he could go where things would be different, where he could go about freely, where a girl might look at him the way Ling looks at him. At least, it never occurred to *me*, and if it ever crossed his mind, he said nothing.

But Ling is not looking at him now. She is slurping her soup, eyes fixed on her book.

"The girl studies nonstop," says Wyn, noticing me looking at her.

Mei says something tart about hope and their family, and Dek translates: "She says all their hopes of a better life lie with Ling."

Ling slams the book shut at that, her face empty of expression. She takes a pair of peculiarly shaped dice from her pocket and tosses them onto the table, looking at me and saying something that sounds awfully like a challenge.

"*Look* at these!" exclaims Wyn, picking one up and rolling it. They are twelve-sided, white as bone, with black characters carved into each side.

Mei grunts disapprovingly as Ling takes a different book out of the pocket of her tunic and waves it at us—a fat little book that fits in her palm, with red binding and soft, worn pages. It looks well loved, all right.

"If we're going to play dice, we ought to drink," says Wyn. He brings a bottle of *shijiu* from the larder and pours us each a cup. Ling drinks hers down very quickly and explains the game to Dek. Best I can understand, it is some kind of fortune-telling game. She scoops up both dice with her bandaged hand and rolls them over to me.

"What happened to your hand?" I ask her. Whatever the damage, it's almost better, by the way she moves it. Dek gives me an irritated look, so I try again in Yongwen. "Your hand," I say, and then just tack "what?" onto the end of my non-sentence, which makes Dek roll his eyes. Ling pours herself another cup of *shijiu* and says curtly, "Broken."

The way she says it—bitter, guarded—makes me think of Casimir snapping my wrist, my fingers. I shake off the memory and the wave of nausea that accompanies it. Mei says something warningly to Ling about not drinking so much. Ling gives her a defiant look and knocks back her second cup.

"Stars, the girl can drink!" says Wyn, refilling her cup. Mei glares at him.

Ling wipes her mouth with her sleeve and leans across the table toward me, asking me a question.

"What is my . . . what?" I ask, catching only half of it.

"Your destiny," says Dek, raising an eyebrow.

"How would I know?"

She slows her Yongwen down for me, like she's speaking

161

to a young, rather stupid child, so that I can understand her without Dek's translation: "What is your birthday?"

I can't remember the Yongwen names of the months, so I fumble out, "One month . . . later." I think that's what I say, anyway.

"How old will you be?"

At least I know numbers in Yongwen. "Seventeen."

She flips through the book furiously.

"The dominant constellation on the date of your birth, along with the dominant constellation right now, and the characters you roll combine to tell you your destiny today," Dek explains. "It's called *The Book of Ten Thousand Rooms*. It's actually a book of philosophy, but it's more commonly used for fortune-telling."

"Your destiny *today*?" says Wyn. "Does destiny change day to day? Not much of a destiny, then, is it?"

"Your destiny can change—indeed, it *does* change—depending on the choices you make," says Dek. "But in a larger sense, you keep heading in the same direction via different routes. No matter what, though, we're all trapped in the House of Ten Thousand Rooms."

"Why trapped?" I ask.

"Because no matter what we choose, we're within these rooms for the duration of our human lives," he says, and then flicks the book in Ling's hand. "Or within this book."

"So what's outside it?" I ask, and Dek translates this to Ling.

She looks at me, her eyes bright and her cheeks flushed

with the drink now. She licks her lips and says, in harshly accented Fraynish: "The beasts."

I can't explain it—I've not touched the *shijiu* myself— but a cold fear uncoils in my gut when she says this. I think of those things in Kahge pointing at me, shouting at me, emerging from the shadows. I think of how *I* am changed in that place.

"What beasts?" I whisper. Her lips part again as if she's about to speak, but suddenly she breaks out into peals of laughter instead. She says something scornful about witches.

"Ask the philosopher-witches," Dek translates, and then he says to her, "Take it easy on the drink or you'll get sick."

She gives him a look so coquettish I almost blush to see it, and she pours herself another cup. Mei mutters something under her breath.

"Roll," says Ling to me, so I roll the dice.

She examines the characters, flips madly through the book again, running her finger down the lines. Then she reads aloud.

Dek translates it, clearly amused: "Who dares defy his ruler has no honor."

I grin. "That's my fortune? Dishonor and defiance? Not bad."

Imperious now, Ling scoops up the dice and hands them to Wyn, demanding his birth date, flipping through the book when he rolls.

Dek translates again: "In the sight of the gods, a peasant and a king are the same."

Mei shakes her head like a disapproving mama from the Twist.

"Julia's and mine seem contradictory," says Wyn. "Hers is about not defying the ruler, and mine makes it sound like there ought not to be a ruler at all."

Mei explains this one, via Dek: "We have to abide by the rules of the world and submit properly to our role on earth. The gods don't view us according to our role but according to our submission. Our place in the world is only a costume we have to wear in order to become what we are, but we must *wear* it humbly."

Wyn shrugs. Mei cracks a rare smile and says something.

"She called you an idiot," says Dek cheerfully. A sharp exchange between Mei and Dek follows, and he amends it: "An affectionate word for an idiot, then. Someone who doesn't think deeply."

"Well, not about junk like this," grumbles Wyn.

Ling offers the dice to Mei, who shakes her head, scowling again. Ling laughs, jiggles the dice in her hand, and then rolls for herself. She finds the page and reads it in a high, mocking voice.

"Ambition is a mountain with no summit," translates Dek.

Ling shoves the dice at him, almost angrily. He rolls, and she finds the right page.

"The thirsty man in the desert must learn to drink sand." Dek laughs a bit ruefully. "That works as a summary of the past, but I'd hoped it wouldn't be my future. I've drunk enough sand."

He pushes the book closed. Ling leans against his shoulder, the angry light in her eyes going out all at once. She looks almost wan.

I think Mei is scoffing that Ling cannot hold her liquor, but Dek doesn't translate, so I'm not sure. I'm thinking about Dek drinking sand. Suppose I'd been the one to get Scourge, left crippled and an outcast? I can't help thinking that Dek would have found another kind of life for me, even if it meant crossing the world, leaving our home behind. I'm thinking ten thousand rooms are not nearly enough, if every room requires submission.

"I don't believe in destiny," says Wyn, taking out a pack of cards and winking at me. I can't help my smile—it gives itself to him, whether I will it or not. "Chance rules the day, in the end. You play the hand you're dealt as best you can and that's the end of it. Isn't that right, Brown Eyes?"

"To chance, then," says Dek, raising his cup.

"To dishonor and defiance," I laugh.

"But no more sand," says Dek.

I meet his eyes and say: "No more sand."

Wyn shuffles and deals out.

TWENTY-TWO

The following evening I am vanished near the entrance to a posh dining hall not far from the monastery, in Xishui's first tier. The dining area is arranged in a square around a pond full of water lilies so that those eating can look over the water. At the center of the pond, seated on a little stone island, one musician plucks at a stringed instrument and another plays on something like a flute. Huge rafters crisscross the ceiling, and the wood floors are polished to a deep shine.

Jun wasn't there when I spoke with Count Fournier earlier in the day. I asked after him, and the count told me he was quite recovered from the dart Dek shot into him. I didn't dare ask how angry he was. Now, at Count Fournier's request, I am waiting to see who is having dinner with the Fraynish ambassador tonight.

The hall is packed with the elegantly dressed members of Tianshi's elite, eating and drinking and listening to the music. Only one table by the water remains empty. When I see the two Fraynish men being escorted to it by the serving girl, my heart gives a sickening lurch in my chest.

I recognize the taller of the two men. He is unforgettable. The last time I saw him, I was crammed inside a cupboard in Mrs. Och's reading room and he stood next to Agoston Horthy, saying nothing while the prime minister sparred with Mrs. Och. I do not know what name he goes by, but I know that Bianka has met him too, and that he had an interest in Theo. He has a sweep of thick gray hair and a swarthy face that would be handsome except that his fine features are less noticeable than his one yellow eye and the patch he wears over the other eye.

The Fraynish ambassador is a heavyset man with thinning hair and a sunburnt face like an undercooked meatball. His waistcoat is adorned with medals of rank. The two men arrange themselves at the table, the fellow I recognize with his back to the water.

He wants a view of the place, I suppose. Here in the open, it would be impossible for anyone to lurk near enough to overhear a soft-spoken conversation. Unless, of course, that somebody happened to be invisible and standing right at the speaker's elbow.

The serving girl brings them rice wine and tray after tray of Tianshi's finest delicacies. The ambassador eats very fast, his eating sticks clacking against the ceramic dishes. He jams the food into his mouth, gives it a couple of chomps with those big jaws, and then gulps it down like some bulky but efficient eating machine.

"I'm afraid you will find that they are going to make us wait, Lord Skaal," says the ambassador nervously between enormous mouthfuls. "Si Tan likes to show foreign petitioners that they are of no importance, even when they are very important men like yourself. There is nothing to be done about it."

Lord Skaal is one of a rare type of man who has no tics or mannerisms. When he speaks, I am not expecting it because he does not lean forward or clear his throat or shift in any of the ways that most people do before they speak up. He has a pleasant voice, the tone of a friendly cabriolet driver meshing oddly with his upper-crust accent.

"We shall see how long we have to wait," he says. "I rather thought the grand librarian might be curious to meet me."

"Well, perhaps, perhaps," says the ambassador. "But you see, it's all about status here. They like to make you feel your lack of power."

"I did not come here to feel powerful," says Lord Skaal.

"Of course not," says the ambassador. "I only mean, it is a game, you see. He sometimes refuses to see me at all. It is most embarrassing."

"He will see me," says Lord Skaal, quite serenely. He glances over his shoulder at me—no, through me, though my heart leaps into my throat for a moment—and then he begins to ask the ambassador about Tianshi and the sights worth seeing. They talk for half an hour, no more, and leave together. I follow them back to the ambassador's house in the embassy section of the Beijin Triangle. Then I hop on a trolley to Dongshui.

Jun meets me at the door this time, his expression stony.

"Hullo," I say, heart sinking at the look on his face. "I've got news for your boss."

He nods and lets me in, leading me through the outer courtyard to the main house.

"Are you all right?" I ask, my voice stupidly bright. "I feel badly about yesterday. I never meant for any of that to happen."

"If your friends come here again, I shoot them," he says. "I ask Count Fournier to buy me a gun and he say yes. Look."

He shows me a sleek little pistol that fits in his palm. I'm rather sorry that meeting me and my crew has made him feel he needs more than his sharp stick and clever tricks.

"I'll pass that along," I say.

Count Fournier is asleep at his desk, and it takes a good few minutes for Jun to rouse him, but he livens up as I tell him what I've seen and heard tonight. He fixes himself a drink, not bothering to offer me one this time. When I'm done talking, he looks at Jun and asks: "Is that right?"

Jun nods.

I stare, uncomprehending for a moment, and then give a snort of exasperation. "Well, why'd you ask me to do the job if he was going to follow me anyway?"

"Not follow *you*," says Jun. "I cannot see you. I follow ambassador, check if you tell us the truth about what you see."

"What a waste of my evening." I am irritated, but my irritation gives way to curiosity. "Hang on—where were you in the restaurant, then? They had a view of the whole place."

The dimples come out in his cheeks and something flutters behind my rib cage.

"Ambassador is stupid to choose that place," he says, bouncing on his toes a bit in that restless way he has, like he might start turning cartwheels any moment. "There are big rafters on ceiling. I was on rafter, right over them."

I can't help laughing at that, and for a moment he seems to forget his grudge, and we just grin at each other—two spies appreciating a clever bit of spying.

I pull my eyes away and say to Count Fournier, "Have you heard of Lord Skaal before?"

"No," says the count. "But my contacts tell me that he is important, very close to Agoston Horthy."

"I saw them together once in Spira City," I say. "But why is he trying to meet with Si Tan? If he wants to get into the monastery, isn't it Gangzi he ought to be petitioning?"

"Si Tan is likely more open to negotiation," says the count. "And if there is anyone who holds some sway over Gangzi, it is Si Tan. In any case, it is bad news. I need to get the princess to safety as soon as possible. Will your people help us?"

He says *your people* with an avid sort of gleam in his eyes.

"That depends," I say. "Are you going to help *us* find Ko Dan, or do I have to jump through some more hoops?"

"No hoops, my dear," he says. "I've already put the word out. But I'm going to need money. For bribes, you understand."

"I'll bring you some," I say.

Count Fournier shoots Jun a pleased look, but Jun's gaze is snagging on mine again, another smile twitching at the corners of his mouth.

"Well," says Count Fournier, clearing his throat. "What I *do* know about Ko Dan is that he is a man-witch. Male witches are exceedingly rare, as I'm sure you know, and there was a lot of resistance, back in the day, regarding his joining the Shou-shu sect in the first place. Of course, they work a kind of magic with those bells, but the magic is *in* the bells, inscribed by witches a thousand years ago or more. He is the only one who can write magic himself. He was not born in Yongguo. He is from the Muyriki Islands, in the southern sea, but he came to Tianshi alone as a boy, bearing only a letter of recommendation from the Muyriki high holy, asking to apprentice with Gangzi. Gangzi made quite a pet of him. I don't know how or why he left the monastery. There are various stories. Some say he went mad, some say he was executed, and others say he became a secret advisor to the emperor. I never paid the rumors any mind, but I found him a curious fellow when I met him."

"What does he look like?"

"He is a young man, small, a gentle expression. He had a scar under his eye, shaped like a little star. Marked by magic, they said, or touched by the spirits. Who knows the truth of it?"

"D'you think they might have executed him?" I ask. I'd hate to think we came all this way looking for a dead man.

"It's possible, but I think Si Tan, in particular, would consider it a waste. They would want to make use of him somehow, I suspect. Still, if they considered him too dangerous or impossible to control, then yes, they would kill him. I do not know the nature of his crime. The penalty for misuse of magic that harms no one is ten years in prison."

"What are the penalties if someone *is* harmed?"

"It depends on who and how. Witches are drowned here too, you know."

"Witches who hurt people or use magic for their own gain," I say.

"Witches who are accused of that," he says, and then laughs at my expression. "I've been here too long, and I am a cynic. Witches may be useful to the empire or they may pose a threat. The empire keeps them close not because it loves witches but because it seeks to control them in the most efficient way. In Frayne, Horthy and the king drown witches indiscriminately, which is clumsy and brutal and stupid. There is more art to the managing of witches here, but don't imagine they are *not* managed. The penalty for not revealing yourself as a witch—by which I mean for *being* a witch without a license, even if you do not practice witchcraft—is death."

I am a little shaken by this. I suppose I'd imagined Yongguo as some kind of idyll for witches.

"A ruler cannot afford to ignore the fact that some small number of the population can alter nature itself merely by writing something down," he says.

"And what does your aunt, Lady Laroche, think about that?" I ask.

He smiles slyly. "Why, *she* believes witches cannot be ruled. It follows, then, that witches ought to rule. Now don't look so shocked, my dear! You've done very well. My contacts know everybody in this city. If you have money, I will find you Ko Dan."

TWENTY-THREE

I am hoping to find Dek at home, but he isn't there. Wyn is asleep on a mat on the floor with Mei at his side, her arm flung back. An aching, dark space opens up inside me as I look down at them. I used to love to fall asleep in his arms, to wake up next to him.

But he's not mine anymore, never really was, and I have other things to do besides wallow in self-pity. I give him a sharp nudge with my foot.

"Ow," he mutters into the pillow. I nudge harder. He sits up and stares at me.

"Brown Eyes," he says blurrily, and then looks at Mei and back at me, uncertain.

"I need money," I say. "Where's Dek?"

"I don't bleeding know where he is," he grumbles. "It's the middle of the night. What do you need money for?"

"Dek said Mrs. Och gave you money for bribes. I need some."

"So she'd give some to you as well. Why d'you need to come waking me up?"

He gets up off the mat, careful not to disturb Mei. He is completely naked, all beautiful long limbs and ... well. I look away.

"Aren't you precious," he scoffs, snatching his trousers from the floor and pulling them on. "Nothing you haven't seen before."

"I'd rather not wake Mrs. Och in the middle of the night," I say. "And I was hoping to see Dek."

The truth is, I want as little to do with Mrs. Och as possible. I want to find Ko Dan and get out of here. I follow Wyn into the other room, where he pulls up a floor plank and takes out a jar full of coins on strings and wads of paper money.

"How much?" he asks.

I help myself to most of the paper money, filling my pockets.

He gives a low whistle and asks, "D'you want me to come with you?"

"No."

"You're sure? It's not dangerous?"

"I'll be fine."

He sighs and rubs a sleepy hand over his face. "If you say so. You know if you ever need me ... well, just say the word."

"You'd leave your poor girl alone in the bed?" There's more bite to my words than I really intended.

"Yes," he says.

We look at each other. He is all shadow, his bare chest a darkness I know so well. My loneliness opens wider and wider until I feel I am a small thing within it. I shake it off. I'm used to climbing out of this particular pit of regret and desire by now.

"Look, I'm sorry I woke you. I'll come by tomorrow if I get a chance. Tell Dek to stick around."

I can't really see his expression in the dark, and I am already turning away when he says, "I still love you, Julia."

He never told me that he loved me until I left him.

"I love you too," I say lightly, without turning around. Because I do, I always have, in a thousand different ways. I go out and close the door on him.

I don't go straight back to Count Fournier's with the money. I am restless, and my legs carry me, almost of their own volition, to the other side of the Imperial Gardens and the empty road outside the Hundred Lantern Hotel. My heart tightens in my chest as I look up at the lit windows. It is one of the few establishments still open this late. I should be keeping an eye on Pia. I could disappear and get into her room, if I knew which one, without her seeing me. But when I think about it, my breath catches in my throat and I am, quite simply, too frightened. Like a child closing their eyes and pretending the scary thing doesn't exist—if I don't see her, I don't have to think of her in Tianshi, hunting me, hunting Theo.

"What is here?"

I spin around, and there is Jun, just a few feet away.

"Are you following me?" I try to sound annoyed, in spite of a startling rush of gladness.

He jerks his chin at the hotel. "You look at this place like there is ghost inside."

I shake my head, start to turn away.

"Julia," he says, and I stop. There's something new in his expression, two parts mischief and one part uncertainty. "I can tell you what is here at Hundred Lantern Hotel."

"What?"

"Best red bean soup in Tianshi. Maybe in all Yongguo. Maybe in the world."

He arches an eyebrow invitingly, tilting his head toward the door. I can't help smiling, but I shake my head.

"I can't go in there."

He nods and says, "Come with me."

I don't ask where. He takes me across the Zhuque Road and through a maze of narrow streets to a small eatery with a single lantern hanging outside. I follow him down the steps into a candlelit cavern, where a girl of maybe twelve is serving drinks and filling pipes for old men. She sees Jun and waves, then points to a curtain at the back of the room. We sit down at a little booth behind the curtain. The girl brings us tea, and Jun signs at her with his fingers. She nods and disappears again, letting the curtain fall shut.

"What was that?"

"She is not hearing," he says. "She use signs. You know it?"

I shake my head.

"Can be useful if you are hearing or not," he says. "Maybe I will teach you one day."

I hope I'm not going to be in Tianshi much longer, but it gives me a warm feeling, the way he says this—as if he's taking it for granted that we are on the same side, that we will continue to know and help each other. And what *is* this? Why did he bring me here? I pull my hair out of my face, trying to comb through the tangles with my fingers. I would have washed my face and brushed my hair, at least, if I'd known I was going to end up in a candlelit booth with him.

He leans toward me across the table. "How you disappear?" he asks me.

"I just . . . do."

"Show me?"

Stars. He says it so sweetly.

"All right," I say. "There are . . . I mean, I can disappear just a little, or a lot. If I were to try and disappear just a little right now, it wouldn't work, because you're already looking at me. But I can go back farther. I won't move, so when I do it, grab my hand, all right?"

He nods, and I vanish. Two steps back. His eyes widen, and he reaches across the table for my hand. Everything pulls into focus as I'm yanked back into the world by the contact. I laugh at the stunned look on his face, and he gives his head a little shake. He's still holding my hand.

"If you disappear and I touch you, I can see you again. But before, you disappear while I am holding you."

"If I'm just vanished partway, a bump or something kind of . . . knocks me back," I say. "It's hard to explain it, but it's as if there are *layers* of vanishing." I don't know why I tell him this—it's dangerous territory—but I add: "I can even take you with me, if I try."

"Take me where?"

"I'll show you."

I hold his hand tightly, and I pull us back carefully, pull him with me. Two steps. The little room blurs around us, but he—he stays in focus.

"Nobody can see me now?" he whispers. His face is like a light in the faded nowhere, our own invisible cocoon just beyond the edges of the world.

"That's right," I say. My heart speeds up, and I let go of his hand. The room sharpens around us again. The girl from before pulls back the curtain and puts a plate of steaming pork buns in front of us. Jun thanks her with his fingers, and she lets the curtain fall shut again.

"You are afraid of somebody at Hundred Lantern Hotel," he says, splitting open one of the buns so steam pours out. It smells delicious, and my mouth starts watering immediately. I grab the other bun. "Is it same person who put up pictures of you and your boss?"

"Yes."

"This person is dangerous to you?"

"Very," I say.

"Why this person is looking for you?"

"It's complicated."

He nods, accepting this.

"This place is safe. Nobody will tell they see you."

We demolish our pork buns at the same lightning speed. He licks a finger to pick up the crumbs off the plate. I'm tempted to do the same but decide to make some effort at appearing ladylike.

"What about you?" I ask. "Where did you learn . . . well, the sorts of things you can do?"

He grins at me, the dimples reemerging. Blast ladylike—I lick a finger and help him finish the crumbs. From the pouch at his waist he takes out a grayish rock like the one that shot out a bolt of flame when he threw it at the ground. I recoil, and he laughs.

"Count Fournier buy me this," he says. "Touch."

I touch the rock with my fingertips, but it is not a rock at all. It is spongy and warm.

"It is just trick," he says. "The fire does not burn. But looks very hot and bright. If I throw it down, it can scare someone, give me a chance."

"It did scare us," I say. "I saw you leaving the monastery one night. You had a jar of wasps or something."

He grins at me again. Oh, I am utterly slain by this smiling, laughing, candlelit version of Jun.

"I learn that back home," he says. "Get nest at night when wasps are sleeping, trap in a jar, and you have like a bomb you can throw if someone is chasing you."

"So how long have you worked for Count Fournier?"

"Two years. Before that, I am acrobat in children's circus."

"An acrobat!" I'm impressed. "So did you run away with the circus as a kid?"

"Yes," he says. No more than that.

"What about your family?"

"They are not good," he says. His expression does not change, but I know how to recognize practiced nonchalance.

"Not good?"

"Not good." He says it firmly, and I let it go. "I love the circus. When I am getting bigger, I start training for the trapeze. I do dancing on horseback. It is so much fun." There is a longing in his face that twists my stomach into knots. "But the circus leader like young boys too much and I cannot stay with them. When I am thirteen, we come to Tianshi. This is great city with many chance, so I leave the circus. I do many kind of job here, but after one year Count Fournier hires me. He is best boss, so I stay with him. Good pay, safe place to live. He is not happy man, but he is good man."

We look at each other by the guttering candlelight.

"I was seven when my ma died," I offer. "She was a witch. They drowned her."

"I am sorry," he says. "You have father, or brothers?"

"A brother," I say. "You met him. The one with the crutch."

"He shoot me with sleep drug."

"I know. He was trying to help me."

"Maybe I forgive him, for you," he says slyly. And then changes the subject: "I love Tianshi. It is great city. Greatest in the world. You think so?"

"It's amazing," I say. "In Frayne, if you're born rich, you

stay that way, and same if you're born broke. Here, talent really counts for something."

Jun snorts. "Not so different here," he says dismissively.

"But the Imperial Examinations," I say. "I mean, a peasant can take them!"

"How can a peasant learn to read to take this exam?" he says. "And what is on this exam? Maybe I am great painter or great poet, but how can I know when I have no paints, no paper, no time? This exam is for people with money and people with time. If you can do rich person's thing, you can live in the Imperial Gardens. But they do not invite farmer who can make crops grow in a dry year, or goatherd who can deliver calf safely and keep his herd alive through winter, or fisherman who can catch most fish. Maybe if you take away the meat and rice and fish of the rich, they will think those talents are also important. But the men and women who feed this city are poor. I have great talent too, and I am more clever than many men who read poems all day, but I will never have my place in the Imperial Gardens either."

He says all this without rancor, but it stirs me.

"I reckon you're right," I say. "The deck is stacked no matter where you go."

"What does it mean?" he asks, and I try to explain the expression *stacked deck* to him.

"You play cards?" he asks me, eyes gleaming with mischief again.

"I'm all right," I say.

"I show you some trick next time," he says. I want to ask,

Next time what? but I'm afraid to spoil the moment. He is drumming rapidly on the table with his fingers again. I think I've never known someone who can be, at different moments, so restless and so still.

"What about Spira City?" he asks.

And so I tell him about home, all the things I miss. His eyes are black and shining, the angles of his face all the more dramatic in the flickering candlelight. I want to tell him I know what it's like trying to find a life large enough to fit who you are and what you can do. I want to ask him if he feels a pang whenever he sees children with their parents, children who are safe and loved. But instead I cast around for stories and descriptions that will make him laugh, and whenever he does, my heart belly flops all over the place. He tells me about the circus and traveling around Yongguo, and I try to imagine him as a slim young boy dancing on the back of a horse. The girl brings more tea, and we talk about our lives as they used to be—so much safer than talking about the here and now—until the candle burns down to a nub and goes out.

TWENTY-FOUR

"Hey!" cries Frederick.

Cackling with glee, Theo tries to make off with his notebook, filled with the transcriptions of the bamboo strips from the Imperial Library, but Frederick gets it back and puts it on the table. "You mustn't touch these, Theo."

"Stoy!" Theo shouts.

"I'll tell you a story," I offer, looking sadly at my failed attempt at scallion pancakes, burnt to the pan.

"*Feyda* stoy," says Theo. "Buk!"

"I got him a book of fairy tales," explains Frederick. "They're in Yongwen, but I translate as I go. He likes the illustrations."

"Feyda umma *buk!*" insists Theo, trying to snatch the notebook again.

"We had better be careful of that," says Mrs. Och, watching him.

"Careful of what?" I ask.

"Theo learning language," she says. "No matter how it is bound, *The Book of Disruption* is a part of him."

"What do you mean?"

"I mean that his learning language might be dangerous. Oh, probably not so long as he cannot read or write. But even so, we should keep a close eye now that he is beginning to speak. Words have power, and his might have more than most."

That is an unsettling thought. I look at Frederick, who is stacking his notebooks and papers out of Theo's reach.

"Yes, yes," he's saying. "I'll read you a story."

"So nothing useful yet?" I ask him, gesturing at his notes.

"Nothing we don't know already," he says. "Although here is something interesting. Kahge might be described as an echo or reflection of the natural world, but it is not a perfect reflection. There are many reasons for this, one being that the elements in Kahge are not in balance. Because it is made of magic, fire is dominant. That might explain why what you see is like a reflection of the world on fire, or burning, or burnt. I am going to need a different dictionary to translate the pictographs on the rubbing—it is the oldest form of Yongwen I've seen. But there is a bookseller in the Beimu Triangle who has been very helpful. I'll go and see him today. *Yes, Theo, all right!*"

Theo has found the book of fairy tales and is waving it urgently at Frederick. Then he runs outside, and Frederick follows. I don't want to sit at the table with Mrs. Och, and so I take my burnt scallion pancakes out onto the steps, where

Bianka is sitting in the thin morning sunlight, carving a toy for Theo out of a block of wood.

She is carving much too fast. She is very jumpy about Lord Skaal being in the city, and I reckon carving is not the best activity for her at the moment, but I daren't say so. As soon as I sit down next to her, she says, "I don't care what Mrs. Och says. He's here for Theo."

"I think she's right that he's here for the princess," I say. "Casimir might know that we're here, but Agoston Horthy doesn't."

It is early, and the clouds in the east are gold-rimmed as the sun comes up. Frederick and Theo have settled on an empty crate by the pump, and Frederick is reading to him. Theo is riveted by the brilliantly colored illustrations that fill up most of the page, pointing out this and that. I doubt he'll be asking *me* for stories anymore.

"No," says Bianka. "I remember him. He was the first to come for Theo. We need to get out of Tianshi."

The knife in her hand is going still faster.

"Not yet," I say. "Count Fournier has put the word out. We need to sit tight. We'll know something about Ko Dan soon."

"I can't just sit in this courtyard and wait for them to appear and try to take Theo!" she cries. "Oh *blast*." She has whittled the wood away to nothing, her lap full of shavings. "I said I'd make him a toy. He has nothing to play with, and he torments the chickens."

"Mo! Mo!" cries Theo when Frederick reaches the end of the story. Frederick laughs and turns the page.

"You were wrong, you know," I tell Bianka, pointing at them. "When you said I was the only one besides you who loved Theo."

She looks at the two of them bent over the book together, almost cheek to cheek, Theo's chubby little hand fondling Frederick's beard, and her face softens.

"You're right," she says. "They adore each other."

I am about to reassure her again that Lord Skaal is surely here for the princess when a tree pipit flies over the wall and nearly crashes into my face. I give a yell, trying to fend it off. It drops a piece of paper in my lap and lands on the step next to me, cocking its head at me. I unroll the paper quickly. Dek's handwriting: *We've found him.*

The trolleys on the first tier road are always crowded in the morning, but I vanish and step onto the outer ledge, holding on to the window rail. I've seen people try to ride this way for free, though usually the driver spots them and shoos them off. The voices of merchants sing out from their shops and stalls along the side of the road, delicious smells waft up from the food stalls, and the peaked rooftops shimmer in the morning haze. I get off the trolley in Dongshui and buy sticky red rice wrapped in bamboo leaves so I can eat as I walk. I keep my hat down and my head low, hoping the seller doesn't look at me too closely and recognize the foreign girl whose picture is plastered on the walls of the city with a promised reward. Then I head in among the narrow dirt streets where the ramshackle houses practically lean up against each other, old men sitting outside playing Zhengfu and smoking while scrawny chickens run loose, shedding their feathers.

When I get to Dek's house, Mei and Ling are there again. Dek and Ling are at the table, flour-dusted to the elbows, making dumpling wrappings. Wyn and Mei are playing cards, and they both look bored out of their minds.

"These two seem to have moved in," I say.

"Julia!" Dek grins at me. His hair is braided Tianshi-style. "You got our message?"

"I hope by all the holies you mean you've found Ko Dan, or Bianka's going to have a fit and probably turn you into a toad."

"Ling told us. He was readmitted to the monastery at dawn. Apparently, word got out and there was quite a crowd gathered outside to watch him knock on the door and request entry, so for all that we've been pretending we've got the pulse of the city, we're obviously out of the loop. The girls went with their uncle and saw him themselves."

"You saw him go in?" I ask Ling in Fraynish. Dek translates, looking vaguely annoyed with me.

Ling nods, wiping her hands off and fetching me a rolled-up piece of paper. I unroll it and look at the drawing of a solemn, round-faced man with a star-shaped scar under his eye.

"Who drew this?"

"Ling did," says Wyn. "She's not bad, is she? Good technique."

"Can I ... um ... ownership?" I ask her in fumbling Yongwen.

Mei smirks a little at my bad Yongwen. Ling just shrugs, as if she doesn't care one way or the other, but when I fold it up to slip it into my pocket, her brow creases in an expression of surprise and hurt, and I wonder if it's some kind of insult to fold it. I've nowhere to put it rolled up, though.

"Where were you last night?" I ask Dek. "I wanted to talk to you."

"We went to the theater!" he says enthusiastically. "It costs almost nothing for standing room. All the rich people pay for balcony seats above and watch through their little binoculars, but we were right in front of the stage with the rabble. I've never seen anything like it—it was this kind of dance with masks. Ling was explaining it to me. Every movement means something; every mask has significance. Each animal is symbolic. What did we decide? Ling is a lynx, I'm a cormorant. . . ."

"Panda," says Ling in Fraynish, pointing at Wyn, and I snort.

"What would I be?" I ask.

"Hmm, what do you think?" Dek asks Ling in Yongwen. He looks so happy. I can't remember seeing him look so happy. I should be glad to see it, but it makes my heart sink—that *this* place and this girl should be what makes him happy. That there is no hope of freedom or love for him back home, the home I long for.

Ling studies me and then says, with the faintest smile: "Wolf."

I raise my eyebrows at her, not sure if I ought to be offended.

"Wolf?" says Dek, taken aback.

"Wolf," says Ling firmly.

"Are you going to the monastery now?" Wyn asks me, tired of the conversation and probably annoyed at having been declared a panda bear.

"No. Mrs. Och told me to report back to her after I'd spoken to you," I say. "I've got to report to her before I take a piss, apparently."

Dek laughs.

"Wait a bit if you're hungry," he says. "Ling is teaching me to make steamed dumplings."

"I *am* hungry," I say. "But Bianka's waiting too, and probably going mad. If it's really him, we'll be moving on soon, I reckon."

I look at Dek as I say this, but he shows no sign of having heard me, flattening the dough into perfect little circles.

"I'll walk you to the trolley," says Wyn.

"I don't need an escort."

"I'm not escorting you. I want to talk."

"Oh."

"Come back when you're done," says Dek. "We'll have dumplings ready!"

I don't know what to make of this happy, busy version of

my brother. I thank Ling for the picture again, and Wyn walks me out.

"Mail goes out from Shou-shu today," he says. "I was going to snatch one of Gangzi's letters if you still want it. Or should I not bother now that we've found Ko Dan?"

"Might as well get one just in case. Is that what you wanted to talk to me about?"

"No. Well, that was one thing." He clears his throat. "I'm just going to say it. I promise I'll drop it if you tell me that you don't feel anything for me anymore. But I think that you do, and I want you back, Brown Eyes. I want things to be like they used to be."

"That isn't going to happen," I say quickly, before I can say anything else. "Everything's changed. *We've* changed. Or I have, anyway."

We pass an old couple sharing a pipe outside. They look at us curiously, and I duck my head so that the brim of my hat hides my face.

"People don't change that much," says Wyn. "I'll own that I spoiled things. I was selfish and stupid. But it would be different if you'd give me another chance."

"You just finished telling me people don't change. Everybody knew what was happening except me. If I wasn't enough for you then, I don't see why I would be now."

"Because I wouldn't risk losing you again. But you should talk to more girls, Julia. The way you carry on, you'd think I was this roach among men for spending a night or two with Arly Winters."

"I don't carry on," I say, getting angry now. "*You* brought

191

it up. I'd just as soon not talk about it at all. And if you *must* talk about it, don't lie to me and pretend it was only a night or two. What would your girl back at the house think about you telling me this?"

"This isn't about Mei."

"Of *course* it is! She thinks you're her fellow, and here you are trying to sweet-talk me back into bed with you. As far as I can tell, you want every girl you look at, especially the ones you haven't got."

"Don't be so bleeding naïve, Julia. All men are the same. Yes, if I see a pretty girl, I want her. Hounds, if I see an ugly girl, I want her. I wish you could understand how little it has to do with you, or with love. But that's what I'm trying to tell you: If it matters to you, I can just . . . resist all that. Be yours. Really yours. Haven't you been angry long enough?"

"I'm not angry," I say, deflated. "But things are different now."

"You haven't told me you don't feel anything for me anymore."

"Hounds, I'll always *feel* something for you. But not the same way I used to. I'm past it, all right?"

I hear myself saying it, and for the first time I almost think it might be true.

"Flaming Kahge, Julia—what do you want from a fellow?" He kicks a rock down the road, frightening a pair of chickens. "I'll own my mistake, but if you think there's a man out there who's any different, you're deluding yourself!"

I've heard enough.

"Fine, maybe men like you are common as dirt. That doesn't strike me as much to brag about. But I don't go around figuring everybody is just like me, and d'you know why not?"

He gives me an unhappy look.

"Because there is *nobody* like me," I tell him, and vanish, leaving him staring at the place where I was, where I'm not anymore.

TWENTY-FIVE

"He's at the monastery," I tell Mrs. Och, showing her the picture Ling drew. She takes the paper from me and examines it. "Dek's girl saw him going up to the gate, said that everybody was talking about Ko Dan's return, and she drew this."

"What now?" whispers Bianka, watching the goat knock Theo over into the mud in the courtyard.

"I will go and see him myself," says Mrs. Och, rising and giving me back the picture. "Julia, you will come with me to make sure nothing is amiss and that I am not followed back. Frederick! I need strength."

He comes when she calls him. I can see the apprehension in his eyes even though he tries to hide it. He stretches out his hands. She reaches for him, and there is an awful hunger in her gaze. I can't watch. I turn away, leaving the room in a hurry, but I hear him gasp behind me, his knees hitting the floor.

"How are you going to get in?" I ask.

Mrs. Och is striding down the street, and I find myself half skipping to keep up with her, like a child whose long-legged parent won't slow down for them, taking two steps for every one of hers.

"I'll knock," she says.

"But doesn't that blow our cover? Then everybody knows we're here, what we're after."

"If Pia is in Tianshi, it is because Casimir already knows that we are here and what we want," says Mrs. Och. A fair point. "I expect that the grand librarian has a good idea as well. But if it is indeed Ko Dan in the monastery, and if he agrees to help us, then we will not need to hide much longer."

"What if it *isn't* him? What if he won't help us? What if he *can't* help us? Or what if he can't do it without hurting Theo?"

She gives me an impatient look. Her face is bright and alive with what she took from Frederick. I wonder, when I see her like this, if she takes only what she needs or perhaps more. How much she likes it. How much she does it just because she likes it.

"We did not come all this way to harm Theo," she says. "There is no point imagining a thousand possibilities before they come about. It is a drain on the mind."

"Fine. Say you get the text out of Theo. What will you do with it?"

"Perhaps destroy it."

"Destroy it? Really?"

"If it is possible, yes. The Book has been trying to unmake itself for centuries. The time of the Xianren is already past. Casimir is grasping at straws, but they are dangerous straws indeed, and best kept out of his reach forever. Julia, when the witch at the library searched your memories, did she uncover our purpose here? Does she know we are looking for Ko Dan?"

"I don't know," I say. "It was all moving very fast. She knows about Theo and the Book, I think, but the memories she seemed to stop over were from a long time ago. When I was little."

She frowns, dissatisfied with this answer, and boards a trolley at the second tier road. The other passengers make way for her instinctively. I go along vanished, no more chances for asking questions. We ride the trolley to the northwest part of the city and walk from there to the monastery.

"Behind me, Julia," she murmurs. "Unseen, if you please."

I do as she says. She pulls the bell at the main doors of Shou-shu. A panel is pulled back, and a face appears in the gap.

"Who are you?" the face asks in Yongwen.

She says "Och Farya," her Xianren name. No more hiding indeed.

"No woman may enter here," says the face.

A harsh laugh. The air hums. Her cloak billows, and she casts it to the ground. Fur ripples out of the back of her neck and along her outstretched arms, her hair moving and changing to match it. Bony spikes tear out of her back through the fabric of her robe and unfold into wings.

Her voice resonates when she speaks—making the point, presumably, that she is not exactly a woman, and not to be denied. Another face appears at the panel. The two faces deliberate, the panel is slammed, and we wait. The wings lie resting against her back like the wings of a great swan.

And then the doors creak open. The monks back away as she enters, with me vanished in her wake. The doors slam shut behind us.

TWENTY-SIX

We are taken to the tiny, wooden Temple of Atonement behind the Treasury. There he is, kneeling before the many-armed statue of Gu'ama, West Arrekem goddess of repentance—the man from Ling's picture. Ko Dan. My letter-writing friend Prune Face—Gangzi—kneels next to him. They look up as we come in, and although his face is slightly blurred by my vanishing, I can make out the star-shaped scar under Ko Dan's left eye. He rises and bows to Mrs. Och. There is something loose and easy in the way he moves, as if he is more at peace inside his skin and bones than most. Gangzi rises rigidly, grimacing like his joints pain him, and gives a terse nod.

Mrs. Och remains in her startling Och Farya form, but the two men do not seem alarmed. They all greet each other politely in Yongwen, and then the three of them sit down right on the floor together, legs folded under them, which seems to cause Gangzi some difficulty, but he angrily brushes off Ko Dan's attempt to help him.

At first I try to follow their conversation, but it moves too quickly, so I give up and look around the temple instead. Painted on the wall behind them, lovely Tisis, goddess of mercy and forgiveness, is offering her golden cup. Behind her, a whirlwind in her fist, Haizea, goddess of vengeance, bares her teeth. Of course she is here too—she appears in nearly every story and illustration of Tisis. It's bewildering to me the way gods and goddesses from all over the world are welcome under the broad umbrella of the religion practiced in Yongguo, but Professor Baranyi says that they are all regarded as metaphors for the same essential truth. What that truth is, I couldn't say.

Ko Dan—if it is really him—is speaking at great length, low and urgent, illustrating something with his hands, and Mrs. Och is leaning forward, a greedy look in her eyes. I wonder about the purpose of this temple. Is it really possible to atone for one's misdeeds by just kneeling in this room and . . . what? Does he even know what he's atoning for? Does he know the consequences of what he did, the people who have died—people who had nothing at all to do with the Xianren or *The Book of Disruption* or any of this but whose lives were swept away by the storm he unleashed? The battle over that fragment of *The Book of Disruption* should have been between Gennady and Casimir. Instead, Bianka's life was turned upside down, Theo's life defined by this, my own life changed forever, and so many other lives upended or snuffed out. I'm thinking of the dead governess on the bridge in Spira City, dead by the mere accident of sharing a cabriolet with Bianka, and the other innocent victims of the Gethin. I'm thinking of the guard in Casimir's fortress, the one whose neck Bianka snapped because he was in her way, and she could think only of saving her son, and no other life meant anything to her. Is that her fault, or Ko Dan's, or Casimir's? Are we all unwittingly creating chaos we can't imagine, setting off chains of events whose brutal, bloody endings happen so far from us that we never even hear of them? Perhaps he's just doing what he's been told, finishing up his punishment, jumping through the final hoop before Gangzi lets him back.

My stomach rumbles, but nobody seems to hear it, thank the Nameless. I wish I'd asked Mrs. Och how long this was likely to take. Ko Dan stops speaking. Gangzi is looking at Mrs. Och with something like anger. She puts her hands together and seems to think very hard, and then she begins to speak and I hear *the witch* and *the child* and *Lan Camshe*. My heart speeds up.

When she is done, Ko Dan looks at Gangzi, who gives a single nod. Ko Dan says, in formal Yongwen, "I will try."

Mrs. Och walks south from the monastery. I watch the main doors awhile before running after her, vanished two steps back, the city blurred around me, my own footsteps muffled. I follow the silhouette of her cloaked figure. We pass along a street of silk shops in the Nanjin Triangle. A man smoking in a doorway tosses his cigarette aside and falls into step with me, though of course he does not see me. Mrs.

Och turns toward the Imperial Gardens and walks along its outer walls, and so does he. I gather she is going to walk the whole way back to Nanmu. I'm sure now that this fellow is tailing her, so I take one of Dek's darts from the pouch at my waist, unscrew the cap, and jab him in the arm.

It's effective, I'll say that. He stumbles sideways into the wall and goes down hard. A woman drops her basket of wish papers and runs to him, old wishes scattering in the gutter at the side of the road.

Mrs. Och keeps going, following the wall to the Dongnan Canal and crossing the bridge into Nanmu. I keep her in sight, but at a distance. When she is safely back home, I wait outside the courtyard for half an hour, vanished and thrumming with impatience, to be certain nobody else managed to follow us. Nobody comes and so I go in at last.

Frederick is slumped in a chair, still ghastly pale and weak from what she took from him. Bianka is leaning close to Mrs. Och at the table, her expression caught somewhere between terror and hope.

"Well?" Mrs. Och says to me when I come in.

"There was somebody following," I say. "I got rid of him." She nods briefly.

"So is it really him?" I ask. But I know the answer just from looking at her. Her eyes are fierce and bright, her lips parted in a near smile that is almost girlish in its excitement.

"I believe so," she says. "He was able to explain things about how the magic was done that have puzzled me for some time. They have . . . an item that I believed lost forever."

She shakes her head wonderingly, and then continues: "He believes that he can undo the binding of text to Theo without harming him. At least, he is willing to try, and Gangzi is willing to let him."

Theo looks up from the line of ants he is pursuing across the floor, interested because we are talking about him.

"He's willing to *try?*" says Bianka. "We need to be sure it isn't dangerous."

"Such magic does not come with guarantees," says Mrs. Och. "This is what we have come for. If you will not risk it, then it is only a matter of time before Theo is found and somebody else does the same thing without his well-being in mind."

Bianka stares at Mrs. Och, twisting her hands in her lap.

"All right. Yes. All right," she says rather mechanically.

"Good," says Mrs. Och. "Ready yourself and we will take him at once."

"Now?" Bianka whispers.

"Delaying will only increase the danger," answers Mrs. Och. "I want to get this done before Si Tan becomes involved."

Bianka looks at me, and suddenly I have to sit. I know exactly what she's feeling. Of course this is what we came here for, but it feels too sudden and too uncertain.

"Trust me a little further," says Mrs. Och softly. "You cannot hide him away forever, Bianka. Here is the chance to end it."

I wish she'd found another way to say that. Theo is

standing at Bianka's knee now and looking back and forth between us, aware that an important conversation about *him* is taking place, surely aware that his mother is afraid. I want to snatch him up and refuse to let them take him. But what am I thinking? We've crossed the world for this moment. I swore I'd make it right, and we've done it, we've found him.

"I'll come too," I say.

Mrs. Och gives me an impatient look. "No. We will need to move quickly once this is done. I want you to take a message to Count Fournier. We will meet with him first thing tomorrow morning."

She hands me a sealed letter addressed to the count, and I take it, but I repeat, "I want to come with you."

"Do what is *useful*, Julia, not what your guilt demands."

That lands like a blow, knocking the breath out of me.

"Bianka," says Mrs. Och sharply, and Bianka jumps. "You must decide now."

"Yes, all right," she whispers. She puts a trembling hand on Theo's curly head.

"Theo. Shall we take a walk, love?"

"Wawk?" His eyes go wide. He has not been allowed out of the courtyard since we got here.

Bianka nods at him, but her face is rigid as a mask, her smile desperate. "Let's get you into some trousers, shall we? Oh blast, where *are* his trousers?"

Theo begins a little jig, crowing, "Wawk! Wawk! Wawk!" Heart in my throat, I go digging through our things in the bedroom until I find a pair of his trousers. Once Theo figures out we're going to try and put him in clothes, he screams as if this is the greatest betrayal we could have enacted and puts up a tremendous fight, determined to maintain his mostly naked status. It takes both of us to wrestle his kicking legs and arching body into the little trousers. We got the fabric in Ishti, and Bianka sewed them, but already they are short on him, he is growing so quickly.

Bianka scrabbles in Frederick's writing box for a charcoal pencil, tucks it into her bodice, and gives me one more impossible look. I know I am mirroring all the terror and hope I see in her gaze right back at her. She puts on a large straw hat to hide her face and picks Theo up. Having completely forgotten the trouser battle within seconds of losing it, he waves to me cheerfully from her arms.

"Bah-bah, Lala!"

I walk them out and wave back from the gate as they round the corner to flag down a motor carriage. Turning the envelope in my hand, I half want to ignore Mrs. Och's instructions and follow them anyway. But she's right, of course—what good could I do, how could I help, when he has both his mother and Mrs. Och with him? *Do what is useful.* All right, then, I will be useful, since the Nameless knows I can't stay still another moment. I run for the second tier road and get a trolley to Count Fournier's house.

Count Fournier studies the letter from Mrs. Och, puffing his cheeks out.

"Thank the Nameless One," he says. "This Lord Skaal

you saw the other day has been granted a meeting with the grand librarian *and* Gangzi tomorrow! Ordinarily, Si Tan makes the Fraynish delegations wait for weeks, and Gangzi never agrees to meet with *anybody*. He must be seriously considering the Fraynish position. Nameless only knows what they are offering him! I won't put a reply in writing, better not, but tell your Mrs. Och we will expect her in the morning, as early as possible."

Jun brings me a cup of tea.

"An exciting time," he says, all dimples and shining eyes, but glad as I am to see him, I can barely smile back. My stomach is in knots.

"By the way, I've had some news about your monk," says Count Fournier, lighting a match and setting fire to Mrs. Och's letter. He drops the flaming, curling paper in an ashy bowl on the table apparently set there for the purpose of receiving burnt correspondence. "Very reliable source. This fellow has contacts all over the city, high and low. He claims Ko Dan has been imprisoned in Tianshi ever since his disappearance, on Si Tan's order. But not in an ordinary prison, he says. Somewhere secret in the Imperial Gardens."

I stare at him, not quite taking this in at first. Then I say, "No, he's back at the monastery. He got back yesterday."

Count Fournier shakes his head. "I heard there was some rumor to that effect, but no, this fellow is never wrong. I would believe him above any rumor in the streets."

"No," I say again, putting down my tea. "I *saw* him, at Shou-shu."

Count Fournier frowns and says, "How odd," and suddenly I go cold all over. I fumble in my pockets and find the picture Ling drew. I unfold it, my hands shaking as I do so, and shove it across the desk toward him.

The count peers at it through his spectacles and laughs. "But that's not him," he says.

"But the scar . . ." Panic rises hot and bitter in my throat.

He snorts. "Not hard to fake a scar. Well, look, it may just be a bad likeness. This looks nothing like him."

"It's a *very good* likeness of the man I saw," I say between my teeth.

"Then the man you saw was not Ko Dan," says the count. "Please stop looking at me like you're about to cut my throat, poppet. I am not trying to make you angry. I am telling you that this picture does not look like Ko Dan and that, according to my best informant, Ko Dan is in some kind of secret prison."

"Then why . . ." But I know why, of course. He says it anyway.

"Somebody has gone to a good deal of trouble to deceive you, my dear," he says, waving the paper at me. "This fellow is a fake, an impostor."

"They've taken Theo," I whisper.

"Who is Theo?" asks the count, annoyed.

Jun touches my elbow, his face full of concern. I am shaking all over, am back in the moment when I handed Theo over to Pia and my whole world collapsed. The thing I can never undo, the thing I am meant to make right, and Theo, dear little Theo, never again, I promised, *never again* would I let anybody harm him, and now . . .

"I have to go," I say. "Please—"

Jun nods. "I go with you."

TWENTY-SEVEN

Jun keeps pace easily with my panicked sprint. In the Xi-shui Triangle, he pulls me down an alley and into a derelict hut, the roof half caved in, chicken dung everywhere. He moves a rusted pot from the hearth and then lifts the grate. There is a ladder leading down.

"This way," he says.

I start down the ladder, and he follows, pulling the grate back over the tunnel. My heart is crashing against my ribs like it's trying to break out, my mind just a roar of *TheoTheo-TheoTheo*. I see him frightened and alone, I see him cut open, I see him screaming, I see him dead and blank-eyed, and I hear myself sobbing loudly as I go slipping and scrambling down the narrow ladder. "More quiet!" Jun hisses down at me, but I can't control myself.

A voice from below calls up a question in Yongwen, star-tling me so badly I nearly fall, and Jun answers. There is the smell of lamp oil, and a light blazes up. A scrawny kid, maybe ten, hands the lantern to Jun when he reaches the bottom of the ladder. Jun presses a coin into his hand, says something or other about his mother, but I'm not paying attention.

"Come on," I urge him.

He starts down the tunnel at a swift jog and I follow. Little Theo, so excited to set out this afternoon, holding on to Bianka, his face bright and happy. Oh, Bianka. They won't get him from Bianka, she won't let them, she'll find a way, *TheoTheoTheoTheo*.

The tunnel forks a few times, and I stay right behind Jun. A couple of times I hear voices as we pass lit chambers dug out of the ground. In one of them, I glimpse a cluster of armed men dismembering something that I hope is not a body, but I think it is. We pass by fast.

"This is smugglers' route," says Jun over his shoulder, though I haven't asked. "Tunnels all under city. Tell me what you need."

"We need to save a little boy, get him out of the monastery, get them all out of there. My friends . . ." I break off, my voice shaking so much I don't know if I can make myself understood. Jun doesn't ask any more questions. We reach another ladder, and he snuffs out the lantern, leaving it there on the ground. He goes up the ladder, a fast-moving shadow, and I follow with sweaty palms and shaking knees. *I'll save him*, I think. I don't know how, but I'll save him.

Light pours down as Jun pushes aside the flagstone and slithers out. There is nobody on the path, but I hear chanting from the Hall of Abnegation.

"Where?" he asks me.

I head for the Temple of Atonement, the last place I saw Ko Dan—though if he is not Ko Dan, then who is he? Inevitably, we round a corner and run smack into a monk. I've got my knife out and pointed at his throat before he can open his mouth. Jun circles around behind him.

"Ask him if Gangzi has visitors," I say, not trusting my own Yongwen. Jun asks.

"The Main Hall," the monk tells us, wide-eyed.

"What are we going to do with him?" I ask Jun, pointing at the monk with my knife.

Jun looks at me like I'm deranged, and I don't know what I'm asking anyway. What *are* we supposed to do with him?

"Shouldn't we tie him up?" I suggest, rather ashamed of myself.

He shakes his head. "Only hurry," he says. "In, out. Come."

I am so grateful to have him with me. I slide my knife back into the fabric bands of my boot, and we leave the monk standing stunned in the path. The long alley to the Main Hall is walled on either side—easy for me to sneak up on, perhaps, but not for Jun. Two of the Ru are outside, armed with crossbows. I vanish. Jun is on top of the low wall in a flash, running along it. He throws a pale stone that goes rolling down the middle of the path toward the guards. They are aiming their weapons when there is a bang, and a burst of white smoke envelops them. An arrow wings its way by me, down the path. I run straight into the smoke, straight past the shouting guards, crashing through the door, tripping and tumbling to the wood floor.

There is Mrs. Och, but not as Mrs. Och—she is Och Farya, winged and terrible. Bianka is clutching Theo to her chest, stepping back, startled by the sudden noise. The false Ko Dan and Gangzi are with them, Ko Dan reaching for Theo.

They all freeze and look at me sprawled on the temple floor. One of the Ru from outside comes in after me and then falls forward, a wire twisting his ankles, thank you very much, Jun. I yell at Bianka, "He's not Ko Dan!"

I run for her as the second guard from outside charges into the hall. I can see Theo's mouth open in a wail, but I can't hear it over the roaring in my head, and everybody is in motion at once except Bianka. Her eyes are fixed on me, and I can see everything in her eyes in that moment. I know I am asking her to make an impossible decision in a split second, and she does.

She hands me Theo, and I vanish. An arrow strikes the wall right next to us. Ko Dan lunges for Bianka, and she hurls him across the hall, where he hits the wall and slumps to the ground.

Mrs. Och opens her mouth and lets out a roar that shakes the walls and knocks Gangzi off his feet. The guard that fired at me regains his footing quickly, aims his crossbow, and shoots her in the chest. She staggers and goes down on one knee, yanking the bloody arrow out. Bianka has the charcoal pencil she took from Frederick's writing box in her hand; she is writing something on the floor. Gangzi points at her and shouts a command as the smell of rotten flowers sweeps through the hall. The guard Jun tripped with wire shoots at her, but the arrow goes wide. He drops the bow and clutches his eyes.

Theo is crying into my neck, but there is so much noise and shouting now that I am not afraid of anybody hearing him, and I am ready to pull him all the way to Kahge if any more arrows start flying. The two guards, Ko Dan, and Gangzi are all grabbing at their eyes, and Gangzi is shouting something about magic. I see what Bianka has scribbled on the floor in charcoal: *blind*.

She drops the pencil, staggering a little. Her nose is bleeding, and Jun is next to her. I am weak with relief to see him unharmed.

"I am friend of Julia," he says. "Follow me!"

The two of them help Mrs. Och toward the door. There are three more of the Ru on the path ahead, running for the hall.

"Blast!" gasps Bianka. "I can't . . ."

Mrs. Och pulls herself upright, one hand clutched to her bleeding chest, and speaks in that awful, summoning voice. She raises a furred fist and pulls it down. A torrent of rain follows. We are soaked to the skin in seconds, the Ru briefly stunned, and then lightning blasts them. We run straight past the bodies, one of them scrabbling at the ground, the other two still.

Jun takes Mrs. Och and Bianka at a run to the flagstone by the swallow coop. Bianka is screaming, *"Julia!"* and Theo is thrashing in my arms, howling, "Mama, Mama!" I step back into the visible world full of people trying to kill us, everything so sharp and clear, the smell of blood and smoke and rain filling my nostrils. Theo practically leaps from me into Bianka's arms, and she pulls him close to her.

"Hurry!" says Jun. "Down ladder!"

Bianka goes first, with Theo in her arms, and Mrs. Och follows, looking up at me only once to say, "Get the impostor and bring him to me."

I've no idea how I'm going to manage that.

"I'll catch up," I say to Jun. "Thank you."

I want to say more, but it's all I can manage. He nods, and then he is gone too, the flagstone sliding into place over him. I stand still a moment to catch my breath. The storm has gone as quickly as it came, the sky clear and bright. I feel something sharp and stinging on my arm and look down to see a little red dart sticking into me. A sick feeling sweeps over me. Two of the black-clad Ru are striding toward me. One of them has a pistol-like contraption at his side. They blur into multitudes and then blackness spreads fast over everything, like ink spilled over a page.

TWENTY-EIGHT

When I return to myself, I am lying in a comfortable bed like a convalescent. Sitting at my bedside is the witch from the Imperial Library, with her stitched-over eyes and her tattooed skin. She is bent over a little writing table, a sheet of rice paper and a pot of ink before her, and she is licking ink from the brush pensively, her tongue and lips quite black from it. She doesn't notice that I am awake. I keep very still and quiet, trying to figure out how I came to be here. It comes back to me slowly, the haze lifting bit by bit: the battle in the monastery, the dart in my arm. But they got away— Theo is all right. I remember that with a great rush of relief. Now I just have to get out of here, wherever *here* is.

The witch is so busy sucking on her brush that I figure I'll just vanish and walk out, but when I try to pull back, I find I can't. It's like being paralyzed, except that I *can* move my limbs, if only slightly. It is some deeper part of me that is fully immobilized—the part of me that pulls out of the world. That is when I notice the ribbons looped around my ankles, wrists, and waist—spools of red ribbon with untidy Yongwen script all over them. I must have made a small sound of dismay, for suddenly the witch's head shoots up and she points her awful face toward me.

She croons something at me in her scratchy voice and rings a little bell on the table. Then she goes springing over to the door and opens it. I lie helpless on the bed, looking around at the small, bare room with old-fashioned weapons displayed on the walls—double-edged axes, a scimitar, an ornate musket, a set of gleaming throwing knives. Hardly the most cheerful decor.

The witch returns to my bedside, and the oddest apparition comes rolling into the room. It is the old woman I saw the grand librarian whispering to after our first meeting with him. She is clothed in shapeless, beautiful silks and seated on a wheeled sort of platform, a pile of cushions supporting her bulk. Si Tan, the grand librarian, is pushing this contraption.

"A pleasure to see you again," he says congenially to me, in Fraynish. "How do you feel? Any headache or nausea?"

I nod. Bit of both.

"You look well, though. The young are so resilient." He adds something in Yongwen to the old woman, and she answers in her deep rasp.

"The empress dowager asks me to welcome you to the Imperial Residences," he says, bowing.

At least now I know where I am and who I'm dealing

215

with. Again, I find Si Tan's impeccable manners, his elegant clothing and long beard, somehow out of keeping with his physique, which suggests such brute power, the intensity and focus of a predator.

"You make it sound like I'm a guest," I say, struggling to sit up in spite of the ribbons looped carelessly over me.

Si Tan's smile is an awful baring of yellowed teeth. "So you are. But this is a city with laws, and the laws must be upheld. You have come here under an assumed identity, not declaring your true intentions or your abilities. Witches must be registered and licensed in Tianshi."

"I'm not a witch," I say.

The tattooed witch is hovering near Si Tan now, a quivering, hopeful look about her that I don't understand.

"That is a good place to start," says Si Tan. "Why don't you tell us who you are, and what?"

"My name is Julia," I say. I'll die before I tell him where Theo is, but he's welcome to my name. "I reckon your witch here has told you a bit about me already. She attacked me in the Imperial Library."

"Attacked? I am sorry. She can be difficult, this one, and what information she brought me about you was rather a jumble." He gives her a hard look, and she begins to weep, falling down before him and clutching the hem of his robe. The empress dowager looks disgusted and says something to Si Tan. He nods and speaks to the witch. I might be misunderstanding, but it sounds as if he is offering her a treat. She brightens, kissing his hand with her inky lips. He produces a little pipe from a pocket in his robe. She scurries to the corner with it, lighting it with a snap of her fingers. I recognize the sweet smell.

"Opium?"

"She is an interesting case," says Si Tan. "Her name is Cinzai. Her parents brought her to the Imperial Gardens when she was just four years old. They were farmers from the central provinces, very poor, and they had this girl, their seventh child, stronger than an ox and taking naps in the burning hearth. They were glad to be rid of her. She is an idiot, in fact, and it was a terrible task teaching her to read and write at all, but she is one of only a handful of witches in all the world who can write magic with symbols drawn in the air. Now, it is a difficult calculation that needs to be made with one so powerful. It is perhaps safer simply to drown her, and there were many on the Imperial Council in favor of that. They considered her too terrible a beast to master. If you are going to keep a witch such as this, you need a strong leash. Opium is a strong leash."

"That's revolting," I say.

"More humane than drowning, don't you think? Or perhaps not. What would *you* do with an insanely powerful woman with the intellect and impulses of a child?" He waits, as if he is seriously interested in my answer. When I say nothing, he continues placatingly: "I have the good of the empire to consider, you see, but I am open to suggestions. Now I want to talk about your business in Yongguo. I dangled Ko Dan in front of your friends and out came

Och Farya of the Xianren! The little boy she brought to the monastery is the receptacle for Zor Gen's fragment of *The Book of Disruption*. Is that right?"

"He's not a receptacle," I say.

Si Tan's smile this time is genuine—almost warm. "Pardon me. It was a poor choice of words. But the text is inside him, and Och Farya wants it removed. What does she intend to do with it?"

"I've no idea. Keep it away from her brother, for starters."

"That does seem prudent. I have met Lan Camshe, or Casimir, as he goes by now."

"So have I."

"What did you think of him?"

"He's a lunatic," I say.

"I agree with you. Not a man I should like to see with more power. Frayne is a well-placed pawn in a world that is changing, and the Xianren have been competing for control of it. We have kept them out of Yongguo's politics, but now they have brought their business to my doorstep and I cannot ignore it. We have rules about magic here. Och Farya should have come to me from the beginning."

"If you let me go, I'll tell her so," I say.

Si Tan gives a perfunctory smile, as if at a bad joke. The witch lets her pipe fall to the ground and slumps back against the wall in a happy daze. The empress dowager says something to Si Tan, and I hear the Yongwen word for Kahge. Something in his gaze sharpens, and my stomach turns over.

"At the library, Och Farya's friend the professor was

interested in Ko Dan, but another young man in your group transcribed a number of the philosopher-witch treatises on Kahge, on Marike, and on the Gethin. Why?"

"He's writing a book," I lie, not very convincingly.

Si Tan stares at me like he can rout the truth from me with his eyes. Then he says, "Have you heard of Ragg Rock?"

I shake my head slowly. But, in fact, I *have* heard of it. I rack my brain trying to remember where.

"I understand you asked a question about Lidari."

"A friend of Marike's, wasn't he?" I say, trying to sound merely curious. Fear is running cold through my veins now.

He seems to be thinking about my answer. He strokes his beard, watching me. The empress dowager mutters something to him, and he nods.

"Your mother was a member of the Sidhar Coven in Frayne," he says. "She was drowned, yes?"

I nod.

"Barbaric," he says softly—but if he's trying to win me over, he'd have done better not to dose his own witch with opium in front of me. I say nothing.

"I can see why Och Farya would value you," he says at last. "Don't we all wish that we could pass through the world invisible at times! It is a remarkable gift. I've heard of spells that hide a thing from view, but they work on the senses of the viewer, not the object itself, and as far as I know, they do not allow for movement. Besides, as with any magic affecting the senses, they are notoriously unreliable. *You* can travel freely, unseen, and yet it is not magic, or at least you do not use writing or language to do it. How *do* you do it? How does it feel?"

"I don't know how," I say. "It's just something I can do."

He turns and speaks to the empress dowager. She is watching me in a way that makes me anxious. Like I'm a snack. She replies to him in her gravelly voice.

"I understand your reticence," says Si Tan. "I am interested in you, Julia. I think we could be friends and help one another."

"Not sure I like how you treat your friends," I say, nodding at Cinzai in the corner.

His lips curl back in something that could be a grin or a snarl.

"She is not my friend," he says. "She is a weapon. Tell me, where can I find Och Farya? She and I need to have a conversation."

"No idea," I say. "She contacts me when she needs me, but I don't know where she hides out."

"If I keep you here, will she come for you, do you think?"

"Doubt it," I say. I have a feeling Mrs. Och would as soon let me rot.

"Well, we shall see," he says, and then there is a knock at the door. The empress dowager answers sharply. I think she is telling the knocker to go away, but the door opens and a young man in a splendid yellow robe comes in. He is maybe twenty-five or thirty, dark and very handsome, with the kind of simmering gaze that would turn my knees to jelly under somewhat different circumstances. He sees me on the bed, and his face registers astonishment. His eyes travel to the drugged witch in the corner, and his expression turns to one of distaste. He asks a question in Yongwen, and Si Tan answers, bowing deeply and calling him *Your Highness*. I realize with a jolt of surprise that this is the young emperor.

The emperor speaks to the dowager, ignoring Si Tan, his eyes straying to me a couple more times. She answers him curtly, flicking her long golden nails at him. He starts to reply, raising his voice, but the empress dowager cuts him off, ordering him out. The emperor gives me another long look, and I can't help thinking I'd enjoy this whole thing a good deal more if *he* were the one taking me prisoner.

"Are you . . . treated well?" he asks in halting Fraynish.

I look at the ribbons binding me. "I'm not sure. I'd like to go home."

The empress dowager lets out a stream of invective. The emperor scowls while Si Tan just stares off into the middle distance. Then the emperor bows to his mother, saying something between clenched teeth, and he goes out, slamming the door—sadly, without any more smoldering looks in my direction. I think to myself that if I make it out of here alive, I'll have quite a story to tell—watching the supreme head of the great Yongguo Empire being ordered out of a room like a dog by his mother.

In the silence that follows, Si Tan takes out the now familiar sketch of me, Mrs. Och, and Bianka. It seems everybody has got their hands on a copy.

"Somebody else is looking for you in Tianshi," he says. "Who is it?"

I shrug.

"Casimir's people?" he asks.

"Not sure *people* is the word I'd use," I reply.

"I was curious about you in particular when I saw these," he says. "I knew the moment I first laid eyes on you that you were not the educated, aristocratic girl you were pretending to be. I saw in you something far too shrewd for a girl who'd led a sheltered life."

"So you told your witch to chew on my face?" I ask.

"When you vanish, where do you go?"

The question is sudden, less considered than most of what he says, and there is something alert and hungry in his expression. It strikes me that nobody has ever asked me that before. It has never occurred to anybody else that I *go* somewhere.

"Nowhere," I say. "Just . . . nowhere."

He stares at me for a while and then says, "What is she like?"

"Who?" I ask stupidly.

"Och Farya. I have wanted to meet her for a long time. The eldest of the Xianren!"

"She's . . . I don't know. The more you get to know her, the scarier she is, I suppose."

He laughs politely, like I'm trying to be funny, which I'm not, and then a loud bell starts jangling somewhere outside the building.

The empress dowager grunts and draws a little pistol out from under a cushion. Si Tan hauls the drugged witch up by the arm and murmurs in her ear. She goes stumbling out, her jaw slack.

"Do you suppose it is Och Farya come to rescue her precious vanishing girl?" he asks me.

That doesn't seem terribly likely to me, but I am holding out some hope for it. I hear shots and shouts at a distance, then footsteps running nearby, more shouting, an awful scream, and still the bell clanging on and on. My heart is pounding, but I lie there bound in Cinzai's ribbons, unable to move.

The door swings open and the witch comes reeling back in, screaming. She's clutching her head, flailing and lurching around the room. There is something dark hanging from her left ear for a moment, and then it is gone—*inside* her ear. Si Tan sees it too and lets out a cry of rage. He snatches the scimitar from the wall and swings it. Her body goes limp and drops. Her head rolls toward me. A scream reaches my throat and gets stuck there. The black thing that vanished into her ear drops out of it and scuttles across the floor. It looks like a bug, a big centipede or something. Si Tan slices it neatly with the scimitar and it sparks and smokes and goes still. It is some piece of tiny machinery. Something small and red crawls out of the broken metal shell on threadlike legs. Si Tan's lips curl. He stomps on the thing, leaving a wet scarlet mark on the floor, and curses bitterly in Yongwen. We all look at the door then, and I see with a sinking heart who has come for me. It isn't Mrs. Och, of course. It's Pia.

TWENTY-NINE

She stands in the doorway, cool as anything, with a carbine the length of her forearm pointed at the dowager in one hand and a short sword in the other. The dowager is pointing her little pistol at Pia, her chest rising and falling fast.

"Get up," says Pia to me.

"I can't," I say. "They've got me all tied up."

She jumps, kicking herself off the wall so that she ends up behind Si Tan, the muzzle of her carbine pressed against his jaw while the empress dowager's shot explodes against the wall. She shoves him closer to me with the gun, and then she cuts the ribbons around me with her short sword and tosses them aside. Si Tan watches me, expressionless, from the corner of his eye. My limbs feel heavy and slow, but I can move again. I get up off the bed unsteadily, trying not to look at Cinzai's head, her body bleeding blackly all over the floor, her tattooed fingers still twitching like they are trying to write something.

"Go get her gun," Pia orders me. To the dowager, she adds in Yongwen something to the effect that if she gives it over nicely, Si Tan might come back to her in one piece. Once I've got the gun, Pia tucks it into her belt and unloops a sort of harness on her back.

"Climb in here," she tells me. It is an awkward thing to attempt with my limbs still feeling so rubbery, but I manage it. The empress dowager watches us, her eyes little points of rage, her chins quivering.

"Casimir is bold," says Si Tan, very coldly, but Pia makes no reply. She yanks a strap on either side of her and the harness tightens around me, fastening me to her back so that I am like an overgrown child piggybacking on her psychotic mama. She shoves Si Tan's face with the carbine and instructs him to go down the hall ahead of us.

The bell is still clanging, and I hear what sounds like a great many footsteps approaching at a run, but Pia seems unconcerned. At the end of the hall, she takes a small cylinder from her belt and releases a blast at the ceiling, leaving a smoking hole above us. Then she swings her elbow, striking Si Tan in the face. He goes down like a log. Pia clambers up the wall with me on her back. I'm terrified I will throw off her balance, but as far as I can tell, my weight does not even slow her down. Broken wood and tile scrape against my back as she hauls us both through the hole in the roof. I bury my face in her shoulder to protect my head.

When I look up, she is running along the rooftop gable, and then she leaps a terrifying distance to the slanted edge of another roof. I am certain we will fall, but her footing never fails her, and she goes running up the side of that roof and over it. The Ru are milling in the streets below us, pointing crossbows. Something whizzes by us, but Pia is moving too fast to make an easy target. She flies from rooftop to rooftop and then suddenly down into the Imperial Gardens proper. Through gardens and galleries and residences—it is dizzying, and I have to close my eyes again. The clanging bell is receding in the distance now.

I open my eyes a crack when I feel that we are going straight up. She is climbing the outer wall. She reaches the top as the Ru are converging on us, but she is over the side before they reach us, dropping to the city below. I feel the impact when she lands jolt through me, but it doesn't slow her for even a second. I am bouncing on her back along the streets of Tianshi, people pointing and shouting as she sprints through the city, tireless. I think I'm going to be sick.

We reach the Hundred Lantern Hotel from the side. Up and through a window of a room, where a woman screams and ducks into the closet and a half-naked man leaps from the bed, scrambling for his pistol on the night table. Pia kicks the door wide and is down the hall, over the railing of the stairs to the floor below, and through another door. She closes the door and lets the harness loosen. I fall in an ungainly sprawl to the floor, scrambling out of the ridiculous contraption. I am gasping for breath even though she was the one running, my heart hammering. She is pointing the carbine at me now.

"I need to speak with you," she says. "Don't disappear."

I disappear.

⁓

The sun is getting low by the time I reach the house in Nanmu. I can hear Frederick's voice in the main room, loud and desperate: "You haven't the right! We must be allowed to discuss—"

"There will be no discussion of what I deem necessary," Mrs. Och is saying, pure ice, when I come in. She turns toward me, her expression unchanging. "Julia, where have you been?"

Bianka is crumpled on the floor like a rag doll. Her face has a sickly yellow tinge to it. Frederick looks a little better than when we left him this morning, but not much.

"The Imperial Gardens," I say. "Si Tan got hold of me."

"Are you hurt?" asks Frederick.

I shake my head, still trying to put together the picture before me and make sense of it. Mrs. Och is practically bursting with vitality and power. The table is covered with Frederick's notes, and the stele rubbing is spread out across it.

"Did you reveal our whereabouts?" Mrs. Och asks sharply. "Were you followed?"

I shake my head again, and her face relaxes.

"Tell me everything he said."

"He just wanted to know what we were up to. And he wants to meet you. He said we should have gone to him from the beginning."

She gives a short laugh at that. "I walked right into his trap," she says bitterly. "The impostor was most convincing. He knew things that he could only have heard from Ko Dan himself, wherever he is. There were details about the magic he worked with Gennady, and I was so eager to see . . . well, it doesn't matter now. I am glad you are safe, Julia. These two wanted to run off into the city to rescue you, but given your propensity to set off on your own little jaunts without informing anybody, I felt we ought to wait."

"I wanted to tell her brother," growls Bianka, trying to get up. "I knew she wouldn't stay away if she was all right . . . not without checking that we'd made it back safely."

"Well, she is here now," says Mrs. Och. "If you have all calmed down, we have a great deal to do. I must send a message to the professor immediately. Julia, you will take the message, and there is something else I need you to do."

"You're going to send her on an errand?" cries Bianka, managing to get up this time but looking rather like she wished she hadn't. "Look at her!"

"What do I look like?" I ask. And then my legs fold under me and I sit abruptly on the floor. "I could use something to eat," I say. I haven't eaten since breakfast.

"Get her some food," says Mrs. Och, and she sweeps off into her room to write her message.

"Where's Theo?" I ask.

"Sleeping," says Bianka. "Quite worn out from today's adventures."

"There's some stew," says Frederick. "I'll fix you a plate."

"I'll get some water," says Bianka, teetering a bit.

"You're worse off than me," I say. And then we get the giggles, all of us so utterly used up and pathetic we can hardly get a plate of food and a cup of water between us. It isn't really funny, of course—to be so helpless when we're being hunted. But I'm giddy with relief to have made it back safely, and touched beyond what I can say that Frederick and Bianka were so concerned about me, set to go and find me.

"What *happened?*" asks Bianka.

"As soon as you all went down the tunnel, I got shot with some kind of sleeping serum. I'm still woozy. I woke up and got interrogated by Si Tan and the empress dowager."

"The *empress!*" cries Bianka, impressed.

"You were amazing at the monastery," I tell her. "That spell!"

"Very quick thinking, to blind them," agrees Frederick admiringly.

"I dropped the bleeding pencil, though," she says. "I suppose they've broken it by now and undone the spell."

"Never mind. It held long enough for you to get out," I say.

Frederick goes tottering out to fetch some water, and when he brings me the cup, I empty it. I hadn't even realized how thirsty I was. He puts a plate of beef stew in front of me. The smell makes me queasy at first, but as soon as I have a bite, my hunger takes over. He offers some to Bianka, putting a tentative hand on her shoulder. She shakes her head, smiling up at him wearily.

"It was a clever trap, all right," I say. "Si Tan is keen to meet Mrs. Och."

"He can have her," mutters Bianka, but in a low voice.

"How did you get away?" asks Frederick. "They let you go?"

"No. I think they hoped Mrs. Och would come for me. But . . ."

Suddenly, I don't know why, but I don't want to tell them about Pia. I don't know what to make of her rescuing me—if that's what it was—and I am not ready to share it yet.

"Well, I got out, anyway," I finish lamely, and they don't question it. After all, haven't I always been able to get out of everything, out of everywhere, so far?

"I can't tell you how relieved I am," says Frederick with a warmth that startles me. "We've been worried sick."

"How did you know the man pretending to be Ko Dan was a fake?" asks Bianka. "It was just looking funny to me, with the guards there, but I was going to hand him over, Theo"—she shudders—"and then you turned up."

"Count Fournier," I reply. "I showed him the picture Ling drew, and he told me it wasn't Ko Dan."

"Thank the Nameless," says Bianka. "Your friend Jun was fantastic, got us all the way back to Nanmu underground before Mrs. Och sent him off. But then you didn't come back."

"We wanted to look for you," Frederick says, and then trails off.

"Thank you," I say. "Really." I point to his notes spread across the table and ask hopefully, "You've been working?"

"Professor Baranyi was kind enough to find me the dictionary I needed. The stele rubbing you brought back is about a place called Ragg Rock."

"Si Tan mentioned that," I say, frowning, and then I remember where I'd heard of it before. When I was a spy in Mrs. Och's house, I read about Ragg Rock in Professor Baranyi's study. One of his books claimed that the Xianren had joined forces to look for it but did not succeed.

"According to the stele rubbing, it is . . . I'm not sure how to translate it, exactly, but something like the way station at the edge of the world, just beyond what we might call our reality. It is a place that lies between the world and Kahge, and creatures from either place might be granted entry. They can go as far as Ragg Rock but no farther."

"Granted entry by who?" I ask.

"By . . . Ragg Rock," says Frederick. "That part is a bit confusing. I've been reading about Lidari too. I have seen him called a general of the Gethin army, but also Marike's son and, elsewhere, her lover. The references to him span centuries. He was an important figure, in any case, and closely connected to Marike. It's written that when the Eshriki Empire fell, Casimir hunted him down and killed him. You told me that the creatures you saw in Kahge were calling his name. If the essence of the Gethin do return to Kahge after their physical death in the world, he might have been among them. Did you see—were they directing it to one of their group?"

I glance at Mrs. Och's closed door. Feeling rather sick, I say: "They were pointing at me and saying it."

I can see that shocks him, which makes me feel even worse.

"I wonder if it could mean something more general, beyond the specific name. May I tell Mrs. Och and the professor this, Julia? They will have a better idea than I do of how to interpret it."

I grimace.

"I promise that I will keep you informed," he says gently. "But I don't think I can find out much more without their help."

"Fine. If you tell me everything they say."

He laughs a bit unhappily. It's an awkward position for him, I know.

"All right," he agrees.

Bianka puts her head in her hands and moans. "I feel awful."

"Did she take your strength?"

"Didn't even ask. Just grabbed my hands, and—yes," says Bianka.

"She was very weak when we got back—she'd been shot," says Frederick. "And she didn't want you running around the city when your likeness is all over the place and the Ru are out looking for you."

It's a bit halfhearted, I think, compared to his usual defense of Mrs. Och.

"I knew *you'd* never just leave one of us behind without going to look for us," says Bianka to me rather fiercely.

"And were the roles reversed, Julia might even have found

you and been able to assist you, and I would have agreed to let her try," says Mrs. Och, coming back into the main room with an envelope in her hand. "But the idea that the two of you would be able to find her, let alone *rescue* her, was simply ludicrous. Julia is more than capable of taking care of herself—and here she is."

I want to tell her that today I was not so capable of taking care of myself . . . except I don't want to tell her about Pia.

"Count Fournier thinks Ko Dan is imprisoned somewhere in the city, possibly in the Imperial Gardens," I say. "We could still get him out."

"Perhaps," says Mrs. Och. "But if Si Tan is aware of our presence and our designs, then we are running out of time. When it was only Pia, I thought we could hold out awhile. She hunts us alone, in a city unfamiliar to her, a city where she has no allies. Si Tan controls this city completely. We cannot stay hidden here if *he* is looking for us—not for long. However, I still intend to meet with your count first thing in the morning. He may have more information about Ko Dan, and I would like to get Princess Zara to Frayne as soon as possible."

"Do we have . . . *time* for that?" asks Bianka uneasily, and I can see she is worried that, having failed to find Ko Dan, Mrs. Och is shifting her interest to the princess.

"Princess Zara is the key to a Frayne that will be safe for you," says Mrs. Och. "Removing Agoston Horthy from power will diminish Casimir's influence in Frayne as well. It will turn the tide in our favor. These are matters far more important than . . ." She stops, and for an awful moment I think she is going to say *Theo's life*. But she doesn't say that. "Mere trivialities," she finishes.

It hits me like a thunderbolt, and then I feel a true idiot. "You *knew* Princess Zara was in the monastery," I say. "We didn't come all this way just for Theo. You came for *her*."

Horror breaks across Bianka's face. Mrs. Och doesn't bother to deny it.

"If all goes well, we will return to Frayne with the heir to the throne, *The Book of Disruption* safe from Casimir, and Theo safe too," she says.

I have a horrible feeling she may be listing these goals in order of priority.

Mrs. Och holds out a piece of paper to me. I try to hide my shock when I see it. She has drawn a picture of the double-spouted pot—the one I saw my mother holding when the witch was sorting through my memories, the one painted on the wall in the Imperial Library.

Her eyes narrow. "You recognize it?"

"I saw a picture of it in the library," I say, taking the paper and showing it to Frederick. "Do you remember?"

He nods.

"It is called the Ankh-nu," says Mrs. Och. "It dates back to the beginning of the Eshriki Empire—you see the hieroglyph on its side, the symbol for life. There are a few physical objects in the world that have magic written deeply into them, like the bells of Shou-shu. The Ankh-nu is far beyond any of them."

"What does it do?" asks Frederick, examining the picture.

"*This* is what Ko Dan used to put Gennady's fragment of *The Book of Disruption* into Theo. At least, that is what the impostor told me, and I believe it must be true, for there is no other way it could have been done. It is for transferring a living essence from one physical vessel to another. The essence is what some might call the soul, the spark of life, whatever it is that animates the mind, holds the memory, makes us who we *are*. The Ankh-nu can lift the essence of self from its physical bindings and put it into another body, another vessel. It is said that Marike created it for the purpose of bringing the Gethin from Kahge into the world, although where their *bodies* came from is still a mystery. There are even stories that she extended her own life to near immortality by means of the Ankh-nu."

"How would it make someone immortal?" asks Bianka.

"The essence is bound to the body," says Mrs. Och. "It lives and dies with the body, but it is the *body* that grows old and decays. If the essence can be transferred to another body, it will continue to live in that one. And so as one body began to age and die, Marike would choose another. She would *switch*, in other words, leaving her victim inside the body she was leaving behind and taking possession of the new body. It is said that until the Sirillian emperor captured and executed Marike, she had changed bodies more than three hundred times. Indeed, there are those who believe that she lives still, that she was never caught."

"But it's not really possible, is it?" exclaims Frederick.

"I have never seen the Ankh-nu myself," says Mrs. Och. "They say the greatest witches in Eshrik gave their blood and their lives to assist Marike in its making."

"Why would they do that?" cries Bianka.

"It may be only a story," says Mrs. Och. "But Marike was very good at persuading others to do things for her, even to give their lives for her. I remember her. She was . . ." Her mouth tightens suddenly. "It was not that she was so powerful, even, for a witch, but she was clever, charismatic, and she knew how to manipulate people."

"But if the Ankh-nu is for the transferring of a living essence— Ah, I see, *The Book of Disruption is* alive, in a sense, isn't it?" says Frederick.

"Yes," says Mrs. Och. "The Book has an essence of its own. In the beginning, it was text, but certainly alive. Later, after the Eshriki Phars tried and failed to read it, the Book began to change form, trying to unmake itself and become part of the world, part of nature, as the spirits had done. I hid my own fragment underground. It took root and grew into a huge cherry tree. Casimir lived then in a great castle in the foothills of the Parnese Mountains. His fragment became a brilliant green lake that swallowed the castle. Gennady traveled the world, carrying his fragment with him, and it became an implike shadow, clinging to his back—it rooted itself in *him*, since he would not let it root itself in the earth. But Casimir's witch Shey has been able to return Casimir's fragment and mine to their original form, I believe. Ko Dan—the *real* Ko Dan—used the Ankh-nu to transfer Gennady's fragment to Theo's body and bind it to his essence, to live and die with him. He made the fragment *mortal*."

"While I slept," Bianka mutters, and her eyes narrow dangerously. I think that it would be much better for Gennady if he never sees her again.

Frederick asks Mrs. Och: "How did Ko Dan come to have the Ankh-nu?"

"They claim it has been in the monastery for centuries," says Mrs. Och. "I don't know. The Shou-shu monks have acquired some remarkable treasures, but this . . . well."

How did my *mother* come to have it? What was she doing with it? The vision of my mother with the Ankh-nu, those creatures in Kahge pointing at me and hissing *"Lidari"* . . . My heart is thundering in my chest now, a terrible thought beginning to take shape. I need to see Dek. Oh hounds, I need my brother. My hands begin to shake.

"If the true Ko Dan is to take the text fragment out of Theo without harming him, he will need the Ankh-nu again, I believe," says Mrs. Och.

And perhaps it is a sign of how much of a natural thief is left in me, but I feel something close to relief break through my panic when I realize what she's saying.

"You want me to steal it," I say. "It'll be in the Treasury."

I'll have a reason to break in there after all.

"Yes," says Mrs. Och. "I want the Ankh-nu, and I want the princess, and I want Ko Dan, and we have very little time in which to find all three."

I shovel the last few bites of food into my mouth and get up. "All right," I say. "I'm feeling better."

A faint smile plays around the edges of her mouth.

"I am glad. First you will take this letter to Professor Baranyi. I would like him to attend the meeting with Count Fournier tomorrow morning. Esme should come as well."

"Your tree pipit could deliver a letter," protests Bianka.

"This is important. I must know it has reached his hands."

"At least you trust me more than a bird," I say, too exhausted and wound up to watch my mouth. I put the drawing of the Ankh-nu in my pocket and take the letter as well.

"I too was worried for you," Mrs. Och says stiffly. "I must choose the most prudent course, but I hope you do not see it as a lack of concern for your safety."

"Oh, it's all right," I say, surprised by this little pronouncement. I rather *do* see it as a lack of concern for my safety—I have never thought Mrs. Och was particularly concerned for my safety—but I don't say that.

"Be careful," says Frederick. "If I have to worry anymore, I might turn into a mother hen."

"You're quite close as it is," teases Bianka. "Those red feathers."

She tousles his hair. He laughs and takes her hand, their fingers twining together. At first I'm startled, but then I feel foolish not to have seen it before—how close they were becoming. Of course, they're shut up in this courtyard much of every day together. I feel a little pang—not jealousy, not really, only everybody seems to have a hand to hold but me. Stupid thought at a time like this.

"I'll be back soon," I say, fetching my bag with the rope and hook. I put a small lantern in it, and matches, and hurry out into the evening. As soon as I'm away from the house, I open Mrs. Och's letter. She has written it in some foreign language I can't read—not even in Yongwen, for which I might have found someone to translate. My heart sinks. There is no reason for her to write to Professor Baranyi in a language I can't read—unless she doesn't want *me* to know what she's written.

THIRTY

I deliver Mrs. Och's letter but don't stay long to chat with Esme, though I can tell she wants me to come in. In the doorway, I fill her in quickly on the false Ko Dan and on Mrs. Och's plans. When I ask after Gregor, she tells me he is still having tremors and is quite ill from lack of drink but has not asked for it once.

The trolleys stop at sundown, and the sky is already a rich orange in the west, so I say goodbye and run for the second tier road. It is dark by the time I get to Dek's place. Mei is making supper, and Wyn has set up an easel and is working on a Yongguo-style ink-brush painting. No sign of Dek, though the trays and bowls and flour from the dumpling making are still all over the table, attracting flies.

"Bleeding hounds, where does he *go* all the time?"

"Enjoying the freedom he has here," says Wyn, shrugging, but I think there is something else in his expression.

"Why do you look that way?"

"I think I look the way I always look. Don't I? How do I look, darling?" he calls to Mei.

She answers in Yongwen, and he shrugs cheerfully.

"How do you even talk to each other?" I ask.

"We don't," he says. "It's beautiful. I should have found a girl I couldn't talk to ages ago."

I raise my eyebrows.

"I don't mean that," he says quickly. "Look, Dek is going a little wild, but then, he won't be able to do this when he's back in Spira City, will he?"

"If *you're* worried he's overdoing it, he must be on a terrible binge."

He laughs. "Well—it's not the booze and roaming around that worries me. It's this girl and how attached he's getting right before we're planning to clear out. But I reckon he knows what he's doing. Look, Brown Eyes, I'm sorry about this morning. I was out of line. Friends?"

"Of course," I say, relieved.

"So how did it go today? Have you got Ko Dan?"

"It wasn't him. Things are a bit of a mess right now."

"Maybe this will help."

With a flourish, he hands me a piece of paper shut with a red wax seal. I'd almost forgotten about Gangzi's letters, but I am very glad to have one in my hands now, when we desperately need a lead. I break the seal open and look at the letter, but I can't read it, of course. I fold it up and slip it into my pocket.

"Thanks. I'll show this to Frederick." I point at his

painting, which is a fair imitation of a landscape, with a mountain furred with trees, and say, "This is new for you."

He grins. "Watch this."

With a few deft strokes, he paints an enormous frog peering over the mountain. The perspective shifts, and it is not a mountain at all but a mossy rock. I laugh out loud. "That's clever."

"How's this for a character reversal?" he says. "Dek's off carousing, and here I am at home studying art. Informally. You know, if I lived here, it wouldn't matter about my being an orphan or a crook. If I could show I had talent, they'd give me a grand house in the Imperial Gardens and I'd live like a king, drawing pictures all day long. It doesn't matter what you come from here, it matters what you can *do*."

I think of what Jun said—how the most downtrodden have no time to pursue things like painting and poetry, how their skills are not prized by Tianshi's elite.

"You don't want to stay, do you?" I ask Wyn.

"Not bleeding likely. I miss Spira City. Don't you?"

I nod.

"I think about it all the time, what I'll do when we get back." He puts down his brush. "We'll go to Reveille and hear who's playing. I miss Ma Fole's hot cakes, Fraynish coffee at the riverside cafés. Hounds, I even miss my drafty little room and feeding pigeons on the roof. If we're back by summertime, we'll go dancing at the village festivals and drink good Fraynish wine—no more of this *shijiu* rot."

Tentatively, like probing a nearly healed wound, I think

about how it used to be when we did those things together, coming back after midnight and falling laughing into bed, his hands unlacing my dress, his breath hot on my neck. I've never been happier. Mei comes in from the kitchen with plates of overcooked meat and vegetables, nodding at me with a stony expression. There is hardly space on the table, but she shoves some of the clutter aside and puts the plates down at one end.

"D'you want some?" asks Wyn.

I shake my head. "I've just eaten. You won't believe the day I've had, Wyn—"

The door bangs open, and Dek and Ling come in.

"Lost my crutch," he rasps. He is leaning hard against Ling, who looks like she's going to topple over from the weight of him. I jump to my feet to help. They both smell of liquor. Mei says something sharp to Ling—she's speaking dialect, and I doubt even Dek understands her—but Ling doesn't answer. The two of them collapse into chairs at the filthy table. He looks greasy and unwashed. His hair is still tied back.

"Where've you been?" I ask crossly.

"Gambling," Dek says, and laughs. "You ought to come next time, Wyn. It was the strangest place. I've lost all our money, I'm afraid! Oh! Did you find Ko Dan?"

"It wasn't him," I say.

"No? Stars. Too bad." He shoves at a dirty tray so that he can put his elbows on the table. "What a mess. We'll have to fire the housekeeper."

He winks at Ling, who is chewing ferociously at a fingernail on her bandaged hand. The bandage is looking grubby and frayed.

"You used to be so good about cleaning up," I say. It occurs to me only now that I never really helped with the cleaning, that Dek always kept our room spotless.

"I used to be trapped in a flat all day," he replies.

Mei stacks the dirty trays and bowls from the morning with a good deal of angry clanging and banging, staring hard at Ling. Ling keeps working at her fingernail, her eyes cast down until Mei goes back into the kitchen. Then she smiles at Dek. It's a luminous smile, and he smiles back like he can't help it and puts a hand to her cheek. She leans into him, sighing. They look happy as anything, if a bit drunk and worn out. She's bitten her nail so badly it's bleeding.

"I need to talk to you." I'm trying to sound measured but it comes out like I'm yelling. "Things are very bad right now."

"What's going on?"

"We need to talk in *private*. But first you need to wash. You stink."

Wyn and Dek exchange a look, and Wyn goes back to his painting.

"All right," says Dek, getting up. "But the well water is freezing. I want you to know I'll be cursing your name the whole time."

"That's fine," I tell him. "Curse away."

THIRTY-ONE

Half an hour later, we are climbing the narrow steps up the city wall. There is a walkway along the top of the wall, and the view over the city is spectacular. Bats swoop among the trees, and the rooftops make a sea of dark tiles, pointed like waves, around the walls of the Imperial Gardens. Behind us, the fires on distant Tama-shan are coming out. Without his crutch, Dek has to hang on to my shoulder and sort of hop and shuffle along, something that would have wounded his pride terribly not so long ago, but now he doesn't seem to mind.

We perch on the ledge of the wall, legs dangling over the city below. Before leaving the house, I told them about the false Ko Dan and my confrontation with Si Tan and the empress dowager. I didn't want to ask the obvious question in front of the girls, but now I do: "Listen. Ling and Mei told you about the fake Ko Dan, and Ling gave you that picture. There's no way they could have known, is there?"

"No," says Dek firmly. "It was general gossip. Ling drew

the fellow she saw, but there was a whole crowd watching him return to the city and go up to the monastery, people following the whole way. Everybody believed it was him. Besides, the girls aren't connected. They're nobodies in this city."

"All right," I say. "You haven't told her anything, have you? About Mrs. Och or Theo?"

"Of course not," he says, shocked, and then adds: "Not because I don't trust her. But I don't want her to know anything that could be dangerous to *her*."

"And she hasn't asked any questions?"

"Julia, stop it," he says, irritated. "Of course she's asked questions. About you, mostly, because you come banging in and out in a foul mood all the time, and she wonders why we're here. But they are normal, curious sorts of questions, and I've put her off. She doesn't push."

"She doesn't know about the house in Nanmu?"

"No!" He gives me an exasperated look.

And then—I can't help it—I blurt out: "Since when do you go to *gambling* dens?"

His face changes, and he laughs at my expression. He is handsome, my brother—even with the Scourge scars and blots, his right eyelid stitched shut over the missing eye. I am so used to him keeping his hair over his face, but when he ties it back, and when he looks happy, the disfigurement barely matters.

"I'm trying new things, Julia. Don't worry, I won't make a habit of it."

"It's just . . . it's not like you. I never know where you are anymore."

"What's not like me?" he says lightly. "Not like me, I suppose, to have a girl, to have a good time, to go anywhere or do anything. Does it really bother you?"

"That's not what I mean," I say, but I'm not sure, maybe it is.

"I never know where *you* are," he says. "But I had to get used to that a long time ago. Tianshi is a city of wonders, and I want to see all of it, try everything!"

I am afraid of his answer, but I ask him, "Will you be sorry to go back home?"

The silence stretches on so long my stomach drops.

"What if we didn't go back?" he says at last. "Once we get paid, we'll have plenty to live on here—for years, even, if we live modestly."

"I barely speak Yongwen," I manage to say.

"You'd learn if we stayed," he says. "Esme's already said she's going to retire, and I know you don't want to take over from her. I can't go back to living in a dark room, people spitting at me or running away whenever I show my face. We've seen a bit of the world now. I want more."

"But what by the holies would we *do* here?"

"What are we going to do back in Spira City?"

"I just . . . I don't know . . . it's *home*."

"Not to me. Oh, don't look that way. If you want to go back, we'll go back." He says this so lightly, but I feel as if my heart is breaking. The idea of living in Tianshi feels impossible, but who am I to drag him back to a city where he can never have this kind of freedom? No more drinking sand, we said.

"I'd have to get used to the idea," I say, hating how broken my voice sounds. What a spoiled child I've always been with my brother.

"Never mind it, Julia. I'm not going to insist on staying if it makes you unhappy."

But how long have we both put my happiness ahead of his?

"Are you in love with Ling?" I ask.

"I don't know," he says, suddenly vague. "She makes me happy."

"She looks at me funny."

"You're an unusual girl—always running around on secret errands—you're about her age, and you're my sister. She's curious about you." He sighs. "When I mention Frayne to her, she talks about it like it's this terrible, backward place. She says she's heard it's dirty and full of sickness and rats, not to mention the indiscriminate drowning of witches."

"Maybe things will be different. Esme and Gregor seem pretty fixed that there's going to be a revolution. We're meeting with Count Fournier in the morning to see about getting the princess out."

"The last revolution was a bloodbath. Half the revolutionaries were slaughtered before the thing even began. I wouldn't bet on another one going any better. I hope Esme and Gregor come to their senses before getting involved."

"Gregor's still not drinking," I say. "I think . . . I mean, Esme says he's really trying."

"Good luck to him." He sounds unconvinced, and I can hardly blame him. Then he puts his arm around me and says, "Don't worry, Julia. If you're really fixed on going back to Spira City, we'll set up again, just like old times. Maybe you'll meet some handsome fellow and settle down."

I roll my eyes at him.

"Go on—wouldn't that be grand? Little dark-haired tots running around calling me Uncle Dek? And it turns out you like children more than you thought, isn't that right?"

"I like *one* child," I say. "Not *children*."

He's laughing, but I can't laugh along.

"Oh, come on," he says. "What's the matter?"

My heart twists itself into a dark, painful knot. I take out the picture of the Ankh-nu and show it to him. "Mrs. Och thinks this thing is in the monastery Treasury. She wants me to steal it."

"What is it?"

"She says it's what Ko Dan used to put Gennady's bit of *The Book of Disruption* inside Theo. The story is that Marike made it, and it's for separating a person's essence—or the essence of anything alive—from the physical parts and putting it into . . . well, into another body."

"And *The Book of Disruption* has an essence?"

"Apparently. So Ko Dan used *this* to bind the Book fragment's essence to Theo. And apparently, *Marike* used it to stay alive by switching bodies whenever the body she'd been using got too old."

Dek makes a sound halfway between a laugh and a cry of horror. "And what happened to whoever's body it was she was hopping into?"

"I don't know. I suppose they got stuffed into the previous body and died of old age or whatever she was about to die of before she switched with them."

"How revolting!" He shakes his head, and I can tell he doesn't believe it.

I take a deep breath and tell him: "When I was in the Imperial Library and the witch there was looking through my memories, there was one memory . . . I saw our ma. She had the Ankh-nu, and she was talking to somebody, telling them she had it and that she was ready or something."

"You remember this from when you were little?" he asks carefully.

"No . . . it was somebody else's memory, or that's what it felt like. I'm not sure. But there's more." I can't look at him while I say this. I stare at my hands and get it out in a rush. "When I disappear . . . if I pull back as far as possible, I end up . . . somewhere else. It's like Spira City, but burning and made of shadows. I pulled Gennady there by accident when we were in Casimir's fortress, and he said it was Kahge. Now Mrs. Och has got Frederick *researching* me. And in the memory I saw, there was Ma, making some kind of deal with . . . I think it might have been a creature from Kahge. It wanted to go to the world. I felt that—how much it wanted to go to the world. What if she used the Ankh-nu and put the creature in *me* and that's why I can disappear?"

I don't know if I feel better or worse now that I've said it out loud. My heart is thundering in my ears.

"Hounds, Julia—don't go jumping to wild conclusions!" he cries.

I make myself keep going: "Frederick says Kahge isn't like Rainists make it out to be, under the earth and the Dark Ones. He says it's like a . . . a shadow of the world, but made of magic."

"And how does Frederick know that?"

"Well, that's the old idea of Kahge. It doesn't really matter what it's called, the point is that I go *somewhere*, and it's not of this earth, I can tell you that."

"Then stop," he says firmly. "Whatever magic you've got . . . if it takes you somewhere else, don't go there. Stay close. Stay here."

"But why *can* I . . . what does it mean?"

"I've no idea. But look, this memory you're talking about could just as well have been *planted* by the witch at the Imperial Library. You don't know that it's real at all. I don't know why you can vanish, and Nameless knows I don't know a thing about Kahge, but it doesn't mean Ma *did* something to you. Maybe it's good to have Mrs. Och looking into it. Wouldn't it be better to find out the truth?"

I nod, though honestly, I think that depends on what the truth is.

"Just don't leap to conclusions yet," he says. "All right?"

I nod again, because I can't say anything around the lump in my throat. He pulls me to him, and we hold each other there on the edge of the wall, the dark city below us, for a while.

"I feel like I can never quite forgive her," I admit at last. He doesn't ask who. He knows.

"Forgive her for what?"

"Oh, for . . . I don't know, going after Casimir, being part of the Sidhar Coven, getting involved. Sometimes I think that if she'd loved us more, she wouldn't have risked her life that way. She wouldn't have risked leaving us behind."

"It wasn't lack of love, Julia. She tried to be a mother and a revolutionary both, and she died trying."

"I know."

"What about our pa, then?"

"What about him?"

"Do you forgive *him*?"

That gives me pause. "I don't think about him much," I say at last. "I reckon I loved him when I was very little, because he was there, and Ma loved him and you loved him. But mostly I remember him like a stranger who stumbled around and took up space and upset everybody, and then he was gone, and I never missed him."

"I was hard on him when he was around."

"Well, somebody had to be."

"It didn't help," he says. "Being hard on him didn't help, and being soft on him didn't help. There was nothing any of us could ever do for him. But the thing is, I remember him before. You were too little. By the time you were three or four, he was an opium eater through and through. But before that, he and I would go to the track together. I remember his pipe smoke back when he just smoked tobacco. I remember sitting in his lap, and he'd pretend I was riding a horse, his knees galloping along. Before you were born, Ma would go away a lot—hounds, I don't remember, for days, sometimes longer, seemed like weeks—and it would just be me and Pa. We'd do everything together, eat from the same plate, I'd sleep right next to him. After you were born, she was around more, and he had that fall and broke his hip. When he started to disappear, bit by bit, I hated him for it. Hounds, I hated him. He left us years and years before he walked out."

"I know." I'd never thought how much harder it must have been for Dek, who remembered him as something else.

"He was an athlete, very physical, like you. He didn't know how to be a cripple. He didn't know how to be a man with a bad leg looking for work, or a father who couldn't chase after his kids. I still wonder why Ma didn't do something for him. You know, help him with his hip or the pain somehow."

"With magic?"

"Yes. If she could save my life . . ."

"But it took so much from her. She was never the same after that. And people would have suspected."

He looks miserable, and I stop. It's unkind to remind him how she destroyed herself saving him. That last year of her life, she was a shadow of who she'd been before. "Why are we talking about Pa anyway?"

"Because we're talking about forgiveness. Isn't it always our parents we have to forgive? Either for not being there, or for what they did when they *were* there?"

I laugh at the way he puts it, but I reckon he's probably right. "You're the one I couldn't have lived without," I say. "You still are."

"Well, you won't have to," he says, mussing my hair.

"We'll stay together," I say. "Wherever we go."

"Of course. Hounds, Julia. Of *course*."

"If you don't want to go home, we'll stay here."

I make myself say it, and I make myself mean it. I can't imagine a life for myself outside of Spira City, being a foreigner forever in this strange city—but it's my turn to think about Dek's happiness now.

He kisses the top of my head. "Let's get this job done first," he says. "Then we'll talk about what's next."

I fold up the picture of the Ankh-nu and put it back in my pocket. I'd like to stay here with Dek, looking over the city and feeling like I am myself, just a girl, just his sister. But I've got some thieving to do.

THIRTY-TWO

There are two guards outside the Treasury, as always. The squat, steel-doored building is separated from the Temple of Atonement by a row of bushes. Jun crouches behind the bushes, a silent shadow, while I stand next to one of the guards, vanished, and count in my head. When I reach twenty, Jun tosses a handful of gravel at the roof of the Treasury. It skitters along the tiles; both guards startle and look up. Jun aims the little handheld crossbow I got from Dek and shoots one guard with a dart while I stab a dart into the neck of the fellow next to me. They sway and fall together. Neither has time to raise the alarm. I reappear, grinning like crazy.

"That is easy part," says Jun, but he's smiling too, his dimples showing. How he can go from looking so fierce to looking so sweet in less than half a second astounds me. I could watch the change all day. "How we can open this door?"

"*That's* the easy part," I tell him, producing Dek's magnetic pick with a flourish. I am showing off, I admit, and while either one of us could have managed this job alone, doing it together is more fun. I was touched by how relieved he was to see me when I turned up at Count Fournier's. When I described the job to him, assuring him that it was not common thieving but necessary to save Theo's life, his eyes lit up. He is a boy after my own heart, all right.

Dek's pick gets the door open in a jiff, and once we are inside, I take out the lantern and light it. Jun gives a low whistle, carrying the lantern along the shelves. I have never seen such a sight myself. Paintings, ancient scrolls, crowns, weaponry, pottery, jade sculpture, gem-studded goblets, a diamond the size of my fist, and chest after chest filled with bricks of gold—the Shou-shu Monastery is wealthy beyond anything I've ever imagined.

"Why they have all this?" says Jun. "They are monks! What they need gold for?"

"Everybody likes gold," I say. "I don't see it, though. How often does the guard change?"

"Three hours," says Jun.

"All right. We should be able to check every inch of this place in three hours."

And we do. We empty every chest, feel every stone and beam for hidden panels. Jun climbs along the rafters of the ceiling with the lantern, then comes swinging down, landing in front of me. The lantern flickers, making his face go dark and then light as he holds it up and looks around the room again.

"Your treasure is not here," he says. "I think they guard ordinary treasure in ordinary way—locks and guards. But if they have magical treasure, they would guard in a magical way. We cannot find it like this."

"I reckon you're right," I agree. I'd hoped at least *something* might come easily.

"Guard will change before too long," he says.

So we leave, locking the door behind us and giggling at the idea of the guards waking up and how confused they will be, with nothing missing from the Treasury. Still, going back to Mrs. Och empty-handed when she has made it clear that we are out of time leaves me with a pit in my stomach.

We walk slowly through the Xishui Triangle. I'm trying to think of something to say that will make him smile at me again when he grabs my hand and pulls me up a quiet road toward an ancient-looking tree, gnarled and twisted, its branches a darker black against the night sky. Only when we are right under its branches do I see the twists of paper, as numerous as the leaves.

"Look," says Jun, squatting by the thick trunk. I kneel on the ground to see what he is showing me. It is a little wooden box nestled between the tree roots, and inside it there is a pot of ink, a brush, and hundreds of blank strips of paper.

"Do you ever write wish?" he asks me.

"No," I say. "I don't understand why people do it. If you're not a witch, writing something down isn't going to do anything."

"The magic does not come from witch," says Jun. "You don't know that? The magic come from *writing*. From words. Some people—witches—they can bring that magic out. But there is power in any writing. If I write, I cannot make magic happen, but still the writing has some magic in it. Maybe it can change some small thing. Give me some luck, or some chance."

From what I've seen of witches and magic and luck, I'm not sure I believe this. But Jun is already unscrewing the cap of the inkpot, dipping the brush. He writes something in swift characters on a slip of paper, then gives me a mischievous look and goes scampering up the tree, looking for a good spot.

"I like to put my wish near top," he says from above. I cannot even make out the shape of him among the dark leaves.

"Why?"

"I don't know. Feels more lucky."

I pick up the brush, dip it, and pause. I have the overwhelming urge to write *Forgive me* on the paper and tie it to the tree. I think it, brush poised: Forgive me. Forgive me. But who am I asking for forgiveness? Frederick would say that in the eyes of the Nameless I am already forgiven, that we are all forgiven for our mortal errors, and that every moment of our lives is a clean slate, starting over. And what does it matter if I am forgiven by those I've wronged? If I forgive myself? What does it change? Not what I did, nor what I mean to do.

And so I write, *Keep Theo safe*, and I climb up the tree after Jun, twisting my wish onto a twig with no other wishes.

"Come here!" he calls, and I climb higher, to where he sits astride a branch, his head poking above the leaves at the top of the tree. The branches are thick and sturdy even this high up. He reaches for me and pulls me onto the branch next to him, so we are facing each other. My back is against the trunk, and he is balanced out on the branch, seeming entirely at ease way up here. It is a clear night, and the moon is just a sliver, the sky strung with stars. I look straight up, thinking of the map of the planets Frederick showed me once, how tiny the world looked in the endless sea of space, and I try to hope that what I've written has some power.

"I am sorry we cannot find your magic treasure," says Jun. "But I am glad you ask me for help." He smooths my hair back from my face with soft fingers, and that touch ripples right through me, setting my skin alight. He is looking at me very seriously.

"What you wish for?" he asks.

"Doesn't it spoil the wish if I tell you? Make it not come true?"

He looks puzzled. "Writing wish is not like that," he says.

Looking at him in the moonlight, the dark leaves around his face, I almost want to tell him everything, open my heart like a box and take my secrets out one by one to lay before him. I can't, of course—I can't tell him my secrets. But I can tell him my wish, and so I do: "I wished for Theo to be safe."

He smiles. "You are good person."

That brings me all at once to the edge of weeping. "Not really."

"You are," he says, nodding. "I make selfish wish."

"All right, what was yours?"

He smiles that wicked smile again, the dimples coming out, and I hold on harder to the branch beneath me. "Every night since I meet you, I do not sleep enough. Do you know why?"

"Why?"

"Because instead of sleeping, I am lying in my bed and wondering, What it is like to kiss Julia? I am trying to imagine it, and not sleeping, just imagining. So I wish for a kiss from Julia. Maybe if I know, I can sleep again."

"Waste of a wish," I tell him, laughing, and the sky seems to tilt dangerously overhead. "You could have had that anytime."

I lean in to kiss him. He kisses me back with the softest mouth. I think of Wyn, but fleetingly. Jun's kisses don't allow my mind to wander far from the feeling of his mouth on mine. I pull him closer, fit my legs over his thighs, leaning back against the trunk.

"You are strange girl," he murmurs, which isn't exactly the most romantic thing anybody's ever said to me, but I don't care. I'll pretend he meant *dazzling* and it got lost in translation.

"Hush. Get your wish's worth."

He smiles that irresistible smile, leaning in so his lips catch mine again, his hand sliding round to the back of my neck, pulling me deeper into his kiss. The image of that antlered, fox-faced beast pointing at me across the steaming river in Kahge flashes through my mind. *Lidari*. But none of it can be true, not with Jun kissing me this way, not with everything I'm feeling right now. My longing expands, filling up with something else, something like defiance. I put my hands under his tunic and yank it roughly over his head, this hunger opening wider and wider. I surrender to it, let it root me in my body, my *self*. There is a tattoo over his heart, a Yongwen symbol. I run my fingers over it.

"What is that?" I ask.

"It means *luck*," he whispers, and I almost want to cry. Instead, I move his hands away to untie my own tunic. He lifts it over my head, and we let the tunics drop and tangle on the branches below, his eyes fixed on mine. I feel lighter and lighter—more and more real. His skin is brilliant in the moonlight, and he pulls me up against the length of his smooth torso, whispering to me in Yongwen.

"I don't know what you're saying!" I laugh.

It feels desperate and effortless at the same time, and I'm drinking in the sound of his laughter, the warmth of his skin. For a little while I am only Julia, and I think of nothing else.

THIRTY-THREE

"What are you doing still up?" I ask.

Bianka is sitting at the table, sewing by candlelight. She speaks softly, as if she doesn't want to be heard: "Shut the door. Quietly."

I do as she says, put down my bag with the hook and lantern in it, and slide into the chair next to her. My legs are still wobbly, like I've got water in my knees. She's making a new pair of trousers for Theo.

"Any luck tonight?" she asks me. She's still whispering, and so I whisper in reply.

"I've just searched the entire Treasury. No Ankh-nu, no Ko Dan. It's not looking good."

"Are *you* all right?" she asks.

"Oh, fine."

I'm thinking that this has been the longest, strangest, worst, best, most terrifying, most remarkable day and night of my life, but I don't say that, of course. Still, from the hope of finding Ko Dan this morning and then the rescue of Theo and the others from the monastery, to my encounter with Si Tan, then charging across the city with Pia, breaking into the Treasury, and making love in a treetop with beautiful Jun, I desperately need to get some sleep and then have a minute or two just to breathe and think.

I lay my head on my arm. My skin is cool from the night air and my sleeve smells of sweat, and I can still feel everywhere Jun touched me and kissed me. I'm worn out but still hungry for him, his fingers and his mouth, and if I feel all this, then how can I be anything but a girl, the girl I've always been? A shudder of pleasure runs through me, but at the same moment my mind throws images back in answer—of my clawed hands in that burning city, those impossible beasts hissing *"Lidari"* at me. I squeeze my eyes shut.

"I'm awake because I'm waiting for you," says Bianka in an odd voice.

I sit up and look at her.

"Professor Baranyi is here," she whispers. "Frederick is with them. Mrs. Och asked me to tell her when you got back." She pauses, and adds, "I'm just going to finish this row of stitches, and then I'd better let them know you're here."

My blood cools rapidly. "Thank you," I murmur, and she nods, bending over her sewing again.

I go outside. The crack under the blinds is just enough. I am more confident, having done this before. I vanish, and aim myself for the dark corner near Mrs. Och's bedroom door.

Frederick looks downcast. His head is bowed, and he is silent.

"You will find Silver Moya here," Mrs. Och is saying to the professor, the two of them bending over a map at her desk. The professor looks very flustered.

"Yes, yes," he mutters.

"If you are granted entry, you must ask in particular about Lidari," she says. "We need to know for certain what became of him."

"Yes," he says again. "Of course, yes. Do you think . . . ? Well, we shall go at once."

Frederick looks up. "I'm to go with him?" he asks. He looks as if he's been arguing for a while and is exhausted from it. "Is it dangerous?"

"To be turned away is not dangerous," she says. "But if you are granted entry, I do not know! I gave up on Ragg Rock a very long time ago. You should hurry. I want to know what we are dealing with before daybreak, if possible. I am trusting Julia with a great deal at the moment, and I do not like risk."

If Jun's touch seemed to draw the rage and fear away from me, it comes back now in a rush, a metallic taste on my tongue, a bitterness in my throat.

"I am sure she can be trusted," says Frederick, but in a weary, halfhearted way, as if he doesn't expect to be listened to. "She's frightened. She's . . . stars, you only have to talk to her for five minutes to see who she *is*."

"I seem to remember you vouching for her trustworthiness

when she was posing as Ella the housemaid as well," says Mrs. Och bitingly, and Frederick's shoulders slump. "Your confidence does not reassure me in the slightest. It may be that she has simply traded one disguise for another, and I need to be sure."

Professor Baranyi is putting on his coat. He and Frederick go out together, past Bianka stitching by the fire. Frederick says good night to her, but she does not look up. Mrs. Och watches them go, and I go with them, vanished.

They go to a little clock shop in the third tier of the Beimu Triangle, near the east gate. The shop is shuttered and closed for the night, but the professor knocks anyway, and at length an old man with a candle opens the door for them. They exchange a few words and are ushered inside. The clock shop looks quite ordinary. Through a door behind the counter is a workshop, dark and empty. The old man lights a lamp, and a tired-looking woman comes through the door, wrapping a robe around herself and nodding greetings. She asks something in Yongwen, and the professor answers very formally. She asks Frederick then. He confirms whatever it is she has said, and she indicates that they should sit at the broad worktable.

Carefully, deliberately, she takes out a scroll of rice paper, a pot of ink, a small bowl, and a brush and lays them all out. Then she scatters some seeds across the table and fetches a bird from a cage hanging near the ceiling. Cages with sleeping birds inside hang all around the room. This one wakes up and begins pecking at the seed. The woman unscrews the back of her ink brush to reveal a little blade, then reaches for Professor Baranyi's hand. She slices his finger and squeezes some blood into the tiny bowl. She pours some ink from the pot into the bowl, mixing it with the blood, dips the brush, and writes something on the page.

They sit there silently for a bit. She smiles apologetically, raising her shoulders in a shrug, and asks Frederick if he is willing. He does not look as if he wants to try, but he offers his hand and lets her slice his finger. She does the same as before with a fresh bowl, and again they all sit there awkwardly. Then she gets up, puts away the writing implements, and takes the little bird back to its cage. I don't know what I've just seen. Professor Baranyi and Frederick look rather relieved, I think.

The professor asks something politely, taking a piece of paper out of his coat pocket. He unfolds it and shows it to the woman. She looks at it and shakes her head. I look over her shoulder and give a start. It is the picture of me, Mrs. Och, and Bianka that has been circulating, and he is pointing at my picture, asking her if she's seen me before. Frederick looks quite miserable. Professor Baranyi tucks the picture back into his pocket, thanking the woman, and we all go back to Mrs. Och's house, where Bianka is still sewing by the fire, looking like she's about to fall asleep over her needlework.

Mrs. Och is in her room, a candle burnt down to nearly nothing on her desk, her back rigid.

"It didn't work," says Professor Baranyi.

"Frederick, make the professor a bed in the servants' quarters so he does not have to go back to Xihuo tonight," she says, sounding angry. "I am going to bed. We will visit the count in the morning."

"And Julia?" asks Professor Baranyi. "Silver Moya claimed not to have seen her."

Mrs. Och hesitates. "We will have to trust her for now," she says at last. "We can't do it without her. Not without attracting a good deal of attention, anyway. I hope you are right about her, Frederick."

Frederick and the professor go to the servants' quarters, and when Mrs. Och closes her door, I reappear, startling Bianka.

"Well?" she asks me.

"They're suspicious of me, but I don't know why," I say, and I tell her what I saw. She is as baffled as I am, and for a few minutes we say nothing, puzzling it over.

"I'd better tell her you're back," she says at last. She goes and knocks on Mrs. Och's door.

"Julia is here," she says when Mrs. Och opens it.

"Ah. The Ankh-nu?" she asks me eagerly, swinging the door wide.

I shake my head, trying not to let my anger show on my face.

"Worse and worse," she mutters, and gives me a long look, like she's not sure she should believe me. "Go to bed. We will speak in the morning."

"I'm going to sleep as well," says Bianka. She squeezes my hand. "Coming?"

"In a minute," I say.

She nods and goes into the room we share with Theo. I find Frederick in his room in the servants' quarters, sitting on the edge of his narrow cot with his face in his hands.

"Did you find it?" he asks me, looking up.

"No."

"Well, we will have to hope that your Count Fournier has some leads for us tomorrow. Oh stars, it nearly *is* tomorrow." He hesitates, and I can see he is trying to decide what to tell me, who to betray.

I spare him the struggle and say: "Why has she got you going to some witch in the middle of the night? What was that about? Who's Silver Moya?"

He gapes at me and then lets out an unhappy laugh.

"I wish she would agree to talk to you directly," he says. "There's obviously no point trying to keep anything from you."

"Don't tell her, please," I say, suddenly frightened at the thought of what she might do if she knew I'd been spying on *her*.

He sighs. "I won't," he says. "Only because she'd be furious. But I'd be very glad if my life contained less *Don't tell hers*, on both sides."

"I need to know what's going on. It isn't fair to keep it from me."

"Silver Moya is a witch," he says. "Or, a kind of witch.

There are hundreds of her particular sort around the world. There is one in Spira City, as a matter of fact. They are called in adolescence—I am not sure of the details, but my understanding is that they begin to have visions of Ragg Rock and may then choose to accept the role and the name of Silver Moya. Only they can make a request of Ragg Rock. As for Ragg Rock—well, I am not sure if it is a place or a creature . . . or what exactly. We know only that a number of witches throughout history *claim* to have had entry to some in-between place via a Silver Moya. She did not ask us for money, only a bit of blood."

"I saw," I say.

"You were there?" He looks torn between amusement and annoyance. "Well then, you know that nothing happened."

"But what does Mrs. Och want? She told you to find out about Lidari."

"I told her about those things in Kahge calling you Lidari, as you said," he tells me. "She was disturbed."

"She thinks I'm connected to them," I say.

"I don't know what she thinks. She has not shared any theories with me. I'm not sure she has any."

"And she thought I might be . . . what, visiting Ragg Rock myself?"

"Perhaps. Mainly she wanted to know about Lidari. What had become of him."

"Frederick—did *you* know that Mrs. Och wanted to come to Yongguo for the princess?"

"No. She doesn't take me that far into her confidence."

"The professor must have known."

"I imagine they spoke of it. But you mustn't think Theo's safety is not important to her."

"Oh, I believe *The Book of Disruption* is important to her," I say, not very nicely. He looks unhappy but doesn't argue. Suddenly I remember that I've got Gangzi's letter in my pocket. I take it out and hand it to him. "Look, Wyn got hold of this today. It's a letter from Gangzi to . . . somebody."

He reads it and raises his eyebrows. "It's addressed to some minor official in Gumao—a city bordering Rossha, in the north. I'll show this to Mrs. Och in the morning. She'll be glad to have a clue, at least."

"What does it say?"

"See this symbol?"

He shows me the letter. I hadn't picked it out among the Yongwen characters, but there is the Eshriki symbol for life—the *ankh*. "He is asking this official to conduct a search of the city. He describes a double-spouted pot with the hieroglyph on each side."

"So the Ankh-nu is in Gumao?" I say, confused.

"See if you can get a few more of these," says Frederick.

I rest my head against the doorframe and feel myself drifting toward sleep, everything that has happened today a tangle in my mind: the stars, Jun's hands on me, the taut muscles of his arms and chest, Si Tan's horrible smile, Cinzai's head coming off—I raise my head with a jolt. Frederick looks concerned.

"Are you all right?"

"Exhausted," I say, which isn't the half of it.

He hesitates and then says, as if he's been trying to work out the phrasing and hasn't quite got it: "Whatever we find out . . . about Kahge and all that . . . it doesn't really change who you are, Julia. You must believe that."

"I do," I say. But I'm lying.

THIRTY-FOUR

A tugging at my scalp wakes me up. Theo is busy with my hair, knotting and matting it.

"Oh, Theo, what a mess!" I cry, feeling my head. It is sticky and smells of honey. I must have been sleeping like a log.

"Lala umma ebby ebby sump," he says cheerfully.

The early-morning sun is filtering through the curtains. I pick him up and hurry outside, still in my nightdress. Bianka is washing her face at the pump. Mrs. Och sits on the steps, looking bent and ancient.

"Did Frederick show you Gangzi's letter?" I ask her.

She nods.

"Well, what do you think? He's lost the Ankh-nu, hasn't he?"

"I don't know. I've sent a pipit instructing your brother to get some more of the letters," she says. "How are you feeling?"

"Better," I say, and it's true. I don't know how long I slept, but it was a deep sleep, and now I'm hungry. I put Theo down, and he runs to Bianka, who scoops him up and kisses him.

"Good," she says. "Eat something, and we will go see your Count Fournier."

She retreats to her room, and I boil myself an egg, glad to see there is still bread as well, a little stale, but we have some butter that will make it edible. The honeypot is nearly empty and full of small, dirty fingerprints. I bring my breakfast outside to eat in the sun.

"You were talking in your sleep," says Bianka, coming and sitting with me on the steps. Theo clambers up onto her shoulders, singing to himself a gibberish song.

"I'm sorry." I dread to think what I might have been saying. I think of Jun and fight my smile. Oh Nameless, the look on his face! Only an acrobat could manage the things we did in a treetop. Just thinking of it makes me shiver.

"Sounded like you were fighting all night," she says. "I'm surprised to see you so well rested, to be honest."

"I'm on edge. I just hope the count has something useful to tell us."

She avoids the subject and says instead: "What on earth has happened to your hair?"

"Your son," I say dryly. "I don't think it's going to comb out."

She tries to work her fingers through the sticky tangles.

"Hounds, is that *honey*? Oh, Theo!"

Theo scrambles off her shoulders to examine his handiwork with pride and then goes to dig a hole at the bottom of the steps with a stick.

"Ow," I say as she pulls at my hair.

"Well, if you ever brushed it in the first place, he might not have been able to make such a mess of it," she says, laughing. "But you're right, it'll have to be cut. I can cut it to your chin if you like—some girls make that look very stylish and modern."

I think of Pia, the sharp line of hair ending at her jaw.

"No," I say quickly. "Just cut it like a boy's. I've been dressing like one anyway. Given the way things are, the less I look like me, the better, I reckon."

"All right." She fetches her sewing scissors and settles behind me on the steps, snipping away. I watch the long hanks of matted hair falling to the ground and listen to Bianka humming—an unexpectedly happy sound.

"So. You and Frederick," I say.

"Yes." I hear the smile in her voice.

"I had no idea you felt that way about him."

There is a pause, and then she says, "Well, proximity changes things. And he's good to Theo. I want to be with someone I can count on for a change."

I think that that's not terribly fair to Frederick, but I don't say so. It's not really any of my business.

"Listen," she says, lowering her voice. "I wanted to tell you—just in case. You know the bag I've got hanging from a hook in the bedroom?"

"Yes."

"Have you ever looked inside it?"

"No," I say, hurt she had to ask.

She hears my tone and says placatingly, "Well, you *are* a spy. And I wouldn't have minded. Anyway, there's some dry food in it—just emergency rations—a fair bit of money, a few diapers, and a change of clothes for Theo."

"All right," I say. We are quiet for a moment, just listening to the *snip snip snip* of the scissors around my ears and neck. "And?"

"If something happens to me and . . . I don't know, if you need to run, you take Theo and you take that bag."

"Nothing's going to happen to you," I say.

"One has to think about these things," she says, and then Frederick and Professor Baranyi come through the gate. Frederick is carrying a basket laden with fruit and vegetables from the market in one hand and a stick with something shaggy at the end of it in the other. The professor glances at me nervously and asks, "Is Mrs. Och inside?"

I nod coldly, and he goes in. Frederick joins Bianka and me on the steps, putting down his basket.

"What on earth are you doing?"

"Theo made a mess of Julia's hair, so I'm cutting it off," says Bianka.

"I'm going to look like a boy in a minute," I say.

"Feyda!" cheers Theo.

"Hullo, monkey," says Frederick. "Look what I've got you! It's a horse!"

He presents Theo with the stick, and I realize that the shaggy bit at the end is meant to be a horse's head, its mane made of rags. I grab a hard little apple out of the basket and take a bite. Frederick shows Theo how to ride the toy horse, and Theo goes galloping around the courtyard, shouting with glee.

"That was nice of you," says Bianka.

"I thought he might like something to play with besides chickens and rocks," says Frederick.

Bianka brushes the stray hairs off my shoulders and says, "There—you look absolutely terrible."

"Good thing we haven't got a mirror." I touch a hand to my shorn head. It feels so strange, the weight of my hair gone.

"It's not so bad, actually," says Frederick kindly. "It's a bad haircut, but it brings out your eyes."

A strange humming feeling washes over me all of a sudden, the courtyard somehow too bright, the sky too high, everything too much, not right. Theo has stopped galloping around on his horse and is squatting with a stick, drawing something in the dirt.

"What's happening?" asks Bianka, alarmed. Her voice sounds echoey and unreal.

Something rises up out of the dirt. It is huge, with the head of a goat and a great furred body staggering on enormous chicken legs. *Kahge*—that is my first thought. Theo laughs in delight at the thing looming over him. The look on his face is one of amazed recognition.

"Theo!" Bianka leaps toward him.

"The stick!" cries Mrs. Och from the doorway, and I realize what has happened the instant she says it. Bianka snatches Theo away from the lumbering creature, and I dive for the stick he has dropped in the dirt, lying next to his clumsy drawing. Hairy arms grab at me, catch me around the waist, but I've got the stick, and I snap it in two. The thing crumbles to nothing, to dirt, and the air and the courtyard return to normal. I sit panting in the dirt, Bianka clutching Theo to her, Frederick wielding the sewing scissors next to me like he is going to take down a magicked monster with them.

"Well," says Mrs. Och, coming over to look at Theo's picture. It just looks like a scribble in the dirt, although there is something resembling a head and a body, I suppose. "I was afraid of that."

"Afraid of what? What was that thing?" shouts Bianka.

"Teo stoy!" crows Theo, delighted with himself, trying to wriggle out of her arms.

"It's *The Book of Disruption*," says Frederick. "He's not a witch, but still, a part of the most powerful text on earth is inside him. He can write magic . . . in a way."

"He can't *write*—he's just a baby! Those aren't even words—it hardly looks like *anything*!" cries Bianka.

"The earliest writing was pictographic," says Mrs. Och. "Until we can get the text out of him, we must keep him from making pictures. His imagination combined with the act of writing is much too strong."

"Oh hell," says Bianka.

"Teo tick," says Theo, picking up half of the broken stick and looking at me indignantly.

"Put that down at once," says Mrs. Och, snatching it away from him so hard he topples over. He gapes at her and begins to cry.

"Keep a close eye," she says to Bianka and Frederick. Then she turns to me. "Julia, come. We are leaving."

THIRTY-FIVE

"Oh, your lovely hair!" cries Csilla when I arrive at Count Fournier's house with Mrs. Och and the professor. Mrs. Och looks vaguely annoyed that Csilla and Gregor are there as well.

"Pish," says Esme. "What use has Julia for lovely hair?"

Which I might have found insulting if I didn't have so much else on my mind.

"Ah, well," says Csilla forlornly. "It'll grow back."

Jun is standing by the door. I am absurdly nervous to look at him, but I do. He makes an O of surprise with his mouth and then grins, and my stomach somersaults wildly. I smile back and then can't wipe the smile off my face, so I look down to try and hide my ridiculous expression. Hounds, I'm an idiot. I want to drag him into the hall with me, away from the others.

Count Fournier looks overwhelmed to have us all in his dilapidated parlor: Gregor, gray-faced but upright, his mouth a line of grim endurance; Esme, long-limbed, benign, and genderless; and Csilla, who always looks set for a night at the opera, though her face paint is a little brighter and more careless than usual. Professor Baranyi helps Mrs. Och to the smelly sofa, where I was held at gunpoint just a few days ago. It's so strange now to think of Jun pointing a gun at me. Count Fournier seems uncertain about kissing Mrs. Och's hand, and in the end just clasps it loosely and then goes springing over to his liquor cabinet. He is wearing shoes for the first time since I've met him.

"Thank you all for coming! Och Farya, it is a great honor. I never imagined I might host one of the Xianren! May I . . . Brandy, anyone? Or whiskey?"

He is already pouring a glass, which he then holds toward Gregor, beaming.

"No!" says Gregor hoarsely, and stuffs his trembling hands into his pockets. Csilla rushes to take his arm.

"Please put it away," she begs the count. "We don't want any!"

He looks confused, but he puts the glass down. "Well then," he says, a bit sadly.

I sneak another look at Jun. He winks, and a wave of heat goes through me, thinking of his hands slipping under my tunic, his ragged breath in my ear.

"Do you have word of Ko Dan?" asks Mrs. Och sharply. Nothing to kill a pleasant fantasy like the sound of her voice.

Count Fournier shakes his head nervously. "There are a hundred different rumors. The source I trust the most believes him to be imprisoned in the Imperial Gardens by order of Si Tan, but even that I cannot confirm beyond doubt, and nobody can tell me exactly where."

"And you say that Old Zey is ill?" says Mrs. Och, leaving the question of Ko Dan behind rather quicker than I like.

"Dying," says the count. "The Sidhar Coven has been reassembling."

"What little is left of it," says Mrs. Och dismissively.

"I have no money, no means of returning, but if you take me back with you, I have contacts all over Frayne—the names of well-connected people who are waiting for a revolution."

"Witches and a few Lorians might be ready to rise up, but are the people?" asks Esme. "It cannot be a revolution of witches. That is not a revolution. That is a coup, and the people will not support it."

"The people will be ready if they have a princess," says Gregor. "I am sure of it."

"We have met with one impostor recently," says Mrs. Och. "Are you certain this is Zara, daughter of Prince Roparzh? What proofs does she have of her identity?"

"She has in her possession the family's royal seal, her father's ring, and a certificate signed by a holy at her birth. These will be contested, of course, but it will be enough to convince the people. More important . . . well, you will see when you meet her. She is obviously of royal blood. She has been educated broadly and has lived in many countries, sometimes under very difficult conditions. She is intelligent and thoughtful and wise well beyond her years. She will be a fine queen, you can be sure of that. But we have to act quickly—Si Tan and Gangzi are meeting today with the Fraynish ambassador and Lord Skaal."

"Meeting where?" asks Mrs. Och.

"The Imperial Gardens, I assume," says Count Fournier. "That is where Si Tan receives guests."

"We will take Princess Zara to Frayne immediately," says Mrs. Och.

I understand now why she wanted to bring all of us on this journey to Tianshi. She knew Gregor and Esme were involved in the Lorian Uprising, that they would be perfect for this task. She did not bring them here for Theo at all.

"I have no money," says the count again, humbly. "But Zara trusts me, and I have connections. I have been involved for years. I wish to help."

"Julia will go now to fetch her," says Mrs. Och, ignoring his plea. "How can we ensure that the princess goes with her willingly?"

The count has a frantic look, like he realizes he is being left behind, cut out of the whole business.

"She will know," he says. "She has a sense of these things, of whom she can trust. I cannot get in myself, but Jun could manage it unseen and he knows the monastery. . . ."

My heart leaps, and Jun and I grin at each other like lunatics. Esme's eyes narrow a bit, looking at us, but I don't care.

"Julia will go alone," says Mrs. Och. "She does not need help."

Jun's smile falls away, and he looks from Mrs. Och back to me.

"He helped tremendously the other day," I say. "In a pinch, I'd like him with me. If he's willing," I add, looking at Jun. He begins to smile again, but Mrs. Och puts an end to it.

"No. Julia will get the princess and bring her to my house. Julia alone. Thank you, Count Fournier. I will be happy to pay your passage home if you wish to return to Frayne."

We all stand there uncertainly as Mrs. Och rises to her feet, Professor Baranyi taking her arm to help her.

I look at Jun. He says, "You cannot take tunnels. They are flooding them. Everybody running like rats."

"Who is flooding them?" I ask.

"I don't know. Somebody. Not much places to hide in Tianshi today. Ru are out searching homes. Maybe they are looking for you?"

"Julia!" Mrs. Och says sharply. "There is no time to waste. Fetch the princess and take her to my house. Do not let anybody see you."

So I leave them all there: Jun, helplessly watching me go; Mrs. Och, counting paper money out onto Count Fournier's desk; and Gregor, looking at everything except the brandy on the side table, Csilla on his arm like an anchor straining against a storm.

THIRTY-SIX

The monastery is surrounded by the Ru. There is no chance of going over the wall with my hook. The only way to do it is to vanish farther than I like—back through the foggy space at the edge of the world to that reeling nowhere where I must angle my perspective to make sure I don't lose the wall completely. My aim is off; I land on a temple rooftop and slide down, grunting.

The old woman meets me at the door of the little house, pointing the blunderbuss at me with a look in her eye that says, *Yes, this thing will break my arm if I fire it, but don't think I won't.* Princess Zara, stout in a brilliantly patterned silk robe, her frizzy hair pinned up with jade combs, is holding a pistol, but her eyes are clear and unafraid. She says something to the old woman. The old woman just grunts and keeps pointing the blunderbuss at me.

"Count Fournier sent me," I say, my hands raised and visible. "You're not safe here anymore. King Zey is dying, and we mean to take you back to Frayne to, um, claim the throne."

She receives my news with an equanimity I find hard to believe, just nods her head and tucks her pistol away inside her wide sleeve.

"I'll need my bag," she says, and fetches a battered valise from under her bed. Then she speaks to the old woman in Yongwen. Slowly the blunderbuss lowers. The old woman's chin crumples and wobbles. Tears pour down her wrinkled cheeks. Princess Zara embraces her. They cling to each other for a long moment while I stand there feeling increasingly awkward. When at last they pull apart, Princess Zara presses a clinking bag of coins into the old woman's hand.

"The thing is," I say, "the monastery is surrounded, and so to get you out . . . it's going to be a little strange. You'll have to hang on to me. Just close your eyes and don't let go."

"Are we going to fly out?" she asks, her eyes twinkling, as if I'm joking.

"Not exactly," I say. "You might be scared, or startled, but please hang on."

She says simply, "I trust you"—which, under the circumstances, is one of the strangest things she could possibly say, but I'm not complaining. She kisses the old woman one more time.

"Well," I say awkwardly, "just put your arms around me."

As if we are going to dance, she puts one arm around my waist and the other across my shoulders, the valise in her hand bumping against my hip. For a moment, I think I don't know how to do this and the whole thing feels utterly absurd and embarrassing, showing up here and telling her to hold me. I grab the princess around the waist and yank back. For a horrible split second, I'm afraid we're just going to fall over on the ground, but then we're through. I can feel her heartbeat quickening as the world fades around us and I pull up, up, and everything is spinning under us. Too high, I feel like we are soaring way over the city, like a balloon whose string has been cut, like we are going to get lost in the sky. I panic, and we are zooming in close, too close, and then I'm afraid I am going to dash us to bits in the street. I come back to myself right outside a shop selling painted silk fans. I hear somebody scream. The princess is struggling to get out of my grip, so I grab on to her, pull us out of the world again, trying to control it better. A few streets at a time. I vanish far enough that it seems as if we are hanging over the city but not too far above it, then pick a spot farther along, reappear there, stop and breathe, ignore the shouts, pull back again. In this way we cross the city—leapfrogging in and out of the world.

Once, I pull back too far—or it feels as if something is pulling *me*. I hear a whispering sort of hum behind me— the city gone, a rising roar—but no, here it is, the street, the trees swaying in the breeze, blossoms and wishes floating down, a beautiful day, and the princess's breath hoarse in my ear, her arms tight around me, hanging on for dear life. I find the house in Nanmu and put us in the courtyard, startling Bianka, Theo, and Frederick. Not bad, I think, quite pleased with myself. Faster than a trolley.

I let go of the princess, and she staggers a little, her face very pale, but she composes herself quickly. No shrieking from the walls, so I suppose they must have gotten rid of all the protective warning spells in preparation for her arrival.

"Thank you," she says, and puts down her valise.

"This is Princess Zara," I say to Frederick and Bianka, trying to look steadier than I feel after leap-vanishing across the city.

Bianka drops a curtsy. Frederick bows hastily as well.

"Oh, don't bother," says the princess, laughing. She recovers fast, I'll say that for her. "Well, that was . . . different. Might I ask for a cup of tea?"

THIRTY-SEVEN

The others return soon after we've made tea. The house feels smaller than usual as they all come pouring into the main room and greet the princess with bows and curtsies and noisy exclamations of concern. Princess Zara, for her part, is all smiles and graciousness, as if quite in her element. More tea is made, and maps are rolled out across the table. Theo is delighted by the hubbub, getting in everyone's way and shrieking with excitement. Bianka hovers close to him, watching his hands anxiously.

"I mean, what do I do if he draws something with his finger? I can't break his *finger*," she whispers to me. "I'm going to go mad watching him like this!"

After greeting the princess, Mrs. Och goes immediately to her room, indicating that Professor Baranyi and I are to follow her.

"Well done," she tells me, sinking into her chair. I can see the morning has taken a lot out of her, but I'm not much inclined to sympathy.

"All very well to have the princess," I say. "But what about Ko Dan? Or the Ankh-nu?"

"I will visit Si Tan tomorrow," she says.

For a moment I'm speechless, and then I splutter: "You'll *visit* him? Why am I sneaking around getting assaulted and kidnapped when you're just going to go sauntering into the monastery or the Imperial Gardens for a chat? Why didn't you do that to begin with?"

"It is a last resort, Julia," Mrs. Och says wearily. "Perhaps I can persuade him to help us. If not, we will have to leave immediately."

I want to kick my chair over and storm out of there, but not as much as I want to hear what she's going to say next, so I stay put.

"I need to know what passes between Gangzi and Lord Skaal today. We may have even less time than we think. You will go to the Imperial Gardens now and report straight back to me."

"Fine, I'll go," I say. "But d'you really think you can just go have a chat with Si Tan and he'll say, *Oh, I understand completely, look, I've got Ko Dan stashed in this cupboard, you can borrow him whenever you like, and here is the Ankh-nu as well?*"

She stares at me unsmilingly. "No, I do not anticipate that. But I will see what I can get from him."

I can tell I've been dismissed, so I get up. I'm almost out the door when she says, "You are doing well, Julia. You really are . . . most remarkable."

"Thank you," I say, a bit taken aback by this. She looks

terribly tired. Professor Baranyi helps her toward her bed, and I go out, closing the door behind me.

⁂

Spira City will be only beginning to shake off winter's clutches, but today feels almost like summer in Tianshi. The air is warm, and the Imperial Gardens are full of the smell of flowering trees, pollen drifting on the breeze. For all that it frightens me to think about what I am, what might be *in* me that enables me to walk the edge of the world, unseen, I can't deny that at times like these I enjoy it tremendously— walking right past the Ru, slipping through the gate and making my way through this forbidden sanctuary and up the steps toward the pavilion.

It seems that I am just in time. Si Tan is there with Gangzi at his side, exchanging elaborate greetings with the ambassador and Lord Skaal, who is dressed unprepossessingly in a long black coat and riding clothes. A servant comes with drinks and little cakes, and Si Tan begs his visitors to sit. His tone is gracious, as always, but his eyes are like flint. He is an intimidating figure, but Lord Skaal does not appear to be intimidated in the slightest.

Once the servant is gone, Si Tan breaks the brief silence: "Lord Skaal, I am pleased to meet you. I have heard some interesting things about you. They say you are Agoston Horthy's most prized official and that you have almost single-handedly eliminated magic from Frayne. Which seems surprising, given the rumors I have heard of your own background."

"People love to invent stories, and I'm sure my exploits have been exaggerated," says Lord Skaal coolly.

"Your prime minister is lucky to have you," says Si Tan.

"It is I who am lucky to serve under him," Lord Skaal returns. "Please, thank Gangzi for agreeing to speak with me. I am most grateful to have you here as a translator, Lord Grand Librarian. I'm afraid I speak no Yongwen at all."

Si Tan smiles thinly. "If you mean to take up this matter of visiting the monastery, I am afraid you will have no more luck than your predecessors in persuading Gangzi to go against his honor."

"Indeed, you have refused all that the good ambassador here has offered you thus far in exchange for the girl pretending to be the traitor Roparzh's daughter," says Lord Skaal. "I wonder if there is any inducement we *can* offer."

He doesn't pose it as a question, but he pauses. Si Tan murmurs to Gangzi in Yongwen, and Gangzi, in a cracked, angry voice, responds at length. Si Tan seems to do some editing in his translation, which is briefer:

"There is nothing, no threat or reward, that your tiny kingdom can realistically offer to tempt or compel Gangzi. He is not interested in anything more you have to say. However, I would be glad to give you a tour of the Imperial Gardens."

"I do hope you appreciate the fact that we haven't just gone and snatched her," says Lord Skaal.

Si Tan raises his eyebrows. "If you made an assault on the monastery, Lord Skaal, Yongguo would crush Frayne utterly in swift and justified vengeance."

The ambassador's jaw drops. He would be a terrible poker player. But Lord Skaal is unfazed.

"To be sure. As a matter of fact, I didn't come here only to plead for entry to the monastery. I have some news, as well. Agoston Horthy wanted me to inform you in person that Lady Laroche has been captured, charged with witchcraft and treason, found guilty, and sentenced to death."

Lady Laroche. Count Fournier called her his aunt, said she was the head of the Sidhar Coven in Frayne. No wonder he hasn't heard from her in a while. I'm not going to enjoy delivering that news to him.

Si Tan doesn't miss a beat. "The penalty in Frayne for treason is hanging, and the penalty for witchcraft is drowning. Which did you choose? Or did you attempt both?"

"The prime minister's intent, after getting whatever information from her he could, was to behead her first, before casting her body into the river Syne, so that the head could be sent to you as proof. I understand your reluctance to break your agreement with such a lady, but now that the lady herself has expired, surely we can come to our own agreement."

Si Tan translates this to Gangzi, who rises and does a fair bit of shouting and spitting and finger waving before hunching back into his seat.

"He doesn't seem happy," remarks Lord Skaal. "Was he fond of the lady?"

"He is expressing disgust at your barbarism," says Si Tan. "You are such backward fools, he says, with your heads in the sand, imagining you can eradicate something as elemental as magic. Might as well try to fight the air we breathe, et cetera, et cetera."

"Perhaps he is right," says Lord Skaal. "Nevertheless, the lady is dead by now, as are most of her associates. There is no reason for you to keep hanging on to the girl. What use is she to you?"

Si Tan translates. Gangzi creases his face and mutters something in reply.

"Gangzi does not intend to do anything for you because he does not like you," says Si Tan. "Shou-shu is peaceful and independent. The monks have no quarrel with outsiders, and outsiders have always given them the respect due to them. The monastery stood unguarded for centuries because it had no need of guards. If you desecrate that place by breaching its walls without Gangzi's permission, I have promised him that Yongguo will destroy Frayne. Shou-shu is a jewel in our country, and it is under our protection. Any defilement of the monastery will mean the annihilation of your little kingdom."

"Frayne is rather a distance," remarks Lord Skaal. "An awful lot of mountains to cross in one direction, and an awful lot of ocean in the other. Can't think it would be worth your while invading us for a girl that means nothing to you."

"I say nothing of a girl. I am talking about respect," says Si Tan. While his voice remains calm and polite, it seems to me that his entire body thrums with violence. "You have no knowledge of magic, only your fear of it. You have no idea what our empire can do."

The ambassador has gone quite white. He bursts in: "No need to talk of war, my friends! We have come here openly and honestly. There will be no desecration of the monastery."

"No, of course not," says Lord Skaal smoothly. "I just thought the threat of invasion rather out of proportion."

Si Tan says nothing, and I'm thinking that our snatching the princess might have repercussions we hadn't imagined, since surely the Fraynish delegation will be blamed for it.

"Well then, it appears we have gotten nowhere," says Lord Skaal. "If I can persuade this fellow to like me, might he give me the girl? Is that really what all this hinges on? Shall I buy him a drink or let him beat me at cards? What do monks like to do, anyway?"

"I do not think he can be persuaded to like you," says Si Tan, smiling slightly.

"Pity. In spite of all my charm. It causes me to doubt myself." Lord Skaal rises, and the ambassador scrambles to his feet as well. They both bow to their hosts. Si Tan stands up, taller than both of them, and bows in return, but Gangzi just turns his head aside, staring through me, his face crinkled with contempt.

"If you wish to extend your stay in Yongguo, come and see me again," says Si Tan to Lord Skaal meaningfully. "I could find you a position here, if you wanted one."

The ambassador gapes again, but Lord Skaal only says, "That is very kind of you, but I am happy with my current position."

I follow closely as the two men are escorted to the gate by

the Ru. The ambassador's entourage is waiting outside with a small battalion of motor cabs.

"The prime minister will not be pleased. What are we going to do?" says the ambassador in a low voice.

Lord Skaal shrugs. "Lady Laroche is dead. The girl is no use to them; they're just being disagreeable. They'll turn her out eventually, and we'll be on hand when they do. The main thing is that we know where she is and that we find out who is supporting her here. Clear *them* out of the way and the girl will be hung out to dry. Cheaper than the alternatives, honestly. Don't worry, my good fellow."

"Well, you seem to have it in hand," says the ambassador uncertainly.

Lord Skaal laughs—the same pleasant laugh I remember.

"I'd like to think so," he says. "But nothing ever goes as one expects. Especially when dealing with people like these. We will speak again later. I have some other business I need to attend to in the city. I'll go on foot."

"Alone?" asks the ambassador, shocked.

"Yes."

"We'll dine at six?"

"I look forward to it."

Lord Skaal shakes the ambassador's hand and sets off into the city with me at his heels. I am still so preoccupied with the fear of what our kidnapping of the princess might mean for Frayne that I don't notice where we are going until we are right at the door of the Hundred Lantern Hotel.

THIRTY-EIGHT

The girl behind the counter is rubbing her eyes with the heels of her palms. Lord Skaal approaches and drops a string of heavy coins on the counter, startling her. She gives him a wary look.

"Looking for a foreign woman," he says in Fraynish. He makes circles with his fingers, holding them up to his face like goggles and mimicking a whirring sound. "You know who I mean. Which room?"

She shakes her head. He drops another string of coins in front of her, then draws back his coat to show her the pistol at his hip. "Go on," he says. "It only gets worse from here."

She looks at the coins for a half second, then sweeps them off the counter into the pocket of her apron. She makes for the stairs, beckoning him to follow. Suddenly I have the feeling that we are being watched. I turn around, scanning the dining hall, but I see nobody, and Lord Skaal and the girl are already halfway up the stairs, so I run after them. In the hallway, the girl is pointing to a door. Lord Skaal mimes unlocking it, but she shakes her head vigorously and he shoos her away. My heart is in my throat as he knocks. No answer. He sniffs at the door, gives an impatient sigh, then backs up and kicks it down.

"Sorry, were you sleeping?" he calls out, backing away from the door. He knows quite well who is behind it and what she is capable of. Still no reply. He approaches the broken door cautiously.

"I came to say hello, since we both happen to be here in Tianshi. Thought I could buy you a drink."

He inches into the room, and I go after him.

"Ah. There you are."

She is standing by the window, her curved knife in her hand. I find myself fixating on it, unable to look away from the bright blade. Hello, Pia's knife edge, old friend.

"You broke my door down because you want to buy me a drink?" she asks dryly.

"Sorry—bit extreme, perhaps. Only I'm short on time and you weren't opening up. Shall we call a truce and go down to the bar?"

"No," says Pia. "Tell me why I should not kill you."

"Because my mother would weep for me," he says lightly. "Come, there is no reason for either of us to be killing the other. Though I'd feel better if you'd put that knife away."

She sheathes the knife and says, "I don't need a knife to kill you."

"I'm sure you don't," he says. "But I really did come here to chat. After all, we're very nearly allies, aren't we? The prime minister thinks of Lord Casimir almost as a brother."

"A brother?" Her lip curls.

"A mentor, perhaps," says Lord Skaal.

"A benefactor," suggests Pia. "And too fearful an enemy to risk provoking."

"Well, that describes my relationship to my own brother quite well," says Lord Skaal. "You see, it is as I said."

"Why are you in Tianshi?" she asks.

"Do we have to do this standing across the room from each other? Can we at least sit down?"

But there is nowhere to sit. The room is bare except for a bed that looks as if it has never been slept in and a nightstand.

"No," says Pia.

"Very well, we'll be uncomfortable if that is what you prefer. You know, I've been curious to meet you for a long time." He looks around, looks at *me* with that one yellow eye, as if perturbed. For a moment my heart stalls, but no, he is only looking through me.

"Why are you in Tianshi?" she asks again.

"For Princess Zara, or whoever she is," he says. "You know Lady Laroche?"

"I know the lady," says Pia, all ice.

He looks in my direction again and says, "Somebody else is here."

Horror threads its way up my spine. Pia's goggles whir. He steps toward me, and I pull back farther, far enough that I can barely make out his features and he is just a blurred silhouette, my fingers and toes tingling, that nothing-nowhere right at my back, ready for me to fall into it.

I hear his voice only faintly, as if from very far away: "It is gone. Almost."

And Pia's voice: "There is nobody here. Why are you asking me about Lady Laroche?"

"She cut a deal with the Shou-shu monks a few years back and they took in Prince Roparzh's daughter, or someone pretending to be his daughter. The ambassador tried to get her handed over as soon as he learned of it, but there was no budging Gangzi. We set about cutting off the princess's organization at the roots, drowning the witches who made the deal and supported her. Capturing Lady Laroche was the final blow to the girl's support system, and once it was done, I was sent here to try again to get hold of the girl and identify her."

I feel faint, so far back from the world. I ease a little closer so that I can feel my fingers and toes again. Their voices come clearer, though I still cannot make out the expressions on their faces.

"You captured Lady Laroche?" asks Pia.

"Personally," says Lord Skaal with a bow. "I hope she was not a friend."

"No," says Pia. There is something odd in her voice. "She was not that. Is she dead?"

"Yes."

"I do not believe it."

"I assure you, it was quite the operation, and Agoston

Horthy's greatest triumph since he crushed the Lorian Uprising. What remains of the Sidhar Coven topples with her."

Pia is quiet.

"Anyway, that's what *I* am doing in Tianshi. Casimir supports Agoston Horthy's efforts to get rid of this girl, particularly now that King Zey is so ill, but I doubt his interest in the matter is strong enough to send *you*, and I received no word. So what *are* you doing here?"

"I am here for something else," she says.

"Yes, that's what I was just implying," he says, sardonic. "Is *Casimir* in Tianshi?"

"No."

"His sister? Mrs. Och?"

Pia's goggles whir.

"I am only curious. My orders concern the princess, that's all." He looks toward me, through me, again. "There it is again. This scent has been with me since I met with the grand librarian. I assumed—"

"There is nobody here," says Pia again.

He gives a sniff. "Somebody *is* here," he murmurs very softly, like a threatening purr. He can't see me, I tell myself. He can't see me.

"I am tired of this game," says Pia sharply. "It is time for you to leave."

He is uneasy now. "I have a very keen sense of smell, you know. I trust it over my eyesight. There *is* somebody else in this room with us."

"This is my room. It is not your concern."

"Then you know who it is?"

She pauses and then says, "Yes."

I am torn between panicking and laughing. So they both know I'm here, but neither of them can actually *see* me.

"You've been having me followed?" he asks, and when she doesn't reply, he says, "Well, that seems unfriendly, but I'll let it slide. Are you here because of that same old matter with the little boy? That has been bothering me a long time."

"Why should it bother you?"

"I saw him once, you know. Obtained some samples—blood, tissue, hair. His pretty witch mother did not like me much. What *is* he?"

"I don't know."

"Really? You don't know?"

"Nor do I care."

"Would you be interested to know what I found out about him when I ran my tests?"

"No."

"What an incurious creature you are!" He glances toward me again. Since they know I am here anyway, I have allowed myself to draw a little closer. "You and I both know that there are a great many variations on the human. Some of us are born a little different, or become so later on. This boy, however—he is woven through and through with something potent, something incomprehensible. He is not touched by magic, he is *made of* magic, as far as I could tell. And the Xianren covet him. What could he be? How can you not wonder?"

"I am done with all manner of wondering."

"But you *are* here for him?"

Silence.

"I'm not going to try to find him myself," Lord Skaal assures her. "I haven't the manpower here, and those are not my instructions. To be honest, I have wondered about you quite as often as I've wondered about him. I hoped we might find we had things to talk about."

"I am done talking to you."

He nods, looking almost relieved. "It's lonely being different, don't you find? Sometimes I think I want to talk with somebody else who is . . . well, also *different*. But the trouble with people who are *different* in the manner that you and I are different is that they are so often such flaming arseholes. Well, if you change your mind, you can find me at the ambassador's house. I'll be staying there awhile. My apologies for the door."

He looks in my direction as he goes out and bares his teeth at me. Even though I know he can't see me, I flinch. I stay in the corner of the room, watching Pia, waiting to see what she will do next. She looks out the window for a few minutes, perhaps watching Lord Skaal depart on the street below, and then she says, almost gently: "Julia. Show yourself."

Run, I tell myself. *Go home, you stupid girl. Too risky.* But a dangerous mix of curiosity, fear, and longing is pulling at me, outweighing all my reason and better judgment. I step back into the world, and Pia's face comes into focus.

THIRTY-NINE

"You've cut your hair," she says, looking me over. Back in the world, closer to her, I feel the broken-ice pitch of her voice grating against my eardrums.

"It was getting in the way."

"You have been following Lord Skaal?"

"Yes." No point lying—she knows I have been.

"Then Mrs. Och is here for the princess too. I suppose that is not surprising. What do you make of him? Keen sense of smell!" She starts to laugh. It is not a pleasant sound. "I am glad you have come, Julia, even if only because you were led here. It was not kind of you to run away after I rescued you from Si Tan. I have been thinking of how to draw you out, and none of the ideas I had were pleasant. But I need to speak to you. It is not about the boy."

"All right. Here I am. What is it about?"

"I am instructed to tell you that Casimir's offer of employment stands. Should you become disillusioned with your

Mrs. Och—or should you decide you want more gold and more freedom than she can give you—well, in that case, it appears that you know where to find me."

"I'd have thought it was clear by now what I think of Casimir and his offer."

Pia grins, wolflike. "I told him you would say as much. But why, then, have you yoked yourself to Mrs. Och?"

"If you can't see the difference between Mrs. Och and Casimir, then we're not alike at all," I tell her, and instantly regret it.

"You are deluded if you think the difference between your master and mine is such a great one," she says. "And you are a fool to imagine that the outcome of their conflict really matters for the likes of us. I am Casimir's creature, as you are Mrs. Och's. We are very alike indeed."

"I'm not her creature."

"Then what are you?"

"I'm just . . . me." As if that answers anything at all. And anyway, maybe I'm not.

"I am to ask you what you want. Casimir is willing to give you whatever you ask if you will accept his contract."

"Safety for Theo," I say immediately, without really thinking about what I'll do if she agrees.

"Except that," she says. "But anything else. Anything you desire."

"No."

She tilts her head at me, the goggles whirring in and out again.

"You fight so hard for this boy, sacrifice so much. But what is he to you, after all?"

I just shake my head. There's no explaining love to Pia.

"And when I find him? You will weep, I assume, and then you will carry on with your life. Or will you be bent on revenge? Will you come looking for me?"

"You won't find him. But if you did, I'd come looking for you."

A vivid image of Haizea and her whirlwind rises up in my mind: her bleeding eyes, her fist clenching the storm.

"Then we are sure to meet again," she says. "Even once this business with the boy is ended, however it ends, Casimir will not give up on you. He longs to understand and harness this power of yours."

I feel a chill closing around my heart. "Casimir's contract—it's not a piece of paper, is it?"

She grins, but there is no joy or even humor in her expression.

"Can I see it?" I ask.

She pulls off her leather glove, and I walk over to her at the window. She turns the inside of her wrist to me, and I see the silvery disk, which I know to be scalding hot, nested in folds of shiny scar flesh. My stomach curls.

"How does it work?"

"It is a living contract. The surest way to allow it to take hold is to insert it at the wrist—a minor operation—and allow it some days to grow toward the brain. It is less likely to kill you if introduced in this way. It can also be inserted via the ear, which is faster but much riskier—it results in death about half the time, and even if the person survives, it leaves them deaf in one ear and a little mad. Once it enters your brain, your will is bound to his, inextricably. I could not disobey him even if I wished to."

"That's what you put in Cinzai's ear," I say, remembering the witch flailing and screaming, the thing that crawled into her ear. "That's why Si Tan killed her."

"In a matter of minutes she would either have belonged to Casimir or she would have been dead," says Pia. "In her case, the gamble was worth it, the loss nothing to him. But Casimir wants *you* undamaged, as much as possible."

"Does it hurt?"

"Not anymore."

"Why would you let him do that to you?"

Her face is so white, her lips a thin line, those goggles masking any expression I might have been able to read if she'd had eyes.

"I was broken," she says—her voice suddenly losing that shattering, high edge. "He said that he could piece me back together. Make me whole. Oh, there was gold too, plenty of gold. What difference did it make to me? Every servitude looked alike, and this one came with more money."

"Did he make you whole?" I can't stop myself from asking.

"If you are broken the way I was broken, there is no way to be whole again."

"Broken how?"

We are standing so close together, heads bent toward each

other, and she answers me as if we were friends, as if we trusted one another.

"Casimir destroyed me bodily and put me back together, but before that . . . you heard Lord Skaal speak of Lady Laroche and the Sidhar Coven? I belonged to them for a time, and they broke my body and my spirit in a thousand ways, but I came to them broken, as well. When did it begin?" The goggles whir—out, in. "There was a man, a long time ago. My first memories are of being frightened of him." Then she shrugs. "But there is always a man; there is always a dark corner and people who pretend not to see. That is a common story. It seemed at the time that I was broken already, born broken, and that my brokenness summoned him to me, thick-fingered and stinking, out of the dark. It was all so long ago, and I have no memory further back, no memory of being whole."

I feel sick. I hear myself saying, "I'm sorry. . . ."

The goggles give a sharp whir, and she snaps her chin up. "But why?"

I don't know how to answer that. She studies my face. I can't imagine what she sees there.

"My mother was part of the Sidhar Coven," I say.

"Yes. Did Casimir not tell you?"

"Tell me what?"

"Before they sent Ammi, your mother, to bind him in stone and bury him in the sea, I was sent to kill him. I was the coven's pet assassin, their little attack dog. I did not succeed, of course. He smashed me to pieces. He shattered my bones. He put out my eyes. He did all manner of things to me, and still I did not die, I did not die. Casimir is not one for a quick kill. He likes to see what he's dealing with. Pain and fear, in their most extreme forms, reveal so much. He saw I was a resilient sort of dog, and that I had no will of my own. How convenient, how ideal! And so he did not kill me. He repaired me, more or less. What you see"—she spreads her hands—"is the work of his mechanic. His greatest work, so he says. He had me put back together, he offered gold, and he put his contract into me. I submitted to all of this. I could not go back to the coven, for they had made it clear what the result of failure would be."

I want to ask, but I can't. She answers anyway.

"I did not know Ammi. I knew *of* her, of course. But she moved in higher circles than I did."

"But you're not a witch," I say.

"No—and so I was never part of the coven. Only their dog, as I say."

"You didn't have family?"

"None that cared to be so. I was a stray dog for some time, and that is a hard life. I was glad of a leash. I didn't mind being beaten if it meant I had a hearth to curl up on. They were cruel to me, the witches who took charge of me. Casimir destroyed me, yes, but once I submitted to him, he was a good master. Plenty of gold—not that I care so much for gold, but I enjoy a comfortable bed, a fine meal. More than gold, he gave me honesty, and he was the first to do so. Casimir does not pretend to be other than what he is, nor does he pretend I am other than what I am. There is something to be said for that. It is more than you receive from your Mrs. Och, I think."

My mouth is dry. "What do you mean?"

"I mean that you are her dog," she says, "but neither of you will call it what it is."

"I'm not her dog, and she'd be a fool to think me so," I say.

"You are so young—it would break my heart, if there were anything left to break. You do not understand what is happening. You think it is about a little boy. It is not about the little boy. It is about power. The world is terrible, has always been terrible, and the striving and seeking and suffering of powerless mortals is a great waste of effort. I do as I am told and that is all. Casimir never needed to put his contract in me. I would be his, regardless. Do you understand what I am telling you?"

"No! I really *don't* understand what you're on about. Why don't you tell it to me straight?"

"I am trying to explain." She sounds more agitated than I have ever heard her. "If I cannot make you understand, then there will come a time, soon, when I must hurt you or kill you. I do not wish it, but I will do it."

"I'm leaving," I say, backing away from her.

"Wait! Please wait." She puts up a hand, entreating. "Let me explain something you cannot fail to understand. The strong think that they cannot be broken. I've seen it a thousand times—that unfounded confidence before the fact. The truth of the matter is that everyone can be broken.

Everyone. Any person who has known real pain knows this to be true. I can take you to a place, Julia, where you will no longer care what becomes of that boy, or anything, or anyone. A place where all that matters to you is that the pain should stop. There is a place even beyond that where you would worship me as the god who brings you pain or relief from pain. It is a very nasty and time-consuming business, but I have done it before, and if I must, I will do it again. I wanted to speak to you first, to tell you of my own life, my own history, because I hope it will not be necessary for you to endure what I did or become what I have become."

"You can't lay a hand on me," I say. "You know it." But my voice quavers a little. I feel the emptiness at my back; I am ready to fall into it, to leap out of the world and away from her whirring goggles, her dead white face.

She goes over to the nightstand by her bed. From the drawer she takes the ribbons Cinzai, Si Tan's witch, bound me in.

"You are not invulnerable," she says. "I have seen you rendered helpless, tied to the world by that poor brute's magic—and Casimir employs a far more powerful witch than her. Think on it, Julia. I would rather we find another way to bring you to Casimir's side."

Panic comes in a great wave. Stupidly, blindly, I reach for the knife in my boot. She moves faster than I can think. Something strikes my chin—her foot, perhaps—and I am scrabbling on the floor, stunned. Then the sound of glass shattering, the thunk of something landing on the floor, a

310

figure running toward me, and a bolt of white flame in the middle of the room, shooting up to the ceiling. Pia snarls, raising one arm to shield her goggles from the glare. I see him first, Jun, right next to me, aiming his pistol. Pia is moving toward us, knife in her hand now. He fires the gun, but she doesn't stop. I grab him as her knife flashes toward him, and in my terror, I pull him straight through that invisible space—through and through and through to the other side, to the gray street, whirling with ash, and the burning air.

FORTY

The street shimmers. There is a man walking toward us. Not a man—it is the top hat that makes me think so, but he is transparent, I can see the street right through him, through the fixed grin on his skeletal face. A girl creeps up behind him, reaches deftly into his pocket, and pulls out a snake. She looks at us and winks, and I hear a horrible noise in my throat because it is *me* as a little girl, but with pooling black eyes and a chalk-white face. No—something shifts, and it is little Pia with goggles for eyes. My own scream startles me—not a human sound. Jun is struggling against me. My hooked hands grip his shoulders, holding him fast.

I hear hoofbeats. Or perhaps it is just my heart beating. The street has gone whirling away from us. I am running with him, and I am so much stronger than he is here—he seems to weigh nothing—and then we are outside the little flat I grew up in, the laundry shop at street level. I've run home. In the doorway stands the antlered, fox-faced creature I saw before. He has a curved blade in his mottled, half-decayed human hand, a blade with a jagged, strangely glittering edge. His teeth are bared in a stiff snarl.

"Lidari," he says.

"Who are you?" I cry in a not-mine voice.

There are more of them in the street now. A crocodile head is snapping atop the rangy, rotting body of a lion, ribs showing through the torn flesh. Some apelike thing with a starved panther face is loping toward us. Another one looks human but *dead*, with the bright yellow eyes of some other creature rolling about in its head. They are closing in on me, holding long, narrow stalks with hooks at the end. Everything feels horribly slowed down. Fox Face's blade comes swinging toward me. I move, but not fast enough. The blade catches me on the arm, though for the moment I feel nothing but heat where it strikes me. My legs buckle and I fall down on the street, Jun shouting something, the gun going off, cries of triumph from this mob of patched-together beasts. The blade goes up again, up into the burning sky. I am fixed on it. It comes down. I grab Jun and pull back hard, right through the street. I hear something like rushing water, the long, anguished hiss, *"Lidariiii."* We are above Pia's room, broken glass all over the floor, Pia crouched, knife in hand, listening for us. There is shouting from the hall.

I aim for the window, trying to catch sight of the road below. We end up on the opposite rooftop, jarred back into ourselves and the world. The sun is low in the sky, and there is hardly anyone in the road. I can still see Pia through her broken window.

A click. Jun has pressed the muzzle of his pistol to my head. He speaks through clenched teeth.

"What. Are. You?"

I swallow. My throat feels burnt dry from the terrible air of that place. I gulp in a breath of Tianshi's fragrant springtime air, with its hint of warmth and honey.

"I'm sorry," I manage to get out.

He slides down the other side of the roof and drops into the alley behind. I follow. He backs away from me, pistol pointed at my chest, his face closed and tight and pale.

"You are monster," he says, and his voice shakes.

"I didn't mean to," I say. I feel so weak, like I can barely stand up. "Jun, please. When we were there . . . what did I look like?"

"Like *monster!*" He screams this last word at me and gives the pistol a threatening jerk, breathing hard.

I put a finger to my lips. Pia is only one street over, may be out looking for us now.

"Stop pointing that thing at me," I say, trying to sound reasonable and halfway calm. "We need to get out of here."

"Stay away or I shoot," he says. The gun is shaking in his hands.

"Please lower that thing," I beg him. "She would have killed you. I was trying to save us, and I . . . I didn't mean to go there. I'm scared to death myself. I'm sorry."

"Go where? What is that place?"

I say, "I don't know," because I can't tell him, not when

he is looking at me that way, scared out of his wits already. Saying *Kahge* isn't going to calm him down. I'm terrified he's going to put a hole in me just from nerves.

"Please . . ." I don't know what to say to him. "Look, *you* followed *me.*"

But then I realize he couldn't have. He must have been following Lord Skaal.

"Stay away," he says, backing down the alley. Then he ducks around a corner and is gone. My arm gives a dull throb, and that's when I notice I'm standing in a puddle of my own blood. My knees give out under me.

Later it feels like a dream: I can't say for sure that any of it happened, nor can I think of an alternate theory for how I got home. Lying there bleeding in the road. Her boots beside me. She crouches next to me, and if I didn't know her better, I would say her voice sounds sad.

"This is not the day for you to die, Julia."

Lying in her bed as she binds my arm. Her face looms over me, taking up my whole view of the world. Those awful goggles.

"If you could tell me where you live, I'd take you home," she says. A brittle laugh. "Here, this will give you strength. Think of what I said and come back to me tomorrow, or I will have to find you. One more chance. I want you to choose. I want to give you that much."

Her fingers in my mouth, a bitter pill dissolving on my tongue. Then everything is sharp and clear. I am running, the evening air cooling around me, my heart hammering with something like joy. I could run forever. Blood rushes and pulses in my arm, the bandage soaked through in no time, but there is no pain, no feeling at all except for the speed of my limbs, almost like flying, because I barely feel my feet hitting the ground. The wind is roaring in my ears—or maybe the roaring is inside my head, I can't tell. I vanish when I reach Nanmu, as is my habit, and something tugs at my arm, hard. Blood flows out into the air, flows straight out and away, out of the world.

I vault over the courtyard wall, everything coming into terrible focus, the hard planes and edges of the world, Frederick's voice banging about inside my skull: "What's happened? Are you all right?" And I am on the ground—how did I get on the ground? I feel as if my heart is going to explode from my chest. They are all in a knot around me, and I hear Princess Zara saying, "Give her space," Esme saying, "Her arm—she's hurt."

Bianka lifts me in her arms. We are indoors, the ceiling swinging over me, the floor buckling under me. She holds me and tells me, "It's all right, it's going to be all right."

"I need to clean and stitch this *now*," says Esme.

Something wet and burning on my arm. I let out a strangled yell. It sounds like a dog barking; the world narrows down to Frederick's anxious face peering over Bianka's shoulder, Bianka holding me fast, and then Esme's needle biting my arm again and again.

FORTY-ONE

Professor Baranyi holds a little vial under my nose. It burns my nostrils, burns my mind clear. Mrs. Och's room settles around me with a jolt, my heart thudding back to sudden slowness. Mrs. Och is at her desk, hands folded before her, and I am seated opposite her.

"Better?" asks the professor, corking the vial.

I nod and finger the bandage on my throbbing arm. I'm relieved to see Frederick is here too. They won't do anything to me with him here. But then I wonder why I think they might do anything to me.

"What happened?" asks Mrs. Och.

"May I have some water?"

I'm only partly stalling, trying to remember what happened and what I can tell her. My mouth is dry as dust. She nods at Frederick, and he goes out.

"I went to the Imperial Gardens, like you said," I tell her, my mind groping back through the day.

"Did Si Tan mention us to Lord Skaal?"

"No," I say. "But he threatened to invade Frayne if they tried to make off with the princess, and surely he'll think it *was* them."

Frederick comes back in with a cup of water, which I drink gratefully. Mrs. Och waves my concern aside. "I will tell him tomorrow that it was me," she says. "Once the princess is out of the city."

"They said Lady Laroche is dead," I add, remembering how casually Lord Skaal talked of sending Si Tan her head. The leader of the Sidhar Coven. She must have known my mother.

"Lady Laroche?" cries Professor Baranyi. "That is a blow indeed, if we hope for a revolution."

"Perhaps not," says Mrs. Och. "Go on, Julia. How were you injured?"

"The meeting didn't go very well, and then Lord Skaal headed off into the city, so I followed him, and he went to the Hundred Lantern Hotel. He wanted to talk to Pia."

This is where it all gets difficult to explain, but I tell her as much of their conversation as I remember, and how he seemed able to smell me, which makes her chuckle for some reason. Not particularly funny from my perspective. Her face reveals nothing when I tell her about Pia's offer and her threats, how she said Casimir would give me *anything*, and how Jun appeared, crashing through the window. If he was following Lord Skaal, watching through the window, I can only imagine his surprise at suddenly seeing *me*

318

in the room with Pia. But he broke his cover to try and help me, and what must he think now? I think of his face when he screamed *Monster!* at me in the alley, and my stomach curls with misery. I refrain from mentioning Pia's remarks about Mrs. Och: *You are her dog, but neither of you will call it what it is.*

"Pia cut your arm?" suggests Professor Baranyi when I stop.

"No," I say.

Now the hard part. I stare at my hands in my lap—my ordinary hands—and I tell them about what happened after: Kahge, the nightmare quality of it, my home and my childhood distorted and horrifying, those revolting creatures, the bright blade cutting my arm.

I look up at her. There is no point hiding it—Frederick has already told her—so I say, "When those creatures in Kahge shout at me, I think they are calling *me* Lidari. Why?"

Professor Baranyi gives her an anxious look, but she keeps her gaze trained on me, unmoving and revealing nothing.

"Lidari was Marike's associate," says Mrs. Och. "I never met him, of course. Marike was the first ruler to defy the Xianren. We suffered our first true defeat at her hands. Casimir claimed to have had Lidari killed . . . oh, a thousand years ago or more. Why the creatures in Kahge call *you* Lidari, I cannot fathom." Suddenly she laughs—an odd and humorless sound. "Are you sure of your parentage, Julia?"

My heart goes cold and heavy at that. Well, I asked, and now I may be getting the answer I dread more than anything—the half thought that sits at the back of my mind like a grinning goblin, taunting me: *You are not what you think you are.*

"What do you mean?" My voice shakes, and I hate myself for it.

"Only that your mother, being a witch, might have sought some connection with Kahge," says Mrs. Och. "The fact that she was able to bind Casimir—she must have had some very great magic to assist her, and you were born shortly after that. Could your birth be the result of some deal made with the half beings of Kahge?"

She is halfway there herself, without knowing the memory or vision I had of my mother with the Ankh-nu. And how casually she suggests my deepest buried fear, that I may not be of this world, not human at all, not *myself*. I begin to shake. No, no, I am Julia, I have always been Julia, this is a mistake, they are all mistaken. Frederick comes to my side quickly, putting his hands on my shoulders.

"I look like my mother," I whisper. "I look like *Dek*."

"Oh, indeed," says Mrs. Och, watching me very carefully. "I did not mean to upset you." She smiles a strange, false smile. "Julia, I want you to work for me."

"I do work for you," I say.

"You work for me now because of Theo. But soon I will return to Frayne. There may be a revolution, and if there is not, there will still be the work of trying to get witches out

320

of the country and protect those that remain. You would be a tremendous asset, and you would be well compensated. It is dangerous work, of course, but it is important, and I would be glad to have you working alongside the professor and Frederick and myself. I would also help you to untangle this mystery of your unusual gift. It would serve us all well to understand why you can go to Kahge."

Frederick lets go of my shoulders, as if he's just noticed how tightly he was hanging on to me.

For a moment I am speechless. Is it that easy? Can I join Mrs. Och's inner circle, working to destroy Agoston Horthy and save women like my mother? Isn't that a dream come true—to put my skills and strengths to work, not for theft and blackmail but for helping those who need it, righting the wrongs that have shaped my own life? Surely it beats mopping floors for a pittance. It seems like the answer to all my uncertainties and fears about the future. And to have her help me find out why I can vanish as I do—when surely she is the only one who *can* help me— should be irresistible. Still, the idea of working for Mrs. Och does not sit right with me. Pia has planted her poison in my ear.

And Dek doesn't want to go back.

I lick my lips and say, "Thank you," because what else am I to say? And what does Pia know about Mrs. Och *or* me?

"Good," says Mrs. Och. "Tonight some of our party will take the princess out of the city. They will wait two days for the rest of us to join them at a farm a half day's journey from here. I will meet with Si Tan in the morning and hope we can come to some agreement regarding Ko Dan. If we cannot—well, I fear we shouldn't stay in this city much longer."

I look at my hands again, my dirty fingernails—or is that blood? They are trembling, and I ball them into fists to make them still.

"Perhaps we should let Julia rest a bit," says Frederick gently.

"Indeed," says Mrs. Och. "But, Julia, next time you must consult me before you do something reckless like visit Pia. I can only captain this ship through the storm if all members of my crew keep to their posts."

"I didn't exactly mean to *visit* her."

"How is your arm?" she asks.

"It hurts, but I reckon I'll be all right. Esme knows how to patch a body up."

"She is quite formidable, your Esme," says Mrs. Och. "We will speak again in the morning."

Frederick and I go out. He looks like he wants to say something to me, but Theo catapults into me as soon as we emerge from Mrs. Och's room. I twist sideways, trying to protect my hurt arm, and a hush falls over the table. The main door is open to the cool evening air, cicadas screeching in the trees outside the courtyard.

"Come," says Esme, breaking the silence and pulling out a chair for me. "Eat something."

I sit down in the chair she offers, across from Princess Zara, and they all watch me carefully, their faces yellowish in the candlelight. The plates are cluttered among the dripping candles—strips of mottled beef, black mushrooms, bowls of steaming rice, stewed duck, figs, persimmons, and bamboo tips. I am too tired to be hungry, but I let Csilla fill my plate anyway.

"I hope you weren't injured on my account," says the princess.

Of course—I turned up raving and bleeding and generally behaving like a lunatic. No doubt they'd like to know why. I give them a much-altered abbreviated version of what I've just told Mrs. Och, leaving out Kahge and blaming my injury on Pia. Frederick, sitting down at the other end of the table and filling his own plate, doesn't correct me or even look at me.

"I'm grieved to hear of Lady Laroche's passing," says Princess Zara. "I owe her a great deal."

She doesn't look particularly grieved, but I suppose it's a lot to take in all at once.

Theo makes a circuit of the table, crawling onto laps and eating everyone's bamboo tips, all of us keeping a nervous eye on his every gesture lest he start drawing. Soon the conversation picks up again. Gregor, Esme, Csilla, the professor, and Princess Zara are leaving tonight, via a smugglers' tunnel that will take them to the other side of the city wall. It is not part of the regular tunnel circuit—which is flooded anyway—and I am given to understand that the use of it has cost Mrs. Och dearly. They will wait two days at a farm we used on our way to Tianshi and then carry on to Frayne without us if we have not joined them by then. Now they are discussing an alternate route that would avoid the Kastahor Mountains—hiding on a cargo train to the southern border and then passing through the kingdom of Xanuha to the Parnese states.

"We didn't come that way because we understood the Xanuha warriors to be ruthless about their territory, and it is a mountainous region also," says the professor.

"But nothing like the Kastahor Mountains," says the princess. "I have ties to that kingdom, I stayed with them for some months when I was younger. I'm sure the queen of Xanuha will grant us safe passage and guides. I am amazed that you survived the journey through the Kastahor Mountains."

"Barely," says Esme. "I would prefer to take almost any route but that one."

"I would still rather brave a sea voyage," says Csilla.

"No," says the princess. "Not unless we can find a *very* well-armed vessel. The pirates off the coast here rule the seas, and about half of them are in Casimir's pay."

"How did you know to trust me?" I interrupt.

They all go quiet and stare at me again.

"I have a sense of such things," says the princess, with an easy smile.

"What kind of sense?"

She folds her napkin, suddenly brisk, and says, "It is a

small gift compared to your own. But I can sense the intentions and emotions of everyone nearby. I can tell if they mean me well or ill, if they are at ease or afraid, lying to me or telling the truth. These things are as clear to me as the color of a person's eyes to you."

"Stars," says Csilla. "That must be useful."

"It has kept me safe a great many times," the princess acknowledges. "There is a wealth of goodwill and noble intent here. I am grateful to have such friends."

"Do you *want* to be queen?" I blurt. Perhaps it's a stupid question, but she is not much older than me and has spent her entire life running around the world hiding from people who want to kill her. I wouldn't wonder if she just wanted to go live a peaceful, quiet life somewhere, if that were possible. Be free.

"It isn't a matter of wanting," she replies. "Although I have never wanted anything else. My family was executed unjustly. My father was murdered by his own brother, and that man still occupies the throne and allows his prime minister to devastate Frayne through his fanatical vendetta against magic and folklore and the traditions of our people. I believe in the Nameless One, but I believe in the spirits too, and I know magic can be a force of good as well as a force of evil. I believe I have the power and the purpose to change Frayne for the better, to lead New Poria toward a more tolerant age. I believe it is my destiny."

She says all of this calmly and evenly. Only upon the word *murdered* does an edge come to her voice. We are all quiet, and into the silence, the bells of Shou-shu chime the closing of the city gates and nightfall. The princess rises and begins to stack the dishes to take out and wash at the pump. Theo is dozing in Bianka's lap now, full of bamboo tips. Bianka watches Princess Zara go out with the dishes, a rapt expression on her face. I wonder how many princesses share in the washing up after meals. I think I am falling under her spell myself, imagining what Frayne might be if this strange girl ruled it.

While the others are cleaning up and packing their belongings, I go out for some air and find Gregor smoking on the steps.

"Quite something, isn't she?" he says.

"Yes."

There is a cup full of some dark liquid beside him. An unexpected anger wells up inside me.

"What's this?" I ask, picking up the cup.

"Tea," he says.

I give him a scathing look and sniff it. It is tea. I put it back down on the step and sit next to him. "Stars. I'm sorry, Gregor."

He waves my apology aside. "You're quite within your rights to be suspicious."

"It's none of my business. I shouldn't be sniffing your tea."

"You think I'll fail," he says flatly. When I don't answer,

he looks down at his trembling fingers, takes another savage draw on his smoke. "You've told me enough times that people don't change."

"That's true, I have." But I have a good deal at stake in believing otherwise now. I need to believe that we *can* choose or change our paths, ourselves, that we are not trapped like flies in amber, held by our pointless or terrible destinies.

I examine his face, full of a younger man's anger. It's the kind of righteous anger you would need, I suppose, to try and overthrow a tyrant, to believe it is possible to change a world that remains so stubbornly cruel from one dynasty to the next.

"You've seen this before, I know," he says. "You've seen me fail, just like you saw your old man fail. You've seen it a hundred times."

"Yes," I say.

"It's different this time," he tells me, stabbing his cigarette out on the step.

It's true, I *have* seen it a hundred times. This failure of a man to change, to love the people who need him more than the drug that feeds him, is something I broke my heart on when I was still cutting teeth. I don't know why it's so hard for me to say it, and I don't know if I mean it or not, but I want to mean it, and so I say: "You'll do all right this time, Gregor. I'm sure of it."

His face is like dawn breaking, the way it brightens, and I think, it hurt only a little to give him that.

"It *will* be different. *I* will be. It's all going to be different," he whispers.

"I know it will, I know it," I say, the last part a wheeze as he crushes me in a hug. I put my uninjured arm around his big shoulders. The booze has had Gregor on a leash for so long I don't really believe he knows how to walk the world without it, but by all the holies, I am going to let myself hope for him just a little this time.

⌒

The goodbyes are brief and hushed. Esme has gone out and returned driving a horse cart with a hollow bottom for the princess and the others to hide inside until they get to the tunnel, after which they will go on foot.

I hear the professor murmuring to Frederick, "You *will* take care of her, won't you?" and Frederick offering reassurances. I am surprised that Frederick is staying and Professor Baranyi is going, but nobody questions Mrs. Och's decisions. I suspect that she is not willing to let my crew carry off the princess without one of her own going along too. She might admire Esme, but she does not want to cede control to her.

I wish them luck, half asleep on my feet by now, dread closing like a dark fist around my heart. Csilla tells me again that my hair will grow out, and Esme gets down from the cart to plant a kiss on my forehead. Gregor, Csilla, the professor, and the princess climb one by one into the false bottom of the cart and lie flat. Esme lays the planks back over them, and I am queasily reminded of a coffin being shut. I have an awful feeling that this is the last I will see of them, but I banish the thought, bury it deep. Esme gets back onto the front of the cart, gives the reins a jerk, waves at us, and they are gone into the night.

FORTY-TWO

We are still at our breakfast the following morning when Mrs. Och strides out of her room and says, "I will go to Si Tan now. Bianka, I need strength."

Bianka's expression darkens. "I might need it myself. I've a little boy to take care of."

"Teo," says Theo placidly from Frederick's lap, and I think again that he understands so much now and we need to watch what we say.

"Julia and Frederick can tend to Theo," says Mrs. Och.

"That's not what I mean," says Bianka through gritted teeth.

"Take mine," offers Frederick.

"I need more than that," says Mrs. Och. "I need Bianka." She looks at me. "Or perhaps Julia would do."

"No," I say.

"She's hurt," says Bianka. Mrs. Och swings her eyes back to Bianka, and Bianka breaks her gaze first.

"This is our last attempt to find Ko Dan," says Mrs. Och. "You have seen what Theo will be capable of. We need to remove the text from him not only to protect *him* but to protect the world from a child with such terrible power. I do not know what to expect from Si Tan. I need strength."

Bianka curses under her breath.

"I'll take Theo outside," says Frederick.

"Coward," mutters Bianka, which is unkind, but I think she's right that he does not want to watch. They both look at me then, as if they are expecting me to leave. I stand my ground and stare at Mrs. Och. If she is not ashamed, let her do it in front of me.

Her eyes were blue in Spira City and now they are nearly black, but her piercing glare is the same. She takes Bianka's hands in hers. Bianka's limbs go loose at once, and she sinks to her knees, the deep brown of her complexion dimming, her eyes rolling back, broken sobs shaking loose from her throat—while Mrs. Och's back straightens, power flowing into her, making her seem instantly younger and stronger. It lasts only a minute. Mrs. Och releases her and Bianka crumples to the floor, gasping.

Mrs. Och turns to me, her expression bright and fierce, almost exultant. "Fetch me my cloak," she says.

"Fetch it yourself."

For a moment, I think she will strike me, and if she does, I don't know what I might do. But instead she lets out a little bark of laughter.

"Such children," she scoffs, and strides to her room.

Bianka recovers faster than Frederick or I would, that much is true. Her face is grim and faded, but she gets back up again. I try to help her, but she pushes my arm aside. Mrs. Och sweeps past us with her cloak over her shoulders, out into the sunshine, where Frederick is reading to Theo from the book of fairy tales. In the doorway, Bianka plucks my sleeve. I look at her, our eyes locking—like in the Main Hall at Shou-shu, that moment when she handed Theo to me and let me vanish with him. *I trust you*, her eyes are saying. *I trust* only *you*. I know what she is asking me.

"Shall I come with you?" I call after Mrs. Och. "I could keep an eye out."

"No," says Mrs. Och, already at the gate now, brimming with Bianka's youth and power. "Wait here."

But I go anyway.

⁓

I ignore the sharp twinge deep inside my arm when I vanish. Mrs. Och hails a motor carriage, and my heart sinks. I can't run behind the carriage vanished, certainly not with my arm throbbing under its bandage, the pain jarring me with every step. I manage to hold on to the back of the carriage with my uninjured arm, and I thank the stars for the smooth, paved roads of Tianshi.

She gets out, paying the boy at the Huanglong Gate, and announces herself to the Ru. In no time she is being marched along the broad streets within the compound. I follow, vanished two steps back, everything a muffled blur around me. Something still tugs at my stitches, insistent.

This time we do not go up the steps to the Imperial Residences but stop at one of the sprawling white courtyard houses at the foot of it. We pass through a leafy outer courtyard, through an archway, and into an attractive outdoor pavilion in one of the inner courtyards. A woman dressed in silk, with black hair hanging straight down her back, brings delicate wafers and green tea. She speaks sharply to the Ru, who remove themselves by several feet but do not go away. She seems too young to be Si Tan's wife but too elegant to be a servant, and who knows which is more plausible—that he should have a very young wife or a very elegant servant.

Mrs. Och seats herself on a pillowed bench in the pavilion, and I position myself slightly behind her. We do not have to wait long before Si Tan emerges from the main house in a gorgeous embroidered robe. The woman in silk has disappeared. He comes toward Mrs. Och, bowing, his manner quite different from every other time I've seen him. There is a tension and an eagerness about him now. He almost seems nervous.

"Och Farya," he says in his flawless Fraynish. "It is an honor to meet you."

She nods, and gestures for him to sit down, as if this is her place. I want to see her face, but even vanished two steps back, I feel safer out of her line of sight. The stitches in my arm are straining, something pulling at them.

"You tried to trick me," she says.

"I beg your pardon. I did not know for certain *whom* I was tricking. I met an unusual group of foreigners in my city, lying to my face and seeking Ko Dan, and I wanted to find out why."

"You know what the boy is."

"Gennady's son, and vessel to one-third of *The Book of Disruption*," he says placidly.

"What does the grand librarian of Yongguo want with a fragment of *The Book of Disruption*? Surely you do not intend to put it in your library."

"I want what your brother Gennady wanted, but sooner."

"The text fragment destroyed," she says. "*The Book of Disruption* rendered forever incomplete, unreadable."

"Yes. The world belongs to human empires now, and I do not like to think what kind of world Casimir would make. But my understanding was that you were against the idea of the Book's destruction."

"I was," says Mrs. Och. "But Casimir has lost his senses. I see no other way to keep him from reassembling the Book now."

"If the fragment is destroyed, *The Book of Disruption* will be broken forever. The spirits have faded already. Witches here and there will be all that is left of magic in the world. You are at peace with that?"

"No," she says. "Not at peace. But it is inevitable."

"I am glad we agree," says Si Tan, though he looks more wary than relieved.

"Where is Ko Dan?" asks Mrs. Och.

"You do not need Ko Dan to destroy the text, Och Farya. If the text is bound to the boy, it will perish with him."

"I know that," she says impatiently. "I want Ko Dan to take the text *out* of the child. Then we will destroy it."

"It cannot be done."

"I would like to ask Ko Dan himself whether it can be done."

"That is impossible."

"Where is he?"

"It is not your concern. Is that really why you have come all this way? For the child's sake?"

"Yes—for the child's sake," says Mrs. Och. "But not only for the child."

"The princess," he says.

"She is gone," says Mrs. Och. "My people are taking her to Frayne."

A long silence stretches between them. "You took her from Shou-shu," he says slowly.

She nods once. Si Tan steeples his fingers.

"Och Farya, you are making things very difficult for me. If you had come to me from the beginning, we could have worked out this business with the princess together with Gangzi. She was still under his protection, and he is not a man who takes lightly his honor being slighted. What am I to tell him?"

"You may tell him that the princess left the monastery and is returning to Frayne to claim her throne," says Mrs.

Och. "She left of her own accord with her own people. She was never a prisoner, surely."

"Were you responsible for the raid on the Shou-shu Treasury?" he asks.

She inclines her head.

"But nothing was taken. What were you looking for?"

"The Ankh-nu."

He gives a gruff bark of laughter. "You come here brazenly, with no respect for Shou-shu, no respect for me, and admit that you are trying to steal one of the world's great treasures from us? Your lack of grace surprises me, Och Farya."

"Does it? But I do not respect you or that ridiculous sect of monks pretending they can live forever. Why should I? I am not interested in the rules you've invented or the games you play with ancient objects and people whose power runs deeper than your own. I have my own goals."

His expression hardens. "I am sorry to disappoint you, but you will not find the Ankh-nu in the monastery."

"You have lost it, then. I am afraid of who might have it. Did you really hope to use it as Marike did?"

"It's true, then?" he asks her, something greedy and avid coming into his expression. He leans forward. "Did she really live for hundreds of years, using the Ankh-nu to move her essence from one body to another?"

"I believe it is true," says Mrs. Och. "But no one else besides Marike has managed to use the Ankh-nu in that way. Nobody else has been able to coax any magic from it at all . . . except Ko Dan."

Si Tan looks horrified for a moment, like she has struck him. Then he returns to himself and says curtly, "Indeed, Ko Dan *was* able to use it. If he could transfer the essence of the Book into a living body, I dared hope perhaps he could learn to do more than that."

"I suppose it is more likely than your monks learning to live forever by way of asceticism and force of will or some such nonsense."

"The human body fails us all," says Si Tan. "But the *essence*, our inner selves, our intelligence, the *truth* of what we are . . . all of that needs only a vehicle to live on! You cannot understand it. You are not bound as we are to some mortal sack, a frail and aging cage of meat and bone. Surely the spirit of a great man is larger than his fleshly prison and should be able to live beyond it. I will not let all that I am be snuffed out by oblivion. I am *bigger* than that."

"All mortals feel so," says Mrs. Och dismissively. "But they die all the same. I have no wish to lay claim to the Ankh-nu. I only want Ko Dan to use it once. He may be able to save a child's life, destroy the text fragment, and thereby keep the world safe from Casimir. Is it not all to the good?"

"What you ask is impossible."

"Then Ko Dan is dead?"

He lifts his chin, eyes flashing with sudden anger. "You have come to my city without announcing your presence, and every act you have taken has been one of subterfuge or sacrilege. You admit freely that you have no respect for me. What right do you have to demand information, let alone help?"

"Yongguo is the greatest empire in the world, which makes you one of the most powerful men in the world, if not *the* most powerful. I use the word *power* here in the sense of authority, of course. You have no *true* power, nothing that cannot be taken from you. The balance will shift if Casimir reassembles *The Book of Disruption*. Kahge was created by the splitting of the Book, but if the fragments are bound together again, Kahge will be pulled back into the world, everything will be changed, and the order you so cherish will be shattered. We have a shared interest in keeping the Book from my brother. If you fear him, you should help me."

"How can I trust anything you say? How do I know you do not wish to make use of the Book yourself, or that you are not allied with Casimir, as in the past? You ask so much of me, and you have offered me nothing."

"Ah. You want me to offer you something. Do you have any suggestions?"

"Your vanishing girl," he says without hesitating, and I go cold all over.

"No," says Mrs. Och. "She is mine."

I see his lips moving, but I can't hear him anymore. My ears are full of a distant roar, and my arm is bleeding freely, the stitches split wide. The blood is not running down my arm but seeping through the sleeve and out into the air in crimson threads, then vanishing. The pavilion keeps blurring and then brightening, fading in and out of view, and something is pulling, pulling, pulling at my arm, at my blood, the roaring sound rising and drowning them out, then receding again. I need to get out of here. I need to get back to the house. Esme will fix my arm. No, Esme has left already. I need to tell Bianka.

Si Tan is on his feet now, his voice barely controlled: "One single life! For the sake of a hundred thousand lives or more, for the sake of a world that, for all its ills, can still be changed for the better, I beg you to destroy the child and with him *The Book of Disruption*."

My heart gives a horrible jolt. I need to see her face. I try to move closer, but the twinge and tug at my arm becomes a yank, the roar drowning out whatever else they are saying. Blood gushing. I see the pavilion from every angle for a single blurred second—Mrs. Och's face, her lips moving, her yellow teeth—and then I am nowhere, and I can't get back.

I land in the steaming courtyard outside Esme's old building—a gutted wreck here. The statue in the fountain is all tentacles reaching, blood-dark water boiling inside it. From every side of the square, those patchwork creatures are coming.

Some of them have human faces, some of them have wings and are swooping overhead, and many of them are holding those peculiar hooked stalks to their mouths. Everything is pouring out of my arm—all thought and breath and strength—and *he* is bounding toward me with something close to grace, the fox-faced beast with his majestic antlers. In his gray rotting hand he has the jagged, glittering blade that sliced my arm open.

I try to pull away, back to the world, but I can't feel the edge of things. I can't find my way out of here. As if this is everywhere. As if the world I know is gone. The antlered beast is closing on me fast, and I jump.

It is almost like flying. I feel like Pia. I go right over his head, landing on the other side of him, and stagger, amazed at myself. More and more of them are swarming. A jackal-faced thing comes at me, and the hook on his stalk bites my shoulder. I grab the creature by the neck and toss him aside, pull the hook out of me. Oh, I am strong here, *strong*. Even dizzy and bleeding, I am stronger and faster than they are.

Still, there are too many of them. Another hook bites at me, and another. Talons rake across my back. I hurl another off me—this one knots of muscle without skin, wielding something that looks like a common garden hoe. A boar-headed monster with a spear charges me. I dodge and grab the spear, yanking it from its owner, and his half-rotten arm comes away with it.

Then something pulls at my very heart, an awful lurching, like when Mrs. Och took my life force to save us from Casimir—something deep and fundamental being grabbed, stolen. A hook has got me on the arm, and the stalk seems to have come alive, turning a fleshy pink, bending and swirling.

A bat-faced thing sucks on the other end of it, poised on several hairy legs. I can barely feel my hands to move them, but I pull the hook out of me with fumbling fingers, and immediately I feel my strength returning.

They are closing in around me, shuffling, monstrous, and now I know to fear the hooks, to get them out of me before they sap my strength. Shouts of *"Lidari! Lidari!"* rise up. I feel a sharp burn and push in my side. The antlered fox-beast is looming over me, making to swing his blade again. I tear the hooks out of my skin and bound away from them as fast as I can. Now a bright, hot pain is radiating out from my side, and I can feel blood running out of the wound.

I flee, and they follow, screeching *"Lidari!"* Near the river, with a little distance from the mob, I can feel it again, the space around me. I pull away so fast, thinking of nothing but escape, and I land, hard—right between Mrs. Och and Si Tan in the pavilion.

In seconds, the Ru have closed around the pavilion, bows drawn. Mrs. Och throws off her cloak, wings tearing out of her back, her face blooming into its half-animal self. She stretches out her arms as if to ward off the Ru, and in a voice that echoes like a hundred voices, she cries: "She is mine!"

Si Tan's face is truly fearful for the first time. He is shouting at her in Yongwen. I stagger to my feet. My tunic is sticking to me, blood on my arm, on my side, everywhere.

"I'm sorry," I sob at Mrs. Och. Throwing myself on her mercy. The Ru are waiting for Si Tan's command. She scoops me into her arms like I'm a child and cries: "Make way!"

Si Tan makes an angry gesture at the Ru and they fall back. Mrs. Och carries me through the Imperial Gardens to the Huanglong Gate, but I pass out before we reach it.

FORTY-THREE

A light rain is falling when I wake. My side and arm are clumsily bandaged. I scramble out of the bedroom. Frederick is in the main room, scribbling in his little notebook, but he drops it as soon as he sees me. The front doors are open, and I can see Bianka washing diapers outside, Theo galloping around her on his toy horse.

"Bianka," Frederick calls to her in a low voice. She leaves the diapers and comes running up the steps. Theo drops the horse, darts past her, and throws his arms around my leg.

I cry out with the impact, my side exploding with pain. Bianka pulls him off me.

"Ouch?" he says in surprise.

"What happened?" whispers Bianka.

"Si Tan's not going to help us," I gasp, fighting my nausea.

"I know that. But what happened to *you*?"

"It's complicated. How angry is she?"

"Difficult to say. She hasn't come out of her room."

I touch the bandage wrapped around my middle. "Who fixed me up?"

"I did," says Frederick. "Stitches too. Sorry—I'm not very good at it."

"Hounds. Well, thanks. Have I been out long?"

"Not so very long," Bianka begins, and then Mrs. Och emerges from her room.

"Julia." Her voice would freeze live flame. "Explain yourself."

"I followed you." No point lying now. "I'm sorry. I was . . . I don't know what happened. I was *pulled* into Kahge. I was vanished, just like normal, but they pulled me right through and . . . they were trying to kill me—but I got out. They can *pull* me there!"

"Why did you follow me?"

Her face is terrible. I've never seen her in such a rage, but I realize suddenly that she is *afraid*. But of what? Of *me*?

I look at Bianka. She says nothing, holding on to Theo and staring at the ground. I suppose that's only fair. She depends on Mrs. Och far more than I do. She can't come out and say, after everything, that she doesn't trust her. So it's on me.

"I wanted to know what passed between you," I say, lifting my chin.

Her face twists. She grabs my shoulders and pulls me close to her, peering into my eyes, searching for something. I gasp with pain, my arm and my side crying out.

344

"Lidari?" she whispers, so close to me I can taste her stale breath. I shake free of her, staggering back.

"No!" I yelp. "It's me, Julia!"

She straightens and says stiffly: "Yesterday I made you an offer of permanent employment. I withdraw that offer now. You no longer work for me. Not in the future and not now. I gave you a second chance after you betrayed me, and you have betrayed me again. I am done with you. Leave my house now and do not return."

All the air goes out of me.

Bianka's hand flies to her heart. Theo has wriggled out of her arms, and now he is hanging on to my leg, staring up at us with big, frightened eyes. He knows something important is happening.

"Promise me you won't do what he said," I say. "You won't harm Theo. Promise me that. Promise Bianka."

Bianka picks Theo up and takes a step back.

"I did not cross the world in the evening of my life to do him harm," says Mrs. Och evenly. She has recovered and is quite in control of herself again. "I shall do everything within my power to protect him, as I have done since I knew of his existence. But it is no business of yours any longer. Now go."

"I need help!" I beg her. "Those creatures *pulled* me into Kahge and tried to kill me!"

"You'll have no help from me."

Frederick's head is bowed. If he won't speak up for me, I really am done here. I force my voice to be steady. "I reckon you owe me some of that gold, then."

"I owe you nothing," says Mrs. Och, her voice rising again. "You will leave now, or I will destroy you where you stand."

"You can't!" cries Bianka. "This is Julia!"

"Julia, who was a spy and our enemy, who kidnapped your son, who has proved herself untrustworthy yet again, and who may not be who she claims to be at all," says Mrs. Och. "She is lucky I am willing to let her go."

I am trying to think of some response—*may not be who she claims to be?*—but she cuts me off before I can find words: "Your brother will be paid in full and dismissed. You may return to Frayne or wherever you like with him, but do not let me see you again."

"Lala!" says Theo urgently, reaching for me. I look at Bianka, who has pressed a hand to her mouth, her eyes filling.

"You'll be all right," I say to her, which is completely senseless, of course. I ought to say something more, but I can't bear to say goodbye to them, and I can't bear Mrs. Och's eyes on me anymore. So I just go.

FORTY-FOUR

Even without vanishing, I can feel it—the tug at my stitches, under my bandages. Suddenly it is like a hook to the wound in my side. The street blurs and slides sideways, and I am hanging above it all, my perspective widening, wheeling outward. I fling myself back into my body in the road, and as I do so, I feel the stitches tearing again. Panic pours through me, fast and cold. *They can reach me here where I stand, here in my body, in the world.* The wounds are straining under the bandages, blood seeping out of the lesser scratches on my shoulders, neck, and forearm. I break into a run. At first I think I am going to Dek's, but I change my mind halfway. I go to Count Fournier's house and bang on the outer door. Nobody answers.

"Jun!" I shout. I go down on one knee and pick the lock, go through the outer courtyard, and bang on the next door, then pick that lock as well. When I get the door open, there he is, pointing his gun at me.

"Get out," he says.

"I need your help," I beg. "Please. I'm hurt."

The gun doesn't scare me as much as it should. I am as sure as I can be that Jun isn't going to shoot me. I lift my tunic so he can see the blood-drenched bandage around my middle. "Look," I say.

He stares at the bandage and then at my face, bouncing lightly on his toes. It breaks my heart a little. How quickly I've come to love that coiled restlessness in him, the way he looks like he might, at any moment, break into a sprint or start turning cartwheels. Just the other night he kissed me in the tree until I didn't know up from down anymore, and now here we are.

I grope for words to persuade him. "It's just me. Julia." Is that the truth? Oh Nameless, please let it be the truth! "What happened before—it was an accident. I need help or I'm going to bleed out."

I feel faint, but I can't tell if it's from blood loss or if I am being pulled out of the world again. I grab the doorframe like I'm clinging to this place, this moment, gripping so hard that the wood digs into my hand. That brings me back to myself a little. *"Please."* I'm weeping openly now. "It's me, it's just me."

He tucks the gun into his belt.

"Come."

I follow him through the inner courtyard to a narrow room at the back of the house, the roof collapsed. It is all boxes and clutter and bits of broken tile everywhere, half open to the sky. He picks his way through the wreckage, never turning his back on me for more than an instant, and finds somewhere a metal box with antiseptic, bandages, and such.

"Hullo."

I hadn't seen Count Fournier, and I jump at his voice. He is sprawled in a corner, an empty bottle of brandy next to him. As I turn toward him, everything blurs again, that dizzying pull at my wounds coming from nowhere. I fall to my knees, press my hands to the floor, breathing hard. I need to concentrate just to stay here, in this place, in this body.

I try to focus on him leaning against the wall, legs loose on the floor, head bobbing, a silly grin on his face. It's so oddly familiar. I used to come home to find my father like this.

"Jun says you are some kind of monster," he says, sounding entirely happy.

"I'm not." But maybe I am. I don't know what I am.

"Sit here," says Jun, finding an unbroken chair. I pull myself into it. He removes my tunic—an unhappy echo of the other night—and unwraps the bandage. I hoped then that he thought I was pretty, that he liked my body. Now I only hope not to terrify or disgust him. With my unhurt arm, I hold my bloody, torn tunic over my chest, because even in this state I feel self-conscious sitting half naked in front of Count Fournier, drunk as he is.

"What happen?" asks Jun, touching my side with such soft fingers. "These stiches are rip right open."

"Something's after me," I say between clenched teeth. There it is again—pulling, pulling. Jun backs away, eyes widening in horror. The blood does not run down my side. It flows outward, away from me, into the air, and disappears. Wisps of blood are escaping from the lesser scratches and floating away from me too.

"Make it stop," I whisper. I'm so afraid he's going to run away and leave me. I watch him get a handle on himself, make a decision.

"I give you some whiskey."

"I may have drunk it all," drawls the count.

"I'll manage without," I say.

Jun stares at me a second and then gives a short nod. He kneels next to me, setting straight to work. He is not as fast or as steady as Esme, but he stitches my side back up. Maybe it's pointless—they will just rip me open again. But the hot, sharp pain of the needle focuses me. I try not to jerk away, to hang on to the pain that keeps me in my body. The blurring and the sense of slipping out of myself stops.

"You're not a monster," says Count Fournier, watching me. "I've known a few. Believe me."

"Thanks," I manage to grind out between my teeth.

"How is the princess?" he asks.

"Gone. They left last night."

"Good."

Jun breaks off the thread and sets about stitching up my arm. I squeeze my eyes shut, but that's worse. I need to see the world and feel the pain as much as possible. I stare at the sky through the gaps in the roof and grind my teeth.

"I get you clean bandages," he says when he's done. I turn toward him, and a deep tremor goes through me, looking at his face up close—close enough to kiss. The slant of his cheekbones, the line of his jaw, those full lips and black eyes—I think of his mouth against mine, his hands moving over me. How I can still want him in this condition, I don't know, but I do.

"Can I have the needle?" I ask.

He looks at me, his eyebrows going down.

"It helps," I say. "Pain helps . . . keep me here."

He hands me the blood-slicked needle wordlessly and goes rooting around for bandages.

"What will you do?" I ask the count, trying to ignore my blood battering against the new stitches. My arm and my side are burning, but I'll take the pain gladly over the other-worldly pull. "Don't you want to go home?"

"This is home, as much as anywhere, by now," he says, waving a hand around the broken, cluttered room. "But as for what I will *do*—who knows? I worry about Jun. He'll have to find other employment."

"I like his prospects better than yours," I say frankly.

He chuckles at that. "Well, I'm an old toad now. I've stopped caring much what becomes of me. Oh, I would like to see Princess Zara on the throne in Frayne. To see my childhood home again. To feel I had something to give. But the distance from here to there is . . ." He holds up the empty bottle and examines it. "Unmanageable," he says at last. His eyes fall closed for a long moment, and I think he might be asleep, but then they flick open again and he smiles at me.

Because I think I have to, I tell him: "I heard that Lady Laroche, your aunt, has been executed. I'm sorry."

"I feared it might be so," he says. "You know, when I was little—hounds, I was afraid of her." He laughs. "But she won me over. She wins everyone over, given a chance. I can't quite imagine . . . I've never known anybody so alive. It is hard to imagine her dead."

Jun wraps my side and my arm firmly with the clean bandages and helps me pull the bloody tunic back on. Whenever I feel the edges of things starting to blur, that tug, I stab myself in the thigh with the needle, which jolts me right back to myself. That is something, at least. Jun backs away, watching me, and the wariness in his gaze hurts almost as much as my stitched-up wounds.

"What you will do now?" he asks me.

"Have you heard of a witch called Silver Moya?"

"Everybody know Silver Moya," he says.

"Silver Moya!" cries Count Fournier. "The plot thickens!" He begins to giggle.

"She is unlicensed witch," says Jun. "But she never get arrested. Just small things. Luck charms, bone casting, illegal potion."

"I need to go see her," I say. "Later . . . I'll explain everything. Or I'll try, anyway."

"Explain," he says, his voice hardening.

"I will."

"Now."

The pull, the drift, the slide. I see his eyes widen, and I think I must be fading. I drive the needle into my leg a bit too hard and yell with pain. He flinches as I return to myself.

"Explain now," he says. "Or do not come back here."

I roll the needle between my fingers. I can get through this, I tell myself. Deep breaths and needle jabs. I can confess the whole bewildering, ugly thing to the only person I've known who seems so much *like me*, except for one enormous difference—that I might not be a person at all.

So I tell him.

When I was a child, my parents never talked about witches or magic or the Lorian Uprising. We saw the wreckage of the old ways around us for a few years, and then even those last hints of the way things once were disappeared as well. I remember the smashed shrines in the woods outside Forrestal, the old folks sitting on their stoops and muttering to one another, many of them with scars and burn marks, and, of course, the Cleansings, where women, young and old, quaked on the big government barge and were tossed into the river Syne to drown.

One of the stories my mother told us was about a bear and a girl who switched bodies. They woke up one morning, each in their own home, but in the wrong body. They had to flee their families and homes, for the bear-in-girl's-body would have been eaten, and the girl-in-bear's-body would have been shot and killed. They were not safe anymore among their own kind, having ceased to *be* their own kind. The bear-in-girl's-body ended up begging in the city. She did not speak any human language, and she was friendless and alone and confused. The girl-in-bear's-body had to learn to hunt in the forest, and she was shunned by other bears, who sensed that something was amiss. But as the years went by, they learned how to be what they had become. The bear-in-girl's-body learned language and how to use it, she learned the rules of the human world, and she even fell in love. Likewise, the girl-in-bear's-body learned how to be a bear—how to catch fish in the river, gather berries, and be with other bears. Still, they both thought often of their old lives, their true families.

One evening, when the moon was full, the bear-turned-girl crept into the forest. She wanted to wade in the stream, dig in the earth, feel her old world around her. That same night, the girl-turned-bear crept into the city. She wanted so badly to see a human face, to smell bread baking, to hear speech and laughter and song.

Well, this being one of my mother's stories, you can imagine how it ended. The bear-turned-girl romped through the woods, happy as can be, until a pack of wolves set upon her and tore her to pieces. When she died, her body turned back into the body of a bear. The girl-turned-bear was spotted in the city and shot. The bullet did not kill her, but the moment the bear-turned-girl in the woods was killed by wolves, the spell lifted. The girl-bear turned back into a young woman, bleeding from the gunshot wound in her side. The people thought she must be a witch, and they threw her into the river. She was bleeding heavily, and they would not let her swim to shore, and so she drowned.

My mother stroked my hair as I wept and said, "Oh, come now, it's only a story," but I know she didn't believe that, and she would not have told me such a terrible story only for my entertainment. Now I wonder what she thought the story meant. Wonder if it means that magic is random and brutal, that we cannot choose it, and it can change us, take us from ourselves and from the lives we might have wished for if we had not been somehow chosen. Or if the point is that you can never stop being who you are and loving what you love, no matter how you change on the outside.

Or perhaps it means that you will never stop longing for who you *thought* you were before you became something else.

I think of that old story again as I am telling Jun about who I used to be—a pleasure-loving girl with a skill that set her apart and with no moral compass to speak of—and who I am now, the big question mark. I tell him about the Xian-ren, and Kahge, and *The Book of Disruption*. I tell him about Pia and Si Tan. I tell him how afraid I am of what I might be, of why I can vanish. I tell him about Theo, and I tell him the awful thing I did. I tell him everything.

When I'm done, he meets my eyes for a long moment, and

he looks more thoughtful than afraid. I want so much to touch his face, but I don't dare.

"I forgive you what you did to me," he says gravely. "Do not do that again."

"I promise."

"Good. I go with you to Silver Moya."

FORTY-FIVE

We enter the clock shop Professor Baranyi and Frederick went to the other night. The benign-looking old man who opened the door to them is at the counter. When Jun asks him for Silver Moya, he waves a hand at the curtain behind him. In the workshop behind the curtain, the same woman, dressed in simple peasant garb, is sitting cross-legged on the dirty floor, tinkering with a clock. She has a wide, sweet face—the kind of face you trust instinctively. She puts down the clock and the screwdriver when we come in and pushes back her dirty hair.

"You talk," says Jun to me.

"I want see . . . ," I start in hesitant Yongwen, but then I don't know how to say it, and so I finish in Fraynish: "Ragg Rock."

The woman rises and puts away her clock, clearing the worktable behind her. She climbs up on a stepladder at the back of the room and takes a little bird from one of the cages onto her crooked finger, brings it over to the table, and gestures at me to sit. The tabletop is sticky, and the stool is so high that it leaves my legs dangling like a child's.

In a very businesslike manner, as if she's about to take an order for a custom-made clock, Silver Moya scatters a bit of seed on the table, then unrolls a piece of rice paper, opens her inkpot, pours a little ink into a bowl, and takes out her brush with the sharp blade on one end. The sparrow hops around, pecking at the seed. Silver Moya reaches for my hand, her face smiling and kind.

"I need a little blood," she says in careful Yongwen. "May I?"

I offer my hand, still holding the needle Jun gave me in the hand of my hurt arm. She slices the soft pad of my thumb and then holds it over the inky bowl, squeezing out a few thick, scarlet drops. I'm relieved that this blood, at least, does not float away and disappear. She releases my hand, then bunches her mouth up and dips the brush.

I see everything up close for a moment—the bristles of the brush emerging from the bowl, heavy and dripping with darkness. The brush comes down on the page, and I feel the jolt of it, the potency of this magic, all natural law crushed between the ink-black brush and the empty page. Dark, wet lines move across the paper, and everything shifts. I smell rain. Lightheaded, I fumble the needle and it slips between my fingers. Sound is amplified—the needle hits the floor with an awful crash—and then the final stroke of the brush sweeps everything aside, leaves the world changed.

The sparrow hops around on the table, chirping. The room has gone shadowy and still. The little bird is the only thing properly in focus. It is bright and moving, every feather twitching with life and color. It cocks its head and chirps at me. Silver Moya is still as a statue—Jun, likewise, motionless, a silhouette. The bird takes off from the table, flying out an open door I had not seen, a bright door leading into the world. The bird's movement is like a hook inside me, and I twist after it, nearly falling off the stool in my hurry to follow. I want to say something to Jun, but words are far-off, sticky things, and I am light as air, flowing after the bird.

Outside, the city is like a painting, one-dimensional, unmoving. Only the bird and I are alive, in motion. The bird shoots down the street, dipping and rising, and I run after it, light on my feet. Like the bird, I am real, I am alive, fluid and shining. I pass people in the streets, but their faces are blank and wooden, their expressions painted on. The road curves, and I follow the bird up stone steps that wind and twist up a craggy hill that has never been in this city before. Tianshi seethes below, falling farther and farther behind us. The air turns sharp, acrid. The bird falls like a stone and lies smoking at my feet, its feathers singed.

Before me, there is a crumbled archway—or what must have been an archway once, but now the top is broken and so it is two curved pillars in the road, crusted with lichen. My blood hums, and I step through it, over the scorched bird.

The road runs straight into a muddy swamp. A mist lies over the swamp, obscuring whatever is beyond it. Behind me, the stone stairs are crumbling down toward the painted city. I can go back or I can go forward. I step into the mud and instantly sink up to my thigh. I wade a bit, and it gets deeper, rising over the wound in my side. What am I to do? Then the ground is gone and I am flailing, looking for something to hang on to, but there is nothing. I swim through the thick muck and into the mist, where I can see nothing at all.

FORTY-SIX

My hand touches slippery rock. Weak with relief at finding something solid, I clamber up onto the shore, my clothes heavy with mud. The fog around me lifts, and there is—I want to say a woman, but she is not quite that—a creature shaped like a woman on the path before me, pointing a bow, with arrow drawn, at me, but the bow and the arrow are made of fire. I blink, but the apparition is still there.

"Hold on, don't shoot." I scramble to my feet. A rope of mud bursts out of the ground and wraps itself around my ankle. I scream and try to kick it off, thinking it a snake or some creature living in the mud, but then another one bursts forth and grabs my other ankle. The mud vines give a yank, and I am flat on my belly, winded, on the ground before the woman-thing and her fiery bow and arrow.

"Please . . . ," I begin, but I can't decide—please, *what?*

She is naked, a reddish brown color, and there is something odd about her skin—something claylike about its consistency.

Her face too appears to be made of wet clay and is not holding its shape very well. Her eyebrows are mossy clumps, her hair a shag of weeds and reeds, her eyes black stones, shiny and unmoving. When she bares her teeth at me, they look to have been stuck haphazardly into her gums—each one sharpened to a point. She is a terrible thing to behold.

"Raaaa," she gurgles at me—a thick, muddy sound.

"Is this Ragg Rock?" I cry.

She jerks her head at me, as if to say, *Go on*. Or maybe *Go away*—who can tell?

"I'm in trouble. I need help. . . ." I realize suddenly that I don't feel it here—that tug from Kahge. My arm and my side hurt badly, but it is an ordinary pain, the kind of thing you would expect to feel after being whacked with a sword and then stitched up without anesthetic. "There's a little boy, a happy, gorgeous fellow, but he's got part of *The Book of Disruption* stuck in him, and he's going to end up killed or worse if we can't get it out of him."

I'm babbling. Slow down, Julia. Figure out what's going on here. What this thing is. Where you are.

"Raaaa," she says again. Then, gurglingly: "Hel-lo."

"Hello," I pant.

"Raaaaaaggh. Tell me . . . more."

"Is this Ragg Rock?" I ask again.

"I am," she says. Her voice sounds a bit less liquid. She folds the flaming bow and arrow into a sphere between her hands and extinguishes it. The tentacles, or whatever they are, fall away from my feet, crumbling into mud. I rise slowly.

"Do not . . . *hurt* me," she says.

The mud around my feet curls up like a wave, threatening, as if to back her up.

"Of course I won't," I say. "I didn't come here to hurt anybody."

She really is made of mud and clay, I realize—like somebody tried to build the semblance of a woman out of earth and moss and stone. There are cracks in the dry clay of her legs, and yet she moves quite as well as I do. Rather better, at the moment.

"Come," she says, beckoning me along the path, up the hill—a craggy, damp rock covered in moss and brambles. The sky is an evening color, a deep blue-gray, with shreds of cloud moving fast over it, but no sun or moon or stars that I can see. Muddy rivulets run down the hill to the swamp below, which surrounds the rock like a moat. A black hut stands at the top of the hill—black, as though it has been burnt, though it stands firm enough—and all at once I recognize this place from the vision of my mother with the Ankh-nu. She was *here*—my mother was here—and the memory comes back vividly, the way I felt looking at her, that awful longing, but it wasn't *me*, please Nameless, it wasn't me.

I climb after Ragg Rock. When I look behind me, I can see Tianshi tumbling at the bottom of the hill, beyond the swamp, a little bit askew. The green rice fields and the forests stream out from the city and its tilting walls. There is Tama-shan, poking up like a red finger, and beyond it, the desert. As I look, I feel the world rushing toward me, or my perspective soaring out over it, over the desert. There are walled cities, the rivers and railroads that zig and zag between them, miles of terraced rice fields cut out of the hills, old fortresses where warlords sit glowering in heavy robes. I put out a hand to steady myself as it all goes zooming past me. A woman drinking from a jeweled cup, out her window the yellow sand whipped by the wind. The grasslands becoming foothills becoming mountains. It is moving too fast—the swaying ocean, palaces, and villages, wild beasts hunkered down in their dark places, old women whispering around fires, children playing on muddy riverbanks. It is like seeing everything up close and from a great distance all at once—an exaggerated version of how I see when I am midway between the world and Kahge. I yank my gaze from the wide world and stagger on the path behind Ragg Rock. Dizzy, I hurry after her, leaving the world reeling and unspooling behind me.

When we reach the little hut, she does not take me inside but, instead, takes me around to the back of it, to the other side of the hill.

Far below us, a ghostly, smoking Spira City forms and dissolves along with other places I have seen, and places I've never laid eyes on too. Cities and forests rise up, take shape, then undulate and collapse, becoming something else. Beyond this shifting, burning no place, black cliffs and mountains spit fire, and beyond those, that giant whorl of purplish green cloud, spinning and roaring.

"Kahge," I say, and Ragg Rock croaks, "Kahge."

"What is that?" I ask, pointing at the roaring storm of cloud in the far distance.

"That? I wonder. Maybe it is the edge of . . . something, or everything."

"*Maybe?* Don't you know?"

"Why would I know?"

She looks right at me, and that is unsettling. Can she really *see* me with those black stones stuck unevenly in the mud of her face?

"Speak more," she says. "Tell me . . ." She thinks for a moment. "Tell me a story."

Oh, for heaven's sake. Now I'm to tell fairy tales to Ragg Rock, whatever she is, wherever this is, and who knows what is happening back at Mrs. Och's. But I don't know what to do except obey. I tell her the story of the girl-bear and the bear-girl that I thought of at Count Fournier's house. She nods avidly while I speak. When it's finished, I say, "It's not a very nice story, is it?"

"It's a very good story," she says, speaking more easily now. One of her teeth has come loose and is hanging lopsidedly from her gums, which are the same red-brown mud as the rest of her. "Come inside—I want to show you something."

I follow her into the hut. There is nothing much here, nowhere to sit, just a cauldron boiling with, as far as I can tell, more red mud, and a hutch made of wire and wood.

"Look," she says, squatting by the hutch. I crouch next to her. Inside it, a thin brown rabbit is sniffing despondently at

365

a pile of grass. Ragg Rock reaches one of her clay hands into the hutch and strokes the rabbit's back.

"This is my bunny," she croons. "He's so soft. I can't decide what to name him."

I have no idea what to say. She looks at me with those pebble eyes. Her voice is much less garbled now. "Do you want to pet him?"

I don't particularly, but I reach in and stroke the soft fur. He is warm, and breathing fast.

"So there are animals here?" I say.

"No—he is from the world. Tianshi's Silver Moya brought him to me as a present. Wasn't that nice? She thought I'd like a pet."

Is that the key to magical, otherworldly assistance? Bring a fluffy bunny to the made-of-mud creature at the edge of the world? Wouldn't Mrs. Och be surprised to hear it.

"He's lovely," I say. It comes out sarcastic. Hounds, be nice to the mad mud woman, Julia. Try not to get killed.

"What should I name him?"

"Oh, I don't know. What about George? He looks like a George."

"Does he?" She turns her gaze back to the rabbit, stroking his back rhythmically. "That's what I'll call him. I like him. I like to touch him. I'm lonely."

"I'm not surprised." It is hard to imagine a more desolate place, and surely there can be no place more isolated.

"You've come to ask me for help, haven't you?"

"I suppose so." It seems foolish now—given that I don't

really know where this is, what she is, what her allegiances might be, if any.

A rumble in her throat, like a growl. She rises, making an impatient gesture for me to follow.

"People want things," she says, striding out of the hut and around to the side of it. "The shadows in Kahge want things too: *Make us whole. Make us alive.* How am I to do *that?* Mothers from the world come, begging me to return their dead children or some such impossible thing, and I can't, and I don't want to watch anybody else drown themselves in the mud. Witches come, and they say they will give me things, but they *do not have* things I want. Sometimes they try to hurt me because I cannot help them. They think they can *make* me do things. They think they can take something from me, from this place. I don't like that. I don't let the strong ones come here, the ones who might hurt me, not them, I don't let them in, never."

So that's why the Xianren could never reach her. Quite right of her to fear them too. I'm confused by her sudden fluency, the casual tone, why she speaks Fraynish when she seemed not to use language at all mere minutes ago.

"I won't hurt you," I say.

She looks at me, and her muddy lips form a smile. "I know. *You* cannot hurt me. But I need more food for the rabbit."

"What kind of food?"

"Silver Moya gave me apples and lettuce, but he ate them all, and now I have just grass and corn for him. He doesn't care for grass and corn so much. The corn isn't right, anyway.

She hasn't come back. She brought me the rabbit because I asked her to live here with me. She's afraid I won't let her leave if she comes again. But I only want food for the rabbit, *nice* things that he likes."

She looks as desperately unhappy as someone with a face made of mud could possibly look.

"I could bring you apples and lettuce," I say. "Where did you get him corn? I don't see any corn here."

She pats the big boulder we've stopped at, and I realize it is not a boulder but a massive dial. The black face of the rock is shot through with streaks of copper and silver and iron. Characters that look vaguely like the old pictorial Yongwen characters I saw in the Imperial Library are carved all around the edges of the rock face. The dial at the center points to a character very like the Yongwen character for *earth* that I've seen at small shrines by the road.

Ragg Rock grabs the dial and twists it to the right with an awful grinding sound that I feel in my teeth and bones. The rock shudders under my feet. A thick blanket of moss crawls over the ground, and trees shoot up like spikes out of the moat at the bottom of the little hill, branches spreading outward and bursting into green. They grow up and up, obscuring the view of the city below, creeping up the hill toward us. Dusky, skeletal butterflies the size of my head come winging out of the sudden woods, spiraling around the hut behind us and into the evening-colored sky, and there are other flickering shapes among the trees, like animals, but not fixed, colorless.

"I can find some things," says Ragg Rock. "The bugs are the most real, but my rabbit does not like bugs. I can find grass and grain." She twists the dial again, and the woods collapse into a cornfield, tall and yellow. I stagger as the moss under my feet recedes.

"Water," she says with another twist, and water pours out of the rock, the cornfield tumbling into a proper moat now, like a river circling the hill, bright and fresh and moving. "Animals must have water, you know. I can keep him *alive*, but he liked the apples and the lettuce best, the things from the world. I've found some trees that bear fruit, but not apple trees. I've found crops, but not lettuce." She yanks the dial again. The ground heaves. I think I'm going to throw up. I grab the boulder to keep myself steady, and the water turns back into mud. She turns a horrible, sharp-toothed grin toward me.

"I liked your story about the girl and the bear. I can tell someone has hurt you. If you bring me some apples and lettuce, you can stay here as long as you like. This is a good place to hide. Nobody would find you. Nobody can come if I don't let them in, and I can tell when somebody asks to come—the blood tells me things—what they fear and what they want, how strong they are."

"I'll bring you apples and lettuce," I manage to say, cautiously letting go of the rock now that she seems to be done changing the landscape. "But I can't stay. I wanted . . . I thought maybe you would know what I am."

"Why would I know?" she asks, impatience creeping into

her voice. "Everybody thinks I will just *know* things. I know *some* things. I have this view"—she sweeps her hand in a circle, taking in both open doorways of the hut, the world at one side and Kahge at the other—"and I've been watching things happen for . . . oh, a *very* long time. But I don't know *you*. You look like a girl. Aren't you a girl?"

I realize with a horrible start that she is sounding more and more like *me*. Not just the way she speaks—her casual, low-class Fraynish, which sprang up after her initial gurgles and foreign-sounding hello—but her *voice*. After several minutes with me, she has learned to mimic me perfectly, borrowing my language and my *sound*.

"Maybe I am," I say. "You said those shadows in Kahge ask you for things."

"They want to come into the world, be real, be whole. This is the closest any of them get. They can see the world from here, if I let them. I don't anymore. Not since one of them got out. I made a mistake. I get lonely sometimes, and I make mistakes."

One of them got out. I feel sick.

"I've been to Kahge," I say. "I can go there."

She looks at me with those pebble eyes and says, "How?"

"I don't know. I just can. And some of the shadows are not really very shadowy. They have bodies. I mean, their bodies are like a mix of animals from the world."

"Oh, *them*," she says, almost sheepishly, if it's possible for a mud woman to look sheepish. "I know the ones you mean. That was a mistake too."

"What are they?"

"Just shadows, like the others. But a witch came to me . . . oh, nearly half a century ago now. I should never have let her in. Too strong. But so much grief that it pushed out everything else I might have seen, and I was curious what she meant to do with all the body parts."

"Body parts?" I say faintly.

"She made a deal with them. She met them here and brought them parts from the world. She fastened those parts onto them with magic so they would have bodies. And she gave them other things too. They can love and feel pain, they can sleep and even eat. I wanted to see if it would work."

"Why did she do it? What did they do for her?"

"They each gave her some essence. A tiny bit. Enough for a terrible spell, to bring life back to someone she'd lost. But I don't think it went how she wanted. She tried to come back here again, and there was so much rage it frightened me. I didn't let her. She tries, and I never let her. And those shadows with the body parts are angry too and trying to get into the world, and I don't let them come here either anymore. Too much trouble. The whole thing was a mistake."

I reckon I can guess what they want with *me*. I think about those hooks biting into me, the sucking tubes, the way it felt like my core was being pulled loose. Perhaps they think they can take from me whatever enables me to cross over. Perhaps they can.

But that doesn't explain why they call me Lidari. So I tell

her: "I saw them in Kahge. They tried to kill me. And . . . they called me Lidari."

The mossy eyebrows go up. Something guarded comes into her expression.

"Lidari was their leader," she says, and then adds after a long pause: "But he's gone now."

"Gone where?" I ask, thinking, Please *not* inside my skin and bones.

"I don't know."

"You said one of them got out. Did you mean Lidari?"

She nods slowly. She is not relaxed anymore. She has gone very wary.

"When?"

"The last time . . . maybe seventeen years ago. The others were so angry that he'd left them behind."

My heart is thundering in my ears now. I steady myself on the rock.

"And a witch helped him, didn't she?"

"I just let them come here to meet. Lidari had always been interesting. He'd been in the world before, and it made him more . . . *human* than the rest of them. After so long in the world, his essence had changed. He had a sort of body of his own even in Kahge—he didn't want the animal parts. And I liked the witch too. I thought she was my friend. I got muddled."

"I think that witch was my mother," I say. I feel as if the pieces are all there before me, but I can't quite assemble them into a picture that makes sense. Not yet. "Her name was Ammi."

"Yes," says Ragg Rock, even more wary. "Ammi. That's right."

"Could my mother and Lidari have . . . *had* me? I mean, could I be Lidari's child?"

I've never longed to claim my father, but I would rather have a pathetic opium eater as a father than some other-worldly half-alive monster.

"No," says Ragg Rock, laughing—an eerie echo of my own laugh. "Shadows from Kahge can't procreate any more than they can die—they aren't alive enough for either. Only the living can make life, and even among the living it is complicated. If a woman mates with a dog or a horse, she doesn't give birth to a little half-dog or half-horse baby. A baby comes from two living humans. I know *that* much."

The hollow fear that has been crawling through me for days now is spreading, widening, opening up like a dark, poisonous flower. I think of Theo, the text that was woven into him as a baby—and my mother with the Ankh-nu, which is for transferring an essence from one being to another. The memory I had that was not mine. Perhaps Lidari's memory.

"Then could Lidari's essence have been put *inside* me somehow?" I force myself to ask. I don't want to believe that I might be carrying around something else, *someone* else, inside me, but I can't shake the idea either.

"I've no idea," she says. "I mean, I think you would *know*. He's not the sort to sit silent."

"I'm different in Kahge," I say. "I look like something else."

"What do you look like?"

"I don't know exactly. Monstrous."

373

"Well, it *would* be a distorted reflection," she says, shrugging, just the way I shrug.

"One of them cut me with a sword, and now it seems like they can pull me to them, right out of the world. Like my blood is a rope crossing the world to Kahge." I don't know how to express it. "They had these hooks and tubes, they were trying to take something from me."

"Solanze's sword?" she says.

"I don't know. Is that the fox-faced one with the antlers?"

"Yes. He's been leading the rest of them since Lidari disappeared," she says. "That was another present from the witch who gave them bodies. It was forged partly in the world and partly in Kahge. It can steal your blood, and blood is important for magic. I'm not surprised he can call you if he got some of your blood with that sword. If that's their bridge to you, you could take it from him, take it out of Kahge. Then they couldn't call you there."

"How would I do that?" The last thing I want is to ever go back there.

She shifts a bit, and suddenly her ankle crumbles, the leg angling down and hitting the ground, separating completely from the dried-out foot. "Blasted hounds!" she curses, falling. Horrified, I don't move fast enough to catch her, and she lands hard, her arm breaking off at the elbow.

"Oh, oh, oh!" she sobs, though it's all sound and a contorted face—no tears from her black pebble eyes.

"What can I do?" I ask desperately. It is horrible watching somebody go literally to pieces before you.

"Get my foot," she whimpers. She grabs her broken-off arm in her other hand and pulls herself up the path to the little hut. I pick up the clay foot—it is surprisingly heavy—and follow her.

Inside the hut, she shifts herself to a sitting position and scoots over to the pot of mud boiling on the hearth. I help her fit the broken foot back to the stump of her leg. With her one hand, she reaches into the mud and scoops out a bubbling handful.

"I hadn't noticed I was getting so dry," she mutters. She slathers the hot, wet mud over her ankle and foot, working it into the cracks. Soon her leg is red and moist and supple and she does not need me to hold it in place. She twists and flexes it, wiggles her toes as she moistens the mud between them, giving them a bit of extra length. She does her arm next, sealing it back together at the elbow and covering the whole thing with another layer of mud. More relaxed now, she keeps steadily wiping the mud over her shoulders, her breasts and belly, between her thighs and then up her neck and cheeks, with gentle dabs.

"Do my back?" she asks lazily.

"It's too hot," I say, looking at the bubbling pot.

"Oh, it cools fast." She scoops up some mud and holds it out to me. It *is* hot, but it doesn't burn me. I take some in my hands and spread it over her back. She rolls her shoulders so the shoulder blades flex as I work.

"I just thought of something better than getting Solanze's sword!" she cries. "We'll stop your wounds up with my mud!

Then they won't be able to reach your blood. Not even with the sword—not with *this* stuff in the way."

I want to say no, but then I think of that tug, tug, tug, and I think I'm willing to do anything to stop those things from pulling me out of the world. If I don't have to go back to Kahge and try to make off with a magical sword, all the better. So I take off my tunic and let her unwind the bandage on my arm. She pulls a pointed tooth right out of her gum and uses it to slice open Jun's stitches.

"Ow!" I shout, tears springing to my eyes.

"Don't be a baby. This will *work*." She scoops some mud out of the pot and fills the wound in my arm. The pain is blinding for an instant, the scalding mud inside me, and I let loose a scream, but almost as quickly as it comes, the pain is replaced by an odd, thick numbness. She goes to work on my side next. I clench my teeth and let her do it, looking at the hardening clay-red streak in my arm where the wound was just moments ago. She dabs a blob of mud on each of the scratches the hooks made.

"They won't be able to get at your blood through that!" she says cheerfully.

"I'm not Lidari," I say, pleading. "Am I? I don't want to be."

"You don't seem like him," she says. "Too jumpy and anxious, for one thing. Lidari always knew what he was about. Your blood when it called me was ordinary, human. Just stay away from Kahge. Those animal bodies are coming apart, and when they do, they won't be able to wield that sword anymore. They'll just be what they were. And they won't be able to call your blood through this mud."

That is a relief to hear but doesn't explain away my thousand questions.

"Who *was* Lidari, exactly?"

She looks cross at first, and I think she isn't going to answer, but then she says: "I reckon he was always a little more alive than the others. A little more gumption, a little more *wanting*. Marike saw something in him, anyway. She brought him over—that whole business with the Gethin." Her mouth points down suddenly.

"So the Eshriki Phars really brought the Gethin from Kahge?"

"Oh yes."

"How?"

"It was Marike." She looks angry now. "She and Lidari made that little pot of hers. They used some of her essence, some of his, some of my clay, and the blood of a hundred witches. I don't know how they made the Gethin bodies. I should have paid more attention. It seemed like it hadn't worked—like her pot just swallowed the essences. But then later there was this army. It's my fault. I didn't know what she meant to do. Marike . . ."

She breaks off and rocks back on her heels, a faraway look on her face. I bend and flex my arm. The wound is entirely sealed up by the strip of red mud. It doesn't even hurt anymore.

"Marike what?" I prompt her.

"The whole of the Arrekem continent was hers, and the Parnese armies were all that stood between her and conquest of the kingdoms to the north. Old Poria didn't even exist then, it was just clusters of warring tribes, some witch-led and some not. I admired Marike. Is that stupid? The Xianren were always trying to get at me, and I was scared of them, and I liked watching her defy them. Anyway, Lidari was Gethin first, but then she put his *essence* in the Parnese emperor's body. She *switched* them and killed the Gethin body with the emperor inside it. So Lidari pretended to be the emperor, wearing his body, and married Marike, and then half the world was hers. For a while, anyway. The two of them . . . they planned to live forever, jumping from one body to another. It worked for centuries, until Lan Camshe captured Lidari and executed the body he was in. His essence came back to Kahge—I don't know how. It didn't happen to the rest of them."

"What happened to Marike?" I whisper.

"She was captured and drowned when the Sirillian Empire rose. Well, there are some who said she switched bodies and lived on."

"She never came back for Lidari?"

"I didn't let her back, nor any of her underlings. Not after what she did with the Gethin. I was afraid of her."

I look down the hill at Tianshi, tumbling below.

"How do I get back?"

"I've been very nice to you," says Ragg Rock, her voice caught now between anger and wheedling. "I've told you all kinds of things, *and* I've helped you. You *said* you'd bring me some food for George. Something from the world that he'll like. I don't want him to be unhappy here."

"Yes," I promise. "I'll come back. I'll bring apples and lettuce."

"Good." She smiles again. "Then just swim back across the moat and go down the hill. Go to Silver Moya when you want to come back. I'll recognize your blood. Come back soon."

"I'll come as soon as I can. But first I have to help a little boy. He's got part of *The Book of Disruption* stuck in him. Do you know about that?"

"Oh yes. Zor Gen's son. That's the Xianren's business. You should stay out of it."

"I can't," I say.

"Why not?"

"I love him."

"Oh," she says, nodding. "Love. Yes. I hear about that all the time. But don't forget what you promised me."

FORTY-SEVEN

The little house in Dongshui is dark, but I knock anyway, knowing better by now than to go barging in. Quite right too. A moment or two, and the door opens, a candle flickering in Wyn's hand. With his other hand, he's tucking his shirt into his trousers.

"Holy stars, what's happened to you?" he cries when he sees me. "Your clothes! Your *hair*."

"Can I come in?"

"Of course." He pulls the door wide and steps back. Mei comes out of the bedroom, tying a robe loosely around her waist. She gives me a startled glare as she lights the lamp. I must look a fright.

"Is Dek here?"

"No. Oh, don't look at me that way. What am I supposed to do, give him a curfew? Mrs. Och sent a pipit. We're supposed to be leaving the city in the morning. Why are you covered in mud?"

"Things have gotten complicated."

"Complicated how?"

"I've been sacked."

"And then Mrs. Och tried to drown you in a mud puddle?"

"Not exactly. Have you got anything to eat?"

He has some cold dumplings left in the larder. I fill him in on what happened with Mrs. Och and Si Tan while I eat, every bite making me feel more rooted in my body and the world. I don't talk about Kahge or Ragg Rock, because I've never told him the whole truth about vanishing to Kahge and I don't know how to tell him now. So I tell him I got muddy going through the tunnels, and he just raises his eyebrows, like he knows I'm lying but isn't going to push it. Mei slouches in a chair for a bit while I talk and then goes back to bed without saying anything to either of us.

"I don't think she likes me," I say.

"You aren't very friendly to her," he remarks. I consider this. I suppose I'm not.

"Does she know you're leaving?" I ask.

"Yes. I doubt she'll miss me. I'm not leading her on, Julia. It's not like Ling and Dek—some great connection. Look, I've got something to cheer you up. It might even get you back in Mrs. Och's good graces."

He goes into the bedroom and returns with a bamboo basket full of letters, all closed with Gangzi's wax seal. I rifle through them. "How did you get these?"

"I had to pull a pistol on the mail carrier. I'll be a wanted man now, so good thing we're leaving."

"You shot him?" I ask faintly.

"No, of course I didn't shoot him! Hounds, Julia. I just threatened to. Anyway, here are your letters."

A soft *tap-tap* at the door. I start up, thinking it must be Dek. Wyn opens the door and manages to look relieved and annoyed at the same time. It's Frederick.

"I'd hoped to find you here," he says, rushing past Wyn. "Holies, what's happened? Are you all right?"

I hesitate. I want to tell him, but I don't want Wyn to hear. I can't bear for Wyn to think me less than human, but Frederick knows so much already, and I need to tell somebody.

"Can we take a walk?" I ask.

"Of course," says Frederick.

I can see the hurt on Wyn's face. "It's not safe around here," he says.

"We won't go far."

I feel more able to speak freely out in the dark street. I don't look at Frederick as I tell him everything. I roll up my filthy sleeve to show him the scar of red mud on my arm. It gives me a chill to see it there, this strip of mud flesh, like a part of Ragg Rock. He touches it lightly with his fingertips, but I feel nothing there at all. A blank spot on my arm, nerveless.

"You mustn't vanish again until we know more," he says to me. "It's terrifying to think that they can reach you now that they've shed your blood."

"I won't," I say. "What's happening back at the house?"

"I'm to get supplies first thing in the morning. We're leaving the city and meeting the others at the farm."

"So Mrs. Och has given up on Ko Dan?"

"He is either dead or locked up, and Si Tan is set against us. The Ru are out searching the city. I shouldn't even have come here, but I had to see you. Bianka and I have both tried to persuade Mrs. Och to reconsider, but she insists she can't trust you."

"I don't trust *her*," I say.

"Do you trust anyone?"

It stings to be asked that. Is that really what he thinks? That I trust nobody?

"Yes," I say. "Quite a few people. Including you. I trust you completely, as a matter of fact."

Silence at that. I don't dare look at him. I carry on in a rush, the words coming out of my mouth before I've thought them through.

"I've just found out that before I was born . . . I mean, *just* before I was born, my mother went to Ragg Rock and made some kind of deal, or I think she did, with Lidari. To bring him into the world using the Ankh-nu. And since she went to try to kill Casimir right after, I suppose she got some power or magic from him in return. I think . . . I'm afraid *that* is what I am—just some monster from Kahge. What if that's true, and everything I think I am is false, and being Julia is a . . . a disguise?" He tries to stop me, but I can't stop now, my worst nightmares fully taking shape in words for the first time and pouring out of me. "What if the *thing* inside me decides to shrug off this disguise, and everything I think I am is gone, just sloughed off, and I'm something else, something horrible? Maybe that would explain it—why I

383

kidnapped Theo, why I have to try so hard—I mean, it feels like such hard *work* just to be decent and to do what is right, and perhaps I'm wrong anyway, about what is right. . . ."

"All of that sounds very human indeed," says Frederick, gripping my hands. "I don't know the truth of it, Julia. But suppose you discovered for certain that your origins were not what you thought? That, in fact, you are somehow from Kahge?" Seeing my face, he holds up a hand. "I don't believe that is true. But I am asking you, if it were—what would change? Would you stop caring about Theo? Abandon your attempt to help him?"

"You don't understand," I cry. "I'm afraid I might not be in control of my feelings. That they could change, if I'm so changeable. That I could be . . . I don't know, overthrown from within."

"You have crossed over to *somewhere*—whether it is Kahge or not, I can't say. You have been something else and yet still who you are, unchanged within, and you have returned. Whatever your powers, whatever else may be inside you, you are and have been Julia, with Julia's feelings and hopes and tremendous courage, with Julia's *goodness*, all along."

"My goodness and a couple of pennies would buy you a cup of coffee," I say—a feeble old joke of my father's. Funny I remember it now.

Frederick shakes his head. "That's not true. You need to forgive yourself."

"I'm trying to earn it."

"Saving Theo won't change what you did," he says. "You

have earned Bianka's friendship, and mine, in *spite* of what you did, by being the brave and selfless person you've chosen to be, minute after minute and day after day."

I feel something collapse inside me, and I practically fall into his arms. He holds me close against his chest, so I can hear his steady heartbeat against my ear. Standing here in the dark road, terrified and exhausted and caked with dried mud, I want so badly to believe that he's right. How could I feel so much, if I am not Julia? Then it occurs to me that I'm getting him very muddy, and I pull away, suddenly awkward.

"I should get back," I say. "I need to speak to Dek when he comes home."

"I'll take up your case again with Mrs. Och," he says. "But she is not easy to sway once she's made up her mind."

We go back to the house, where Wyn is dozing in his chair, and I give Frederick the basket of letters.

"Take these to Mrs. Och," I say. "Maybe there will be a clue about the Ankh-nu, if we're lucky."

"I'll go through them all tonight," he promises.

We say our goodbyes, and I close the door behind him.

Wyn's head jerks up. "Frederick gone home?" he asks. "Is all forgiven?"

What a question.

"I don't think Mrs. Och is going to change her mind," I say.

A pause, and then he says, looking at the ceiling, "I wouldn't have guessed he was your type."

If I were not quite so wrung out, I might have laughed.

"I don't think I've got a type," I say, and leave it at that. I'm hardly going to tell Wyn about Jun. And anyway, Jun thinks I'm a monster now.

"Look, I don't even know if Dek's coming back tonight," says Wyn. "I'd offer you my bed, but Mei's in it right now. You could take Dek's, or we could lay a blanket on the floor. I wish we could put you up in better style."

"I can't go to sleep," I say. "I've got to find Ko Dan before Mrs. Och leaves the city."

"What, tonight? How?"

"I don't know."

Another knock at the door, but it isn't Dek this time either. It is a ragged scamp with a message for *me*, written in Fraynish, a fast scrawl: *Help me please. Come to Old Thien's. Jun.*

FORTY-EIGHT

I leave Wyn at the little house, refusing his offers to come with me. For all that Jun helped me and said he forgave me, I can't forget the look of terror on his face in the alley after I dragged him with me into Kahge. The way he said the word *monster*. It sits like poison in my chest, how frightened of me he was once he'd seen the truth about me with his own eyes. I want so badly to believe that he trusts me, that he would turn to me for help, that there could still be something between us. So I don't stop to ask myself how likely it really is—not until I burst into Old Thien's and see Pia, her booted feet up on the table.

She swings her legs down to the floor and gestures with a gloved hand at the seat across from her.

I don't dare vanish, and so I sit down opposite her. Blast, blast, *blast*. If she knows about this place ... if she knows about Jun ... she's been following me. I should have known she wouldn't just be sitting around in that hotel. Thank the

Nameless I always vanish in Nanmu. At least she can't know where Mrs. Och's house is—where Theo is.

"Have you made up your mind?" she asks.

"What?"

"I know you aren't going to give up the boy, of course. But you could still give yourself up. Then Casimir would go on chasing Mrs. Och around the world, and there's no guessing who might prevail, but it wouldn't be your problem anymore. You'd have gold, adventure, freedom of a kind. Better than being broken. I'm hoping you've thought it through."

"I've had a fair bit going on since I last saw you," I say.

"So it would seem," she says, looking me over. "I wasn't sure you'd make it back at all last night, the way you were bleeding. And yet here you are, walking in as if you'd never been harmed. Remarkable."

"I'm not going to work for Casimir," I say.

The goggles whir but her expression does not change.

"I'm not working for Mrs. Och anymore either, as it happens," I add. "I was a bit too independent for her liking. I've been sacked. So I reckon I'm out of this business altogether."

She gives a shattering little laugh—it sounds like thin glass hit with a stick.

"You'll never be out of it. Not now that Casimir has seen what you can do." She leans across the table toward me. "What happened to you? You disappeared, and you came back bleeding. I thought it was a kind of visual trick, the disappearing. But you *went* somewhere and something hurt you, isn't that right?"

"Yes."

I half want to tell her. She wouldn't stare at me in disbelief or horror. She would not be frightened, appalled, sickened. But I keep my mouth shut.

"Shey could help you, if you need help," she says.

I shudder, remembering the sad-faced, hunchbacked witch.

"I shot her a few times."

"She wouldn't hold it against you."

"Like you don't hold it against me, the way I stuck a knife in you and left you for dead?"

She smiles.

"I am not interested in vengeance, Julia. I am done with the whirlwind."

The image of Haizea, bleeding-eyed, her teeth bared, rises up in my mind.

"Done with it?"

My head is spinning, but she sits back, suddenly chatty and relaxed. "I had my chance with it. Casimir understands vengeance, and he can be generous. He indulged me, gave me a part to play in the destruction of the Sidhar Coven. There was a satisfaction in it, I won't deny. I made my keepers crawl. Some of them I left for dead, and some of them I left with pain and nightmares. But it is an ugly sort of work. The whirlwind has no end."

Casimir. If I had the chance, if I had the power, what would I do to him? Casimir, who drowned my mother. Casimir, who broke my hand and nose. Casimir, who took Theo. But it was me who took Theo. That was me.

"Those who terrorize the weak so rarely imagine the day when their victim might grow to be strong. I even found the man who came to me when I was small, the one I told you about, who took from me things I didn't yet know that I had. He loomed so large in my memories of him, and yet when I found him again, he was an ordinary-size man, getting on in years, with bad teeth, ill health, and a wife who despised him. He was puny and cowering. I let the whirlwind rise. I let it tear him limb from limb and scatter the pieces of him far and wide. There is no right or wrong in the eye of that storm, only the power of it, only the certainty of what it will do, that nothing in its path can stop it. But it is a powerful thing to contain within oneself. If it does not tear you apart, at least it leaves you changed. It empties you out as it does its work. I would say that, yes, there is satisfaction in it, even a kind of joy, but less than you would think, and afterward, well . . . the landscape is changed. Everything that used to matter has been blown apart. There is so much vacant space and nothing to replace the fury."

I don't want to sit here chatting with Pia about what a lunatic she is, and yet I find myself riveted all the same.

"Do you regret it?"

"No. But I have had my fill of it. I have had my fill of strife and rage and even hope. This, here"—she folds up the bottom of her glove and flashes the disk of hot metal on her inner wrist at me—"this is the closest I have come to knowing peace. The freedom from choice. You might find it a relief."

I shake my head, my insides shriveling. "I'd die before I let him take me like that."

"You know as well as I do . . . no, not quite as well as I do, but even so, you *know* that there are a great many things worse than death, and that you will submit to Casimir rather than undergo them."

The silence stretches between us.

"What do you intend now that you are no longer in Mrs. Och's employ?" she asks.

"I'll figure something out."

"Last chance, Julia. Please consider carefully. Am I to tell Casimir that your answer is no?"

"You can tell him whatever you bleeding like," I say, getting up.

I am at the door when she says, in a sort of drawl, "Before you came to Tianshi, I'd almost forgotten that you had a brother."

I freeze.

"The cripple," she says. "Was it Scourge?"

I turn toward her slowly. Her hand is on her knife, ready for me.

"What have you done to him?"

"Nothing. I expect he's out having a good time with his girl. Pretty, isn't she?"

"Stay away from him." But my voice shakes badly when I say it.

She shrugs. "Your friend Jun, though . . . he is easier to follow than you are. You have this irritating habit of suddenly disappearing. I gave Count Fournier's address to Lord Skaal as a gesture of cooperation. He's been looking for anyone who helped the princess. So if you happen to find that either of them has been harmed, it was not by me. Not directly, in any case."

I pull the door wide and run.

FORTY-NINE

The house in Dongshui is empty except for Mei sleeping in Wyn's bed. Wyn is gone. No sign of Dek. I stand there in the dark, listening to my own breathing, but I have no idea where they might have gone, no way to find either of them. I leave a scrawled note on the table: *Not safe here.* Then I wake up a very cross Mei, hustling her into her clothes and out of there. She lets me take her home—a sad little place under the shadow of the north wall—and she closes the door in my face without saying good night.

Count Fournier's house is dark and unchanged from the outside, but inside it has been torn to pieces. I find the count's body on the floor behind his desk, full of bloody holes. His expression is one of frozen dismay. I kneel next to him, and even though his dead eyes are staring up at the ceiling, I say his name, as if he might answer: "Count Fournier!"

I understand now why people close the eyes of the dead. It is too horrible to leave them staring at nothing, their death most apparent in the eyes, which are not windows to anything anymore. His eyelids still feel warm and soft under my fingers when I close them. I leave him there, my heart thundering in my ears, and search the rest of the house.

Jun is slumped against a wall in the broken room at the back of the house, fumbling with the box of bandages he used on me earlier. Tears slip out the corners of his eyes when he sees me. His right side is dark with blood.

"Let me look," I say.

"Bullet is here," he says thickly, pointing to his right shoulder. "I go down, play dead. There are so many—too many."

"I'm so sorry."

"He is dead."

"I know. You need a doctor. Tell me where to go."

His eyes close, and I feel like the ground is falling away underneath me.

"Jun, pay attention! Where can I find a doctor?"

He heaves a sigh. "First I need sleep."

"*Don't* go to sleep. I'm going to get help!"

He gives me a blurry look and shuts his eyes again.

I'm afraid to vanish, but I'm not strong enough to carry him any other way. I pull him to me—he smells like blood and sweat—and back to the edge of that bodiless place, where the room scatters beneath me, all its angles up close and far away at once. Immediately I feel the tumult of my blood under the mud of Ragg Rock, the reaching and tugging from something just beyond the void. I aim for the window and we land in the inner courtyard, hitting the ground too hard, Jun's head lolling back in my arms. A sob catches in my throat. I pull back again, out over Tianshi, the swooping tiles of the rooftops gleaming dark below me, around me the canals rippling black and silent through the city, the stars coming out, and the moon gazing down at it all like a blank, unhappy eye. The sky is full of winged shapes, which confuses and frightens me. I take us down into Nanmu, returning to myself next to a small shrine to the spirit of the earth, piled around with fruit and wine and cups of rice. Ragg Rock was right: for all that the beings in Kahge might pull at my blood, the mud is a total barrier, more effective than my flesh, which melts away and reforms itself too easily between the world and its shadow. I look up with my own eyes; those winged shapes are still coasting over the city, huge birds swooping lower. I take a breath and pull back again.

I carry Jun to Mrs. Och's house in staggering leaps in and out of the world. I hear a hiss behind me, faint but persistent: *"Lidari."*

Shey could help you, said Pia. The only tempting part of her offer, now that Mrs. Och is done with me. I kick open the gate, and the spells in the courtyard walls start to screech like an army of cicadas.

"It's me!" I shout, trying to drag Jun across the courtyard. "I need help!"

Frederick reaches me first, helps me carry Jun inside.

"He's been shot," I say.

Jun is barely conscious now, mumbling deliriously. I am

so focused on him that I don't see her coming. Mrs. Och descends on me and sweeps me outside, depositing me at the bottom of the steps in a startled jumble. Bianka comes running out after us.

"Go inside," Mrs. Och commands her. "And make that racket from the walls stop immediately!"

"You shan't hurt her," says Bianka, her voice shaking, stepping between us. "I won't let you."

"It's all right," I say to Bianka, getting to my feet. "She can't touch me." I direct this to Mrs. Och, who stares me down.

"Go help Frederick," I beg Bianka. "Help Jun. I need to speak to Mrs. Och."

"Call if you need me," she says, going back inside but leaving the door open. Mrs. Och and I face each other in the courtyard. The screeching from the walls goes suddenly quiet, and the night lies heavy all around us. I can hear anxious voices from the neighboring courtyards. The sky is dark, but the darker shadows of hundreds of birds still fill the sky.

"What's going on?" I ask.

"Si Tan is looking for us," says Mrs. Och. "We have to leave. I told you never to set foot in my house again. Why are you here?"

"Jun's been shot," I say. "I didn't know where else to take him. He saved you that time in the monastery. Count Fournier's dead, Jun's got no one now, and he *helped* us. Will you help him?"

"I am not going to throw him bleeding into the street, if that's what you are asking," she says crisply. "But it seems that if I want to be done with you, I must take more extreme measures than simply telling you so."

"Wait," I say. "I've been to Ragg Rock. Look."

I pull up my tunic so she can see the long strip of mud in my side—and then I have the surely rare experience of seeing her stunned and speechless. She reaches out a trembling hand and runs her index finger along the clay scar.

"What did Gangzi's letters say?" I ask her.

She stares at me for a long moment, and then she says, "He is writing to every warlord, every minor official, every town leader and police chief and influential family across the empire. He is enlisting them all in a search for the Ankh-nu. It could be anywhere."

"Then we've as good a chance of finding it as they have," I say.

She smiles mockingly, and I force the question around the lump rising in my throat: "You think I might be Lidari. Don't you?"

"I do not know what you are."

"Well, neither do I!"

"What do you want from me, Julia?"

"One more chance," I say. "Not for my sake—for Theo and Bianka. I don't expect you to pay me. When it's done, you'll never hear from me again unless you ask for me, and if ever you ask for me, I'll come. Let me find Ko Dan and bring him to you."

"How?"

"I don't know yet. But I will. Maybe *he* can help us find the Ankh-nu."

She touches the mud scar again, presses on it. I step away from her, pulling my tunic back down.

"We cannot stay here," she says, and gestures at the sky, the low-swooping birds.

"Just wait a few hours," I plead. "I'll bring you Ko Dan."

"You are confident, Julia."

No, only desperate. I wait while she looks into me, like she's struggling to see straight through to the center of me. Whatever might be there, I can't say. Then she says, "You have until morning, but I will wait no longer than that."

"I'll find him," I say with a certainty I am far from feeling. "But . . . if I don't?"

"Yes?"

"You'd never do what Si Tan wants, would you? I need to know. I need to be sure that you'll never hurt Theo."

"If it came to a choice between his life and a thousand lives or more, what would you do? Would you still want to save him, at any cost to the world?"

"It hasn't come to that," I say. Because I don't want to say that, yes, I would choose Theo. I would choose Theo no matter what.

"I have lived a long time," she says. "Casimir would say that the details do not matter. A life here, a life there. What can it mean, in the great oblivion of time, in this small corner of space, all of it just a brief flare in the emptiness? Casimir tries to make his gestures great ones, his goals, his thoughts, all of them large, so that his life might matter, signify *something* in the great void of time and space. In my opinion, any attempt at largeness is futile. It is easy enough to believe that none of it matters, that life and love are meaningless, that there is nothing worth caring about. But here we are all the same. If I can bring relief to those who suffer, if I can offer help to those who think they are beyond it, if I can act on the side of right in this tiny play, then I shall do so, for I *must* act, whether for good or for ill. Call it an attention to detail. We are here, and we must make our choices. What Gennady did was wrong—creating a living vessel for his fragment of the Book. But now Theo *is* alive, he *is* a child, and if I can give him a chance at life, I shall do so." She passes a hand over her face suddenly, as if she is moved, and I am shocked to see it. But her voice is clear and cool when she continues, changing direction slightly. "Regrets pile up as the years pass. You know it yourself, as young as you are. Live for centuries and the regrets and sorrows and losses can become too much to bear. I will do what is *right*. I will protect Theo as long as it is *right* to do so."

"So where is the tipping point? When is it no longer right to protect him, according to you?"

"Find me Ko Dan by morning," she says, "and you will not need to wonder."

The birds are swooping lower and lower over the city. One of them comes diving straight into the courtyard, right over our heads, so that we both duck instinctively and cover our heads with our arms. It is as big as a swan, and black. It swoops right around the courtyard and drops a scroll of paper on the ground between us before shooting up over the wall and away again.

We dive for the paper at the same time. I get it first, scrambling away from her and unrolling it while she advances on me, her face pure murder, her hand out, demanding it.

"It's blank," I say. I let her take it from me. Her eyes move across the page as if she is reading, and my heart plunges.

"It's *blank*," I say again. "Do you see something? Are you reading it?"

She raises her eyes to me, and the paper crumbles to nothing in her hands.

"What was that?" I shout.

"A warning from Si Tan," she says.

"What kind of warning? What did it say?"

"We are out of time."

We stare at each other for a beat, and then I swing around and go back inside, grabbing my bag and stuffing a coil of rope into it. Bianka is writing magic next to Jun, who appears to be sleeping peacefully now, his bloody shoulder neatly bandaged.

"He lost quite a lot of blood," says Frederick.

"It's fine," Bianka says through gritted teeth. The tip of her pen breaks. "Blast. Get me another, will you?"

Mrs. Och comes in behind me. I can feel her watching me. I turn around, hoisting the bag over my shoulder.

"I'm going to get him right now," I say, heading for the door.

"Julia," says Mrs. Och—a low, threatening hum.

"Wait for me here," I tell her without turning around. "I'll be back with Ko Dan."

I vanish and make my way through the city, where the birds fill the sky, diving at houses. I find the same blank scrolls of paper in the streets, in the gutters, and each one, after I've looked at it, dissolves into air, and none of them show me anything. I break into a run.

I'm thinking of those little hooks the beasts in Kahge had, made to pull something out of me, whatever I had that they wanted; I'm thinking of Casimir offering me anything I desired if I'd bind myself to him, let him harness my power; of Si Tan asking Mrs. Och to give me to him, like I was a head of cattle, and Mrs. Och answering, *She is mine.* Pia's voice: *You are her dog.*

But I am no one's dog, and whatever lies within me, whether Lidari or something else lurks inside Julia's skin and bones, there will be no harnessing of this power by anyone else, and no hooks will draw me out. Those who would make use of me, who want to take possession of me, they've known all along what I am only just beginning to understand: I am stronger than they are. Whatever its source, this power is terrible, unstoppable—and *mine*.

FIFTY

I find Si Tan in the cocoon-like room hung with silk, bent over a map of Yongguo with the empress dowager, both of them smoking fragrant black cigarettes and murmuring to each other. The dowager sees me first as I appear before them. She reaches into her robe for her pistol, and Si Tan leaps to his feet, his face registering shock, and puts out a hand to stop me.

I grab him by the neck. I need less than a moment—less time than it takes for him to throw me off, less time than it takes for the dowager to aim her pistol. I dig my hand into the flesh of his neck and pull.

We cross that boundary of nothingness, the world and our selves receding, and we land in the black husk of the city I grew up in. I pull in a breath of burnt air. My hands like claws, my arms darkly scaled. This is what I am, then—this monster. This too.

Si Tan's eyes are wild, the whites visible all around the quivering irises. I drag him toward the boiling river, and he stumbles along with me. For all his physical power in the world, *here* I am stronger than him—much stronger.

Those patchwork beasts come almost immediately, with their hooks and tubes and rusted weapons.

"Do you know what this place is?" I ask.

"Some illusion," gasps Si Tan.

"No," I say. "This is Kahge. I'm going to leave you here and let these creatures eat you unless you help me."

"Help you do *what*?"

"Is Ko Dan alive?"

"Yes," he cries.

"Then take me to him."

His face contorts, fury and fear together. "Och Farya has sent you to threaten me."

"Not her," I say. "Forget her. Look at *me*. I could leave you here to die and I'd feel *nothing*. Next the empress dowager. The emperor himself. His heir. I can pull you all out of the world one by one, end the imperial line as quick as you please. You can't see me, and you can't stop me, and now you know how quick and easy I can do it. Take me to Ko Dan."

"It will not matter," he gasps. "Ko Dan cannot help you."

And now those awful monsters are upon us. But I am ready for this. I am ready for a fight I can win. I let go of Si Tan, who cries out, reaching for me, and I leap for the fox-faced creature, the one Ragg Rock called Solanze. His sword is about the length of my forearm, bright and curved, the jagged edge glinting and winking at me. I get hold of that arm before he can swing the sword.

We struggle soundlessly for a moment, my face right next

to his snarling muzzle. Something close to joy is rising in my chest—but it isn't joy, it is too bitter for that, too swollen with fury. Trying to wrest the sword from him, I break his arm right off and stagger backward, stunned. A stinking smoke pours from the bloodless shoulder socket. I pry the sword from the dead hand and drop the arm, my stomach heaving with disgust. Their bodies just costumes indeed. Something catches against my back, stinging—those little hooks. I whirl in a circle, cutting the tubes and pulling out the hooks, and then I swing Solanze's sword at the creatures.

They recoil and flee now that I have the sword, ignoring Si Tan as he huddles on the ground and shouts something at me. But I can't hear him over the roar in the air, the buzz of my own blood, the cries of these shadow-monsters. Solanze grabs me from behind with his one arm, pulling me toward him. I break free of him easily and spin to face him. He has got one of those hooks now. It catches me on the cheek, right below my eye, and scrapes a gash down to my lip as I pull away from it. I swing the sword; he raises his arm as if to defend himself with it, and I cut his remaining hand clean off. More foul gray smoke. He goes down on one knee, scrabbling for the hand, screaming words I don't understand, except for *Lidari*.

For a moment, I see myself reflected in a window, standing over Solanze, sword aloft. My hair is moving around my head in smoky tendrils, my eyes are black pools, and there is a crimson line down the side of my face, which is both my face and yet not.

"Take me back!" Si Tan is slowly scrambling toward me,

like he's moving underwater, his face a mask of terror. With the hand not holding Solanze's sword, I drag him to the river's edge and then let go of him, pointing at the boiling river with my clawed finger.

"Take me to Ko Dan. If you don't, I'll bring you back and drop you in there. Then I'll go see if the emperor can be more helpful."

"I'll take you," he gasps. "It won't help. You will see."

I haven't really got the stomach for any of this. I'll take what I can get. We go back. I am this monster, and then I am nothing, and then I am Julia.

Si Tan leads me through the dark to his own house, where he met with Mrs. Och. I have a firm grip on his arm, and I keep us both vanished two steps back, so it is like walking through a hazy tunnel together, the world a blur on either side. I am ready to pull him back to Kahge at the slightest sound or unexpected movement. My cheek is burning, and I have Solanze's sword in my hand.

In the central courtyard, next to a flowering hibiscus bush, is a neatly swept stairway with a door at the bottom.

"Here," he murmurs, and opens the door.

The room is mostly bare. There is a bed, a table, two chairs, a basin, an electric lamp. And there is a young man sitting in one of the chairs, his hands loose in his lap. He looks up at us, his expression bleak. He has a star-shaped scar under his eye. Suddenly I am wild with hope.

"Ko Dan," I breathe. "Just . . . here? In your house?"

"Yes," says Si Tan.

Ko Dan looks me over. "Who is this?" he asks in Yongwen, his voice a low rasp.

"I need you to come with me." I give Si Tan's arm a shake. "Blast. Does he speak Fraynish?"

Ko Dan frowns. "*Who* is this?" he asks Si Tan again.

Si Tan speaks to him in Yongwen. I hear *Och Farya* and *Zor Gen*. The way he talks, and the despairing look on Ko Dan's face, make me think Ko Dan is afraid of him.

Then Si Tan says to me: "You may find Och Farya has changed her mind when you return."

"The birds," I say. "That was you. But the papers were blank."

"A message for her," he replies. "For her eyes only. The city gates are locked. There is no way out of Tianshi for her or for the boy. I have offered her an alliance. For all that she scoffs, she cannot deny the might of our empire. And I have told her the truth: there is no way to remove the text from the child. The Ankh-nu is missing, and Ko Dan remembers nothing. The only way to keep the Book from Casimir is to destroy the vessel—the boy."

"What do you mean, remembers nothing?"

"*He* did not put the fragment of *The Book of Disruption* into Gennady's son."

My heart is plunging and plunging. Here, my moment of triumph, when I've found Ko Dan at last. I hear Si Tan's words, but I can't make sense of what he is telling me.

"Then who *did* it? Gennady said . . . he *said* it was Ko Dan."

Si Tan lets a bitter little laugh out.

"Do you really not know?" he asks. "I thought perhaps you did. That you might be in league with her."

"With who?" I am going to throttle him in a moment. "Start at the beginning."

"Your mother," he says. "Marike."

Ko Dan watches with vague interest as my knees turn to water. I have to balance myself against the wall. Something comes alive in Si Tan's face, and I see the danger in it.

"Sit in that chair," I tell him, pointing with the sword. Solanze's sword does not look so impressive here—the jagged edge rough, not glittering anymore, just a damaged, rather rusty old weapon. "I can still take you to Kahge and leave you there."

He sits. My cheek is throbbing. I touch my hand to it, and my fingers come away wet and red with blood.

"What," I say very carefully. I can't find words. "Tell me. Explain."

"I have been trying to piece it together myself," says Si Tan. "I have spent my life searching for the Ankh-nu. Two years ago, Ko Dan received a letter from a witch claiming to have it. She was offering it to us—for the monastery to keep safe. I sent Ko Dan to meet this witch—with an armed escort, of course. The escort was murdered and Ko Dan disappeared for weeks. When he returned, he claimed that he had been kidnapped and taken many miles away to a mountain cave, where a masked witch came and performed some magic on him, using the Ankh-nu. Afterward, he remained for weeks in the cave. Armed witches gave him food and water and kept him there. But—and here is where it gets really interesting—his body was not his body anymore. There was no mirror for him to see his own face, but his body was older, different, and entirely unfamiliar, until the masked witch returned with the Ankh-nu and gave him back his own body. Then he was set loose and found his way back to Tianshi. I had Cinzai search his memory to try to find the truth, and it was as he told us. More than this—his body has been touched by another essence. The traces are still upon him."

My mind is reeling. I can't untangle this on my own.

"What about my *mother*?"

"Cinzai found the Ankh-nu in one of your memories," says Si Tan coolly. "She relayed it all to us. Your mother used it. But only Marike can use the Ankh-nu. Only Marike and Lidari, in all of human history, have been able to borrow the body of another by means of the Ankh-nu."

"So you mean . . ." But I stop. I can't put it together.

"*Marike* borrowed Ko Dan's body. If alive, of course, she would have feared the possibility of Casimir assembling *The Book of Disruption*. But she would have known too that Gennady would never deal directly with her. She had made enemies of all the Xianren. He would not have trusted her. So she used Ko Dan's body as a disguise to approach Gennady. Young as he is, Ko Dan is well known and respected, even by the Xianren. *Marike* put the text in the little boy, presumably intending to destroy him and thus the text, but she failed in that. And then she returned Ko Dan to his own body once she was finished with it. The question is only how willing he was. I have not been able to discern *that* from his memories—whether he was her prisoner or her accomplice. We are trying to separate out the traces her essence left upon his body. It is a difficult magic, and it has taken its toll on him, as you can see. But I believe that if we *can* isolate those traces, we may be able to use them to find Marike and the Ankh-nu as well." A rather mad laugh, and then he pauses, the avid look in his eyes sharpening, focusing in on me. "But perhaps there is an easier way. Perhaps *you* know where she is."

"Why would I know? Why would you think my *mother* is Marike just because she had the Ankh-nu? My mother drowned years ago."

"Who but Marike could use the Ankh-nu? Who but Marike could defeat Casimir, even temporarily? Who but Marike would dare to *try*? Who but Marike would want to bring Lidari back to the world? She is still alive, playing her games, borrowing bodies. The question is—who are *you*?"

Those creatures hissing "*Lidari*," Mrs. Och searching my face for something—*someone*—else. No. No. No.

"I'm not . . ." I say, but I don't know how to finish the sentence. I need somebody to help me figure this out. If it's true . . . but I can't think it yet.

Si Tan rises, and his eyes are dangerous. I push myself off the wall and stand unsteadily. The sword feels so heavy suddenly.

"Sit in that chair or we go back to Kahge," I tell him. He sits. I take out my rope.

"You will not get out of the city," he says.

"Don't be an idiot," I say. "You aren't going to stop me. You *can't* stop me."

Ko Dan just watches, expressionless, while I bind Si Tan to the chair. I gather he hasn't been treated particularly well. Si Tan curses at me coarsely, dropping his accent, and I realize that he does not come from the upper classes at all, that his accent and manners have been carefully learned.

I stand up, and Ko Dan stiffens, fearful.

"He is *mine*," hisses Si Tan, but I ignore him.

"You're coming with me," I say to Ko Dan, who stares at me uncomprehendingly. I grab his arm and pull him out of the world.

FIFTY-ONE

I am getting the hang of carrying another person with me between the world and its shadow. When we hang bodiless over the streets, I focus on the farthest point I can, taking us there at the speed of my own gaze, then return to the world for a split second before pulling back out, throwing my perspective wide again and finding the next point, and the next. In this way, we reach the courtyard of the house in Nanmu within minutes.

The first gray glimmers of dawn are lightening the sky. Frederick is in the courtyard arguing with Ling in rapid Yongwen, and she is crying. Wyn is standing helplessly by.

"What's going on?" I ask sharply, reappearing. "What is *she* doing here?"

They all stop and stare at me, then at Ko Dan, who has pulled free of me and backed against the courtyard wall. He looks down at his own body, and at his hands, flexing them—I suppose not an unnatural reaction for a man who had his body stolen from him once before.

"What happened to you?" cries Wyn. "Your face . . ."

"I'm fine," I say.

"Is this . . . ?" Frederick takes a step toward Ko Dan and says something to him in Yongwen that Ko Dan appears to find reassuring. He nods, relaxing a little. Ling is still sobbing.

"*Where is Dek?*" I shout.

"He's all right. He and Ling were at a play, and Pia found them," says Frederick quickly. "They got away, and he told Ling this address, sent her here in a motor carriage. He's gone to fetch Mei and bring her back here too. Ling is worried about her, and I was just saying Mrs. Och won't allow it, but—"

Ling bursts out, shouting something at Wyn, jabbing her finger in his face. He looks sheepish. "My *sister!*" she finishes in Fraynish.

"I'm sorry!" says Wyn. And then, to me, he says: "I was sleeping at home after you left, and the pipit came with a message from Mrs. Och, telling Dek and me to go to the farm to meet up with the others. I didn't want to leave without you, and I didn't know where Dek was, so I came here. I had no idea the girls were in any danger or I would never have left Mei alone."

"I took Mei home!" I say to Ling. "She's fine!"

Ling puts her face in her hands, and her shoulders shake as Frederick translates this for her.

"I think we should all just stay here and wait for Dek," says Wyn. "What *happened* to your face, Brown Eyes? Where'd you get that sword?"

"Fighting monsters," I say. "Come on, let's introduce Ko Dan to Mrs. Och."

Frederick speaks to him in Yongwen again, and Ko Dan goes to him, giving me a wide berth like I'm a mad dog. Ling takes her hands away from her face and looks at me, her face blotchy from crying.

"Come inside, then," I say. "It can't matter. We won't be here much longer."

So we all go in together. Mrs. Och and Bianka are poring over a map of Yongguo. Bianka is holding Theo tight. The sash he sleeps with is wrapped around his waist, tying him to her.

"Here is Ko Dan," I announce, but the moment feels hollow because I know it's no use.

Bianka leaps to her feet. Mrs. Och rises more slowly, looking from my bleeding face to Ko Dan.

"Dare I ask you how you have done this?" she says.

"Probably better not."

Mrs. Och speaks to Ko Dan in Yongwen, and he bows and answers.

"Can he do it?" Bianka cries. "Without harming Theo?"

"Teo," says Theo, trying to squirm free of her, but she squeezes him closer.

Mrs. Och holds up a hand, giving Bianka a stern glare. Then her eyes fall on Ling.

"Who is this?" she asks, acid-voiced.

"Dek's girl," I say.

"Pia came across them, and Dek sent her here," says Wyn. "He's gone to get her sister too."

413

Mrs. Och waves this aside and turns back to Ko Dan. Frederick manages to persuade him to sit down.

"We ought to see to that gash on your cheek," says Bianka to me. "It looks very nasty."

I put down Solanze's ugly sword, and we sit around the hearth while Mrs. Och batters Ko Dan with questions, her voice rising sharply. Ling glances at them in horror a few times, and I can only imagine what she's hearing. I can't follow the rapid conversation around the table, so I just sit and let Bianka wash my cheek, Theo still bound to her, tugging at the sash but cowed by the tension in the room.

"I ought to stitch it," she says. "Not sure I'm up for another spell."

"Please don't. I'm so sick of being sewn up."

"Well, it's going to be a whopping scar," she says, and Wyn says, "It'll suit you, very piratical."

I can't bring myself to care at the moment. Wyn fetches me a clean cloth, which I hold to the wound. Mrs. Och bangs on the table with a fist, her voice turning angry.

"Is he going to help?" Bianka asks me in a low voice. "*Can* he help?"

I don't know what to say. "It's a little complicated," I mutter.

Even though I've done what I set out to do, I know it's a flop; the way to help Theo has slipped away from us. We crossed the world to find this man, and for nothing. The things Si Tan said keep turning and turning in my mind. Marike took Ko Dan's body. Marike, wearing the monk's body, made the deal with Gennady, put the Book into Theo, and disappeared again with the Ankh-nu. Years before that, Marike-as-Ammi went to Ragg Rock and brought Lidari across to the world with the Ankh-nu. Somehow she then defeated Casimir and had a child—me. And the creatures in Kahge sensed Lidari's essence in me.

Suppose it's all true. Suppose my mother is Marike. Then she did not drown, it was not her on that boat at all, but someone else in another discarded body, for if my mother is Marike, she was in Sirillia working a terrible magic less than two years ago. And if we're to save Theo, somehow we have to find her.

I feel dizzy. I don't know if it's joy or fear making me tremble. I don't know if I should believe anything Si Tan said. I need to talk to Dek.

"Why is he taking so long?" I say without explaining who I mean, but Wyn nods at me, his forehead creased with concern. Ling plays peekaboo with a restless Theo. She seems calmer now. And then Jun emerges from Mrs. Och's room, taking in the crowd of us.

I leap up, my cheek throbbing. He is a little pale, but upright and moving and still beautiful, his arm and shoulder wrapped in a sling. Whereas, I—well, if ever he thought I was a little bit pretty, I am not now. My chopped hair, my eyes swollen with tears shed and unshed, my face still streaked with mud and now with a great ugly gash across it—I must look a horror, and I see the shock register in his eyes.

"Are you all right?" I ask stupidly.

He nods, easing himself into a chair by the hearth, and doesn't ask me if *I* am all right.

The conversation in Yongwen is carrying on more calmly now, and so Bianka boils eggs and butters bread for breakfast, poor Theo complaining bitterly about the sash. Ling puts on a kettle for tea, as if she's at home.

At last, Mrs. Och says in Fraynish, "No matter what, we cannot stay in the city. But Bianka, Theo, Frederick, and I will not go back to Frayne quite yet." She looks at me. "You will go your own way now, Julia. Wyn should join the others at the farm immediately. They will leave by nightfall, and they will be safer if he is with them."

I wonder if she knows—if Ko Dan understood what Si Tan said about my mother.

"What about Dek?" asks Wyn.

"If he's not here soon, I'll go find him," I say. Trying to push down the fear.

"We'll stick together, you and me," Wyn says to me. But I shake my head.

"You should go. Gregor and Esme can shoot straight, at least, but Mrs. Och is right—it'll be better if you're with them. Get the princess back to Frayne in one piece."

"I want to help *you*," says Wyn. "I want to get you and Dek back to Frayne in one piece."

"This is how you help," I say. "I'm going to get Dek out of here. I'll take him by vanishing, and it'll be easier if it's just him. The others could use you."

He looks downcast, but he nods. I don't want to say good-bye to Wyn, but I want him safely out of here, and I need to save my strength for Dek. I don't reckon we're going back to Frayne yet either. Mrs. Och may think she can shrug me off now, but if she is about to go off looking for my mother, she's not doing it without me.

"How are we going to get out of the city, if the gates are locked and the Ru are everywhere?" asks Wyn.

"You'll need my help," I say to Mrs. Och, but she shakes her head at me.

Jun pushes his plate away. He keeps looking everywhere except at me. "I take you," he says to Wyn. "I know some way out. Secret way."

"Good," says Mrs. Och. "But leave quickly. More and more routes will be shut to you the longer we wait."

This sets us all in motion. Bianka fills gourds with water from the pump, and I pack them some bread and dried fruit. Wyn just sits there looking stricken until Jun takes his pistol, which Wyn has left on the table, and tucks it into his belt.

"Hey, that's mine!" says Wyn, coming to life.

"I should have gun, not you," says Jun. "In case we meet trouble."

"I was thinking that *I* should have the gun in case we meet trouble," says Wyn.

"You are not good shot."

Wyn's mouth quirks a little. "I'm a very good shot," he says.

"You miss when you shoot at me."

"Oh, that. Well, that was more of a warning shot."

Jun pats the pistol at his belt, as if making a final argument. Wyn looks torn between anger and amusement, but he shrugs, then shoulders the bag of food and water.

"Take care of them," I say to Wyn. "Get them home."

"I will," he says. "Don't do anything foolish, Julia. Come home safely."

He pulls me into his embrace. I let my arms go around his too-familiar frame, his heartbeat against my ear, my dear, beautiful boy. But my own heart feels like a stone in my chest. Jun stands in the doorway, watching us with no expression on his face.

"Let's go," says Jun. "Before too light."

"Wait."

I follow him out onto the steps.

"What will you do?" I ask him. "I mean, after."

"I am not decided yet," he says.

"You could come with us," I say, knowing as I say it how stupid it is.

He lifts an eyebrow. "This is my home. Greatest city in the world."

"I know," I say. "It's just . . ." Don't be such a coward, Julia, just say it. "One night with you doesn't feel like enough."

Something in his expression softens a little. "I do not understand many thing about you, Julia," he says. "It is too much for me to not know. I cannot love girl who changes into monster. But I am wishing luck for you."

418

He touches a hand lightly to his chest, where the tattoo for luck is hidden beneath his shirt.

"I'm so sorry . . . about Count Fournier," I manage. "It's my fault."

"Not your fault," he says, and then he leans forward and kisses my cheek, under the gash, and I nearly crumble right there. He turns and walks away across the courtyard.

"Hold up," says Wyn, behind me. "Did you and he . . . ?"

"Go on, hurry," I say, giving him a shove. He gives me a cockeyed look that might have made me laugh under different circumstances, but he goes after Jun, waving from the gate. And then they are gone. I feel something ease in me. The more people I love who get out of here, the better.

I go back into the main room, where Ling is offering around tea. Mrs. Och waves her away impatiently, but Ko Dan takes a cup and raises it to his lips, nodding gratefully at her.

"We part ways here, Julia," says Mrs. Och to me. Something awful in her expression. So much we are not saying. Marike's name, for starters.

"Dek is meeting us back here," I say. "I'll leave with him, and not before that."

But where is he, where is he, where is he?

She scowls and turns back to Ko Dan, directing a sharp question at him in Yongwen. He puts his cup down, and fear flashes across his face. He looks at Frederick, his mouth open but no sound coming out.

"What is it?" asks Frederick, leaning forward.

Ko Dan touches a hand to his chest. His eyes go wide, and he begins to shake. It happens so fast. Foam on his lips, veins bulging at his temples, eyes turning crimson as the blood vessels explode. He falls sideways, rigid and shaking, Frederick and Bianka at his side, shouting. I can't move. Mrs. Och says in a cold, tight voice: "Poison."

It takes only a few seconds, though time feels slowed down horribly: his purpling face, his body convulsing and then falling still. My heart is thumping so loudly in my chest that Bianka's screams seem distant, and my thoughts are moving slowly, like underwater thoughts: Doctor. Too late. Poison. The teacup on the ground—green tea spilling onto the floor.

Ling.

I whirl around, but she is gone. The gate is swinging in the courtyard. I snatch up Solanze's sword and go over the wall. She is running down the road, around the corner. I catch her easily and slam her into the wall. She gives a little cry, like a kitten mewing. I pull her back and slam her into the wall again. I don't know what I'm doing. It's too late, of course. I grab her wrists, pinning her to the wall, screaming *"Why?"* at her—but my question is answered for me. The dirty bandage on her wrist. Even through the fabric, I can feel the heat. I tear it off her.

She has gone limp against the wall, sobbing. There, in her wrist, that little disk of metal, the burnt skin peeled back around it. Casimir's contract.

"You work for Casimir," I breathe.

Of course she and Dek didn't just *get away* from Pia. But he told her Mrs. Och's address. How long do we have? I hold the sword to her throat. "Where is Dek?" I grind out.

She tilts her head back a little, as if daring me to cut her throat, and says in Fraynish: "Safe." Then she asks me a question in Yongwen. It takes me a minute to understand that she's asking if Ko Dan is dead.

"Yes!" I shout. "Of course he's dead. You're a liar and a murderer! We'll all be killed now!"

Hounds, the look on her face. I lower the sword and step away.

"My sister," she says in Yongwen, and her voice cracks. She tries to grab the sword from me, but I yank it away. She lets out a laugh that sounds more like the yelp of an animal caught in a trap. Then she starts biting at her wrist until she gets that metal disk between her teeth. It must be burning her lips, but she doesn't stop. She pulls it loose, her face contorted and gray. A silvery thread follows. She pulls and pulls with the fingers of her other hand now, the bright thread spooling out of her, slick with her blood.

I don't want to watch, but I can't tear my eyes away either. One more sharp tug, and something like a bloody jewel the size of a baby's tooth comes slipping out of her wrist. She drops it with a shuddering cry. Behind it stream countless tendrils, several inches long. They move and flail, then find the ground like hundreds of tiny legs. The little jewel comes crawling toward me, gathering speed. It skitters for my leg, and I jump away, shouting inarticulately. Quick as

421

anything, Ling grabs a loose stone from the ground and brings it smashing down on the thing. The tendrils go limp. She raises the rock cautiously. Whatever it was, it is just a wet red blob on the street now.

"His contract," I say.

Ling looks up at me, and words start pouring out of her, about Dek and Mei and a rich man and the Imperial Gardens, but I can't follow, and her wrist is bleeding badly, her face turning a disconcerting ashen color.

"You need to see to that," I say, picking up the dirty bandage I tore off her.

I wrap it around her bleeding wrist. She stares at me with such a defeated expression, but she lets me bind it. I may not understand her fast Yongwen, but I can read the whole story in her face—I *know* this story, because it was my story too. A talented girl in a big city, stuck, and then something comes along that could really change things. A big chance. In my case, a heap of silver. In hers, maybe the promise of a way to the Imperial Gardens. For both of us, it was a poisoned promise, but how were we to know? By the time we knew for sure that we were working for the wrong side, it was too late. She's killed a man, and I don't think it's really sunk in yet, just like it took a while to hit me that I'd kidnapped a child.

I ask her in Fraynish because, honestly, I can't think straight enough to even try in Yongwen: "They threatened Mei, didn't they?"

I don't know how much Fraynish she understands, but I think she can see in my face everything that I can see in hers. We crouch there in the road together, and she nods. The

422

bandage is already turning dark with blood. I've done a lousy job, but I don't have time to take care of Ling, and I reckon she knows how to take care of herself.

"Does Pia know where the house is?" I ask her. She looks at me blankly, so I point down the road, and put my fingers in goggle shapes around my eyes. She nods again. I need to get back there right away. I start to rise, and she catches hold of my sleeve. She is saying something about Dek, her eyes gone hard and bright. I only understand the word *sorry*.

"I'll tell him," I say. "Get your sister safe. Hide."

Go where Casimir can't find you, can't reach you. I see my own story written so starkly in her miserable expression that it makes me feel ill. We both look at the little blob in the road; then she locks eyes with me one more time, gives a small nod, turns, and starts running. I dash back to the house.

The gate is wide open. Frederick is alone, slumped on the floor next to Ko Dan's dead body. He is chalk-white and limp, his eyes half-lidded. I skid to my knees beside him and grab his shoulders.

"What happened?"

"They left." It is barely a whisper.

"*What?*" I scream.

"She said . . . there was no time."

"She—who?"

"Mrs. Och."

"Mrs. Och," I repeat. "Mrs. Och took Bianka and Theo. *Where?*"

"Leaving . . . the city."

Without Frederick. Without *me*. She wanted to get out of here without me. But there is no way out of the city, Si Tan said.

"Bianka?" I manage to ask.

"She took my . . . force and . . . Bianka's too. Left her just enough to . . . walk. So fast. She said—no time."

Maybe she means to get them away safe, but I don't believe it. *Where is the tipping point?* I asked her, and she told me to bring her Ko Dan. But now he is dead, was not the right man anyway, and if there is no way to get the text out of Theo, then the surest way to keep the Book from Casimir is to destroy it. To kill Theo, who is himself becoming dangerous. Ally herself with the most powerful empire in the world.

My panic is rising fast. I squash it down, trying to clear my mind, trying to think where they would go, how I can find them. They can't have gone far; it has been only a minute or two. If I go now, I can still catch them.

A voice from the doorway: "Is it your blood or someone else's you're covered with this time?"

I look up, and there is Pia.

FIFTY-TWO

Frederick is struggling to get up. I pull back, out of sight, but Pia is ready for that. She yanks Frederick to his feet, her curved knife at his throat.

"Stay where I can see you," she snarls. "And drop that sword."

I reappear and do as she says. She drags Frederick with her from room to room. He almost looks like he's asleep, except that he's so pale.

"Where is the boy?" she calls to me.

"I *don't know*. Mrs. Och has taken him, and I've no idea where. I told you—I don't work for her anymore."

"And yet here you are."

"She left us behind."

"Who is the corpse?" she asks, jerking her head at Ko Dan. My stomach clenches. I found him for this. To be killed within the hour.

"Ko Dan," I say.

"Ah," says Pia. "Then you found him."

"I thought . . . he was a witch. But she poisoned him."

"There are poisons that work well on witches," she says. "Or well enough. The girl succeeded in that, at least. We weren't sure if you had him or not."

"Ling was working for you all along."

"For Casimir," she corrects me.

"For how long?"

"Since you arrived in Tianshi. But this house was harder to find than we'd expected. Your brother didn't give Ling the address until today, and I had to pretend to capture her and threaten her life to pry it from him. She was supposed to get the little boy and bring him to me."

My heart stutters, thinking of Ling playing peekaboo with Theo. But Bianka had him tied to her. Oh, Bianka.

"You threatened her sister if she didn't go along with it, didn't you?" I say.

"Her sister, her grandmother, her uncle, her little cousin," says Pia casually.

"She took the contract out," I say. "That . . . thing. She pulled it right out of her wrist."

"Ah," says Pia, and her goggles whir. "It hadn't fully attached yet. If it had, I wouldn't have needed to threaten the sister. It takes some time. Where has she gone?"

"No idea," I say, relieved that it's true. "Will they be all right?"

"They are no longer useful," says Pia. "We are done with them. But the contract must have been quite far along. Pulling it out at this stage . . . I can't say what the damage will be."

She was able to run, I tell myself. If she could run, she must be all right. I wonder what rejecting Casimir's contract will mean for Ling's dreams of the Imperial Gardens. But I don't have time to think of that—of what she might have lost. There's no winning any game with Casimir, whichever side you're on.

"You really don't know where Mrs. Och has taken the little boy?" asks Pia.

"No."

"Disappointing. I was going to offer you a trade. The little boy for your brother."

It takes everything I've got not to snatch up the sword and try to stick another hole in her. My voice shakes badly, but I manage to ask her: "Where is he?"

Pia lets go of Frederick, and he slides to the floor, gasping. She spreads her hands—I've seen her make that gesture before, a Lorian gesture, the acceptance of mystery.

"I passed him along to my contact as soon as he gave us this address and Ling was on her way here. She was awfully fond of your brother. I had to swear up and down no harm would come to him. Of course, my word is worth less than nothing, and I do not know where they have gone now."

"Did you hurt him?"

"No more than was necessary to subdue him. He will be taken to Casimir, and Casimir will decide what to do with him. It won't be pretty. Unless, of course, you have something to offer in exchange. A little boy, for example."

I feel as if my veins are full of sand, everything slowing

down, everything inside me grinding to a halt, my heart struggling to beat against the terrible pressure of so much weight.

"I can't," I whisper. "I told you, I don't know where he is."

"Casimir might accept another trade," says Pia. "After all, he is very keen on *you*, as well. Then your brother could go home with a nice bag of gold for good measure."

I think of that tentacled little blob Ling pulled out of her. Something starts to beat inside me, something deeper and stronger than my stuttering heartbeat. Like a drum calling forth a different kind of strength. Like the pulse of some other, terrible Julia.

"Give me the day to look for Theo," I say. "If I can't find him, I'll turn myself over to Casimir in exchange for Dek's life. Wait for me at the Hundred Lantern Hotel."

"Wait for you?" Pia's goggles whir. "I don't think I ought to let you out of my sight."

"I'll come," I say. "You know I will, for Dek."

She nods, once. "Very well."

I go and kneel next to Frederick.

"I have to go."

"I know."

"I'll be back."

"You don't . . . have to come back," he says.

His face is pinched and tight, his eyes faded, all the color drained out of him. How much did she take?

"Will you be all right?"

He says, "She wouldn't . . . she wouldn't . . ." But who

428

knows what she would do. His eyes slide toward me, find mine. "I can't move."

"You don't need to move right now. But don't die. Please."

"I'll try . . . not to," he says, almost smiling.

Pia stands on the steps, looking out at the dawn.

"If you hurt him, I *will* kill you," I say. It sounds so hollow.

"I have no interest in him," she tells me. "Not yet. But do not make me wait too long, Julia. Nightfall, or I will work my way through everyone you care for and leave you a trail of corpses by which to find me."

FIFTY-THREE

I run out into the lane with Solanze's sword. They can't have gone far, but I can't risk going in the wrong direction. I vanish and pull back—four steps—hanging over the courtyard, where Pia is sheathing her knife and heading for the gate. I pull myself back a little farther, the city spinning beneath me—too far. I focus again on the area around the house. The streets are quiet. I feel the new core of me beating, beating, beating. Over the rooftops my vanished gaze skims, over the courtyards, the alleys, the main roads.

I find them on the canal. A boy of no more than thirteen or fourteen is punting them along. Theo is sitting in the bottom of the boat at Bianka's feet, and Bianka is slumped over like she has barely the strength to hold herself upright. My heart contracts. Mrs. Och doesn't mean to take them out of the city. She wants them on the water. She's made Bianka weak, and she has taken her—a witch!—out on the water.

I pulled my perspective too far out and I come out of it too fast, forgetting to focus on a destination point. I am plunging through the sky.

Mrs. Och looks up.

For a moment, my heart stalls with panic. I am falling fast. I pull back, vanishing again. Then I am everywhere, nowhere, I can feel myself scattering, the city spreading wide beneath me. I narrow my focus, hurl myself toward the boat.

I miss by a few inches and hit the water. I emerge gasping at the front of the boat, clutching the gunwale. The boy has dropped his pole, is screaming and pointing at me. Mrs. Och moves quickly. She grabs Bianka by the arm—Bianka, still tied to Theo by the magicked sash—and heaves her like a rag doll over the side of the boat into the canal, Theo pulled along after.

Oh, I remember it, it lives inside me—the low path by the river Syne, my screams like those of an animal in a trap, and how my mother fell and the water closed over her and she was gone and I did nothing, I did nothing. But I am not that powerless girl, not anymore. This time, I go after her.

Letting go of the sword, I grab Theo, I grab Bianka's hand, and now I know why witches cannot swim or float. She pulls us both under, fast, like something beneath is sucking her down—something stronger than me, stronger than her, stronger than anything. Trying to pull her toward the surface is utterly futile. I try to pull them out of the world, but something in the water has her and will not release her. We rush downward, my lungs bursting, the seconds drawn out to eternity. I can barely make out her face, but she is yanking her hand from mine. She is tearing at the sash, Theo's body struggling against me. The sash comes free and she is gone so quickly, disappearing into the darkness below, and I am holding Theo and kicking madly for the surface, bright and wavering above us.

I break through it, surging out of the water and nearly capsizing the boat, gasping in a desperate lungful of air. Theo is flailing, making horrible choking sounds, and then he vomits water all over my neck. Mrs. Och is standing in the boat with a long knife in her hand—not Mrs. Och but Och Farya now, winged and terrible. She does not hesitate—her eyes fixed on Theo, still retching in my arms, she dives straight for him with the knife. I let go of the boat and swing my arm for her wrist. As soon as I've got a hand on her, I yank hard, hurling myself back, pulling all three of us out of the world and straight through to Kahge.

We land in another boat, a charred boat with ragged sails moving fast through a river of lava. Both sides of the river are lined with her Spira City house, over and over again, windows ablaze like eyes, and giant white spiderish things are crawling out the doors toward the fiery river.

I shove her away from me, away from Theo. He lets loose a howl that at least means he's able to breathe, followed by more choking and retching.

"I did everything I could for them!" cries Mrs. Och. Her voice sounds strange and thin here. And then she lunges at us with the knife.

I let Theo slide to the bottom of the boat, and I grab her

arm, twisting it with both hands. I can see she is taken aback by my strength here, but she is no patchwork half creature coming apart at the seams. She hurls me off, and the knife flashes toward me. I roll aside and then throw myself at her again, grabbing her around the waist, bringing her down with me. For a surreal moment, it is like the grappling sort of fights I had as a kid in the streets of the Twist. The kind of fight Dek had to pull me out of, dragging me home with a busted lip and raw knuckles, blood humming, defiant. But this is not the Twist, I am not a child, and nobody is getting me out of this. She chucks me against the gunwale and staggers back to her feet, making for Theo, who is screaming on the deck. I dive after her. I snap her wrist back, and this time I manage to wrench the knife out of her grasp. I position myself in front of Theo again. She pauses for half a second.

"Lidari—if you are Lidari—"

"I'm Julia!" I howl at her. "I'm Julia!"

And then she comes at me. I thrust with the knife, my mind full of Bianka disappearing into the canal, tearing off the enchanted sash—handing me Theo once more and for the last time. *Oh, Bianka, Bianka.* The knife goes into Och Farya, right up to the hilt, and she doubles over it, her face livid.

My only thought is to *stop* her. I know a knife wound is not enough to stop her. I keep driving her back with the knife in her gut. I push her right over the gunwale, and she topples into the lava. A high and terrible sound comes from her throat, fading to a hiss. Hanging over the gunwale and holding her under with the knife, I can feel the heat from the river going to the very core of me, the way I felt the ice in me when we crossed the Kastahor Mountains, back when I still hoped I might be a girl with a monster inside her, instead of a monster with a girl on the outside. The fire rolls over her and over her. My throat hurts, and my ears are full of an awful sound, and then I realize I'm screaming. I pull the knife out of her and drop it there on the boat. I pick up Theo, who is shuddering and gasping, canal water seeping out of his eyes and nose and ears, while a terrible form hauls itself out of the lava and back over the gunwale.

I mean to leave her there, leave her behind. I leap up, up into the hot sky, out of this place, feeling too late the hand that clamps around my ankle. When I land back in the boat on the canal in Tianshi, what is left of Mrs. Och has come with us: bones and blackened flesh, a smoking, hissing carcass. Still some noise comes from between her teeth. It sounds like *"Lidariii."*

The punters on their approaching vessels scream when we appear. I see a boat full of the Ru, armed with crossbows, bearing down on us. Arrows fly. I kick loose of Mrs. Och's grip and pull Theo away from it all—into the air, the nothingness, where I can't even feel his arms around my neck, his breath in my ear, his hot tears against my cheek. I leave Bianka and Solanze's sword at the bottom of the canal. I leave Mrs. Och for dead, or as close as she can come to that, her burnt corpse floating down the canal on the boat.

I am so far from pity, so far from mercy—I have forgotten how to feel such things.

Frederick hasn't moved, but he opens his eyes. I grab Bianka's bag, the one she told me about, hanging from a hook in the wall in what was our room—*If something happens to me, you take Theo and you take that bag.* I add the book of Yongwen fairy tales, sling the bag over my shoulder. Then I crouch next to Frederick.

"Hold on to me," I say. Theo between us, I take them to Silver Moya's, coasting over the city, and though I am carrying them in and out of the world and themselves, they hold on to me like I can save them, and they are not afraid of me. Trusting me. Not asking me why, not even when I stop to steal apples and lettuce from the market.

It is so hard to tell Frederick. I'm afraid that he won't believe me, that he will doubt what I saw or what I say, that he will tell me I did not have to do what I did. He weeps silently, his face in his hands. I hold him, Theo still between us. Neither of us can stop holding on to Theo. As if we can keep him safe from what has already happened, what he has already lost, motherless now and unprotected, except by us.

~

She mixes my blood and Frederick's and Theo's into the little bowl with some ink. Theo roars with outrage when we slice his finger, and I can't bear it, can't bear to hurt him even this tiny bit. But I don't know what else to do. Silver Moya's brush flattens the world and makes way for the hill to Ragg Rock. The paper city is full of paper people who do not see us, and we follow the bird, bright and so alive, so terribly alive, but not for long, everything peeling away as we climb.

☞

From Ragg Rock, the city looks farther away than it did before, faded. The same is true of Kahge, the far-off storm steaming and swirling through a thick haze. I squint, trying to take my gaze to the city gates, the roads beyond, but it all remains a distant blur.

"I can't see anything."

"You've taken a part of *The Book of Disruption* out of the world," says Ragg Rock. "Everything is farther apart now."

I remember what Mrs. Och said—that reassembling *The Book of Disruption* would pull Kahge into the world. The world and Kahge were close, I suppose, when Theo was in Casimir's fortress with the other two text fragments— which might explain why it was so easy for me to pass from one place to the other then. Now both seem impossibly distant.

Ragg Rock's pebble eyes are fixed on Theo. Head-to-toe muddy, he is exploring the mossy crags between the world and the nonworld, as if he has forgotten what he saw—his mother disappearing into the dark of the canal.

I try to scour the city for Dek, but from this distance it has become impossible.

Ragg Rock uses a flint knife to slice off strips of apple, and Theo feeds them to the rabbit, fascinated. Frederick is lying in the corner of the hut. I try to explain to him about the stone dial, so he knows there will be food and water for them, in spite of how barren it looks.

"Wabbit," Theo tells Frederick urgently, tugging at his sleeve. "Dat wabbit, Feyda!"

I don't know that he's ever made such a perfect sentence before. I press the heels of my palms against my eyes, inhaling, pushing down my grief and fear, down, down, down, out of my way.

"How long can they stay?" I ask Ragg Rock when I can speak again.

"Forever, if they are nice," she says. "But it will change a person." And she grins at us with her stone teeth and muddy gums.

"I'll bring more food for the rabbit when I can," I say. "But you can't let anybody else come . . . not if they are coming for Theo. Not even me."

"You won't come back?"

"I will. I'll try. But I mean . . . you said you can tell *why* somebody is coming, didn't you? What they want? I'll come to see them. But if I'm coming to take Theo, you can't let me in." I'm choking on my own words. "Only Frederick can take Theo from here. Not me, nor anyone else. That's important. Only Frederick."

She nods slowly.

"Do you promise?" I plead. "You won't let me . . . if I try?"

"I promise," she says. But she says it flatly, and I don't know how I can trust her. I don't really know what she is, how she feels—this bunny-loving mud woman, old as time. And Frederick is still so weak.

Theo tires of the rabbit and wanders out onto the hill, past the stone dial, chasing after one of the giant skeletal butterflies that came out of the now vanished woods. I want to tell her, *Don't let him get too near the mud moat; he could drown.* I want to tell her, *You will need to watch him; he is still so little, he is not as resilient as a rabbit, even.* He runs down the hill, his little legs so much steadier than when I first met him. He is so much more like a boy than a baby already, but Bianka won't see this, won't hear him learning to speak, watch him learning to run. Ragg Rock watches him with no expression on her clay face, and I know I am being ridiculous—she is no child's nursemaid—but I have no choice anyway, can only hope Frederick finds his strength returning soon. This is the only place that is out of Casimir's reach.

"You mustn't let him draw anything," I say. "He can make things real if he imagines them and draws them."

Ragg Rock smiles, like I've told her something charming about him.

"Mama!" barks Theo, running back into the hut, commanding us.

"Mama's not here. You need to stay with Frederick," I tell him, my voice strangled.

"Mama!" he roars, and then he throws his arms around my leg. "Lala umma beppo stoy."

"Frederick will read you a story when he's a little better. Something with a happy ending."

I try to kiss him, but he pulls away from me, cross, and goes back to the rabbit.

"What will you do?" asks Frederick.

"I'm going to kill Casimir."

He doesn't say, *Don't be a fool.* Or *Stay.* Or *Let's go, we'll hide, together we'll hide*—there's another way, there must be another way.

"I'll be praying for you," he says. "Every minute."

And for all that I don't know if I believe in the power of prayer, I find some comfort in that.

I leave them with Ragg Rock and return to the world, the bright and lovely springtime day in Tianshi. I'm not holding out much hope, but I soar over the city in vanishing leaps, pulling back and in again, searching for Dek. I don't find him. When the bells of Shou-shu chime for the setting sun, I make my way, defeated, to the Hundred Lantern Hotel, and there I offer myself up to Pia.

FIFTY-FOUR

It takes two days to reach the coast. Pia secures us a first-class cabin on a luxury steamer. She is not concerned about the notorious pirates off the coast of Yongguo—most of whom belong to Casimir, if Princess Zara was right. Nor does she appear worried that I might try to cut her throat in the night, though I lie in my comfortable berth and think of little else. I suppose she knows I won't risk it, not with Dek in Casimir's hands. Or perhaps she doesn't care if I do. I am beginning to understand her.

She takes me up on deck at sunset one evening. I am dressed like her, because the only clothes she has for me are her own and I could not get the stink of blood out of mine. The other passengers avoid us, and who can blame them? I see islands on the horizon. Dolphins are leaping near the prow, the pink sky full of seabirds wheeling, rainbow-colored fish flying. We stand side by side at the railing, look-ing at the sea.

It's beautiful, but I don't care about beauty. The drum-
beat at my center has summoned a storm, a howling wind
within. It is spinning higher and higher, whipping itself into
a frenzy, a terrible force gathering. The sun dips to touch
the horizon and spills bloody across the water, like a murder.

All right, Dek: I forgive myself. It's past time, isn't it, now
that I am barely who I was? I forgive myself for being such
a stupid child, for being callow and cowardly when I took
Theo from Mrs. Och's house, a lifetime and many selves
ago. I was afraid, and I was a fool, and I can forgive myself
for that.

I can even forgive myself for the rest. For failing Bianka—
just moments too slow. For failing to save Ko Dan or Count
Fournier, for the murder of Mrs. Och, for the many blun-
ders that have led us to this pass. I'm putting it all behind
me. You are the only one with whom there was never any
need for explanations or forgiveness.

And perhaps it doesn't matter—what I've done, what I
am. We choose each moment, Frederick says. I've seen Casimir's contract skittering on its little legs, but in the grip of
this fury, I don't believe he has any magic strong enough to
put a leash around me. At this moment, I believe that I could
gather Kahge in my fist like the edge of a tablecloth and hurl
all the might of hell at my enemies. I believe I could tear
down the world to save you, level cities and leave empires in
ruins behind me—and I'll do it, if that's what it takes.

Pia turns away from the sunset to look at me, and I look back, unflinching. I see myself reflected in her goggles, the new scar a black slash down the side of my face.

"I'm sorry, Julia," she says, and her voice is soft, as I've never heard it before.

But my own voice is like a knife when I answer her: "Don't be."

No more trying to hold on to the girl I hoped I was. I'm finished with the business of atonement. I'm coming for you, Dek, and I am bringing the whirlwind with me.

ACKNOWLEDGMENTS

Sitting down to write this makes me feel lucky, just like sitting down to write every morning makes me feel lucky. It takes a little book-loving army to turn a story into a book that works and isn't riddled with errors and inconsistencies, to make it look beautiful and enticing (and readable!), to get it out into the world and try to persuade readers to give it a try. I know just how tremendously lucky I am to be working with such kind, brilliant, dedicated people. Thank you a million times over to my agent, Steve Malk; to my editor, Nancy Siscoe; to Amy Black in Canada; and to everyone at Knopf and Doubleday Books for giving Julia a home and taking such good care of her. I am beyond grateful.

Thank you also to my generous and insightful beta readers—Dana Alison Levy, Kip Wilson Rechea, and Samantha Cohoe. I owe you all the chocolate in the world.

I dread to imagine where my stories and I would be without my band of stalwarts. Thank you to my beloved brothers; my inspiring grandmother; the people who didn't start out as family but became so—Jon, Giles, Mick; and my parents, who gave me calm waters, a blank map, and bright horizons to start off with, and built my heart into an unsinkable ship fit for the stormiest seas.

ABOUT THE AUTHOR

CATHERINE EGAN grew up in Vancouver, Canada. Since then, she has lived on a volcanic island in Japan (which erupted while she was there and sent her hurtling straight into the arms of her now husband), in Tokyo, Kyoto, and Beijing, on an oil rig in the middle of Bohai Bay, then in New Jersey, and now in New Haven, Connecticut.

She is currently occupied with writing books and fighting dragon armies with her warrior children. You can read more about her at catherineegan.com and follow her on Twitter at @ByCatherineEgan.